THE SUMMER GAMES:
SETTLING THE SCORE

R.S. GREY

The Summer Games: Settling the Score

Copyright © 2016 R.S. Grey

Published: R.S. Grey 2016
authorrsgrey@gmail.com
Editing: Editing by C. Marie
Proofreading: Jennifer at JaVa Editing
Cover Design: R.S. Grey
Cover Model: Lance Parker

THE SUMMER
GAMES
SETTLING THE SCORE

Note to Readers

Although this story is a **standalone**, it overlaps with the world first created in *Scoring Wilder*.

Keep in mind that *The Summer Games: Settling the Score* actually takes place five years after *Scoring Wilder*.

Enjoy!

Chapter One

ANDIE

E VERYONE HAS HEARD the rumors about the Olympic village—not the details of the world-class amenities and supercharged meal plans, but the whispers about the trouble athletes get into once they're off the track and in the sack.

The committee passes out condoms like candy.

The athletes are all sex-crazed maniacs.

The games continue long after the gold medals are handed out.

In 2000, the IOC officials dished out 70,000 condoms. They must have felt the walls shaking harder than expected, because they reportedly ordered 20,000 more after the first week of competition. For the Sochi and London Games, they upped the ante to over 100,000 prophylactics for the 6,000 competitors in attendance. If you do the math, that's 16 to 17 condoms *per* athlete, for an event that lasts less than a month. So, whispers or not, the message rings loud and clear: *when the flame is lit, let the games begin.*

Kinsley Bryant, my mentor on the women's soccer team, assured me that all the rumors about the village were true. She'd competed in the last summer games and lived to tell the tale, but this was different. Her first games had been in proper London-town. This time around, we were in sunny Rio de Janeiro, Brazil, a city well acquainted with debauchery. The moment we stepped off the plane, I could feel the excitement in the air. Tourists and athletes flooded into customs. The crowds were alive, in a rush, and speaking a million different languages all at once.

Outside the airport, I drew in a heavy breath, trying to make sense of the circus. Street vendors shouted for our attention (*"Pretty necklace for a pretty girl!"*) and taxi drivers promised low fares (*"We take you where you want to go! Cheap! Cheap!"*). My first five minutes in the city proved colorful, loud, and intoxicating.

"This way, ladies!" our team manager said, waving her hand in the air to usher us toward a row of waiting shuttles. I hiked my backpack up on my shoulder and dragged my suitcase behind me. I wanted to take my time and soak it all in, but they were already dividing us into groups and shoving us into the shuttles. We were heading toward the Olympic Village and my body hummed with excitement. What would it be like? Would I even be able to walk outside my room without coming face to face with some German rugby player's *überdong?* Would they be shooting condoms at us with a t-shirt cannon like at basketball games, or would there be an attendant in each room with a silver tray full of magnums? *"Boa tarde, here's your room key and some lube."*

Surely they'd be more discreet than that.

"If we have to sit for much longer, my legs are going to shrivel up and I won't be able to compete," Kinsley said, drawing me out of my obsessive thoughts.

She turned from her perch in the middle row and assessed the three of us crammed into the back of the shuttle. Nina, another rookie, sat beside me, quietly working away on a Sudoku puzzle. Michelle was on the other side of her, checking her phone. So far, they'd both proved to be bumps on a log. I had tried to get them out of their shell during the long flight from L.A., but it was no use.

"I agree," Becca said, turning around and propping her elbows on the back of her seat. Kinsley and Becca were both veterans on the team, but at that moment they looked like two detectives about to interrogate us. "I think we need something to entertain us until we get to the village."

Kinsley suggested a round of fuck-marry-kill, but since the other rookies lacked both homicidal and matrimonial tendencies, we ended up just going around the shuttle and choosing which athlete we would have sex with if the opportunity presented itself.

"What about you?" Kinsley asked me, wiggling her brows for emphasis.

I smiled. "Sorry, I don't have a dick-directory going." I figured there would be enough good-looking guys roaming the grounds that I wouldn't have to worry about preparing a hit-it-and-quit-it list beforehand. "Old fashioned, I guess."

She arched a brow. "Seriously, not *one* guy comes to mind?"

I shrugged. "I'm sure I'll find one soon enough."

"Boo! You suck," Becca chimed in. "Who's next?"

"Freddie Archibald!" Michelle exclaimed, finally glancing up from her phone.

"Mmm, Freddie," Nina agreed, pausing her Sudoku game long enough to stare wistfully out the window.

I scrunched my nose. "Who's that?"

"He swims for Great Britain," Michelle explained with

3

a look of horror on her face. Apparently I should have already known who he was. "His full name is Frederick Archibald and he's like British royalty or something. Total package."

With a name like that, I pictured a stuffy prince with a royal stick up his ass.

"Okay then, what about you two? Who would you pick?" I asked, turning the tables on Kinsley and Becca.

Kinsley flashed her left hand with the big fat diamond sitting on her ring finger. "Sorry, can't play if I've already won."

I laughed and rolled my eyes. Kinsley was married to Liam Wilder, a soccer god and an assistant coach for our team. They'd met when Liam started coaching her college soccer team before the last Olympic Games. Becca was also married to a soccer player—one of Liam's old team-mates—and between the four of them, they were quite a photogenic bunch. Every time I checked out at the grocery store, there was a sports magazine with at least one of their faces plastered across the cover. When I'd been called up to the Women's National Team, they'd enthusiastically adopted me into their fearsome foursome. Moving from Vermont to L.A. had been a rocky transition, especially when paired with Olympic training, but Kinsley and Becca had proven to be the older sisters I'd never had but always wanted.

"So do those rings mean you guys can't come to a party with me tonight?" I asked with a sly smile.

Kinsley narrowed her eyes. "What are you talking about?"

"The Brazilian swimmers messaged me on Facebook. They're hosting a themed party and I was planning on going."

"Count me out," Nina said. "Jetlag."

Michelle nodded. "Same here."

Shocker.

Becca and Kinsley exchanged a worried glance over my party plans, but that wasn't surprising. Over the last few months, I'd tried to convince them that I was an adult, but they still saw me as the wide-eyed rookie from Vermont.

I understood their worry; I didn't have much experience with partying and I'd only really traveled abroad during the qualifying matches a few months prior. Not to mention, we'd all been fed the same spiel about Rio's crime rates during a "Safety at the Games" seminar, but it wasn't like I'd be out walking the streets alone at night.

"Ever since you moved to L.A., you've been like a little sister to me," Kinsley had said on the way to the airport. *"I feel responsible for you."*

Technically, I *was* Kinsley's little sister on the soccer team, and though I appreciated her concern, I was ready to live a little. For so long I'd focused all my energy on soccer, but we had one week until our first match and I was ready to see for myself what kind of mischief the village had to offer. *Viva Brazil!*

———

THE VILLAGE WAS spread out over seven compounds with high-rise condos and apartments lined up along one main road. The shuttle drove us toward the entrance of our building, and I counted the amenities along the way. There was a coffee shop beside a flower shop. Cafes were sprinkled in among a doctor's office, banking center, salon, and post office. Anything we could possibly need was within walking distance.

We arrived at a crosswalk and our shuttle paused to let

the crowds cross in front of us. It looked like move-in day on a college campus. Athletes spilled out of cars and vans, sporting their national colors. Everyone was weighed down by their suitcases and duffel bags, tired from hours of travel. We were all there to work hard and represent our countries in the games, but now that we were all mixed together, there was an undercurrent of excitement in the air.

"There he is!" Michelle shouted, tapping her finger against her window. "Freddie! Look!"

I followed her finger, trying to discern a British athlete in all the madness.

"Where?" Kinsley asked, shoving past Becca to get to the window.

"That's my boob, jerk. Get off!" Becca said, pushing her back.

I tried to find him, but the sidewalk looked like an explosion of color. Athletes were weaving between one another and the second I'd spot what looked to be someone sporting British colors, they'd disappear back into the crowd.

"I don't see him!"

Michelle groaned. "Look! He's the tall guy with the brown hair!"

"Right, Michelle, because that really helps," Kinsley said, giving up and falling back onto her seat.

I laughed, prepared to give up as well, but then Michelle screamed and pointed out the front window. "THERE! HE'S RIGHT THERE!"

I wedged myself in between Becca and Kinsley and froze as Freddie came into view, framed in the center of the windshield as he crossed the street.

God save the queen.

"Damn," Nina whispered, clawing her fingers into my

arm so she could push herself up for a better view. Damn didn't begin to cover it. Damn was a word for ugly peasants. This Freddie? The sight of him begged a rousing "good heavens" with a polite undertone of "new pair of panties, please". His face was so handsome I blinked three times before letting myself believe I was looking at a real live human.

"Look at his jawline," Nina said in awe.

"Look at those lips," Michelle whispered.

"He's so tall," Nina replied. "Oh my god…he's *so* much better in real life."

I tried to ignore their assessments so I could take in his features for myself. He had rich brown hair and a pair of eyes that looked to be a few shades lighter. *Caramel.* His skin was tan and clean-shaven and anyone with a pair of eyes could see the muscles hidden beneath his button-down. But for me, it was the slow-spreading smile he aimed at the media liaison leading him across the street. *That* was the moment my stomach flipped.

"I forget," Becca said, turning around to look at the three of us in the back seat. "Is it 'The British are coming' or 'The British are making me come'?"

Kinsley laughed. "We never should have declared independence. Do you think we can take it back?"

"Where do you guys think he's going?" Michelle asked, ignoring them completely.

"Probably to an interview," Nina answered.

There was no doubt he had the looks for TV, but more than that…he was intriguing. Frederick Archibald was an entity unto himself, and as the shuttle pulled forward, I stared back at him through the window and wondered if maybe Michelle and Nina were right. There was definitely something about Freddie Archibald, and if I were going to make a list of sexy athletes in Rio, it'd start with him.

Chapter Two

FREDDIE

"**WELCOME TO GOOD** Morning America. I'm Nancy Rogers, joined this morning by Frederick Archibald, the enigmatic British swimmer with no less than sixteen gold medals to his name."

The camera panned to me and I waved to the audience. The studio lights made it hard to see five feet from my face, but I could just make out Thom, my teammate, standing beside the cameraman having a laugh.

"Welcome to the show, Freddie," Nancy continued, angling her body toward me. "When did you first arrive in Rio?"

"Just two days ago, actually. Flew over with a few of my other teammates."

"I would have thought you all would just swim over! Kidding of course!" she screeched, drawing from the well of manufactured enthusiasm only available to middle-aged morning show hosts.

I took a patient breath before offering a small smile. "Would be a bit cold, that."

"Well nonetheless," she started, eying my physique.

"I'm sure you would have been able to manage it. Your workouts must be so *very* grueling." *Is she hitting on me?* "Tell us, do you plan on breaking the records you set during the London games?"

Fucking hell, I'd forgotten the kinds of questions they asked over in the States. What did she suppose I wanted to do? Lose?

"You've got it, Nancy. That's the plan," I said, deadpan.

She smiled, a fake sort of grin that made her face lopsided.

"You know, Freddie, your reputation definitely precedes you—even 'across the pond'," she tittered. "You're known to everyone as the 'bad boy' of swimming."

The camera zoomed in on my face as I glanced to Nancy and frowned. "Was that a question?"

She stammered and adjusted the lapel mic on her blazer. I wasn't making the interview easy. It was thirty seconds in and I was having a go at her, but there was no point in dancing around it. I didn't like press. I didn't want to do interviews. My manager had insisted I take the interview, so this was what she'd get—ten minutes of awkward air time.

"You're right. Silly me. I meant to ask, how does it feel to be the 'bad boy' of swimming?"

I laughed. "You'll have to ask my mate, Thom. He chats up ladies far more than I do."

It was a lie, but I needed some way to diffuse her question. Who actually refers to someone as *the bad boy of swimming*? I'd never get laid again if I went about saying that.

"Oh, I'm sure you're being modest."

I didn't reply and she had to rifle through her cue cards to find the next question.

"Uhh, Freddie…" she stammered, eyeing the camera

tentatively before turning to me. "It's been four years since your last Olympic games and I understand that a lot has changed for you since then. Would you mind going into a bit of detail about the announcement of your—"

I shook my head to cut her off. I knew my manager had passed along a specific list of topics that were off-limits. "Nancy, this interview was meant to be about swimming."

She smiled wider. "And it will be! I promise, it's just that our viewers are dying to know what your plans are with the lovely *Caroline*."

I stood and reached for my mic. "Sorry Nancy. Until my races are done in a few weeks, my focus will be in the pool and nowhere else."

I passed my mic to the cameraman as I walked off the studio set. Thom wouldn't stop laughing until we were back outside—the wanker. They probably couldn't air the segment. It was less than two minutes, but I didn't care. The media were vultures. They'd write what they wanted to whether or not I pretended to be a well-mannered gentleman.

"Freddie, do you think you'll try to swim *even faster* this time around?" Thom echoed, doing his best impersonation of Nancy.

"Exactly!" I laughed and shoved his shoulder. "Of course I'm here to break my bloody records."

"Did you really mean what you said to her?" He looked concerned. "About only focusing on the pool?"

"What? Have you already got plans for us or something?" I asked, reaching for my mobile. There were already three missed calls from my manager—she'd want to berate me for walking off the interview—but I skipped over them, content to ignore her.

"There's a few swimmers heading over to Brian's place,

but I think we should stop in at this party the Brazilian swimmers are having. Blokes've got a theme and everything."

Sounded ridiculous. "What's the theme?"

"Says 'Rubik's Cube' on the Facebook invite."

I paused and turned to him. "Are they taking the piss?"

Chapter Three

ANDIE

WE'D ONLY BEEN in Rio for a few hours, but Kinsley, Becca, and I had already begun to settle into place. We were sharing a condo on the same floor as the rest of the team and though the three of us each had our own room and bathroom, we'd probably be joined at the hip the whole time anyway. Even then, they sat in my room watching me rifle through my clothes instead of unpacking their own things.

"What exactly is a Rubik's Cube party?" Becca asked.

"It's simple: everyone wears different colors—red shirt, blue shorts, green socks, whatever—and once you get to the party, you have to swap clothes with people until you're wearing all of the same color."

Kinsley tsked. "Sounds like an excuse to see people in their skivvies."

I tossed my luggage onto my bed. "Yes, well, isn't that basically the meaning of life in the first place?"

I didn't have to look over my shoulder to know they were exchanging one of their trademarked worried glances. They weren't used to seeing this side of me. In

L.A., I hadn't gone out much, but that was because my entire day—6:00 AM to 6:00 PM—had been dedicated to soccer.

"Do you guys have any purple or orange clothes I can borrow?" I asked, reaching for a blue tank top and pairing it with red shorts. There was enough red, white, and blue gear stuffed in my suitcase to last a lifetime. They basically shelled it out to us in bulk as soon as we were called up for the national eam.

"I think this will look better," Kinsley said, reaching around me for a giant white fleece I'd packed as an afterthought. It was technically winter in Rio, but it felt more like a mild L.A. summer.

She laid the fleece out over the blue tank top and then offered me a proud smile. "Yeah, see. That's adorable."

Ten minutes later, I had the outfit I wanted to wear: blue tank top, red shorts, white knee-high socks, and a yellow trucker hat I'd picked up at the airport. It had *Rio de Janeiro* spelled across the front in scrolling cursive. On top of that outfit, Kinsley and Becca had laid out their choices for me: black track pants that covered every inch of skin from my navel to my ankles, the white fleece, and a red scarf they dictated should be worn like a burka.

"Oh, and you can keep the white socks," Kinsley said, like she was doing me a big favor.

Becca nodded. "Yeah, and maybe just wear the hat over the scarf?"

"I think I can handle it from here." I started to usher them to the door, sweeping my arms back and forth so they'd get the picture. "You guys have helped enough."

After they left, I used my suitcase to barricade the door. I changed quickly, pulled my blonde hair out of its pony-tail, and shook it out. Loose, long waves framed my face, and when I put the trucker hat on backward, it took the edge off my feminine features. I smirked at my tan reflection in the bathroom mirror. Night one in Rio was going to be a good one.

"ANDIE! Let us in!" Kinsley yelled, banging on my bedroom door.

Or not.

I grabbed my phone from my bed, pushed my suitcase aside, and pulled the door open to find Kinsley and Becca changed and ready for the party. *No. Just no.* They looked absolutely ridiculous in matching red Adidas track suits, black hats, and sunglasses. Either they'd just walked off the set of an 80s music video or they were now officially part of my security detail. Either way, I wasn't going anywhere with them.

"What the hell, you guys? I'm not walking into the party with you two dressed like that."

They followed me out of the condo, adjusting their hats and assuring me they'd blend in just fine. I knew better. Sure they were still sexy, confident, kickass soccer players, but they'd lost a little of that edge. Once Liam and Penn had "put rings on it", there was nothing left to keep them from becoming *real adults*. (They literally got excited over a Friday night spent watching *Parks and Rec* reruns before turning in at 9:00 PM.)

"What about your husbands?" I asked, reaching for some legitimate reason to block them from coming with me. "Surely they don't want you two mingling with a bunch of eligible bachelors."

"While you're correct in your assessment that I've still *'got it'*," Kinsley said with a gesture at her bright red tracksuit. "I'll have you know Liam trusts me and made me promise I wouldn't let you go alone."

I groaned. *Liam too?!* How many parents did I have on this trip? I tried to walk faster, hoping that if I took four steps for every one of theirs, I'd eventually lose them. No such luck. They picked up the pace and linked their arms with me, successfully shackling me to my embarrassment.

"This will be fun!" Becca said with a little skip in her step. "Girls night!"

Kinsley nodded. "We don't have practice until noon tomorrow so we should be able to let loose."

Kinsley and Becca were only four years older than me, but when we arrived outside the party, it felt like I was walking in with my parents.

"Whoa, a disco ball!" Becca said, pulling us through the door. "Who packs a friggin' disco ball for the Olympics?"

The Brazilian swimmers ushered us inside with big smiles.

"Good evening, ladies," one of them said with practiced English and a heavy accent.

"Sorry! Liam Wilder already put a ring on it," Kinsley said, waving her left hand in the air like Beyoncé. Becca did the same, and since they had death grips on my arms, I couldn't slink away. Their wedding rings formed a veritable force field of chastity around us that no one seemed to notice but me.

"Should we get some punch?" Becca asked.

"We should really only be drinking water this close to competing," Kinsley said.

Dear god, I needed to get away from them.

"Guys, I'm going to head to the bathroom," I said, sliding out of their grips.

Becca looked alarmed, as if needing to pee was an admission of some untold guilt. "Oh, should we all go?"

"NO!" I shouted, then lowered my voice to a whisper. "I, uh…I need to poop."

"Oh, someone's *neerrrvvouuuusss*," Kinsley said with a knowing smirk.

"It's her first Olympic party, of course her bowels are moving Kins!" Becca laughed.

I closed my eyes, took two deep breaths, and then slapped on a fake smile. "Honestly, I'm so glad you guys came with me. I'm just going to head over to the restroom and when I get back, we can party together the rest of the night."

My fake speech threw them off, so much so that they let me go to the restroom all by myself; as a twenty-one-year-old, I never thought that would be an issue. Fortunately, the second I was out of their sight, I finally saw the party for what it really was: *a playground*.

The Brazilian guys had a condo that was at least twice the size of ours. The living room was packed from wall to wall with a multinational bevy of Aphrodites and Adonises. Kinsley and Becca were holed up in the foyer, and as I wove through the party trying to find a restroom I didn't actually need, I realized it wouldn't be hard to steer clear of them for the rest of the night.

Everyone was shouting over the music, and I couldn't distinguish one accent from another. I caught passing words in English, but by the time I turned, I couldn't tell who'd said what. I made it past a rowdy group of guys who were blocking my path to the drinks table, but I weaseled my way through, mostly unnoticed thanks to their gargantuan stature.

"Oy! Where you going?" one of them asked with a heavy accent as I pulled a beer from the table and tried to slink back into the madness.

"Oh." I laughed. "Just grabbing a drink."

I wiggled the can back and forth and they all broke out into smiles. Clearly, they approved of alcohol. Between their stature and thick beards, they looked like a group of Vikings who'd accidentally time traveled to 2016. One of them had on a rugby shirt that looked big enough to cover my whole body, which made perfect sense. They were definitely part of a rugby team.

"All right, well you guys have fun," I said, trying to shimmy past them.

The one who was closest to me—a giant with a red beard that stretched down past his chin—clapped me on the shoulder. My knees buckled under the weight. "Stay! Drink!" he bellowed.

I thought it over for a second. Drinking with a bunch of rowdy rugby players hadn't really been in my vision for the night, but if I stuck with the Vikings, Kinsley and Becca would never be able to find me. I scanned across them again, and wide cheeky smiles flashed back at me. Crooked or missing teeth were par for the course, but they seemed fairly harmless—so long as none of them thunder-clapped me on the shoulder again. *It literally felt like getting hit by car.*

Ten minutes later—the details were fuzzy—Gareth (bearded dude) had hoisted me up onto his shoulders and was parading me around the party like a piñata. His teammates formed a scrum around him, and they all taught me a drinking song, one that sounded like a sea shanty borrowed from pirates in the Victorian era.

"What will we do with a drunken sailor? What will we do with a drunken sailor? What will we do with a drunken sailor early in the morning?"

I didn't actually know the words, but I was singing along with them at the top of my lungs just the same.

"What shall we do with an all-i-gat-or? Something-something drunk James Taylor…EARLY IN THE MORNING!" I bellowed, tilting back and forth on

Gareth's shoulders. I'd chugged two beers and the alcohol was sloshing around my stomach in the worst way possible.

"Keepitup, lassie," Gareth said, tilting his head back to look up at me.

"Oh my god! You just called me lassie!"

I threw my head back to laugh, which in hindsight wasn't the most genius move. Shifting my weight back threw off Gareth's equilibrium. Picture a tipsy raccoon on the shoulders of a bear. Sure, he weighed five times what I did, but he couldn't counterbalance my weight and before I knew it, I was sailing for the ground in slow motion. There was a distinct moment when I thought, *This is where a sexy man would catch me if I were a Disney princess.* That thought concluded right as I collided with the ground with a heavy "oomph" and the air whooshed out of my lungs.

The music faded and the laughter died down as people formed a wide circle around me. Did they think I was dead or something? *Wait, am I dead?*

I blinked, and blinked again, trying to make out some definitive sign that I was still alive. The lights overhead swung back and forth, but that could have been the angels calling me to heaven—or y'know, hell, since that's honestly where I was headed for lying to Kinsley and Becca about needing to poop.

A face leaned over me, blocking the heavenly (or hellish) light. I caught caramel eyes, dark hair, a defined jaw, and a pair of dreamy lips.

Was it God? Or...

"Are you the devil?" I asked the floating head. "Because I swear I was going to clean up my act really soon."

The face laughed and I focused on the lips that had been moving and now stretched across a seriously cute face. If Satan was this handsome, I'd probably be able to handle the eternal damnation business.

"All right, I'm going to lift you up. Just give a shout if something hurts," said the devil with a very cute British accent.

Hands wrapped around my shoulders and lifted me up to a sitting position. I could breathe again, and I didn't feel any pain. I patted my elbows and my head. I surmised that I'd managed to fall very gracefully, like the princess I'd imagined earlier.

"All right?" the British voice asked again, coming around to face me.

The bobbing head was connected to a very, *very* handsome body. I took my time scanning over him until I reached his face and realized all at once that I recognized the devil.

"You're Frederick Archibald," I said with a small, shocked voice.

"I prefer Freddie—"

A slow-spreading smirk took hold of my heart just as Gareth rushed forward.

"Lassie!" Gareth boomed. "I'm sorry, but you're too slippereh!"

The rugby team was all there surrounding me, probably awaiting my cue to send me off for a proper Viking funeral. I waved him away and pushed to stand. "I'm fine, really." My wrist hurt, but that wasn't from the fall. "I swear."

There was another five minutes of them picking up my arms and turning me around to confirm I didn't have a bone sticking out or something.

"I think she's fine," Freddie said, hovering just behind the rugby guys.

I stared up and smiled, finally getting my first real look

at him. Either he was stealing my breath, or I'd lied about being okay earlier. Had I punctured a lung? Dislodged my heart?

The rugby team agreed that I was stouter than I looked, or that I looked like I needed another stout. Either way, they departed and I was left standing a few feet from Freddie, trying to work up something witty to say. He was wearing blue jeans and a red t-shirt. I couldn't tell what color his boxers were, but if I swapped my pants for his, I'd be one step closer to completing my Rubik's cube.

"Feeling better?" he asked, taking a step toward me.

I smiled. "Yes, but I need you to take your pants off."

Chapter Four

FREDDIE

"**Y**OU NEED MY trousers?" I asked, confirming that she had in fact said what I thought she'd said.

This girl was cute—more than cute, really. Her blue tank top rode up an inch or so on her trim torso, and one look at her long legs proved she played a sport in which she ran—loads. Her bluish gray eyes were hard to ignore, even with the lopsided yellow cap covering half of them.

She looked like that type of American girl blokes dream about: pale blonde hair and sun-kissed skin, as if she'd just walked off the beach. I told myself this was the reason why I wasn't leaving her alone. She'd had an entire team of titans more than ready to keep her occupied for the night, and yet my curiosity had gotten the better of me.

She pointed to her red shorts and I caught another glimpse of her long legs. "Yes, we have to swap so that I can have blue pants and a blue top. It's for the game. We have to leave the party wearing one color, and I guess my color is blue."

I had no clue what she was going on about, but there

was no way we were swapping trousers. Her shorts would hardly fit around my ankle.

"C'mon, you have to play," she said, jutting out her bottom lip. Something told me she got away with murder having a pair of lips like that.

"I can't give you these," I said, "but my boxers are blue."

Freddie, you dim perv. She doesn't want your boxers.

Her brows rose in shock, but it didn't last. The surprise faded into a smile and she reached out for my hand. "C'mon, we can change in here."

I'd braced for a slap for even suggesting the idea, but maybe American girls were different. She led me past the drink table and we turned a corner down a long hallway. The party was less crowded back there, and every person we passed took one look at us, her hand in mine, and assumed the worst. The lads clapped me on the shoulder and the girls flashed jealous stares.

"Wait, I don't even know your name," I said as she knocked on one of the doors at the end of the hallway.

She turned and smiled at me over her shoulder. "Andie."

I knew that name. "Andie Foster?"

"How'd you know?"

"You and the other football girls are the talk of the games."

She arched a brow and nodded, not bothering with a response.

The room she pulled me into was an unoccupied bedroom. It had the same furniture as all the other rooms in the Olympic Village: standard queen bed, chair, and dresser. There wasn't a suitcase or bag in sight.

"Looks like we'll be safe in here," she said, turning to face me. "But you'll have to turn while I change."

I opened my mouth to reply, but she was already working on the waistband of her shorts. I turned and stared at the opposite wall, trying to talk down the excitement in my pants. I could hear her pushing down her shorts. I pictured them sliding down her tan legs and I shoved my hands into my pockets and pinched my eyes closed. I had as much willpower as any bloke, but this was pushing it.

"Hey, I don't hear you taking your boxers off over there," she said with a laugh.

Oh, right.

I unbuttoned my trousers, pushing them down to the ground.

"Rest assured, I put these boxers on right before the party," I said with a smile.

"I don't care," she said. "Here."

I caught movement out of the corner of my eye and then something landed on my shoulder…a red, silky something.

"Jesus." I groaned under my breath. She'd tossed her panties at me, a red, lacy pair that felt like heaven in my palm.

That's it. I'm moving to America after the games. It's such a beautiful, beautiful *country.*

"Ahem!" She cleared her throat. "I need those boxers. My butt cheeks are cold!"

I'd survived more high-pressure situations than most blokes have by the age of twenty-seven. I'd competed in two Olympic games and swam in hundreds of races at the international level. None of those situations were half as difficult as facing away from Andie in that moment. I knew she was standing behind me. Her bare skin was right there, all I had to do was turn around; she probably wouldn't have even noticed.

"Freddie!"

Bloody hell.

I pulled my boxers off, ignoring the slight tenting situation occurring in the front. I walked backward, trying to hand them off to her like a gentleman. It seemed like a good idea right up until my hand brushed against her bare ass.

"HEY! Hands off the tush," she said, yanking the boxers out of my hand.

"Ah, sorry," I said with a cheeky smile. "My mum told me never to throw my knickers at a girl."

She laughed, though I was more focused on trying to push aside the memory of how soft her skin had felt. I pulled my jeans back up and buttoned them.

"All right, they're a little big, but it'll work."

I turned to find her rolling up my boxers so they wouldn't fall down her hips. They were rather large on her, but by the second roll they seemed secure enough.

"How do I look?" she said, adjusting the hat over her hair.

Un-fucking-believable.

"ANDIE!"

Bang. Bang. Bang.

"ANDIE FOSTER! We're coming in!"

Fists pounded on the bedroom door right before it crashed open. Two girls jumped forward, one with pepper spray and the other with a bottle of beer poised to strike.

"We're too late!" The brunette one had zeroed in on Andie's knickers still clutched in my hand. "HE ALREADY HAS HER PANTIES!"

Chapter Five

ANDIE

I **WOKE UP** to Kinsley and Becca standing over my bed, doing their best impersonation of FBI agents. Their arms were crossed and their glares would have sliced me in half had I not been burrowed safely beneath my covers.

"What do you two want?" I asked, clutching a spare pillow beneath my chin.

"Sleep well, Andie?" Kinsley asked with an arched brow.

Apparently they had practiced the good cop, bad cop routine.

"Or was it pretty...*drafty* down there?" Becca asked, yanking the covers back to expose my blue tank top and matching pair of boxers—the pair Freddie had given me. They were loose around my hips, but I liked the feel of them and, SUE ME, I didn't see the point of taking them off before going to bed.

"Planning on wearing those things to practice as well?" Kinsley asked, eyeing the boxers like they were contagious.

A quick glance at the bedside clock revealed I'd slept right through breakfast. I felt like total shit, but I wouldn't let them know that. They wanted me to suffer after what I'd put them through the night before, but I wouldn't.

I shooed them out of my room and changed into my soccer gear, taking care to shove Freddie's boxers safely into my suitcase. I dragged my shin guards and cleats out into the living room and tossed them near the door before rifling through the cupboards for something of substance. The food court would have been my first choice, but I didn't have time to go down before practice.

"Finding anything, Andie?" Becca asked.

The committee had filled the cupboard with snacks and food prior to our arrival. I reached in and grabbed the first thing my hand touched…a bag of kale chips, salt and vinegar flavored. "Yup. Mmmmmmm. I love the taste of vinegar in the morning."

Kinsley held a granola bar between her thumb and pointer finger. I snatched it without a second thought. It was a peace offering of sorts, and as I trailed them to the bus waiting on the first floor of the condo complex, I decided to push the subject.

"You guys can't be mad at me forever. I didn't do anything wrong!"

"You went off by yourself!" Kinsley said.

"Fraternizing with the enemy!" Becca added. "When you were supposed to be pooping!"

All right, they were being ridiculous, so I had to take extreme measures. I took my seat at the back of the bus beside Kinsley and dialed her husband's number. Most people knew Liam Wilder as the rowdy ex-professional soccer player who'd been forced to retire due to a knee injury, but I knew him as Kinsley's husband, the man who donned a chef's apron on Sunday mornings to whip up enough eggs and bacon to feed a small village.

He answered on the third ring and sounded genuinely happy to get my call. "Andie!? What's up? Are you guys headed to the practice field? I'm already here."

"Oh, yeah, yeah we're on our way LIAM."

"What?" Kinsley tried to reach for the phone, but I pulled it out of her reach. "LIAM—don't talk to her, she's a traitor!"

Fortunately, he didn't hear her. "I just spoke with Kins earlier—"

"Yeah, that's great," I said, cutting him off. "Listen, Liam, when you were in London for the last Olympics, did Kinsley ever go to any parties?"

He laughed, this long, drawn-out laugh that definitely proved my point without him having to say a word. "Ask her about the Russian gymnasts. That's all I'll say."

"HA!" I shouted at Kinsley and hung up. "I rest my case."

She was already firing off a text to Liam, no doubt threatening divorce.

"Was it fun partying with those gymnasts, Kinsley? Did you have so much *fun?*"

By this point, nearly half our team had turned around to listen to our argument. It was in Kinsley's best interest to nip it in the bud to preserve her reputation as team captain.

"What I did in London is beside the point. Becca and I had Liam and Penn to protect us, but since you are basically an old spinster that nobody loves—"

"I'm twenty-one."

"Right. Even still, we love you, and you've left us no choice but to be your chaperones for the remainder of the games. Every step you take, Becca and I will be there."

"Every breath you take and every move you make," Becca continued.

"Every bond you break, every step you take, we'll be watching you."

"Every single day and every word you say."

I covered my ears. "Oh my god. STOP SINGING THAT SONG."

But they wouldn't stop. I had to listen to them going on and on until the bus pulled up outside the practice complex. I ran for it as quick as I could and decided then that I probably needed new friends. Maybe the Russian gymnasts would be down to hang out. I'd tower over them, but that'd be okay. Everyone needs one tall friend for reaching things on the top shelf.

Liam and Coach Decker were standing just inside the entrance of the stadium looking like the start of a bad joke. Coach Decker was fifty-three with short white-blonde hair and a face that promised she hadn't laughed since the Nixon era. She'd worn the same pair of thin black-framed glasses for as long as I could remember and she was a damn good coach, even if she did scare me a little. Liam stood by her side, tattoos exposed down his arms, dirty blonde hair short and fussed up. He and Kinsley made quite an adorable pair, though I refrained from telling them so as their perfectly proportioned heads were already close to exploding.

"Good morning, Liam," I said, tipping an imaginary hat in his direction.

He eyed me curiously and then glanced back to Kinsley and Becca walking into the stadium a few feet behind me.

"Are you three fighting?" Liam asked with what he probably thought was a chastising glare. It never worked the way Coach Decker's did.

"No fighting," I said, holding up my fingers. "Scout's honor. Although your wife is a little crazy. You should have her head examined."

"Liam! Do not talk to her about the gymnasts!" Kinsley shouted.

Coach Decker shook her head and clapped her hands to get everyone's attention.

"All right everyone. I know we're all excited to be here for our first practice in Rio, but it's time to focus. Kinsley and Becca, show the girls where to stash their bags and then Kinsley, I want you to lead warm-up." She paused and turned toward me. "Andie, there's a trainer over there ready to tape your wrist."

I followed her gaze and found a group of trainers stationed near benches off field. They'd propped up a small black table and as I walked closer, a small girl with black hair knotted on top of her head stepped forward to greet me. Her khaki pants didn't fit well, but her team shirt was fitted and embroidered with her name under a soccer ball and an American flag.

"Lisa," I said, reading her name off her shirt and holding out my hand. "I'm Andie."

She nodded and ushered me toward the trainer's table. "Good to meet you, Andie. I'll be your trainer here in Rio and I'll be with you at every practice and every game. We'll set up times for you to come to the training center for some physical therapy exercises as well, but for now, hop up onto the table and I'll take a look at your wrist."

I did as she said and then started to walk her through the injury. It wasn't career threatening; I'd just sprained it back in high school and it flared up every now and then. I'd gone through physical therapy for it multiple times, but unless I laid off it for a sustained period of time, it would never truly heal. Unfortunately, time was not a luxury I could afford.

"How does it feel?" Kinsley asked.

I glanced over my shoulder to find her watching the trainer as she worked. She flexed my hand, working the tape over and around my wrist so that it'd be supported during practice. I tried not to wince at the stab of pain, but Kinsley caught my mask slip. She shook her head and crossed her arms, but I shot her a death stare as the trainer bent to grab another roll of tape from her bag.

The trainer finished up and stepped back to examine her work. "Tell me if it's secure enough," she instructed.

I flexed and curled my hand, twisting it in a circle one direction and then the other. I could still feel a dull ache, but with the tape in place, it was more tolerable.

"How does it feel?" Kinsley asked again.

I nodded and shot her a thumbs up. As far as our coach and team trainer knew, my injury was minor and I was having it wrapped as a precaution. Kinsley knew the truth—that I was stepping into dangerous territory—but she also knew why I was downplaying it. Bones and tendons and ligaments all heal with time, but with the Olympics only occurring every four years, most athletes consider themselves lucky to earn a spot once or twice. So unless my wrist fell off, I'd stay on the field.

"Listen, I'd like to talk to you about Freddie for a second after practice. Seriously, wait for me."

I promised her I would, though I really had no intention of sticking around for another Kinsley and Becca lecture. How quickly they'd forgotten what it was like to be young and single during the Olympic games. For years, my life of training and preparing for the games had left little time for anything outside of soccer. Sure I'd had a few random dates through the years, but nothing compared to what other girls my age were doing.

Giving up boys to play soccer on a professional level was hard, but in the end it was an easy decision. Growing up in Vermont, the only time I ever saw real action was on the soccer field. It thrilled me in a way no boy ever could. Most of the popular girls in my high school had assumed I was a lesbian because I preferred Adidas over Tory Burch and I didn't know the difference between "beach waves" and "curls". *No, really, someone tell me what the difference is.* To put the rumors to rest, I'd forced my first kiss behind the bleachers of my high school's soccer stadium with pimple-faced Kellan who was a year younger than me and had the breath of a walrus. He was tall and spindly, and when he pulled away, he accidentally bonked his head on the bottom of the stadium seats and had to get three stitches. Once that story had spread, no other guy in school thought I was worth the risk.

Fortunately, college was better after I completed the duckling-to-swan metamorphosis that often graces early adulthood. (Goodbye braces, acne, and pudgy cheeks.) College guys weren't so intimidated by my talent and I'd managed a boyfriend here and there. Still, nothing serious. Dating didn't exactly go hand in hand with competing at the Olympic level. For so long, I'd dreamt of going to the Olympics, not only to win gold for Team USA (duh), but also because I wanted the chance to meet other people who *got* it. Just like me, they'd dedicated their lives to a sport they loved, and they understood the sacrifices that came with the territory.

Kinsley and Becca could lecture me all they wanted, but at the end of the day, how could they blame me for wanting more than gold? I would be in Rio de Janeiro for nearly a month and I wasn't going to waste it. I'd work my ass off on the field, but in my free time I was going to make memories that would last a lifetime. And, *sure*, if Freddie Archibald somehow worked his way into those memories, then so be it.

Chapter Six

FREDDIE

I **WOKE UP** thinking of Andie, trying to recall the bits and pieces of her I'd found so appealing the night before. She wasn't like any of the posh British girls I was used to. They'd have willingly thrown themselves over a bridge before tossing their knickers at my head, and yet Andie had done it without a second thought. I was intrigued, but I couldn't pinpoint what exactly made her so different—the light behind her grayish blue eyes, her confident laugh, or her body. *Her body*. It'd taken all night to tear the image of her standing in my boxers out of my mind. Now that I was awake, I wanted to selfishly cling on to it, just for memory's sake.

My mobile buzzed on my nightstand and I rolled over to find I already had two missed calls from my mum, three texts from my sister, Georgie, and one voicemail from Caroline.

I pressed play on Caroline's voicemail first, hoping it would realign my world and push thoughts of Andie to the side.

"Freddie! My gorgeous sportsman, I've missed you so much. I hope you're doing well. Give me a ring later. Kisses, Caroline."

Andie was nothing like Caroline Montague, though maybe that wasn't a bad thing. I knew exactly what I was getting into with Caroline. She'd grown up in British high society, beloved by everyone. There wasn't a utensil she couldn't name, nor a duchess she didn't know personally. I'd grown up alongside her and knew her to be polite, quiet, and predictable—quite possibly the exact opposite of the enigmatic goalkeeper I'd met the night before.

I pressed delete on her voicemail and then read Georgie's texts.

Georgie: Mum is LOONY. She's phoned Caroline and told her you'd LOVE her to join you in Rio. I tried to pry the mobile from her hand, but you know how strong those bony digits of hers are. I think I've strained my wrist…

Georgie: She's absolutely mad. I'm putting myself up for adoption. Think anyone will have an adorable, house-trained eighteen-year-old?

I smiled and sat up in bed. Georgie had been dramatic from birth, though she'd never admit it. I rang her and then reached for my laptop to glance over the day's itinerary: practice, workout, phone interview, more workouts. I'd be running round the village until supper.

"FREDDIE!" she squealed after picking up on the third ring.

I smiled at the sound of her voice. "Morning Georgie."

"You sound dreadful. What have you been doing all night?"

"Nothing. Honest. I just woke up and listened to a voicemail from Caroline."

"Oh."

There was a pregnant pause before she spoke up again.

"Well let's not talk about that. How's Rio? Has it given your pale English arse a tan yet? Or have you been loitering in the shade of Christ the Redeemer all day?"

I wiped sleep from my eyes and pushed the blankets aside.

"Honestly, I haven't seen much of the place."

She groaned. "What a bore. At least give me some details about the village. Is it just as barking as London was?"

"I'm sure it will be. Last night was…"

I mulled over my previous night, trying to compartmentalize the image of Andie that was fighting its way back to the forefront of my mind.

"Last night was what?"

"I've met someone."

Silence.

More silence.

I pulled the mobile away from my cheek and glanced down to check she hadn't hung up on me.

"Georgie?"

"What do you mean you've *met* someone?"

Her usual charm was gone, replaced by a serious tone I didn't much care for.

"It's nothing," I said, trying to backtrack. Maybe it'd been a mistake bringing it up.

"Well 'nothing' sounds quite like *a girl* to me, Freddie, and you haven't mentioned any of *those things* in four years. FOUR YEARS. And you think I'm going to let you drop this?"

My stomach clenched. "Just forget I've said anything."

Georgie wouldn't let it go. "Spill it, Freddie. Who is she?"

I stared up at the ceiling and acquiesced, actually sort

of glad to confide in her about Andie. What would it hurt to tell Georgie about her?

"She's an American."

"Is her last name Kardashian?"

"No, she's called Andie. She's a footballer. You'd like her, Georgie. She's got a natural thing about her and she's really talented."

"Good lord Freddie, you sound like a smitten schoolgirl."

I smiled. "You're the one who asked, Georgie."

"Are you in love already?" she laughed.

My smile fell and suddenly it wasn't fun to talk about Andie any more. The silence was back, louder than before. Neither one of us was going to utter the words, because we didn't need to. The idea of Caroline spoke loudly enough on its own.

Finally, she laughed. "Blimey. It's rotten luck."

I'm glad one of us can laugh about it.

"Yeah, well. Really, it's nothing." I checked the clock on my bedside table. "Listen, I've got to run and get ready for swim practice."

"Fine. On the contrary, I require a little lie down. Between our nutter of a mum and your dramatic love life, I'm feeling faint."

I laughed and promised I'd phone her later.

"Wait, Freddie," she said, just before I hung up.

"Yeah?"

"What are you going to do about Andie? Will you see her again?"

I hesitated before answering.

"It is a rather small village."

Chapter Seven

ANDIE

"**L** ET US IN, Andie!"

Jesus Christ. I reached out for a pillow and pulled it over my face to keep from yelling at Kinsley and Becca to go away. I'd had four, maybe five minutes of alone time since returning from practice. I'd showered and changed, but I should have savored it more and really reveled in the silence before Kinsley and Becca polluted it. On the bus ride home, they'd tried to corner me, but I'd put on my headphones and tuned them out. My plan had worked temporarily, but now, it seemed they weren't going to take no for an answer.

I'd arrived in Rio less than twenty-four hours earlier and the dust had yet to settle. I hadn't finished unpacking, I hadn't called my mom, and I hadn't had a full uninterrupted minute to consider what had happened with Freddie the night before. Had that encounter actually happened? Had I really slung my panties at his head like a bachelor party stripper?

"ANDIE! Let us in, we have a present for you."

I groaned, shoved off my bed, and opened my door to

find Kinsley and Becca—my team captains and the two people I should have respected the most—standing in my doorway dressed in matching unicorn onesies.

"Here, we got one for you too," Kinsley said, shoving a limp, horned onesie into my hand and then stepping past me into my room.

"The three amigos!" Becca confirmed, running and jumping onto my bed. Between the two of them, there was never a dull moment, hence why I'd bonded with them the first day of tryouts.

"I think your mattress is better than mine," Becca said, bouncing up and down in an attempt to confirm her theory.

"They're all the same," I laughed, setting the onesie down on my suitcase.

"What are you going to do for the rest of the day?" Kinsley asked, taking a seat beside Becca.

I shrugged. "Unpack, get settled, finally call my mom."

She nodded. "We were thinking of going down and scoping out the first floor if you wanna come. Our complex has the biggest food court, so I think most of the athletes will be hanging out there."

"I really need to call my mom. She's already texted me like thirty times." Honestly, she had. The woman was clinically insane.

"It's okay, we can wait," Kinsley offered with a smile.

Since neither of them made a move to leave, I stepped out onto my room's balcony to give my mom a call.

My parents, Christy and Conan Foster, were robots. Sweet, well-meaning robots. They grew up in Vermont, my grandparents grew up in Vermont, and my great-grandparents grew up in Vermont. Somewhere during all those generations spent in harsh winters, their personalities had been replaced by good-natured gobs of maple syrup. Their idea of fun was layering a cashmere sweater over a gingham button down and taking a picnic to the park. They belonged to our small town's country club and spent their free time flipping through L.L. Bean catalogs; needless to say, they were shocked to have produced a daughter like me.

Those first fourteen years were a real struggle. My mother had insisted I stay in dance but I'd insisted on playing soccer. It wasn't until I earned a spot on the U-17 National Team at only fifteen years old that she let me tear down the dance posters in my room. Throughout high school, I'd replaced them with soccer stars like Ashlynn Harris, Hope Solo, and Cristiano Ronaldo. Admittedly, Cristiano was there mostly for eye-candy. Also, I liked to rub his abs like Buddha's belly for luck before a big game.

"Andie, are you using that hand sanitizer I packed in the front left pocket of your bag?" my mom asked as soon as the call connected.

That was the first question she asked. Not, how the hell is Rio? The Olympics? Practice?

"Yes." I sighed. "But did you honestly have to pack a sixty-eight ounce bottle in my carryon? I had to shove it in my checked luggage and it spilled on half of my underwear."

"Brazil is *different*." She whispered 'different' like it was derogatory. "Besides, it can't hurt to have *extra clean* underwear."

I rolled my eyes. "Yeah Mom, that is priority number one as I, y'know, compete for a gold medal."

She mm-hmmed cheerily, accepting my sarcasm as truth.

"Well, just let me know if you need any more underwear."

I edged closer to the balcony, embarrassed by the

conversation. "No Mom, don't send me more underwear." I tried to change the subject. "The condos are fun. I'm sharing a space with Kinsley and Becca."

"They've put you all in a *condo?* How can that be safe?"

"Security only allows athletes and coaches to enter. Guests have limited visiting hours and they—"

"Oh! Sweetie, guess what I watched this morning while I was walking on the treadmill!" She didn't even notice she'd cut me off.

"What?"

"I try to walk at least a mile or two every morning. I even put on some Taylor Swift sometimes, but don't tell your dad because he thinks her music is just—"

"MOM. What'd you watch this morning?"

"Oh! It was this little special on the CBS."

She loved saying "the CBS" like it was a thing.

"Have you heard of Frederick Archibald? They did a feature about his upbringing and his special path to the Olympics."

My stomach dropped at the mention of his name. Was there no escaping his celebrity?

"Apparently he's a prince or something in England!"

I laughed and shook my head. "Mom, he's not a prince. He's just on the swim team."

She shushed me. "No no, believe me. Hold on, let me open up the Google."

Oh Jesus.

Ten minutes later—after she'd accidentally restarted her computer and updated her antivirus software twice— she pulled up the article.

"All right! It says here—" She paused and shuffled around, and I knew she was finding her tortoise shell reading glasses. "His father was the Duke of Farlington and before he passed away, Freddie was just called Lord

Frederick Archibald, but now he is His Grace, Frederick Archibald, Earl of Norhill and Duke of Farlington!"

Wait. *What?* I laughed. That couldn't possibly be right. She made it sound like Freddie was living in Middle Earth. I didn't even know dukes were still a thing that existed.

I turned away from the window and pressed the phone closer to my ear. She kept rambling on about the CBS special, but I couldn't wrap my head around what she was saying. Freddie was a DUKE? He'd touched my hand! He'd touched my *butt!* He'd basically knighted me and I'd tossed my panties at his face like a commoner. Jesus.

"Mom, I have to go," I said, overwhelmed by the discovery.

"Oh? So soon? All right, okay. Just use that hand sanitizer and try to find Frederick. I'd love to show your meemaw a photo of you with British royalty."

Oh my god. "Okay Mom. Sounds good."

"Oh wait! It's also says here that three weeks ago——"

I hung up before she could continue to ramble. I loved her, truly I did, but once she got going, there was no stopping her. It was either cut her off midsentence or turn into a mummified corpse out on that balcony.

By the time I made it back inside, Kinsley and Becca had exchanged their unicorn onesies for jean shorts and t-shirts. We started making our way down to the food court, and though my stomach was rumbling nonstop, I couldn't help but focus on what my mother had just told me. If Freddie really was British royalty—wait, are dukes royal? *Who cares.* If Freddie really was a *duke*, the chances of him and I ever getting another moment alone were slim to none. He probably wouldn't be hanging out around the Olympic village like other athletes. He'd be off sipping tea with baby George.

"Are you thinking about Freddie?" Kinsley asked as we stepped out of the elevator on the first floor.

I shrugged and lied. "No."

"Because there really is something you should know before—"

I held up my hand. "Honestly, could everyone please stop talking about him?"

Between my mom and Kinsley, I'd never get him out of my head. I was in Rio to play the field, not get hung up on a guy after day one.

———

I'D GROWN USED to Kinsley's popularity back in Los Angeles, but walking around with her in the village felt like accompanying Taylor Swift to the Grammys. When we stepped into the food court, heads snapped in our direction. Athletes, families, friends, coaches—it didn't matter what country they were from—they all knew who Kinsley Bryant was, thanks to her marriage to Liam Wilder and her meteoric rise to soccer fame.

I slipped behind her and let her take the brunt of the attention. She delighted in it in a way I knew I never would. I liked the sponsorship opportunities and perks that went along with being an Olympic athlete, but I also enjoyed walking through the grocery store in sweatpants without having to worry that the paparazzi would be waiting to snap photos of me outside. Kinsley didn't have that luxury.

"Better get used to this," Kinsley said, glancing back at me over her shoulder. "Once you carry the flag in the opening ceremonies, people all over the world will know who you are."

I bristled at the thought. When the Olympic committee

had asked if I'd like to be one of the flag bearers during the opening ceremonies, I'd been honored and had agreed without a second thought. Now, as I followed Kinsley past tables and noticed the curious stares, I wondered if maybe I'd made a mistake. I wasn't quite ready to exchange my relative obscurity for fame.

"Woah, watch it," Becca said, pulling me out of the way just before I collided with a group of athletes weaving in the opposite direction.

The food court was a bona fide watering hole for sports stars of all countries. We headed toward a juice bar nestled near the back wall and I scanned over the crowd, taking it all in.

It was remarkably easy to spot the different sports; the telltale signs gave each one away. The rugby and weightlifting guys made their way through four or five different lines, stacking up their trays with enough sustenance to last a normal human a full year. A group of Serbian basketball players had taken up residence in the corner of the food court, towering over the crowd and making the team of Australian gymnasts sitting beside them look like hobbits.

Though there were clearly differences in body sizes, there was no denying one fact: every single person was young and in the best shape of their lives. It was no wonder there were so many rumors about the Olympic village; hundreds of attractive athletes with energy to spare were bound to get into a little bit of trouble.

"What kind of juice are you going to get?" Kinsley asked, pulling me out of my survey of the room. We were nearly at the front of the line and I hadn't even glanced over the menu.

"I think I want a smoothie."

She laughed. "Well there's like fifty of them, so—"

Kinsley was cut off when the girl behind us in line squealed so loud I nearly lost hearing in my left ear.

"HOLY SHIT," she squealed, nudging her friend's arm. "There's Freddie!"

"Shut up! *Shut up*," her friend chimed in.

My gut clenched as I glanced over my shoulder. The girls were a good deal shorter than I was, and when I spun to face them, the faint smell of chlorine spiked the air. They were definitely swimmers, and judging by their identical mannerisms, I guessed *synchronized*.

"Oh my god. He's coming this way," the first girl said. "Do I look okay?"

If Freddie was coming their way, he was coming *my* way. My heart pounded in my chest as I scanned past the girls to see Freddie walk up to the back of the juice line with what looked like a few other guys from his swim team. He hadn't noticed me yet, which was for the best, because I couldn't drag my gaze away from him. At the party the night before, it'd been dark, and the alcohol had cast him in hazy soap opera light. Here, now, in the food court, there was no denying his appeal.

I stood immobile, accepting the punch to the gut that came with the realization that Freddie's good looks hinted at years of mischief managed through sly smiles and charming words. His kind brown eyes and endearing smile suggested he'd never been grounded a day in his life, but the chiseled jaw and sharp cheekbones whispered that he probably should have been.

He was trying to look over the menu, but there was too much excitement surrounding him. A line of athletes began to form to the side of him as if choreographed beforehand.

"Could I get an autograph for my mum?"

"Freddie! Where are you staying for the games?"

"Can I see your abs?"

Question after question came his way, and I realized that whatever popularity Kinsley had, it didn't hold a candle to Freddie's. He drew attention like he was born for it, and as he smiled down and graciously signed autographs, I remembered that might well have been the case.

I used the crowd to conceal my gaze as I continued watching him, or at least I thought I did. I was openly gawking at him as he handed off an autograph and turned in my direction. His eyes locked on me and he smiled out of the right side of his mouth, a slow, cheeky smile that grew the longer I stared.

"Andie," Kinsley hissed, trying to break through the spell.

I blinked once, twice. Freddie offered me a subtle wave, and then I spun around with cheeks on fire and embarrassment coating my skin.

"Holy shit," I said, exhaling a breath I hadn't realized I was holding. "How long was I staring at him?"

Kinsley gripped my hand and squeezed it, hard. "I thought you went catatonic there for a second."

I squeezed my eyes closed and groaned under my breath. Then, a hand reached out and tapped my shoulder. It was the girl from before—the swimmer with the nails-on-a-chalkboard squeal.

"Um, excuse me. Do you *know* Freddie?"

Before I could answer, her friend chimed in.

"If you do, could you introduce us? It's just that—"

Kinsley held up her hand to stop them. "She doesn't know him. He was clearly waving at the juice man," she said, motioning to the elderly Brazilian man behind the counter.

I forced myself to move forward in line and I kept my eyes trained ahead of me, but the excitement behind me was too hard to ignore. People whispered, girls squealed, and cameras flashed as Freddie took photos with his fans. I moved forward and ordered a strawberry banana protein smoothie, and as I turned to find a seat with Kinsley, I ignored every urge to look in his direction as I passed. It was painful to deny myself that simple pleasure, and I was still lamenting that fact when he bent out of line and reached for my hand. His palm touched mine and my heart stopped. He gripped my hand tightly, just for a moment, then let it go.

Hhhhooooookkkkaay. I was definitely having a heart attack. *This is the end. I'm going to die in a smoothie line.* I couldn't breathe and my chest hurt, and then he smiled and started speaking, but I couldn't hear him over the sound of my heart.

"I'm sorry," I accidentally shouted. "What?"

He smiled wider, reveling in the fact that he'd knocked me off my senses. I could only focus on his eyes, at the exact shade of light brown that promised to be my demise.

"Your smoothie," he said with a smooth British accent. "You've left it."

I whipped around to see a girl behind the counter waving my smoothie in the air like a metronome. "Don't you want this?" she asked, confused.

I cringed. Had I not grabbed it already? Apparently not. I hid my face as I walked back and took it from her hand. Every single person in line trailed my movements, either because they thought I was a little off my rocker, or because Freddie Archibald had just reached out and held my hand. His touch had been warm and his palm was massive, wrapping around mine with no effort at all.

I'd stood in line for a smoothie for a solid twenty minutes and then I'd walked away empty-handed, too dumbstruck to care. All because of Freddie-freaking-Archibald—who, by the way, was still watching me.

I forced myself to make eye contact with him as I passed, and he smiled a secret little smile I knew I'd be dissecting for hours.

"See you around," he said, and the words felt more like a promise than a dismissal.

Kinsley and Becca didn't say a word as we took our seats at a table far, far away from Freddie and his adoring fans. I purposely positioned myself with my back to him and stared at my smoothie.

"Honestly, Andie, you need to cool your jets with Freddie—"

Kinsley started rambling on again, but I wasn't listening. She was going to tell me to "focus on soccer" and "stay away from boys" and "don't party" and "keep your head in the game", and I didn't want to hear it.

I pulled my phone out of my purse to find a text message my mom had sent right after I'd hung up on her. I swiped it open much to the dismay of Kinsley.

"Andie!" Kinsley said. "Are you listening?"

Mom: You didn't let me finish! Frederick is betrothed. Can you believe it? Maybe if the two of you become friends you'll be invited to a royal wedding! Or maybe he has a friend…another duke perhaps! Meemaw would be so excited!

NO! Betrothed? *Betrothed?* No. No. No.

My stomach hurt. This wasn't right. He was supposed to be single. We were supposed to touch hands and exchange sly smiles and…

"He's betrothed?" I asked, hearing the shock in my voice.

I dropped my phone on the table and Kinsley leaned

forward to read the text message. When she was done, she glanced up at me with a pitiful frown.

"That's what I've been trying to tell you all morning. Freddie is set to marry some girl named Caroline Montague. The betrothal was announced a few weeks ago."

That made no sense.

Who the hell was Caroline Montague?

Chapter Eight

ANDIE

AFTER **HEARING THE** news of *Frederick's* betrothal, I sat immobile, absorbing the news in shocked silence as my smoothieless stomach began to grumble. My mother had attached a Daily Mail news story to her text message and though I didn't want to, I read it. It highlighted the life and love of Caroline Montague and chronicled her high society British upbringing. Her father, while not titled himself, had invented the software used in most vending machines, and subsequently leveraged his earnings to put his hand in just about every business operating in London. She was worth more than most countries and the news story hinted that their betrothal would unite two illustrious European families, from the old world and the new.

There was a photo of Freddie and Caroline from their teenage years at the very bottom of the article. Apparently they'd been friends since childhood and it had come as a shock to no one when their families announced the betrothal. Caroline Montague was beautiful with delicate features and long blonde hair. She was styled "The People's

Princess Diana", beloved by all and philanthropic to the core. How lovely.

I wanted to feel heartbroken and betrayed by the news. My gut told me I'd been wronged, but then common sense chimed in and leveled with me. I was *not* in love with Frederick Archibald. People do not fall in love overnight. I was merely excited by the idea of Freddie the same way I got excited by two-for-one ice cream sundaes at McDonald's. I couldn't fault myself for it. I had working lady parts and a pulse, therefore the sight of Frederick Archibald had seemed alluring. No big deal. I could move on. There were plenty of other fish in the sea (probably the most applicable that phrase would ever be). The games were filled with sexy athletes whose only baggage was of the carryon variety. Sure, Freddie's jaw was chiseled from Grecian marble and his boyish grin had topped a BuzzFeed poll in 2014 entitled "Panty-Melting Smiles", but there were plenty of attractive people in Rio. Thousands of them, in fact. On to the next.

"Andie, yoohoo! Earth to Andie."

I glanced up to find Kinsley staring at me over the back of the couch. Becca sat beside her, flipping through TV channels at a rate that made my eyes water.

"Becca and I found this really good Netflix documentary series about baby arctic whales, and if we start it tonight, we can probably finish all the episodes before we head back to L.A."

She seemed really excited about the prospect, but there was no way I was joining them. I was putting the finishing touches on a sandwich in our condo's tiny kitchen, and instead of replying, I took a giant bite and offered her a vague head nod.

"Wait. Why are you dressed like you're going out?" she asked, narrowing her eyes.

Becca turned back to assess me as well and I swallowed down the glob of peanut butter lodged in my throat.

"Oh. Well." I glanced down at my jean cutoffs and a cream, off-the-shoulder blouse. "Because I am."

Kinsley threw up her arms. "But Liam will be over here soon, and you are supposed to be our little baby beluga."

"I thought you loved whales," Becca added.

They knew I had a love for whales and they'd likely picked the series because they thought I needed cheering up. They assumed I was upset about Freddie's betrothal, but I couldn't have been further from upset. I didn't need to mope around our condo like my love life was over, because in fact, it was just getting started. I'd received an invitation on Facebook to a poker night hosted by a few members of the Portuguese men's soccer team, and there was no way I was going to pass up that opportunity. They were all tall, tan, and ridiculously handsome. I hadn't played poker in years, but I figured I could skirt by on luck long enough to find a replacement for my Rio boy-toy. I mean, what isn't cute about two soccer players in love? Nothing, as evidenced by Kinsley and Becca's storybook romances.

"As fun as the documentary sounds, I think I'm going to go out."

They frowned in tandem.

"Look, I don't expect you guys to understand. You're both married, and well, boring."

"Hey!" Becca said.

I threw them an apologetic smile. "I mean, it's the truth. If you guys were single, you'd be coming to this poker night with me."

"Not true," Kinsley argued.

I laughed. "Right. Let's see. Remember when you

broke the rules to date Liam Wilder even though he was your college soccer coach?"

Becca burst out laughing, but Kinsley turned and narrowed her bright blue eyes on me. "That was different."

I shrugged. "It just seems strange that you're so adamantly against me going out and meeting a cute guy here when you both have had your fair share of fun."

Becca hummed in thought. I knew I was making a valid point.

"I just think I should get the choice to make the most of being in Rio."

Kinsley nodded. "You're right. But just so you know, you're gorgeous, Andie. And I'm not just saying that because I like you. You could be betrothed to a million Freddie Archibalds if you wanted to be."

I shook my head. "Thanks for your confidence in my polygamy skills, but really, I'm not even thinking about that —*him*—any more."

"And if you want to go out and have fun, be my guest, but I'm not going to stop being overprotective of you. I made a promise to your mom that I'd watch out for you while we're down here."

"My mom called you?!"

Kinsley shot me a glare. "Christy has me on speed dial."

Of course. I should have known.

I grabbed my small clutch from the dresser in my room and then slipped on my favorite pair of brown leather flip-flops. When I walked back into the living room, Kinsley and Becca stared up at me, assessing my outfit.

"You're wearing a bra right?"

I rolled my eyes.

"And underwear? Are they *your own* this time?" Becca asked.

I ignored them and walked to the door.

"Stay safe. Text us and don't stay out too late. We have an early practice tomorrow."

"Wow you really have been talking to Christy lately," I teased over my shoulder just as a knock sounded on the door. As anticipated, Liam stood on the other side with a bag full of takeout clutched in hand. He'd just showered and his hair was damp and mussed up a bit. Kinsley had definitely gotten lucky with him. I smiled and stole a handful of French fries as I sneaked past into the hallway.

"Hey! Wait. Aren't you watching the documentary thing with us?" he asked.

"No, unlike you losers, I actually have plans."

"Stay safe!" he shouted as I leaned forward to press the elevator call button.

Staying safe wasn't really hard to do. While Rio at large had issues with crime, the village in contrast was secure and locked down after 8:00 PM. Athletes were free to roam as they pleased. The Portuguese guys were assigned a condo two buildings down from mine. The breeze from the ocean picked up my hair and blew it every which direction. I twisted the long strands in a low bun to keep them from sticking to my lipstick. I'd kept it simple in the makeup department. I still had a tan from outdoor practices back home, so I didn't have to worry about foundation. I'd swiped on a subtle shade of red lipstick and mascara, and felt confident as I rode the elevator up to the third floor.

The noise from their condo could be heard even before I stepped off the elevator. I double-checked the Facebook invite and confirmed that the rowdy, bass-filled condo was the one I was supposed to be heading toward. *312.* I offered a soft knock on the door though I knew it would go unheard. After another try, I turned the handle and stepped inside, surprised by the butterflies that swarmed my stomach as I entered.

Though the music was blaring, the condo was far less crowded than the Rubik's Cube party had been the night before. There were a few guys in the kitchen mixing up a batch of sangria in a cooler on the floor. They waved me in and pointed to the living room where the rest of the party unfolded before me.

The soccer guys had pushed all the furniture aside to make room for three poker tables. I was running a little late, so the first two tables were already full of people drinking and talking and waving at me as I passed. I slid through the gaps in the chairs and headed for the last table where four empty chairs were waiting to be claimed.

I was about to take a seat when a hand reached out to grab my arm. I turned over my shoulder and came face to face with a tan, smiling guy I recognized from the Facebook invite. I couldn't remember his name, but he was definitely on the Portuguese national team.

"Hey," he said warmly.

He looked handsome, but it was hard to tell with the throwback green visor on his head—a prop for poker night. A few other guys around the living room had them on as well.

"Hey. I'm Andie."

He shook my hand and did a poor job of concealing his gaze as it slid down my body.

"Andie Foster," he said with a smile. "I was hope to having you here." He spoke in choppy English with a thick, seductive accent.

He pulled my chair out for me and took one of the open seats beside me.

"I'm Nathan Drake."

My brows rose in shock. Nathan Drake was a popular

54

name and though I hadn't noticed him at first—probably because of his visor—I'd definitely seen him on a few commercials; he was a heavily sponsored European soccer player in the same stratosphere as David and Liam.

My reaction to his name made him smile wider, revealing a pair of perfectly straight teeth and a single dimple that rimmed the edge of his lips. I was staring there as he spoke up again.

"You have done poker playing before?" he asked.

I shook my head. "Not recently, but I'm hoping I can keep up."

I glanced around the table to check out my competition. Poker was a wise choice for an international party, as the game could be played primarily with universal hand signals and gestures. Fortunately, no one seemed like they'd be taking the game too seriously, and Nathan assured me we wouldn't be playing with real money.

Our table was split evenly between three girls and three boys.

"That is Tatiana and Sarah," he said, pointing to two girls across the table. "Eric and Jorge." I waved and smiled as he introduced everyone I'd be playing with for the next few hours. The majority in attendance were Portuguese athletes, but Eric was an American rower and Tatiana was a Russian diver.

Nathan started shuffling the cards. "We will starting soon. There is a few people still to arrive."

"Sangria estará pronto em breve!" cheered the guys mixing the fruity wine in the kitchen.

They started passing out small cups filled with the concoction as more guests filtered inside, filling the empty seats. The sangria looked good but smelled like equal parts brandy to wine, so I politely declined a cup. Kinsley, though overbearing at times, was right about our early morning practice; I didn't need to be throwing up liquor while we did our workout.

"*Sabe* Frederick?" Nathan asked. "The swimmer?"

I pulled my attention from the room and glanced over. Nathan was beaming over at me, proud of himself for something.

"Um, yeah I know him, sort of. Why?"

He smiled wider. "He's coming. Is the guest special for the evening." He hesitated through the sentence, trying out the words for what seemed like the first time. Freddie was going to be a special guest?

My gut clenched at the thought and I stood from my chair like someone had lit a fire beneath me.

"What is wrong?" Nathan asked, staring up at me.

I shook my head and frowned just as the front door opened again. One of the British swimmers I'd seen in the food court walked in with Freddie right behind him. Everyone greeted them excitedly, but my heart rioted in my chest at the sight. He could slip on a pair of jeans and a gray Henley t-shirt. He could put a baseball cap on and pretend like he was Freddie, not Frederick, but I knew better. He had a certain charm about him—a faultless charm he was fully aware of—and when he glanced across the room and leveled me with his dark gaze beneath the rim of his hat, I knew it'd be a hopeless cause to try and get over him by flirting with a few soccer players.

There was *no* getting over him.

I wasn't surprised when he slipped past open seats at the other tables and made his way toward me. I wasn't surprised when he stopped at the seat beside mine, standing a foot away and stealing my comfort, my resolve, and my senses as he pulled the chair out from the table. I tried to focus down on the green felt, but it was no use. I still caught a whiff of his cologne—or maybe it was his body wash; I couldn't tell. It was subtle but strong, and I found myself wishing for a stuffy nose so I wouldn't have to keep smelling it. *We get it. You're a duke and you smell divine.* Did he need to keep rubbing it in?

"I should have expected to find you here," he said with a smirk I couldn't see but knew was there. "Poker definitely suits you."

"Oh yeah?" I said, finally turning to face him. MISTAKE. It was much easier to put up a barrier against Freddie when he wasn't sitting inches away from me, smiling like the devil himself.

"Yeah, you've got quite a good poker face," he continued.

I tilted my head and tried to get a good look at his eyes under the brim of his hat. Who was he trying to hide from in that thing? There wasn't a person in the room who didn't know who he was.

"Why do you think that?"

"You seem wholly unaffected by me."

I smiled, glad I at least appeared that way on the outside.

"I am."

He smirked. "Are you?"

It was a textbook example of dry British banter with just a tinge of good-natured provocation, but rather than giving him the satisfaction, I decided to go on the offensive.

"Congrats on the betrothal," I said with an arched brow. "Caroline's really pretty."

The blow clearly found its mark as his jaw tightened. "She's just a friend."

"A friend that you're *engaged* to marry," I reminded him.

"My family set up the betrothal. It wasn't any of my doing."

I shook my head. "Clearly I don't understand your

archaic English traditions. To be honest, I didn't even realize betrothals were still a thing. In America, we like to be in control of our own destinies."

His light brown eyes met mine beneath his cap and for a moment I thought I caught a glimpse of the real Freddie, not the teasing London playboy, but a man faced with a future he might not want.

He opened his mouth to speak just as Nathan slapped the deck of cards down on the table in front of me.

"Everyone is here! Ready to play?"

Chapter Nine

FREDDIE

I HADN'T BEEN into the idea of poker night. I'd told Thom to bugger off a half dozen times, but he'd guilted me into attending with a sob story about how he "used to do this sort of thing with Henry all the time." He'd have moaned on about it all night, and I didn't want to hear about how my brother had been ace at poker, so I grudgingly accepted with strict terms: we'd go for a little bit, Thom would play a few hands, and then I'd get back to the flat and rest up. I had an early morning workout and I was still a bit jetlagged from traveling halfway around the world.

Of course that plan was tossed out the window as soon as I walked into the flat with Thom and spotted Andie across the room. She was standing up, looking a bit peaky, like she was ready to bolt at the mere sight of me. Maybe I should have given her space, but I didn't. I slipped past a few blokes and made my way toward her table.

Our banter was easy, her presence was welcome, and though it'd surprised me to hear her speak of Caroline, I'd ended the discussion quickly. I didn't want to talk about her, not when Andie was so close.

She enthralled me. I sat watching her out of the corner of my eye as Nathan passed round the cards and went on about the rules. It was dull, but I nodded along and watched Andie, taking in her delicate features and the hair pinned just at the nape of her neck. The pale shade of blonde reminded me of the summer sun. Her shirt fell off her shoulder closest to me and there were a slew of freckles dotting her tan skin there, just at the top.

"Freddie, if you keep trying to look at my cards," she said, "I'll have to ask someone to switch spots with me." She kept her focus on her obscured cards, but I could see the smile she was trying to hide.

"Right." I pretended to glance over my cards. "I was just wondering if you play poker often?"

Everyone was taking their time arranging their hand and assessing their odds, but it wasn't bloody rocket science. I'd been playing poker for years and I didn't have to concentrate hard on the game. I could play *and* focus on Andie; the two weren't mutually exclusive.

"No, actually," she replied. "I like to play games of skill, not luck."

I nodded. "I'm afraid it's not my strong suit either. I tend to wear my heart on my sleeve."

"And where do you keep your spades and diamonds?" she asked with a soft smile.

Her smiles never lasted long enough. She was back to focusing on her hand, worried over the cards that had yet to be overturned, but I wanted her attention. I leaned closer and whispered in her ear.

"What if you and I have our own little wager?"

Her brow arched with curiosity, though she kept her

focus on her cards. "Like a side bet? I didn't bring any money."

I nodded as I rearranged my cards. "Nothing serious. Just some fun since we're both novices."

She didn't answer right away and when I glanced over, I found her eyeing me suspiciously, as if she was trying to see through my disguise. I watched as she brought her full bottom lip between her teeth, mulling over the bet, and for a moment I was worried she'd say no.

"I've not known an Olympian that was afraid of a little competition," I taunted playfully.

She let go of her lip and straightened up. Just the mere mention of a competition lit a fire behind her gaze and I knew I had her.

"All right, you're on Mr. Viscount of WhateverIts-Called. What are we playing for?"

I smirked.

"We both have to workout, so I propose a 'turf war' of sorts. If I win, you join me in the pool tomorrow, and if you win, I'll join you on the pitch."

She titled her head, still inspecting me as if she'd find my true intent written across my features. I arched a brow and she reached out to shake my hand.

"You're on."

We shook on it and I didn't let go until I was good and ready.

"I hope you packed a bikini."

Chapter Ten

ANDIE

"**K**INSLEY!**" I SHOUTED** through the condo. "Did you happen to pack an old, 1850s style bathing suit in your suitcase?

"What?" she shouted back.

I groaned. "Never mind."

She poked her head past my doorway, but I didn't bother glancing up; I knew she'd have judgy eyes.

"Jeez, it's a mess in here."

She wasn't lying.

I'd systematically removed every piece of clothing from my suitcase and tossed it aside after a quick inspection. I was trying to find something to wear down to the pool. I'd packed two bathing suits, both of which were bikinis, neither of which I would be caught dead wearing around Freddie—who was, by the way, either a card shark or a lucky beginner. Or the devil. I still hadn't decided.

"Why do you need a bathing suit?" she asked.

I tossed another t-shirt aside. "Because I have to go swimming."

"Right, so just wear that bikini you have behind you."

She was pointing at the skimpy light blue one. "It's very Rio."

I slapped my hand over my eyes and shook my head. "Yes, obviously. That's the problem. My boobs look too good in that one. I need one that says 'I'm boring and unavailable' which I figured would be right up your alley."

"I'll have you know that Liam still thinks I'm really sexy. Just because we've been married for a few years doesn't mean our sex life isn't still amazing. Just yesterday, we tried this new thing where I spin—"

"NOPE. NADA. NOPE." I held up my hand to stop her from continuing. "You can stop it right there. I don't need to hear how gross you two are in the bedroom."

"Fine, but I'm sorry, I don't have a nun's habit for you to wear to go swimming. Just wear that bikini like a normal person."

I moaned really loudly, hoping it would scare her away, but it didn't work.

"Who are you going swimming with anyway?"

I paused with a t-shirt gripped in my hands. "No one."

"BECCA! GET IN HERE."

"NO!" I shouted.

There was no time to prepare. Before I could run and lock myself in the bathroom, Becca and Kinsley had worked their dynamic duo voodoo magic on me. Becca had my hands pinned to the floor and Kinsley had my feet. I tried my hardest to thrash them off me, but it was no use.

"Who are you going swimming with?" Kinsley asked again.

"You're not supposed to end a sentence with a preposition," I replied.

"Stop changing the subject! With whom do you plan to swim?!"

"No one! I like to swim laps every now and then!"

She shook her head. "Becca, go fill up a cup. We're going to have to waterboard her."

"NO!"

"Kinsley, I think that's a war crime, even in Rio," Becca warned.

"Well if she likes the water as much *as she claims*, it shouldn't feel like torture."

"Let me go and I'll tell you! I promise."

"Tell us and *then* we'll let you go," Kinsley countered.

"Ow, my wrist!"

Becca was technically holding my bad wrist and though she wasn't really hurting it, my ruse still worked. She loosened her grip just enough that I could break free and twist out of their grasp. I jumped off the floor and reached for something to throw at them in case they came near me again. A cleat was the first thing I grabbed for, but Kinsley was faster. She yanked my favorite t-shirt off the floor, the Harry Potter one with a picture of Rupert Grint across the front and the words "King Weasley" underneath.

"Tell me or Ron gets it."

I narrowed my eyes. "You wouldn't dare."

She stretched the material near the neck, just enough to show me she was serious.

I dropped the cleat and held my hands up in surrender.

"Fine, you death eater, I'm going swimming with the duke."

They exchanged a knowing glance and then Kinsley let my t-shirt drop to the floor. I ran for it and picked it up, confirming that Ron was indeed unharmed.

"Why would you go swimming with him? He's betrothed to another girl."

I rolled my eyes. "I know that. But there's been a development."

"Go on..." Kinsley implored, clearly waiting for some kind of explanation.

"Truthfully, it's because we—he—made a little bet about it at poker night. He told me he wasn't good at poker —which was a huge lie by the way—and I lost. So, now I have to go swimming with him."

They did another one of those "oh dear, this situation doesn't look good" glances.

"Would you two stop? Nothing is going on. And even if something was going on, it isn't me that is initiating it."

I wasn't even lying. Freddie and I had played a few hands of poker the night before and it'd been fun to let my hair down and relax. I knew he was betrothed and he knew I was too cool for him, so there was no pressure. We could just be friends. Super hot, super not interested in each other friends. I didn't see the problem.

At the end of poker night—after I'd called him out for being a cheating asshole—he'd laughed and reached for one of the cards on the table. He scrawled something on it and then Thom shouted out for him, telling him he was heading home for the night. Freddie pressed the card into my palm and then turned away. I stood there, watching him leave, ignoring the slope of his muscled back and shoulders as he walked through the door.

When I turned the card over, it read, *1:00 PM - Central Natatorium Training Complex.*

He didn't even bother asking me if I was free to swim then. Clearly I had to go, if only to reprimand him for assuming, and to tell him that if there was a next time (which there wouldn't be), he should ask me about my schedule first.

I explained this to Kinsley and Becca and they both shook their heads.

"That makes no sense," Kinsley said. "You're going because you think the man will look good in the pool."

Becca nodded. "And you want to see him shirtless. You're reverse Ariel; you're trading your human legs for a mermaid tail so you can kiss him."

I gasped. "What? No. That's preposterous."

"You've never used that word, so I know you're lying."

"Right well, thanks for the love you two. Must get ready now. Chat later." I shooed them both out of my room—a bit forcefully at the end since Kinsley is strong for her size. She tried to hold on to the doorframe and dig her heels in, but I pushed her out and then locked the door as quickly as possible.

"You're only fooling yourself!" she shouted back.

I couldn't hear her over the sound of me telling myself how smart it was to go for a swim. Really, as my big sister on the soccer team, Kinsley of all people should have been encouraging my interest in cross-training.

Chapter Eleven

INHALE. **STROKE. STROKE.** Inhale. Stroke. Stroke. I sliced through the cold water as I felt the muscles in my arms start to protest. I'd finished my workout a few minutes earlier, but I kept swimming. It was the best kind of burn, the slow-spreading reminder of how close I was to competing in another Olympic games. I kicked hard, touched the wall, and sprang up out of the water to check the timer. I'd finished half a second faster than my last circuit.

"Good work, Archibald," Coach yelled from across the pool.

I pulled myself out and shook off water like a mangy mutt.

"Think you could manage a break?" Thom asked. "Your arms will fall off before the games have even started." He threw my towel at me and I reached out to catch it before it landed in the pool. He'd already showered and changed, which meant I'd stayed in the pool even longer than I'd assumed.

I shrugged. "Feels good. I haven't had that good of a go since arriving."

"Yeah, well you're already crushing my time, and I'm the fastest bloody swimmer in the world. I think you could manage a breather every now and again."

I wrapped the towel around my neck and walked to my bag so I could check my mobile. There was a text from Georgie waiting for me.

Georgie: Mum tried to phone you this morning, but I hid the charger for her cell. She was stomping around and having a fit. She'll never find it in Chester's litter box. I hid her hideous canary red lipstick there the other day as well. The woman should thank me—she looked like a cherry tart.

I smiled and typed back a reply.

Freddie: I owe you one.

"What are you doing now?" Thom asked. "Off to the gym?"

I shook my head and tossed my mobile back onto my bag.

"I actually have plans."

"What? Who with?"

I shrugged. "No one."

My mobile buzzed in my bag again and I reached for it as a way out. "Actually, I've got to handle this straightaway."

I made it seem like an important email, but it was just Georgie texting me back. It worked though; Thom wandered off and I shouted that I'd see him back at the flat. I knew he'd interrogate me later, but I could work up a proper excuse by then.

Georgie: Oh no. Mum found the lippie.

Georgie: AND SHE PUT IT ON. You should have seen the look Chester gave her.

Georgie: Also she found her charger. Prepare yourself...I think I hear her trying to ring you from the front room.

She wasn't lying. I'd barely closed Georgie's text when my mum's call popped up on my screen. Bloody hell. I had to answer it. It was better to get it over with. Besides, Andie wasn't due for another few minutes and all the swimmers had left the natatorium. I was alone with time to kill, so I swiped my finger across the screen, took a breath, and answered.

"Hello Mum."

"Frederick!"

She and Caroline were the only people who ever called me by my full name. I despised it. Henry had been named after my father, which left me to inherit a moniker from my great uncle, a stuffy bloke with red cheeks and a belly so round I used to wonder how he fit into the chairs in our dining room. He'd moan on about etiquette and the 'old ways of British aristocracy' any chance he got. In other words, he was a real bore and someone I hoped to never become.

"I'm thrilled to have caught you. Are you busy at practice?"

I wrapped my towel around my waist and took a seat on the bench.

"No, I've got a few minutes. How are things in London?"

She sighed heavily as though I'd just asked her to open up during a therapy session. "Dreadful. I've got Georgie driving me mad, but you know how hard it is to stay cross with her."

I smiled. "Nearly impossible."

"Precisely. And well, I've already begun planning the winter ball here at the estate. Of course with your upcoming engagement, it needs to be more lavish than ever before. I'm thinking of bringing on a party planner to help with everything."

My chest tightened.

"Right."

"It's a significant event, Frederick. When Henry passed so soon after your father, I wasn't sure how we'd manage. Whether you like the title or not, you must bear it. You are the Duke of Farlington and your marriage to Caroline is just what this family needs. She's been reared for this since childhood and she'll make a wonderful duchess one day. She's familiar with running an estate and her family is so close to ours. It couldn't be a more perfect union."

I leaned back against the wall and stared up at the ceiling, listening to her go on.

"And speaking of Caroline…I know you're busy with your races, so I've asked her to accompany Georgie to Rio, to make things easier on you."

I sat forward with a start. "What do you mean? You've invited Caroline to Rio?"

"Georgie's only eighteen. She needs a chaperone, and it's not as if you've got the time. I would go myself, but I have too much to do here."

I dropped my head in my hands and squeezed my eyes closed. "I wish you might have asked me first, Mum."

"Oh Freddie. She's going to be your wife. It's time you start actually spending time together."

We had spent time together. I'd known Caroline my whole life. She had been a fixture in our house for as long as I could remember, but she was never someone I imagined myself marrying—and neither had Henry for that matter. Their betrothal had been just as arranged as ours, but Henry had accepted the responsibility without a second thought. He was the dutiful heir I could only try in vain to be.

Honestly, I thought my mum had it in her head that Caroline and I would marry even before we'd arrived home from Henry's funeral. It was my duty and there was no way around it.

It was three weeks before I left for Rio—I'd been in the middle of heavy training—when she'd come to me with the idea of the betrothal. She'd known exactly what she was doing. I was too busy to devote my attention to anything but racing. I'd told her to table it until after the Olympics, but she took my indecision as resignation. She'd made the decision and there wasn't room for negotiations. Caroline and her family were informed before I'd even entertained the scenario.

I still had my head in my hand, listening to my mum, when the door to the natatorium opened. I glanced up to see Andie stride in, and whatever dark cloud had formed over me during the last five minutes vanished. She walked in wearing her team's warm-up gear: windbreaker pants and a jacket. She had her workout bag slung across her shoulder and when she looked up and saw me, a slow smile spread across her face.

"Freddie," my mom continued. "I know you've a lot to think about right now, but just know that I'm arranging everything in your best—"

"Mum I've got to go."

I hung up before she could respond and stood to greet Andie.

"Before you say anything," she said, "I came straight from practice." She pointed to the mess of hair atop her head. The usually light strands were damp with sweat and her cheeks were still flush from her workout. She wasn't wearing any makeup and I swept my gaze over her features quickly, trying to commit the pink shade of her bare lips to memory without her noticing.

"I hope you've worn a bathing suit under that thing," I said, gesturing to her track pants.

She smirked, glanced over her shoulder to the empty natatorium, and then reached for the zipper of her jacket. I averted my gaze as she undressed, though I didn't know why. Force of habit, perhaps.

She cleared her throat and I glanced back toward her, laughter spilling out before I could stop myself.

"What in the world have you got on?"

She was wearing a tight blue spandex top that covered her arms down to her wrists and zipped up the center of her chest until it ended at the base of her neck. It looked like what surfers wore during competitions, and the bottom was even worse: baggy red board shorts that cinched above her waist and fell below her knees, turning her figure into an amorphous blob.

"What is that?"

She smiled. "A swim shirt. I found it in the gift shop on the way over. And the trunks are to dispel any assumptions of…impropriety, should we have any spectators."

"Right well, the place is deserted," I said, waving to the empty natatorium. "Besides, you can't possibly wear those trunks to swim. They'll pull you down like an anchor."

"No. They're light." She proceeded to hop up and down to prove her point. "Look. See how high I can jump?"

My smile spread wider as I shook my head. "Please tell me you've got a normal swimsuit on under there."

She leveled me with an annoyed gaze. "Fine."

With a sigh, she tugged the slip-knotted drawstring and

the baggy shorts fell to the ground, revealing light blue bikini bottoms. Thin strings tied on either side of her slim, tan hips, and I took in the sight with a heavy inhale. The tight swim top stopped just below her belly button, revealing the last few inches of her tiny waist. She had an athlete's body, lithe and strong, but there was no denying she was all woman. She'd put on the swim shirt to hide herself, but instead it served to accentuate the outline of her breasts, full and tempting. She was bloody gorgeous and I needed to get in the cold water straightaway.

"Maybe I should have had you keep the trousers on," I said, standing up and tossing my towel to the side.

The sooner we hopped into the pool, the better.

She laughed. "This was your doing, remember? You made the bet."

Her words reminded me that in travelling down this road, I was betting on much more than poker.

Andie

TRYING TO SLYLY check out Freddie in his swim shorts should have been an Olympic sport in itself. The moment he stood up and shed his towel, I turned my head but simultaneously developed one lazy eye, which pointed at Freddie regardless of which way I looked.

When he stretched by the edge of the pool, I lost motor function and suddenly couldn't remember how normal people stood. *Do they hold their weight on both legs or just sort of casually lean on one? Crossed arms? No that looks angry. Wait, what are arms for again?* I let the now meaningless limbs fall limply to my sides and pretended to listen to Freddie as he went on about proper freestyle form. I didn't care about swimming form, I cared about *his* form. He had the most powerfully fluid body I'd ever seen, like a modern day gladiator. Every square inch of him was made up of layers of tight, coiled muscle. Thick biceps gave way to broad shoulders. His defined upper back and strong shoulder blades tapered to a slimmer waist, but my gaze had to stop there. He was wearing those tight spandex shorts Olympic swimmers wear. The navy material sat low on his hips, slicing his Adonis Vs in half when he twisted around to make sure I was paying attention. To maintain my own sanity, I kept my gaze on the top half of him—though even that wasn't really a safe zone.

"See how my head stays at 45 degrees?" he asked.

I shot him a thumbs up and tried to ignore the feeling of my heart pounding against my breastbone.

The spandex shorts were basically a form of cruel and unusual punishment. He paused then, noticing the color in my cheeks. I assured him I was paying attention but I wasn't. I was staring at his butt. I'M SORRY OKAY. It was just there, testing the elastic capacity of the spandex, and I couldn't help it. It was the most glorious butt I'd ever seen and I couldn't take it for another second. My self-control had reached its limit, and like the clownfish in *Finding Nemo*, I thought, *I'm going to touch the butt.* My hand twitched and started to drift toward him.

"All right," I squeaked, clasping my loyal hand around my traitorous one. I was going to lose it soon if we didn't jump in the water. "I think I've got it; let's get in."

"I haven't gone over the mechanics of the full stroke," he argued, glancing back at me over his shoulder. Every time he moved, I caught a new angle, a glimpse at his quadruple abs or his strong biceps. A woman can only handle so much.

"I'm going to be honest," I said, propping my hands on my hips. "We can be honest with each other right?"

He nodded and for a second I almost told him how fucking good-looking he was, how much I wanted to maul him at that very moment, but I caught myself before the words slipped out.

"This is literally the most boring thing I've ever had to sit through."

He frowned.

"Sorry, I know form is really important, but I just want to swim."

I walked toward the pool and glanced down at the water, trying to ignore the tight tension radiating through my body. This was supposed to be a fun afternoon. I'd told Kinsley I knew what I was doing, but I felt anxious and hot and awkward. I couldn't be my normal self while he was standing there nearly naked.

"Andie?" he asked, taking a step toward me. I caught movement out of the corner of my eye and I knew he was going to touch me, maybe try to brush my shoulder with his hand. I acted first, bent my knees, and dove into the water. If he touched me, it'd be game over.

———

Freddie

I WATCHED ANDIE dive into the water and then slipped into the lane beside her. Her mood had changed in the last few minutes. Had I actually bored her? Maybe I could have laid off the form talk a bit. Not everyone was trying to win gold, after all. I surfaced and looked out to find her halfway down the pool, swimming a lap faster than I'd expected. I inhaled and kicked off the wall to catch up to her.

"I'm faster than a gold medalist!" she taunted once she'd reached the other side.

I smiled and picked up the pace. My workout had been longer than usual, but being with Andie had reinvigorated me.

"No! Slow down," she shouted, kicking her feet faster to get away from me. She was making exaggerated splashes and I slowed, acting as though she really was beating me. Every few strokes, she'd swirl onto her back to see how close I was to passing her, and each time she did, I had to slow down more and more. Once we'd reached the starting point, she clung to the lane divider between us and shook her head.

"Oh god, this is hard."

"That was only one lap," I said, treading water beside her.

I dipped beneath the lane divider so I could see her properly.

"I'm in good shape," she promised once I'd surfaced again a few feet away from her. "It's just that I've already worked out today and my legs are a lot stronger than my arms."

I made a show of studying her biceps bobbing up and down in the water. "They look fit to me."

She grinned. "So, did I make the team?"

"Definitely, although I'm not quite sure of any protocol for incorporating an American girl into Her Majesty's Olympic men's swim team."

I studied her smile as we spoke, watched as her cheeks flushed when she laughed. Her eyes held a sense of mischief as we treaded water there and I wondered if she was enjoying herself as much as I was. It'd been ages since

I'd hung around a girl and had a laugh, so long in fact, that I couldn't even remember it.

"Well, let's try one more lap," she said. "I really think I can beat you this time."

I nodded. "Do you want a head start?"

Instead of answering, she pointed over to the side of the natatorium with a puzzled look on her face. When I turned to see what had gotten her attention, she splashed a wall of water at my head and dove under the surface, swimming as fast as she could. I stayed where I was, watching as she made her way across the pool. I waited until she hit the other wall before I took off, and even then, I didn't swim at my normal pace. We were lazy about it, swimming laps together. She tried to grab hold of my ankle under water, to sabotage me and slow me down, but she couldn't grip tight enough. I pulled myself out of her hold and took off, always just a little too fast for her to catch up.

"I can't do it," she said halfway through our final lap of the day.

"What?"

She nodded her chin toward the starting wall.

"I can't make it back. My arms don't work any more."

I smiled.

"Well, I guess you live here now." I made out like I was going to swim away and leave her there, but she shouted after me.

"No! Stop!"

She could have pulled herself out of the pool and walked round the slow way, but I had a better, more selfish solution.

"Hop onto my back. I'll swim us back to the other side."

She narrowed her eyes at me and added a little smirk for emphasis.

"I've seen enough movies to know where that leads."

I tilted my head as though I didn't understand.

She shook her head. "We shouldn't cross that line. If I get on your back and you make out like we're just casually crossing the pool, it'll be a sham. I don't want to turn this afternoon into something I'm going to have to feel sorry about later."

"Do you feel sorry about it now? Because I don't. This has been the most fun I've had in a long time."

She smiled. "Me too. So let's not ruin it."

After we made our way back to the starting wall—me swimming back and Andie walking around the side of the pool—she and I sat on the ledge with our feet kicking up water. I passed her a spare protein bar and she tilted her water bottle in my direction to let me know I could have some if I wanted. There was nothing but silence while we caught our breaths. I could see her chest rising and falling out of the corner of my eye, but I kept my gaze ahead, too aware of how close her hand was to mine, too aware of the sound of her heavy breaths. She was right. The moment we touched, everything would change.

"Don't you feel bad inviting girls to swim with you?" she asked, breaking the silence first. "Other women might get the wrong idea, with you in those booty shorts."

"Booty shorts?"

She laughed.

"No," I said, confidently. "I don't feel bad. Not about this."

"Caroline might."

"I don't really care what she thinks."

It felt weird to acknowledge that out loud, like I was

taking the Lord's name in vain inside a church or something.

"Odd," she said, sliding her eyes to me, "considering you're about to be married to the woman."

"If I had it my way, I wouldn't be."

I knew she probably suspected as much, but her brows rose in shock all the same. "So why don't you end it?"

"It's not that simple."

"You already said that last night. I'm beginning to find that phrase really annoying."

"Truthfully, I was never supposed to marry Caroline. She was intended for my brother Henry."

"Wait. Seriously?"

I nodded.

"Were they in love?"

"No."

She kicked up water with her foot.

"What is it with you people and not marrying for love?"

It did seem that way, though I hated to admit it.

"It's sort of a long story."

"Well, I still have half of this gross protein bar to get through, and you can't swim for 30 minutes after eating, so spill."

I smiled. "Right. Well, my brother was the oldest child and the heir to our family's estate. Caroline's family—the Montagues—have been family friends for as long as I can remember and it was established early on that Caroline and Henry would marry."

"Why? To unite two powerful families? What is this, Game of Thrones?"

I laughed. "Actually yes. But with no White Walkers or King Joffreys."

"Whew." She smiled. "So then what happened? Why isn't Caroline marrying Henry?"

I glanced away and focused on the water rippling across the surface of the pool. I knew my answer would shift the mood of the afternoon, but I supposed it was easier to tell her the truth. "Henry died."

"Oh shit," I heard her whisper beneath her breath. It didn't shock me any more, but I was sure she hadn't been expecting that answer. Normal, healthy thirty-year-old men don't just die out of the blue, but my brother had. Heart defect. The shock of it had only begun to wear off a few months back.

I turned back to Andie to find her easygoing smile replaced with a look of shame. Her brows were crinkled and her lips were downturned into a frown I would have kissed away had I the right.

"I'm really sorry for pushing the subject," she said. "We were joking around and I ruined it."

I shook my head and scooted my hand toward hers, nearly touching it. "It's all right. You wanted the truth and that's the honest truth. When my brother passed a few years ago, the responsibility, the title, the estate, and every-thing that went along with it passed on to me—although it feels as if the job inherited me, rather than the other way around."

Her tone sobered. "And that's how you got Caroline."

"So it would seem."

"You don't think you could love her? Even down the line?"

I'd mulled over that question a million times in my head, ever since the day my mother had suggested the betrothal. At times I could convince myself that Caroline was the one for me, but I'd never once deluded myself into thinking I could love her.

"She's…not my match," I answered simply.

"Your match?"

"My soulmate," I clarified.

She smiled. "Your cheeks are red."

Of course the bloody minx would point out the fact that I'd gone red in the face. "Well I sound like a schoolgirl going on about this sort of thing."

She nodded and turned back to the pool. "If it helps, I really hope Caroline becomes your match. It would be sad if you ended up spending the rest of your life with someone you never truly loved."

I nodded and watched her turning small circles in the water with her toes. Her skin was still flushed from the workout and when I looked up, her smile was back but subdued, hanging at the corners of her mouth, ready to spring free if only someone could unlock it. I wanted to be that person.

Chapter Twelve

ANDIE

I **WATCHED MY** trainer Lisa tape my wrist, taking her time to get it right before our practice started. My wrist hurt a little more than it had the day before, but I'd been icing it after practice and there wasn't much else I could do.

"You really need to play it safe," Lisa said as she pulled a small pair of scissors out of her pocket and cut off the excess tape. "Injuries like this seem minor, but they can flare up really easily."

I nodded, absorbing her warning. My wrist wasn't the only ticking time bomb in my life. It seemed everywhere I went, I was walking on a minefield, Freddie included. The day before, after we'd finished swimming, I'd stood to towel off and get dressed and he'd invited me to get a quick bite to eat. He'd made it sound so casual—"supper at the cafe" —and I'd wanted to say yes, but I shook my head and offered up a firm no. I swore I was busy and he swore it was only dinner. Neither of us truly believed the other.

I couldn't quite work out Freddie's motives in my head. Did he truly just need a friend? Did he find me as fun to be around as I did him? Or was he looking for more? Possibly even a way out of a betrothal he wanted nothing to do with? Whether intentionally or not, he was pulling me into murky water. A quick swim, a casual lunch—they were all things that would have looked okay on paper, but I knew better.

"You're all set," Lisa said, tossing the roll of tape into her bag.

I slid off her table and took a shaky breath.

My team was already in the middle of the field, spread out for warm-ups. I took a spot in the back row and started rolling out the muscles in my neck.

"Morning Andie."

I glanced up to find Liam walking toward me. He was in his coaching gear, his soccer shorts in place and his whistle around his neck. The notion that we were supposed to take him seriously had been hilarious to me when I first joined the team. Before he met Kinsley, Liam Wilder had been painted a notorious bad boy, but after a nagging knee injury forced him to retire, he returned to the life of a reluctant coach. He'd settled down with Kinsley, and with time really came into his own in a coaching capacity. Even so, there was no suppressing the fact that he was still young, tattooed, and incredibly good-looking.

"How's your wrist?" he asked, eyeing the tape.

"It's fine."

He nodded. "Good. Three days left before our first game; I want to make sure you're ready."

"I am."

Training for the Olympics had been a fulltime job for the last few years. Once I'd earned a spot on the Olympic roster a few months earlier, I'd moved to L.A. and taken the spare room in Kinsley and Liam's house. Every morning, I woke up and had breakfast by 5:30 AM. I joined my team for practice by 6:00 AM, and we would spend a few hours working through drills and reviewing game footage. After that, we'd get a short lunch break before reconvening in the afternoon for strength training and workouts.

The only social life I'd had outside of soccer was fifth-wheeling on dates with Liam, Kinsley, Becca, and Penn. It was fun, but the days were long and regimented. That was part of the reason why I'd clung to the idea of Rio.

It'd been months since I'd had any sort of real date, even longer since I'd last hooked up with a guy. Sure, there was Tinder and hundreds of other dating apps, but those things took time, which was always in short supply. Unless stolen glances in the grocery store checkout line count, I hadn't so much as locked eyes with a guy since college.

Swimming with Freddie had literally been the most interesting afternoon I'd had in months and that's why I had to be smart, keep my distance, and maintain control of my heart and my head. It'd be too easy for the ground to crumble and wash away beneath us.

Coach Decker started us on drills and I lost myself in practice. It felt good to run, sweat, and concentrate on something so simple. For three hours, the only thing I had to do was draw a line in the turf and keep a soccer ball from crossing it.

"Good work, ladies," Coach Decker said as we huddled together at the end of practice. We sat in a circle, guzzling water and trying to catch our breath. I ripped my shirt off over my head and tossed the sticky thing aside. The cold air felt good against my skin as I leaned back on my palms, listening to our coach. "You all are more than ready for the game in three days. Many of us know France well from last time around, so we know that they're going to come out of the gate with speed and aggression, but if we stay focused, there's no reason why we shouldn't come out on top."

Kinsley leaned closer and bumped her shoulder against mine. I turned and she nudged her chin in the direction of the stadium doors. When I glanced over, it was just in time to see Freddie take a seat on the first row of bleachers. He was dressed down in jeans and a t-shirt, and he'd thrown his baseball hat on as if to stifle his shine. He smiled when he saw me glance over and my already rapidly beating heart pounded against my breastbone so hard I thought it'd be visible when I glanced down.

He'd come to my practice.

Why the fuck had he come to my practice?

I turned away with the image of his sharp features burned into my memory.

Coach Decker wrapped up, we broke from the huddle, and every single woman on my team took in Freddie Archibald sitting and waiting for me. God, he was good-looking. He had those old world, classic features, the kind of face that took generations of good genes to create. No matter how far he tugged that hat down on his head, there was no hiding his beauty.

"I didn't realize we'd invited a royal audience," Becca said as I trailed her and Kinsley to the row of bleachers where we'd dropped our bags. I took my sweet time gathering my things and then dug into my bag for another shirt since mine was still sticky from practice. Fortunately, I had a clean Lululemon tank stuffed in there. I pulled it on before I turned to assess Freddie. Michelle and a few other rookies had gathered around him. Even Liam was over there, chatting with him about God knows what.

Kinsley tried to catch my eye but I ignored her and tugged my bag over my shoulder.

"Did you invite him here?" Becca asked, running to catch up to me.

I shot her a glare. "Of course not."

"Well he looks really happy to see you."

He did. When I looked back in his direction, he'd stood and stepped past the group to get to me. Michelle watched me from over his shoulder with a curious frown. I ignored her and glanced back to Freddie to find a seductive smile stretched across his lips. Yesterday, I'd psyched myself up before joining him for a swim. I'd prepared the whole day, but this—him surprising me at practice—caught me off guard. I'd had no time to neatly compartmentalize him. He was there, standing in front of me, smelling divine and smiling down at me. At least his tush was safely under a pair of jeans this time.

"I thought I'd arrive in time to watch you practice," he said with a touch of disappointment that didn't quite reach his smile.

I looked back at the empty field. "Short practice, we just finished up."

"I can tell," he said, reaching out to drag his finger across my sweaty bicep. Goosebumps bloomed beneath his touch and I inhaled a shaky breath before working up the courage to meet his eyes.

"Yeah, you might not want to come any closer. I'm still pretty gross."

He tilted his head. "I didn't mind yesterday."

Everyone was watching us. Kinsley and Becca had stopped to join Liam. Michelle and a few other girls were behind them, curious as ever. I didn't like being the center of attention.

"Did you need something? Or..."

"Well I actually have a light day today. No interviews or anything."

My throat tightened. I couldn't have this conversation in front of everyone. I reached forward and tugged his hand to pull him out of the practice facility after me. The sun hit my skin and I inhaled a breath of fresh air, happy to be free from the prying eyes.

I let go of his hand as soon as I realized I still had hold of it. "Sorry, everyone was listening to us and I couldn't take it."

He nodded. "I came to see if you wanted to have lunch with me. You haven't eaten yet have you?"

He couldn't do this. He couldn't show up at my practice and invite me to lunch. He couldn't look like that and smell that good and be that nice without expecting me to fall. I really didn't want to fall.

I shook my head. "Actually, I'm going to the gym."

I thought that would end it, case closed, but he smiled wider.

"Brilliant. I'll bring the protein bars."

Chapter Thirteen

FREDDIE

OUT OF THE two of us, my brother Henry was always the one fit to take over as the heir to our family's estate. He was born first and meant for the role, but even still, it was never a duty he tried to shirk. He enjoyed the old traditions: the stuffy etiquette rules that bored me, the hunts that lasted four hours too long, and the dinner parties that, to me, always seemed like a chore.

As soon as I was old enough, I moved from our estate and rented a flat in central London. By the time I competed in my first Olympic games, the fate of our family had long been decided: Henry would follow in my father's footsteps, take over the family business, and later, accept my father's title.

There was peace in the few years following my father's passing. Henry ran the Farlington estate as he saw fit and I was free to swim. It was out of respect that Henry and I never discussed his duties. I pitied him for being shackled to our family's title while I traveled the world doing as I pleased.

When Henry's heart failed suddenly, it was during a

time in my life when I felt untouchable. I'd just finished up at the London Games and I had more medals to my name than most Olympians could ever dream of. I was dating and going out and enjoying my life in London when I got the call that he was in the hospital.

The realizations about Henry's sudden death came in waves. First, came grief: I had lost my oldest friend, my nearest idol, and the shield that held the weight of familial responsibility at bay. But it wasn't until I stood at the wake, shaking hands with stuffy old friends of my father that I fully understood: my father's legacy and my brother's dream were now my reality. The mantle, meant to be worn and passed proudly, had become my own funeral shroud.

My mother, grieving both a husband and son in the span of a few years, couldn't be refused. For all I had lost, she had lost more. This gave her immunity to any protests as she strove to preserve normalcy for our family. I wanted nothing to do with that old world, but I couldn't step aside and let things go to ruin. My mum wanted so much from me and I wanted nothing but freedom. I became a duke, but I wouldn't move home, nor quit swimming. I would not soon become the caretaker for the estate, and I wouldn't take over my father's business. That was when she'd countered with Caroline. After everything I'd already turned down, she slid Caroline onto the table as if a betrothal was a compromise. In her words, it was 'my contribution to the institution to which I owed everything.'

———

I DROPPED MY weights onto the rack near the back mirrors and glanced up just in time to watch Andie step onto the mat behind me. I pulled my earbuds out and smiled. "I figured you wouldn't come."

She and I had agreed on a time to meet up at the gym after her practice, but that'd been an hour earlier. I'd started my workout, lost myself in thoughts of Henry and my family, and slotted Andie as a no-show. Yet, there she was, dropping her water bottle beside mine and twisting her hair up into a messy ponytail.

She shrugged. "Truthfully, I thought it'd be a better idea if I came after you were already finished, but I guess you're more persistent than I thought you'd be."

I didn't ask why she wanted to come after I was done; we both knew the answer.

"I'd like to work out with you. It's more fun with a partner," I said.

She propped her hands up on her hips and tilted her head. "Don't you usually work out with Thom?"

I nodded. "Sometimes."

"But not today?" she asked, her eyes scanning the gym around me.

I smiled. "No. Sometimes you need someone with real muscle spotting you."

She shook her head and walked past me toward the weight rack, doing a poor job of concealing her smile in the mirror. She reached for a set of weights and took up residence on the mat a few feet away—far enough that I knew she wanted some space. It was no use though. The moment she'd arrived, other athletes scooted closer, pulled their weights to the edge of the mats, and lingered nearby her until she'd glance up and flash a smile or a nod. She had a gravitational pull about her and it was hard to keep my distance, especially since these fleeting moments were all we had.

I was in the middle of a set of dead lifts, breathing heavy and trying to focus on my posture, when I caught sight of her out of the corner of my eye. She was at the corner of the mat watching me, and when I dropped the weights and took a deep breath, she stepped closer.

"Impressive," she said with one arched brow.

The fact that she looked that sexy while sweating through her workout clothes was *actually* impressive.

"Thanks."

"I just finished my first round and my legs feel like Jell-O." She laughed, wiggling them out for emphasis.

I glanced over at them, glad to have an excuse. They were long, toned, heartbreaker legs. "They look good to me."

She paused and cleared her throat. "Yeah, well I have soccer to thank for that."

"Football," I corrected with a smirk.

She rolled her eyes. "Yeah, yeah. Listen, I need your help with free weights. I never do them without a spot."

I nodded. "All right, let me just finish up one last set."

She nodded and pulled up a bright blue medicine ball to bounce on while she waited. Her blonde ponytail swished from side to side and her smile was wider than it'd been all day.

"Just going to watch?" I asked with a laugh.

She smiled and bounced. Up, down. Up, down. Up, down. "Why not?"

I swallowed down a shaky breath. Her workout top was damp and I watched as a single drop of sweat rolled down the front of her neck and disappeared down the center of her chest. She tilted her head, watching me watch her. Maybe it was the endorphins or the sweat or the cut of her tank top, but I found it hard to stay away. Why was it so hard to stay away?

"Freddie?" she asked, pulling my attention away from her body. "All done?"

I hadn't even started.

I stepped over the weights and waited for her to stop bouncing. Up, down. Up, down.

She smiled and stood. "C'mon. The bench is over here."

Something changed after that, likely because she was tired of putting up a fight. We stayed together for the remainder of our workout. I spotted her when she needed it, trying my best to keep my focus on her form and not her body. The worst of it came when I was helping her with sit-ups. She was lying on her back and I was leaning over her, holding down her feet and knees to keep her in place. Had we been naked and back in my flat, the position would have meant something else entirely, and my brain was having a hard time separating fact from fiction, right from wrong.

"Ten," I counted as she sat up.

Her lips came within inches of mine. I caught a whiff of her hair, something sweet and scented.

She leaned back for another sit-up.

"Eleven."

Her breaths came heavy and her cheeks were flushed. Her eyes held mine and she broke out in a cheeky little smirk after I counted away another sit up.

"You all good there, Archibald?" she asked, falling back to the mat.

"Brilliant. How about you, *Foster?*"

She glanced away and laughed. "Peachy."

"Good, 'cause you've still got about twenty more."

She exhaled and sat up, coming within an inch of my face. All I had to do was lean forward and her mouth would be mine.

"Freddie," she said, jarring me out of my intense staring contest with her lips. "You didn't count that one."

"What number were we on?"

She huffed out a breath and collapsed back on the mat. "You were the one supposed to be keeping track."

Bloody hell.

"Andie!"

I turned in time to watch Nathan Drake, Portuguese soccer player and all-around chum, walk up onto the mat, eyeing Andie like she was his salvation. I tightened my grip on her knees, feeling her pulse jump against my palm. Sure, I'd known Nathan since London and sure, he'd been fun to have around for a laugh, but now that he was stepping closer and smiling at Andie as she was edging out of my grip to stand and greet him, I decided I didn't like him much. Maybe not at all.

"You two, how you say, exercer together?" he asked, his heavy accent muddling the words. He pointed back and forth between us, but ultimately fixed his attention on Andie as if I didn't exist.

I stood up and stepped behind her. My shoulder nudged hers and though it was tempting, I didn't reach out and wrap my hand around her waist. I had Nathan in height and weight. He was smaller than I remembered, and built lean for soccer. *Jesus*. I sounded like a caveman, even to myself. I couldn't remember the last time I'd sized up another bloke.

"Yeah, just finishing up, actually," Andie said, wiping her hand across her forehead. She was sweaty and beautiful, and Nathan was just as aware of it as I was. He dragged his gaze down her legs and nodded with a smile like he was drunk on the sight of her.

"Good. Good. Tonight we are—a few of us are going to dancing," he said. "Do you want to come?"

Andie glanced over her shoulder at me and then turned back to Nathan.

"Are you inviting both of us?" she asked.

Nathan—as if only then remembering I even bloody existed—nodded his head with a fake smile. "Yes. Yes, the more the marrying!"

He was being overly enthusiastic, with a heavy nod and a thumbs up.

"Oh, okay then. That sounds really fun. I'd love to go," she said, making his day without even realizing it.

"Freddie?" Nathan asked with a flat smile.

If I said yes, I'd have to go and dance about like it was something I actually enjoyed. If I said no, Andie would be at the club alone with Nathan.

I shrugged. "Not sure, mate. I need to take a look at my schedule."

He perked up at that, the wanker.

I didn't pay attention when he rattled off the details, but then he was waving goodbye and I had Andie's attention again. She turned and flashed me a little smile, a nothing smile that told me she knew more than she was letting on.

"You're kind of territorial. Do you realize that?"

No one had ever accused me of that before. I'd never acted the role of the jealous boyfriend. I narrowed my eyes, feigning confusion, and she shook her head.

"Fine. Forget I said anything." She waved back to the spot on the mat where she'd been doing sit-ups. "Let's finish up so we can go get ready."

Chapter Fourteen

ANDIE

I'D PACKED A red dress in my luggage as an afterthought. It was short and skimpy, something I'd never wear in my normal life. I found it in an expensive boutique in L.A. and purchased it on a whim. It was hardly more than a few strips of well-placed fabric, but when I slipped it on in the dressing room of the upscale boutique, I felt sexier than I ever had in my life. It was short and thin, made of a light cotton material that didn't cling to my skin. The front looked innocent enough, though it did hug my hips and cut off fairly high on my thighs. The real detail was in the back—or lack thereof. The dress was a halter that tied behind my neck and wrapped around my waist, leaving most of my back exposed. I'd tried to figure out a bra situation, but the saleswoman at the boutique had assured me you were supposed to wear it *sans* brassiere. I'd laughed in her face— seeing as how I didn't do *anything* "sans brassiere"—but there I sat, in the back of a cab in Rio, letting the girls fly free. I glanced down again, trying to decide if I should cave and turn back to the village. I knew I wouldn't

though; I felt just as sexy as I had in the dressing room in
L.A. The dress felt wild, I felt wild, and I wanted one night
in Rio where I wasn't a soccer player competing in the
Olympics, but a twenty-one-year-old girl out for a night on
the town.

"What is this place anyway?" Michelle asked as we
pulled up at the address Nathan had given Freddie and I at
the gym. The building itself looked unassuming, nothing
more than a warehouse really, and if there hadn't been a
line of people winding around the building waiting to get
in the front door, I'd have assumed we were at the wrong
place.

"It's called Mascarada," I said, handing the driver a
few colorful Brazilian bills before sliding out of the back
seat after Michelle.

Inviting her had been an afterthought. I'd wanted to go
with Freddie, but I hadn't been able to get ahold of him
after the gym. We'd finished our workout and exchanged
numbers. I'd asked him about the club; he'd shrugged and
said he'd think about it.

I checked my phone one last time as we walked toward
the entrance of the club.

Andie: Do you want to ride to the club together?
Freddie: You go ahead. I'm not sure if I'm going.
Andie: Do you want me to wait for you?

I'd sent the last text an hour earlier and he'd never
replied. I'd given up hope and invited Michelle so I
wouldn't have to go alone, and as the two of us flashed our
athlete badges—Nathan had suggested it as a quick way to
bypass the line—I wondered if maybe it was a good thing
Freddie wouldn't be there. I could find a new guy, someone
to focus on who wasn't already spoken for.

"Do you two have masks?" the bouncer asked, handing our badges back to us. I slipped it into my purse and shook my head.

"Are we supposed to?"

"Go in and turn left," he said, reaching past us for the next I.D. "You'll find one there."

Michelle shot me a curious glance as we stepped forward, past the club doors. "What was he talking about? Masks?"

I didn't have to answer her because the moment we walked into the dark club, it made sense. The club was called Mascarada because it was an actual nightly masquerade. Everyone we passed in the foyer was wearing a mask that covered some or all of their face.

"C'mon," Michelle said, tugging my arm and leading me to the left where the bouncer had directed us. The hallway was packed with people trying to get to and from a small room at the very end. We pushed through the crowd and I stood frozen as I came face to face with masks in every shape, size, and color. Feathers, glitter, rhinestones, bows, lace. They were beautiful and exotic, and I knew I'd have a hard time picking just one.

"*Entra!* Come in!" an older woman called from behind a small counter in the back corner of the room. She had white hair, tied up in a severe bun on top of her head. She waved everyone forward, trying to tame the crowd. "Find a mask and then check out with me before you leave."

Easier said than done.

I reached for a white mask hanging on the wall just past the door. It was glittery, cheap, and a bit obnoxious, but I could hardly move in the room, and I didn't care enough to shove through the crowd and try on others. Michelle reached for a blue one next to where I'd found mine, and we edged our way toward the back counter to make our purchases.

It was ten or fifteen minutes before we made it to the front of the line. I'd been jostled and shoved more times than I cared to count, but when I dropped my mask on the counter and reached for the extra money in my small clutch, the woman manning the station shook her head.

"No. No. This one won't do," she said, eyeing me over the rim of her glasses. Up close, she was even smaller than I'd expected. Before I could protest, she abandoned her station at the counter and disappeared into the crowd. I glanced back at Michelle, confused.

"Out of my way!" the woman shouted, though I couldn't pinpoint where exactly she was located in the room. She was a sneaky little thing.

People behind us in line eyed me with annoyance, but I shrugged and turned around. It was a few minutes before the woman sidled back behind the counter with a content exhale.

"Here," she said, dropping a new mask on the counter in front of me and reaching to grab the cash out of my hand. "*Melhor*. Better." She was ringing me up before I'd even confirmed that I wanted the new mask, but I'd have been an idiot to turn it down. It was exquisite, the same red hue as my dress and made completely of brocade lace. It tied in the back with black silk ribbon and I didn't even care to find out what it cost. I *needed* it. Maybe I'd even wear it for the first game. And the one after that too.

Michelle helped me tie it once we'd made it back out to the hallway. The lace was soft against my skin, seductive even. I met my gaze in a hazy mirror hanging on the wall and silently thanked the woman for taking the time to find it for me. With my red dress, red lace mask, and confident smirk, I was hardly recognizable, even to myself.

"All right, let's go," Michelle said once her mask was in place. "I need a drink."

I'd assumed the inside of the club would be less crowded than the mask room, but there were people everywhere. Even with three levels full of private tables, booths, and dark alcoves, I couldn't take more than two steps without brushing against a random person.

The masks had a heady effect on the entire experience. Even the bartenders wore them so that when I leaned in to shout my drink order to one of them, I couldn't be sure he'd heard me. He whipped around to reach for a bottle of liquor and I glanced up, taking in the entire club. The space was shaped like a rectangle with three stories. The center of the room was open from floor to ceiling so that the people on the top floors could lean over the railing and watch the dancers. It was like surround sound for all of the senses.

Michelle tapped my shoulder and I turned to find my drink waiting for me on the bar. We paid and wound back through the crowd, trying in vain to find the group Nathan had promised would be there. We tried the dance floor, curling around the perimeter of jostling bodies without luck.

"Let's try the second floor," Michelle said, pointing to a set of stairs in the corner of the room.

That was where we ended up finding them; they were sitting at a long table, three drinks ahead of us and loud enough to prove it. I'd nearly passed by them without notice, but Nathan had shouted my name.

"Andie!"

I turned and watched him stand to greet me on uneven footing. He smelled like liquor when he pulled me into a hug, but I smiled and introduced him to Michelle. Her smile was wide and genuine—clearly she was interested—and in an instant I felt like a third wheel.

"Michelle quiero mucho dance," I said, hoping my broken Spanish would be close enough to the Portuguese translation.

Nathan arched a brow and held out his hand.

"Should we?"

Michelle's big brown eyes widened behind her mask. "Oh, but I just got my drink."

I rolled my eyes, took it out of her hand, and took a long sip. "There. Problem solved. Now go."

Nathan wrapped his hand around her waist and led her back to the stairs we'd just climbed. Without him there, I didn't have a real connection to the group, and even if I had hopes for recognizing someone, with the masks on, it was nearly impossible. I found a seat at the end of the long table just as everyone held up small shot glasses. The girl closest to me slid Nathan's over and nodded.

"Are you a friend of Nathan's?" she asked, eyeing my dress.

I shrugged. "Sort of. I'm here for the games."

She smiled. "Same here."

Maybe I'd have recognized her, but she was wearing an emerald green mask that covered most of her face, save for a pair of red lips.

"Okay!" a guy down the table shouted, drawing our attention back to the task at hand: shots. He held his glass in the air, sloshing a bit of Fireball Whisky over the side. "Here's to winning gold, and drinking it too!"

"Cheers!" everyone called back as they tipped back their shots. I sniffed the glass and wrinkled my nose. My limit for the night had been one drink, and I already had two in front of me. If I started in on shots, there was no way I'd be a functioning human in the morning.

The shot was a good icebreaker though, especially since they didn't notice me slide mine down the table untouched. Mask Girl and I got to talking and she introduced me to a few other people in the group. Names were too hard to hear over the music, and even the ones I did hear didn't stick to memory. With the masks on, it wasn't like it mattered anyway; we could have been anyone.

The table prepared for another shot and I glanced around for Michelle. I'd assumed she and Nathan would dance to a few songs and then head back up, but they'd been gone long enough that I wondered if they were even still inside the club. I pulled my phone out of my purse, secretly hoping for a text from Freddie. Nothing.

How hard was it to reply to a text?

The table clinked their shot glasses together and I stared at my phone, willing the text bubble to pop up.

"CHEERS!" they shouted as I started typing out another reply. I was breaking the rules by texting him again, but I was too lonely and bored to care.

Andie: I wish you were here.

I had barely slipped my phone back into my purse when it buzzed again. I pulled it out with a shaky hand.

Freddie: Be careful what you wish for.

I read the message twice before I realized my heart was racing with the shock of his reply. Did that mean he was in the club? He'd come after all? I twisted my head around, looking for him, but he wasn't on the second floor, at least not from what I could see.

I hit send on a message that told him where I was, but it wouldn't go through. I'd been able to send a text just a minute earlier, but now the cell reception decided to turn spotty. Perfect. I tried again and then glanced around our table. He wasn't on the second floor. I shoved my phone into my clutch and stood from the table.

"I'll be back," I promised the group, though no one seemed to notice my departure.

My first idea was to go down to the mask shop, but he wasn't in the crowded room. I stood by the door, watching people filter in and out and trying to spot his tall frame. I tried to text him again from that spot, but my phone still wouldn't cooperate.

I walked back into the club and stood just to the side of the dance floor, spinning in a circle. I glanced up to the second and third floor balconies. There were plenty of people hanging over the railing, shouting, dancing, and drinking, but none of them were Freddie. I drew my gaze higher, up to the ceiling of the club. I hadn't realized it before, but it was made of glass. Thousands of pieces of shattered glass fragments pieced together like a puzzle. My broken reflection stared back at me. I looked like a lost red devil in the center of the room. While everyone else moved and danced and drank, I stood frozen, trying to find someone I had no business looking for. It was in those fragmented pieces of glass that I first found him reflected back to me, dressed in black, masked, and walking up behind me.

There's a sensation that comes with shock. That fast flood of endorphins that riles your senses. Your stomach twists and your hands shake and your heart beats so fast that even you aren't sure who is controlling it: you or him. That's how it felt when Freddie stepped up behind me in the club. His hand pressed against my lower back, skimming against my bare skin.

I closed my eyes, listened as he whispered hello in my

ear, and fell into the kind of madness I'd avoided for so many years. For so long, I'd lived in the confines of my regimented life, but now I was in Rio, and Freddie still had his hand on the small of my back.

Inviting him to the club had been a mistake, but he was there and I wasn't going to say no.

I wanted to taste madness.

Chapter Fifteen

FREDDIE

ANDIE WAS A red temptress standing alone in the club, and I wanted to devour her. Her dress was nothing, some fabric tied behind her neck and little else. No bra. *Bloody hell*. Her back was completely exposed and as I walked closer, I dragged my gaze down her spine, getting my fill of the tan skin I wasn't allowed to touch.

I'd spent enough time memorizing her body to recognize it, even behind the mask. She was beautiful. Blonde hair hung loose across her shoulders, silky and long. Gray eyes and long lashes stood out against the red lace. I didn't stop myself from touching her back. She was looking up, watching me in the mirrors when I stepped close and whispered hello.

"You look beautiful."

She didn't reply. She twisted around and faced me, dropping her gaze from the ceiling so she could meet my eyes. There was a darkness there that she usually kept hidden. Her playful, cheeky smile was tucked away. Instead, her full lips held the promise of a smirk—the kind that told me she and I wouldn't be spending the night as friends.

"Do you need a drink?" she asked, eyeing my empty hands.

I nodded and led us to the bar. It was crowded—the whole place was, really. I stayed close to Andie, tucking her into my side so I could feel her body there beside mine. She didn't protest, though I could sense a stillness inside her, a fight over whether she should let this happen. I didn't give her enough time to think it over.

"Is anyone waiting for you?" I asked after placing my order with the bartender.

She shook her head but kept quiet, eyeing the bottles of alcohol behind the bar.

"Do you want to have a dance?" I said, though I prayed she'd say no. I hated dancing in front of other people. To me, if you did it right, dancing was intimate and raw—something better reserved for private rooms and dark corners.

She shook her head again.

The bartender slid my drink across the bar and I took the glass in one hand and Andie's arm in the other. I led us away from the bar before she could ask where we were going, and I found the first flight of stairs that could lead us toward a place I wasn't sure we were ready to find.

The second floor was packed with annoying drunk tourists and locals, so I kept hold of her and took her up another flight, all the way to the top floor. There were no questions or protests from Andie. When we were nearly up the second flight, I glanced back to find her eyes on me, confident and curious.

"I haven't been up here yet," she said, eyeing the space tentatively.

The music was still as loud as it was on the first floor,

thanks to speakers blasting in every direction, but the crowd had thinned enough so that it wasn't hard to find an empty spot.

They'd used tinted bulbs to cast the space in red light. The other floors had been dark, but this was different, red and smoky and intoxicating. The fragments of glass were closer than ever. When we sat and I pulled Andie to the soft leather seat beside mine, I glanced up and took us in from above. My gaze caught on her thighs. Her dress had ridden up when she sat, and she was trying to tug it down, to no avail. I smiled and turned back to her, leaving the mirrors for later.

"Want a sip?" I asked, holding my drink up to her.

She shook her head and took a pull of her own drink. It was after that, when she'd swallowed and worked up the confidence, that she turned to me with a question.

"Why are we doing this? We should go back down with the others."

She sounded resolute in her decision and yet she didn't move. I had my hand wrapped around her waist and I tugged her closer, pulling her into my side.

"Just a bit longer," I said, studying her eyes behind her mask.

The entire time at the gym, I'd been wholesome and restrained. I'd helped her work out and I'd kept my distance as much as possible. It'd been painful at times, and I'd left feeling more frustrated than I had in years. I had contemplated staying home and letting Andie run off to the club by herself, but I wasn't that selfless. I knew that the second she walked in, she would never make it back out alone. I should have let that happen. It might've made life easier on the both of us, and yet there I was, stealing her away to the third floor and dipping close to whisper against her hair.

I knew I'd done the right thing by showing up. I'd only been there for half an hour and I'd already seen the full effect of Andie in her red dress. The bartender had bobbled the bottle when he'd passed over my drink. Most blokes on the stairs had tripped as they watched her slide past. There was a guy, even then, who kept his eyes glued to her from across the room. He was leaning on the balcony railing, too far away for Andie to notice, but I did.

"I meant what I said earlier about you being territorial," she said, turning to face me. I caught a whiff of her perfume and it was enough to distract me from the bloke leaning on the railing.

"I've actually never been that way," I said, meeting her gaze behind her mask. "In the past, I mean."

And that was the truth. In other relationships, there'd been no threats, no insecurity concerning the future, but Andie was a wildcard. We couldn't make each other promises because there was nothing to promise. We had moments, tiny, stolen moments that felt wrong more than they felt right. She wasn't mine and she never would be; I knew that and I felt that every time she was around me. That's why I was territorial, but I was also careful, because Andie was a wisp of smoke; if I tried to grasp her too tightly, she would slip through my fingers. My only hope was to keep the fire burning.

"Do you miss your brother?" she asked, changing the subject so suddenly I had to take a moment to collect my thoughts.

"Do I miss him day to day?" I asked. "No."

She tilted her head and waited for me to continue. I loved that she was willing to listen, but I hated that she was fixated on that topic.

I relented, staring off at a patch of leather sofa past her shoulder. "The worst part is, sometimes I want him to be alive again, not so that he can have his life back, but so that I can have mine."

The words sounded twisted when said aloud; I hoped the music would make it impossible for her to hear them.

"You really don't have to marry her," she said, reaching out to touch my hand. I'd been fisting it in my lap without realizing it.

I shrugged. "Why are we talking about this?"

"Because I've tried to keep my distance from you and yet I'm sitting here, starting to have feelings for a man who is about to marry someone else. How is that possible? Why am I even here right now?"

I leaned forward and dropped my drink on the table in front of us.

"You're here because I want you to be."

She inhaled a shaky breath.

"Look up," I said, tilting her chin back so that she was forced to see her reflection in the shattered glass. Like a good girl, she did, and I followed. She watched me in the mirror as I slid my hand up her thigh, pushing her red dress higher.

"Do you feel how fast your heart is racing? How badly you want me to lean in and drag my lips across your skin? Across this delicate patch of skin right here?"

I swept her hair aside and pressed my lips to her neck. She shivered against me but her eyes stayed locked on the ceiling.

I could see the outline of her breasts, heavy and bare beneath her dress. They'd fit perfectly in my hand, fill up my palm and then some. I pressed another kiss to her neck and her nipples pebbled, begging for my mouth.

She turned then, maybe to push me away or maybe to beg me closer, but I didn't give her the chance to speak. I leaned forward and crashed my lips against hers, hungry with lust. I gripped her waist with one hand, and dragged my other hand up her neck, winding my fingers in her hair. She was shocked for that first second, frozen against me as her pulse beat a wild rhythm. Her hands pressed against my chest to keep me away, but in the end, they worked to pull me closer. She fisted my shirt and kissed me back, hard.

With her caged against the leather couch, I kissed her like I'd never have another chance. The music from the club drowned out our moans, but I could feel her pulling me closer, pushing me to take the lead. I dragged my hand up her bare back and she shivered against my touch.

She leaned against me and I felt another ounce of resolve melt away. I reached up to untie the black ribbon keeping her mask in place, but she pulled away and shook her head.

"Leave it on."

There was a darkness in her that I didn't want to test. I left her mask and trailed my hands down her back to grip her tiny waist. I waited for her to tell me to stop, to end the night right there. She skimmed her finger along my chin, studying my features. Her eyes followed her hand as it burned a path across my skin. She leaned forward and pressed a quick kiss to my lips—a soft, tentative thing that was over before I could close my eyes.

"Tonight, I don't want to us to be Andie and Freddie."

The tone of her voice plucked at my heart.

She pressed her lips against my neck and hid her face against the collar of my shirt.

I shook my head and cradled her against me. "We don't have to be."

And I meant it. We were alone in that corner with a black leather couch to make our own. No one noticed my hand sliding up her dress and no one glanced over when my fingers skimmed along her upper thigh, right past the silky material barring me from her. She pressed her lips against mine and dug her fingers into my arm. As I dragged my thumb between her thighs, her moan was so soft I could hardly hear it. I wanted to reach up and rip the speaker off the wall, anything to make the sound of her pleasure easier to hear.

Maybe it was the masks or maybe it was Rio. There was something in the air, the promise of pleasure that made it impossible to stop.

"You're the one I want. *You*," I whispered to her, airing the truth, even though it meant we'd both be hurt when reality found us again.

Her mouth pressed against mine and I tried to contain her, to keep her there on the couch. Every time I brushed my thumb across her, her hips lifted to meet me. She was soft and beautiful and *wet*. I held her down, hiding her from the dark club as I slid a finger in and out of her. Even if someone did look over, they'd see nothing but our legs tangled together. It was the best I could do. There was no stopping myself. She knew I was a greedy bastard; there was no point in trying to convince her otherwise—not when she pulled my bottom lip into her mouth and bit down hard enough to make my blood burn.

"I want to come," she begged.

I kept one hand between her thighs and palmed her breasts through her thin cotton dress. Her nipples were pebbled, begging to be licked. She filled my hand and then some, so full and sexy I wanted to throw caution to the wind, push her back onto the couch, and lap her up until I'd tasted every delicious inch of her. She was so bloody beautiful, pressed against the couch with red, swollen lips. It wasn't enough though; I wanted to see all of her. I needed to feel the silky skin beneath her dress.

I needed her dress gone.

I needed my mouth on her skin. Her stomach. Her thighs.

I needed to bury myself inside of her until her back arched and her toes curled.

But the words came.

Of course they came.

"We shouldn't be doing this."

She whispered against my skin and still, I tried to pretend I hadn't heard her. I wanted to keep her caged there until I felt her come. I wanted to see it and hear it and then see it and hear it again. Over and over and over.

But she pulled away. I straightened my mask and her fingers pressed against her lips, feeling them as if she was in shock at the fact that they were still a part of her. They weren't, not really. They were mine. I pulled her hand away and stole one last kiss to prove it.

I couldn't get any words out of her as we stood up and straightened our clothes. She grabbed her purse and I downed my drink in one long pass, using the burn of the alcohol to bring me back to my senses.

"Are you all right?" I asked as we headed back down to the second floor.

She nodded and offered me a tight smile.

We were nearly down the flight of stairs when I reached for her hand and pulled her back to look at me. Her mask was concealing so much of her face, but I could see the worry in her eyes. She wasn't sure what would happen next—neither of us were—so I pulled her close and hugged her, whispering the only truth I knew.

"I promise, I'll figure this out."

Chapter Sixteen

ANDIE

I **STARED INTO** the mirror and tried to find something different about my appearance. I could have sworn something was off, but I couldn't pinpoint exactly what it was. My hair, eyes, face—everything looked the same. Even my lips had gone back to normal. I'd lathered them in Chapstick after I got home in an effort to try and erase every detail of the club. It'd been idiotic, wild, and reckless. I'd wanted to taste madness and I had. It tasted like a hot British swimmer who was currently off the fucking market.

God, I'm stupid.

"Andie!"

Kinsley's voice boomed through the condo. She and Becca had been asleep by the time I'd returned from the club, but now everyone was awake and running late for breakfast. I turned and tried to find something to wear. My dress from the night before was crumbled on the floor, but the mask was gone. I'd ripped it off before leaving the club. With it in place, I'd felt like I could hardly breathe.

"Andie!" Kinsley shouted again. "Are you coming?"

"Yes!" I reached for one of our team t-shirts, shorts, and a baseball cap.

I pulled the brim down low so I could hide my eyes and walked out to find Kinsley and Becca waiting by the door, ready to leave. They watched me in silence as I slung my workout bag over my shoulder and prepared my water bottle for practice. The bus would pick us up right after breakfast, so I wouldn't have time to come back up to the condo.

"You look guilty," Kinsley said as she held the door open for me.

Becca nodded. "Yeah, what did you do last night?"

I shrugged and made for the elevator. "Michelle and I went to a club."

They glanced at each other as I pressed the elevator call button.

"And?" Kinsley asked.

"And nothing." I glanced back at them. "What did *you* do last night?"

She narrowed her eyes, clearly annoyed that I wasn't giving her the whole truth. "Liam came over and we had dinner. Oh, and your mom called, so we both talked to her for a while."

I groaned. She'd left me a voicemail the day before but I hadn't had time to call her back yet.

"What did she want?" I asked just before the elevator doors swung open.

"She wanted to know if you'd been kidnapped, and if so, whether or not your captors had brought your hand sanitizer along."

I laughed as I stepped in and found a spot in the front corner. "Sounds like her."

The elevator was completely full of athletes trying to make their way down to the food court, which meant I was momentarily safe from having to answer Kinsley and Becca's questions about the night before. I wasn't purposely keeping things from them, I just hadn't had a chance to process everything for myself. If I told them what was going on in my head, it would sound like *Ummm-mmmmm…right. Well…you see…the masks…and then the kiss…*

I needed a few more hours in my own head, a few more hours of keeping Mascarada to myself.

Once we'd arrived on the first floor, I was content to take in the insanity around the lobby. The opening ceremonies were set to take place the following day and the Olympic village was already in a frenzy over it. Committee members ran around the lobby, setting up rendezvous points and help stations for the people flooding in. Security guards manned the front doors, checking the credentials of everyone entering the building.

We bypassed the lobby and headed for the food court, only to find it was just as crowded with guests arriving for the opening ceremonies. Athletes, coaches, and family members filled every available table, and every food station had a line that stretched for what seemed like miles.

"Here, just hold on to my shoulder and I'll pull us through," Kinsley said, stepping forward and fighting her way through the crowd.

It was impossible. We only made it three steps before hitting a wall of people.

"Let's split up," Kinsley said, letting go of my arm. "Andie, you go grab us a table and we'll find the food."

I nodded and set off, trying to weave through the crowd. I ended up roaming through the food court twice before stumbling on a group of people scooting their chairs back and collecting their trash.

"All yours," the woman said, smiling as she cleared off her breakfast food.

"Thanks."

I pulled out a chair, claimed the table, and then reached for my phone to text my mom. I couldn't imagine what Christy and Conan would do if they were there in the food court with me. My mom would probably be spritzing everyone with hand sanitizer and my dad would be walking around trying to find someone with a shared love of sailing. They'd stick out like sore thumbs in their cardigans and summer whites.

Andie: Kinsley said you called. I'll try and reach you after practice later, but I have that cocktail party, so I'm not sure when I'll be free.

Mom: Cocktail party?

Andie: It's for all the flag bearers, so I have to go.

Mom: Okay. Don't worry, sweetie. Just call when you get the chance.

Mom: Oh, but try and get that picture with Frederick for Meemaw! I'm sure he wouldn't mind, just ask politely, and say it is for your scrapbook.

Oh Jesus. I stuffed my phone back into my workout bag and tried to ignore lingering thoughts of Freddie as a shadow fell over my table.

"Andie Foster?"

I glanced up to find a microphone shoved in my face, the black puff on the end nearly tickling my nose.

"Andie! How serendipitous that we've found here!"

The thick British accent belonged to a tall redheaded woman dressed in an ill-fitting navy pantsuit. According to the pin on the lapel of her jacket, she was a reporter for a

TV station I hadn't heard of. Directly behind her stood a lanky cameraman, angling his hulking over-the-shoulder camera in my direction. The light beside the lens was blinking red and I groaned at the thought of them bothering athletes before they'd even had their morning coffee.

"Andie, I'm Sophie Boyle from Sky News—"

I smiled politely and held my hand up to cut her off. "I'm sorry, I'm not doing any interviews. Thank you."

That didn't stop her. My smile, however fake it was, only spurred her forward.

"Well off the record then: How do you know Frederick Archibald? Are you two friends?"

I angled my head, confused by her question.

"We have reports that say he showed up to watch your practice yesterday. The two of you were seen walking out of the stadium together afterward. Is that not true?"

The intrusive question and her thick British accent reminded me of Rita Skeeter, and the longer she stood there, the more annoyed I became. She was drawing attention to me; every table within a few yards was full of people staring in our direction. For what? Because a guy had watched my soccer practice?

"My love life is none of your business. Are you and your cameraman fucking in the news van?"

She reared back with wide eyes, clearly caught off guard by my brazen question.

"Exactly. It's not fun to be pestered about your personal life."

"That may be the case, but the world doesn't care about Terry," she said with an icy smile while pointing at the cameraman behind her. "They want to know about the person gallivanting around with the man who was once England's most eligible bachelor."

I felt a pang of annoyance for Freddie. If people like

Sophie Boyle hounded me day and night, I'd lose my mind.

"What is going on here?" Kinsley asked, sidling past Sophie to drop our food on the table. She didn't wait for the reporter to respond; she angled her body so that she was blocking me from the camera. "Funny, I thought only athletes and their families were allowed in this section of the village. So, either the committee added 'Bad Eye-Shadowed Reporters' to the Olympic schedule, or you need to leave."

Sophie stammered and though I couldn't see her any more, I imagined her squirming under Kinsley's sharp stare.

"No problem. We've already got everything we need." She angled around Kinsley so I could see her bright red hair and dark, evil eyes. "Thanks for the interview Ms. Foster."

I kept my eye on Sophie as she led the cameraman out of the food court. With his camera clutched under his arm and her microphone hidden away in her purse, they could almost pass as two normal people.

"Who were those people?" Becca asked as she joined our table, half turned around to watch Sophie walk out of the food court. "What the hell were they doing in here?" She slid a plate of food toward me.

"Trying to interview Andie. They must have slipped past security during all the chaos."

"What'd they want to ask you?" Becca asked, sliding into a seat.

I eyed the massive egg white omelet Becca had brought me. I'd been hungry earlier, but Sophie had replaced it with a bottomless pit of annoyance.

"Andie?"

"Oh." I glanced up halfheartedly. "Just soccer stuff."

I didn't have to look to know they didn't believe me. What would Kinsley and Becca think of Sophie's questions? I was making a name for myself in the soccer world —most people had never heard of me—and if that interview aired, I'd be splashed across the internet as the idiot girl at the Olympics focused on men instead of soccer. The Olympic slut, trying to steal Freddie from his beloved Caroline.

"Andie, you okay?" Kinsley asked, reaching to touch my arm.

I flashed her a big, fake smile and nodded. "Never better."

———

I COULDN'T SHAKE the dark cloud Sophie Boyle had cast over my day. Not even a solid practice and a long workout could pull my mind out of the black. I'd regretted kissing Freddie *as* I was kissing Freddie. I wasn't delusional; I knew it wasn't in my best interest long-term. I'd forced us to keep the masks on in hopes that it would help separate fantasy from real life, but Sophie Boyle had confirmed that wasn't possible.

Someone has seen us walking out of my practice together and the media had gotten wind of it. What were the odds they'd find out about the club too? We hadn't been careful. We'd made out in the middle of the third floor. Freddie's hand had been up my freaking dress for half the night.

My stomach hurt just thinking about it. I had made the mistake of thinking Freddie was the only one needing discretion, but if the details of the club ever surfaced, I had no clue what it would mean for me. My career? Sponsorships? Even my personal relationships would take a hit if word got out that Caroline was his betrothed and I was just his whore.

"Andie, how's the wrist?" Liam asked after practice.

We'd just broken from the huddle and I was working at unwinding the tape the trainer had worked so hard to apply a few hours earlier. It seemed like a never-ending process.

"It's fine. I think I'll take something before the game just in case."

"Good idea." He stepped closer. "Kinsley mentioned there was a reporter trying to interview you at breakfast?"

My gut clenched just thinking about it. I glanced up to meet his eye, prepared to shrug off his question, but he was concerned—more concerned than I'd ever seen him. His eyes were narrowed and his dark brows were furrowed, forcing a crease down the center of his forehead.

"As someone who has been where you are, I want to remind you that you're here in Rio to focus on soccer."

I glanced down as a flood of shame washed over me.

"This drama on the side, it seems fun and manageable, but I've seen athletes lose their sponsors over mistakes far smaller than the one you're contemplating. You've been chosen as the flag bearer for the United States and that puts you in the spotlight. Any drama, any juicy detail they can find, they'll print without hesitation."

I opened my mouth to protest, to argue that I hadn't done anything yet, but there was no point in lying.

"I'm not going to tell you what to do," he continued. "I'm your friend as much as I'm your coach. I just think you need to keep your head in the game and leave every-thing else on the sidelines. You have your first game in two days and the opening ceremonies tomorrow. Make sure your interviews are good tonight at the cocktail party and leave your love life at the door."

I finished unrolling the tape from my wrist and threw the ball into the nearest trashcan so hard it drew the attention of a few teammates packing up their workout bags.

Listening to Liam, dealing with Sophie Boyle, and living with my own self-loathing was enough to send me over the edge. I didn't have an ounce of regret as I worded a simple, direct text to Freddie. I pressed send just as I stepped up onto our bus and found the first empty row of seats up front.

Andie: Obviously last night was a huge mistake.

He texted back right away and my blood boiled as I read over the three simple words.

Freddie: No it wasn't.

The bus pulled off onto the road and I typed away furiously, trying to prove to him how naive he was being.

Andie: You're engaged for god's sake, Freddie. I don't care if you don't love her. The WORLD loves her. And if anyone finds out about last night, it's me they'll go after.
Freddie: I'm betrothed, not engaged. And it won't be for much longer.

He didn't get it.

Andie: You're missing the point. I need to focus on the games, not embroil myself in an international scandal. I suggest you do the same.
Freddie: I'll be at the cocktail party tonight.
Andie: Great. You stay on one side of the room and I'll stay on the other.

Freddie: No. I have nothing to hide.

I didn't bother texting him back. Clearly, he didn't understand. I shoved my phone deep into my workout bag, so far down that I wouldn't notice the buzz if he texted me again. I leaned back against the bus seat, stared out at the Rio de Janeiro landscape whipping by, and tried to figure out how exactly I was going to avoid him at an intimate cocktail party without causing a scene.

Chapter Seventeen

FREDDIE

WHEN I'D LEFT Andie at the club, we'd been on the same page. We'd breathed the same air, felt the same things, and agreed that this thing between us wasn't done—far from it. When I read her text after swim practice, I was shocked to find that so much had changed overnight.

I guessed she'd had time to think on it and in the morning, our actions seemed to take on a new light for her. As for me, I'd woken up wanting her just as badly as I'd gone to bed wanting her.

Which was why I had to ignore her text.

She didn't know what she wanted, but I knew what I didn't want to miss.

The cocktail party was something I'd been dreading the last few days. Any event where I had to dress up, plaster on a fake smile, and walk around like a twit answering questions from the press was an event I'd be all right with skipping altogether. But then I took another look at the invitation and saw Andie's name printed beneath The United States of America. She had been chosen to be their flag bearer. They wanted someone new, with a fresh face and a perfect record. To the world, she was Andie Foster, beautiful American girl ready to take on the world from the front of a Wheaties cereal box. To me, she was more.

I stepped out of the car that had shuttled me and fixed my suit jacket. It was a new one my PR team had packed for me and I wasn't yet comfortable in the thick navy material.

"So we'll walk the red carpet, and you'll answer a few questions and pose for a few photos." The media consultant was telling me what to expect, but I was only half listening. I'd spotted Andie getting out of the car in front of me. It was pure luck. Fate. She extended one long leg from the back of the car and her own media consultant rushed forward to help her. He was a tall, skeletal bloke with a giant nose and a mobile attached to each hip. He held her hand as she stepped out of the car and I froze, taking in her simple blue cocktail dress. It was modest compared to what I'd seen her in the night before, but it didn't matter. Her tan legs were enough of a distraction on their own.

"Mr. Archibald, are you prepared to walk?"

My media consultant stepped forward, trying to usher me forward, but I stepped past her grasp and headed for Andie. She didn't notice me until I was there, taking her free arm in mine and gently pulling her away from her media consultant. Her hands were soft and shaking. I couldn't tell if she was nervous about the event or about me.

Her coordinator shook his head forcefully. "Ms. Foster is set to walk the carpet alone."

I smiled and nodded, acting as though I knew exactly what I was doing.

"I've got her," I told her coordinator. His jaw dropped and his gaze flitted frantically between us, but his protests came too late. I was already leading her around the corner, where a hundred photographers were waiting to snap our photo.

"Stop it," she hissed from the side of her mouth. She tried to pull back gently so that no one could tell, but I kept my arm wrapped around her lower back and dipped down to whisper in her ear.

"I won't let you avoid me all night."

"Let me walk the carpet alone and I promise I won't."

I could feel her shaking beside me, and when she glanced up, I realized it wasn't with nerves, it was with rage. She was seething.

"Fine," I said, loosening my grip on her waist. "Wait for me inside."

She promised she would and then her media consultant whisked her away to walk the red carpet in front of me. They had me wait so it wouldn't look as though we'd arrived together. I stood there out of sight, watching as they shouted for her attention. She smiled so beautifully even I couldn't tell if it was real or fake.

"Andie! Andie!" they shouted.

"Look here!"

Her media consultant pushed and prodded her along and when it was finally my turn to take the carpet, I waved and smiled for a photo or two, but not nearly as many as Andie had. These cameramen weren't my mates. They'd shout and beg for a photo one minute and then sully my name in the gossip pages the next.

My consultant flitted around me, trying to get me to stop and pose in specific spots. "If you could stand here for one—"

I shook my head. "That's enough."

I skipped the dozen or so reporters set up at the end of the red carpet, posed with microphones and cameras. They shouted questions as I passed, but there was nothing I wanted to answer. Was I still betrothed to Caroline Montague? *On paper.* Did I plan on breaking my world records? *Isn't that the bloody point?* Was I enjoying my time in Rio? *What was there not to like?*

I brushed by them and walked inside the restaurant, anxious to get to Andie. I'd lost her at some point on the red carpet, and she wasn't waiting for me in the foyer like she'd promised. I swept my gaze around the room, taking in the usual suspects. There was an athlete present from every country, mingling and chatting with the few reporters allowed entry into the event.

A waiter swept past me, holding out a tray of appetizers.

"Chicken skewer, sir?"

I shook my head and pushed past him, stepping deeper into the restaurant. I'd assumed it wouldn't be difficult to find a blonde woman wearing a blue dress, but I circled the room twice without any luck. Then I spotted her in a group of other female athletes. She was laughing at something one of them had said, holding a glass of champagne in one hand and a folded napkin in the other. She looked carefree and happy, not at all concerned with the fact that she'd stood me up at the door. What had changed all of a sudden? Her texts earlier hadn't explained anything.

I made my way toward the corner of the room where she stood with her group. I had the advantage as she listened attentively to one of the women, an athlete I recognized from the Japanese swim team. She was in the middle of a story, but I didn't care.

"Andie, could I speak with you for a moment?" I asked, plastering on the innocent smile I'd learned as a child. It was the smile I wore around the media, the smile my mother had forced from time to time.

"I'm actually busy at the moment," Andie said, smiling politely and then turning her attention back to the woman I'd interrupted. She didn't seem surprised that I'd found her, which said more of my apparent obsession than it did of her lack of remorse.

"Oh, no it's okay if you need to go talk," the woman said. The rest of the group nodded, clearly affected by my smile more than Andie.

"I loathe cliffhangers. Please finish your story," Andie said, waving her hand in the air so the woman would continue.

"It'll only be a moment," I promised, though it wasn't the truth. Not that it mattered; we'd been lying to one another all day.

I turned away before she could protest. I heard a gentle sigh, then the sound of her heels hitting the floor behind me; she was following.

The restaurant was smaller than I'd assumed. There was the main dining hall and a foyer up front. That was where most of the media personnel were stationed, so I steered clear and turned down a side hallway instead. The lights were low and each door we passed was labeled to keep us out. We passed a broom closet and a door marked 'Staff Only'.

I pulled the door open for one of the private restrooms. It wasn't the setting I'd hoped for, but when I turned to see Andie follow me inside, I knew it wouldn't matter.

She was long legs in a tight dress, bright eyes that sparked something inside me. I knew she'd been lying earlier. She was scared and nervous. The easiest solution was to push me away, but I wasn't ready to let that happen.

It was an exercise in restraint to keep my hands to

myself as she walked over to the vanity and turned to face me. I let the door slam behind us and reached out to lock it. The space was tiny, cramped, and dark.

"I asked you to stay away."

Her voice was calm, but curious.

I unbuttoned the front of my blazer and nodded. "I know."

Her makeup made her gray eyes stand out even more against her delicate features. She was watching me, studying me, waiting for me to act, but I stood there for another minute, simply taking her in. Her blonde hair was twisted up high. There was nothing touching her neck, nothing that would get in my way.

One of the straps of her dress was threatening to fall from her shoulder and as I stepped forward, a sudden realization passed over me. The games, my records, the press —none of it seemed important if only I could have Andie. Normally I would have chalked it up to lust, but this need ran deeper.

"So is it a game to you?" she asked. "Getting a reaction out of me?"

I shook my head.

"Because I meant every word I texted you earlier. Last night was a mistake."

I watched the rise and fall of her chest. Every time she inhaled, her breasts pushed against the tight bodice of her dress.

"This isn't a game," I said in reply to her earlier question. "I've been honest about what I want. And now, what I don't."

She crossed her arms around her waist.

"I came to Rio to play soccer and have fun," she said, working up to an argument I didn't care to listen to.

"You don't think last night was fun?" I asked, taking a step closer to her.

Her eyes widened.

"I had fun," I continued.

She blinked, and blinked again. I could see the logic trying to work its way around her brain.

I took another step closer and fingered the strap falling off her shoulder. "You wanted me last night."

She shook her head.

"I could feel your heart beating." I pressed my hand to her chest, to the bare skin above her dress. "Just as wildly as it's beating right now."

Her gaze was on my lips when I leaned in and kissed her, cutting off her protests. My hips caged her against the vanity and my hands wound up through her hair, tilting her head so it was easier to slide my tongue past her lips. She moaned softly, a seductive sound that made me step closer and pull her taut against me. I could have kept her there forever, but I wouldn't force her. When I pulled back, I gave her an out.

"Leave if you want to."

I stepped back and gave us space, staring down at her against the vanity. Her chest was heaving and her fists were clenched by her sides. Her mouth was red and swollen.

"I don't want to be dragged into this," she protested with a fierce warning. "You think the rules don't apply to you, but this is my life too. A reporter harassed me today. About you!"

"Then you should go," I said again. "The reporters will never stop. I wish I could say they will, but they seem intent on capturing every moment of my life from here on out."

She inhaled another breath.

"Go," I said again.

"No."

One word spoken with bated breath.

I stepped closer and she swayed. I let my hands slide up her arms, slowly, giving her time to rethink her answer. By the time my hands had found her shoulders, she looked drunk with lust.

She leaned in and kissed me then. She was hot and demanding as I dragged my lips down her neck and shoulder, kissing a line to the thin strap of her dress. I stilled there as I brushed my hand up beneath her dress. She was velvet and the higher I drew my hand, the quicker her breaths came.

I slid my hand across the center of her thighs, feeling the lace she'd slipped on beneath her dress. I slid my finger back and forth, testing her patience. Her teeth on my bottom lip proved how little she cared for teasing. Her hips arched to meet mine just before I gently pushed the material aside, laying her bare.

"Ahhh…" she moaned, letting her head tilt back and her eyes flutter closed.

I stroked her back and forth. Slowly. So fucking slowly she nearly begged for it by the time I slid a finger inside of her.

"I can feel how much you want this."

I leaned forward and stole a kiss. She wound her fingers through my hair with a punishing grip. She was mine in that bathroom and I could feel her starting to unwind. I could push her up onto the counter and spread her thighs as wide as I wanted. The protests from earlier had died on her lips, replaced with the sexiest moans I'd ever heard.

I was in control.

And then suddenly, no one was in control. I couldn't

stop and I needed to stop. There were voices in the hallway and any minute there'd be a knock on the door.

I ripped my mouth away and pointed to the door.

"You were right. I shouldn't drag you into this. Leave."

She reared back, eyes wide in surprise. "What?"

She sounded wounded.

"Go back to the party."

Her nostrils flared. "You pulled me in here and now—"

"Go back…to the party."

My voice was strained and raspy, but she didn't hesitate.

"Fuck you, Freddie."

She shoved past me and pulled the door open so hard it slammed against the wall. As soon as she was gone, I reached back and locked the door.

Fuck.

I gripped the edge of the sink and leaned over, trying to gather my wits. I hadn't expected to come to my senses at the exact moment she was giving herself to me, but that's when it'd hit me. We couldn't sneak off during a cocktail party and fuck in the bathroom. I didn't care what it would do to my reputation, but it would ruin hers. It didn't matter that Caroline didn't have a ring on her finger —Andie would still be labeled a home wrecker, while I would probably be forgiven for being seduced by her presumed wickedness. And if she was already being questioned by reporters, that meant we had been careless in the club. Understanding that, I needed to get her out of the bathroom before someone saw us leave together.

By the time I'd collected myself and straightened my suit, I had a text waiting for me on my mobile. I read it as I stepped back into the party.

Andie: Stay the hell away from me.

I didn't reply; I turned off my mobile and slipped it into my back pocket. The party had only just begun, otherwise I would have left and taken a cab back to the village. If I left then, the media would spin it into something it wasn't. The media consultant I'd ditched earlier found me at the bar after I'd ordered a drink. She'd become a nervous wreck; apparently disappearing for thirty minutes at the start of a party will do that to them.

"Mr. Archibald are you prepared for your interviews? I tried to find you earlier, but then——"

"I was here," I lied.

"Oh. Right. Of course." She fidgeted with the clipboard she had clutched to her chest. "Well, everyone is waiting near the foyer if you'll just…"

I turned and took the drink from the bartender's hand before he'd even extended it my way. I needed two more, but I didn't dare ask, not when I caught Andie out of the corner of my eye, chatting with a reporter at the other end of the bar. She was beautiful and flush from the last thirty minutes and the lucky wanker she was talking to leaned in closer, probably spewing some excuse about how hard it was to hear over the crowd. She laughed and I turned away.

"Let's go."

Chapter Eighteen

ANDIE

I **WOULD HAVE** let Freddie fuck me in that bathroom. I *wanted* him to do it. He had me caged up against the sink. I could feel how much he wanted me. His hips were right there, pushing up against mine and driving me to the brink of madness. I thought he'd toss me up onto the counter and tear my dress in two—all right, that's a little Tarzan, even for me, but still. I'd been right there with him, ready to let it happen, and then he'd turned away as if suddenly he wasn't interested. Suddenly, it wasn't worth the trouble.

Fuck him. I'd come to win games, not just play them.

After the cocktail party, I'd laid in bed stewing over the turn of events and replaying what it'd felt like to have his hands on me. *I* had been the one to push away first. *I* was the one trying to keep my distance. How dare he pull that stunt and then leave me like that with his hand up my dress and my heart on my sleeve?

Like I said, fuck him.

"Andie! Is that water running in there? Are you showering *again?!*" Kinsley yelled.

I leaned forward and turned off the faucet, letting the last few drops hit the back of my head.

"What the hell are you doing in there?"

"Nothing! I'll be out soon!"

Yes, I'd already showered twice that morning, but it was Freddie's fault. I'd woken up with fantasies playing on repeat in my head (the dirty kind with a happy ending). I'd shoved the blankets aside and run to the bathroom to wash the shame off my body and then I'd tried to go on about my day. I'd returned a phone call from my parents, answered emails, and looked over the opening ceremonies itinerary they'd handed out the day before.

Then, like a dirty little habit, I started thinking about Freddie again. I closed my eyes, imagined what it would have been like if I'd slipped my hand past his belt and tried to affect him as much as he'd affected me, and yes, I couldn't help it; I touched myself at 8:02 AM. Obviously, I'm a terrible person. I'd had two orgasms and no breakfast and I was showering again and hating Freddie for making me crazy.

By the time I walked out of my room, dressed for the opening ceremonies, I couldn't even make eye contact with Kinsley and Becca for fear they'd find an admission in my eyes. They were in the kitchen, preparing breakfast, so I took a seat at the dining table and dropped my phone next to a red beret we were supposed to wear during the ceremonies.

"MORNING SUNSHINE!" Becca said. "Feeling squeaky clean now that you've used up all the water in the whole complex?"

I nodded.

"Want some granola and yogurt?" Kinsley asked.

I nodded again.

"You make our ceremony outfits look really cute," Kinsley said.

She was lying; the outfits were way over the top. The Olympic committee had enlisted a young designer, Lorena Lefray, and she'd decided that every athlete from the United States should rock a bright red jumpsuit. I felt like I was about to parachute out of an airplane so, yeah, clearly, I didn't understand high fashion.

"Thanks," I muttered, staring out past the living room window. I could just barely make out the mountain range in the distance.

Kinsley and Becca carried over our bowls of granola and took their seats at the table. For the first half of breakfast, I ate in silence, more than happy to listen to their conversation take place without me.

"What's wrong?" Kinsley asked. "You've hardly touched your granola when most mornings you almost eat the spoon on accident."

"I'm just not that hungry."

"Are you having cramps?"

I shook my head.

"Diarrhee-ree?"

I smiled. "No."

"She's lonely," Becca offered.

"No I'm not."

"When's the last time you felt the touch of a man, Andie?" Kinsley asked.

I squeezed my eyes closed. "Never," I lied. "I've never felt the touch of a man. Let's drop this."

"I have a brilliant idea!" Becca said.

I glanced up to take in her wide smile. "No thanks. I'm fine. No brilliant ideas needed."

Becca already had her phone out and she was scrolling through the app store. "I've heard this rumor..."

I focused on my granola and tried to pretend my hearing had gone so they'd leave me alone.

"Apparently a ton of athletes are using *Tinder* to find hookups during the games."

Kinsley leaned forward. "Are you serious?"

I caught Becca's nod out of the corner of my eye. "Yeah, Michelle and Nina were telling me about it yesterday. There's like a thousand athletes on there and you can narrow down the distance so you only see the profiles for other people in the village."

"Cute. I hope they find love," I said before scraping my chair away from the table and carrying my half-full bowl of granola over to the sink.

Becca continued, "Look, I know we were being hard on you the first few days we were here. We just didn't want you to go loco. But we can tell you're depressed from all of this Freddie stuff, and sometimes the best way to get out of a slump is to get a good hump!"

"Yes!" Kinsley said, high-fiving her for the rhyme. "It's settled then. We'll make a profile for Andie. I already have this photo of her in a bikini I was going to use for blackmail someday."

"NOPE!" I shouted from the kitchen. "No profiles needed, but thanks!"

They ignored me. Kinsley scooted her chair around the table to join Becca. They dropped their heads together and got to work. I washed out my dish and loaded it into the dishwasher, listening as they giggled like two schoolgirls.

"I think we should say she's 'a fun-loving girl with a heart of gold'."

Becca shook her head. "Boring. How about 'A leggy blonde with lots of room for love'."

I closed the dishwasher. "That makes it sound like I have a huge vagina or something."

They ignored me.

"I think we should just say how it is," Becca said. "'A desperate but pretty soccer player in need of a good fuck.'"

I ran to the table and ripped the phone out of their hands so fast, I nearly took Becca's finger with it.

"No!" I held the phone up above my head so they couldn't get to it. "No Tinder profiles. I don't need to sleep with a random athlete to feel better. Ugh! I'm fine!"

Kinsley turned to Becca. "Hmm. Better add 'cranky' after 'desperate'."

———

EVERY ATHLETE WAS expected to meet in the lobby by 9:00 AM so we could locate our rendezvous point and get placed on buses that would take us to the stadium for the opening ceremonies. It sounded like an easy task, but we had to wait for an elevator on our floor for ten minutes, and when one finally arrived, it was already filled with athletes.

"C'mon, let's take the stairs," Kinsley said, leading us toward a side stairwell where we joined the crowd of people making their way to the first floor.

"OUT OF THE WALKWAY!" shouted a woman standing on top of a chair off to the side of the lobby. She was trying to convince a group of British guys to move and clear a path for people to walk. They'd taken up residence right at the foot of the stairs so that even if we wanted to join the athletes from our country, we couldn't.

"American athletes move to the left of the rope! Great Britain to the right!" the woman shouted again, trying to amplify her voice with a piece of rolled up paper. Most everyone completely ignored her. They were rowdy and excited to see the friends they'd made during the last

Olympic games. Whoever thought amassing a couple hundred athletes in one lobby was a good idea should have been fired.

"American athletes, your busses will leave first! Please find your group and make sure you have your badges with you or you won't be allowed into the stadium for the ceremonies!"

Kinsley dragged me past a group of guys pulling flasks out of their red jumpsuits. (I guessed Lorena had been on to something with all the pockets.)

"Here's to being drunk for the entire Parade of Nations," one of the guys proclaimed. His buddies laughed and leaned forward to clink their flasks against his. I watched in awe as they all took long swigs. Weren't they worried about looking drunk on TV?

"C'mon," Kinsley said, drawing my attention back to the pathway she was trying to make. I let her pull me through, ignoring the groans from the people she was brushing out of the way.

"Where you goin' girls?" one guy asked. "Party's right here."

Kinsley flashed her ring. "I've already got a party of two."

"Boo," he said, waving his hand and moving on to his next conquest.

That's when I first saw Freddie. He was on the opposite side of the lobby, standing on a small staircase that separated the sunken lobby from the hallway that led to the food court. He stood up on the third stair, leaning back against the railing. There were other British athletes around him, talking and joking, but he seemed uninterested, surveying the crowd instead.

I'd seen him in suits, workout clothes, and dressed down in jeans, but seeing Frederick Archibald standing there in his opening ceremonies outfit was physically painful. They'd put him in a tight navy sweater and matching slacks. On everyone else, the outfit looked foolish, but his broad shoulders and strong arms filled out the sweater too easily, making it fit like it'd been designed with exactly his body type in mind.

His medium-length hair was brushed back in one of those GQ cover styles. He'd just shaved and I visually inhaled the sight of his strong jaw, committing it to memory as best as possible before his gaze landed on me in the crowd.

Fuck. He'd caught me staring at him.

My breath caught in my throat and though I wanted to, I couldn't look away.

"Andie?" Kinsley asked.

Someone walked in front of me, cutting us off for a moment, but when they moved, he was still there, watching me from across the room. There was no smile playing on his lips, no hint of friendship, just those caramel brown eyes assessing me coolly. I hated his beauty. I hated the way his attention made my heart race and my palms sweat. I could tell myself to look away, but deep down, I knew that until he was done with me, I'd never be done with him.

Chapter Nineteen

FREDDIE

"**YOU LOOKED LIKE** a knob in that outfit last night."

I groaned. "Georgie, it's too early in the morning for your sarcasm."

"I'm telling the truth. Who designed those things anyway? Why can't they just put you in a pair of normal trousers?"

"Did you and Mum watch the whole thing?"

"She did. I got bored after a few minutes. I did stick around long enough to see this Andie of yours carry the flag for the Yanks though."

"And?"

"And she is quite pretty."

I wiped the sleep from my eyes.

"How's that progressing by the way?"

"Terribly."

"That's because you looked like a knob. No American girl wants a man who wears sweaters. You've probably gone and scared her off."

"Is this why you've phoned me, Georgie? To torment me?"

She sighed. "No. I overheard your conversation with Mum earlier."

I waited for her to continue.

"Are you seriously considering scuttling the betrothal?"

"More than serious. I've made my mind up. I don't want to marry Caroline."

"Because you're gaga over this American footballer?"

Yes.

"No, it's because I've never wanted to marry Caroline, and I shouldn't go through with a marriage only to fulfill some antiquated notion of familial responsibility."

"Won't Caroline's family be cross?"

"I don't really care. If Henry's death taught me anything, it's that life is too short to worry about upsetting people—especially when you're doing what's right."

"Well, Mum explained to me why it's important for you to marry Caroline, how good it'll be for the family, but I agree with you. Caroline is such a bore, Freddie. I'd go mad if I had her as a sister-in-law for the rest of my life."

I smiled. "So you're on my side?"

"'Course. Well, except about the sweater. You really ought to burn that thing."

"I think Andie liked it. She stared at me when she first saw me in the lobby downstairs."

She laughed. "Yes, Fred. She was probably concerned that you'd lost your mind wearing a thing like that."

A fist pounded against my door before I could reply.

"Freddie open up," Thom shouted. "I've prepared a lovely breakfast for you, including *all* the crispy bacon, so stop being a mope and get out here."

I shoved off the bed and opened the door for Thom.

"I'm talking to Georgie, not moping."

"He's moping!" Georgie yelled through the phone loud enough for Thom to hear.

"'Ello Georgie," Thom said, trying to take the phone from my hand. "Goodbye Georgie."

"Not yet, mate." I stepped back out of his reach. "She's advising me."

"When's she coming to Rio?" he asked, ignoring me.

"Next week!" Georgia yelled back.

I worked the door out of his hand and tried to shut it.

"And she's not hanging out with you," I said just before shutting the door in his face.

"Fine, I'll leave, but I'm eating ALL THE CRISPY BACON."

"You really ought to be nicer to him," Georgie said once I'd shut the door and turned back to find a clean pair of workout shorts. "He's the only one who can stand you during competition, and it wouldn't do you any favors if you scared him off."

"I have loads of friends."

"Your eighteen-year-old sis doesn't count."

I laughed and checked the time on my watch where it sat on the bedside table. I had twenty minutes before practice, which meant I needed to get a move on.

"Don't discredit yourself, Georgie. You're just as good as any of my mates. Nearly as hairy, too."

"Ha ha, very funny, Fred. I'll have you know I've morphed into quite a beauty since you've gone. Can't walk down the street with all the drivers crashing from craning their necks."

I laughed.

"Now piss off and DON'T mention the whole betrothal thing to Mum again. She's going mad over here. Wait 'til I've arrived in Rio and we'll get it sorted."

I agreed and hung up, but I wasn't sure how much

longer I'd manage. It'd been one day since I'd nearly had my wicked way with Andie in the bathroom at the cocktail party. Keeping my distance for the remainder of the party and then again during the opening ceremonies was testing my patience in new and unusual ways. I'd already replayed every encounter we'd had in my mind and a bloke can only wank it so many times before it starts to feel shameful.

I'd nearly texted her the night before after returning from the opening ceremonies. It was late and I was missing her, wondering if she'd had a good time carrying the flag. I'd tried to find her during the Parade of Nations, but Great Britain and the United States were separated by too many countries to make it possible.

"Mate, honestly," Thom shouted. "Come get this bacon or I'm going to chuck it out the window."

I laughed and walked out into the living room to find Thom standing at the open window, ready to haul the bacon out onto unsuspecting pedestrians. I yanked the pan out of his hand and plated it beside the eggs he'd made as well.

"We've got practice in fifteen and then afternoon workout after," he said, reading our team's itinerary off his phone.

I shook my head. "I've talked it over with Coach already. I'm going to work out this evening instead."

He glanced up. "What? Why?"

"There's a soccer match I want to attend."

Chapter Twenty

ANDIE

I COULDN'T SLEEP the night before our first game. I'd lain in bed worrying about my wrist and wishing the dull ache would go away on its own. I was nervous about the game. I could stop a ball like no other woman in America, but I didn't trust my wrist. I knew that at any time, my sprain could take a turn and I'd be benched, or worse. I tried to find a sleeping position that offered some comfort, but in the end, I'd lain like a mummy staring up at the ceiling, willing sleep to take me.

When the alarm beside my bed blared three annoying chimes at 6:30 AM, I threw off my blankets with a plan. I'd take three Advil and have the trainer compress my wrist even tighter than usual. It needed to be secure if I was expected to stop balls hurtling toward me at 60 mph. I didn't care about the pain, but I wanted my mind clear and focused.

I was sitting up on the trainer's table when I glanced to the section in the stands where the Olympic Committee had placed the athletes. It was expected that athletes from different sports would show up to support one another in different events, to the extent that the TV channels demanded they be squashed together. Thus, with one quick pan of the camera, viewers at home could see them all—including Freddie Archibald—at once. He was wedged in between a few other athletes in the front row, sporting a neutral white button-down and jeans. When he saw me glance over, he smiled.

"What are you doing here?" I mouthed. My words were mixed with savvy hand gestures, and after two more tries, he finally understood my question.

He pointed to me with a shrug. I was too far away to make out his dimples, but his smile sent a warm swell through me, momentarily numbing my nerves. My family was a million miles away and the only friends I had in Rio were about to take the field with me. Except Freddie. The stands were packed with screaming fans, but Freddie was the only person there for me.

"Good luck," he mouthed with a thumbs up.

I nodded. "Thanks."

———

HE WAS GONE by the time the game ended and I walked off the field sweaty, bone-tired, and cradling my wrist. Adrenaline proved to be the best drug for the pain, but I knew once the shock of our first victory wore off, I'd be in a world of hurt. I stood over the trashcan near the trainer's table, slowly unwrapping the tape between long swallows of my sports drink.

"Good game," Liam said, patting my shoulder as he trailed behind Coach Decker. Kinsley and Becca were right behind him, but they waited until I'd finished unwrapping my wrist before the three of us walked out of the stadium. We looked like a bunch of zombies, and we definitely smelled like them. My jersey stuck to my skin, and though I tried to pry it away, nothing seemed to help.

Once I returned to the condo, I called my mom and tried to recount the entire game as best as possible, but my heart was still racing and my delivery was choppy.

"Your father and I watched the whole thing, sweetie. You played so well."

"Thanks. The crowd here in Rio was the loudest I've ever heard."

"Oh! Speaking of the crowd, you'll never guess who we saw in the stands!"

I already knew the answer, but I humored her nonetheless. "Who?"

"The duke! Frederick Archibald! Can you believe it? Your meemaw said everyone on the news was speculating about why he was there. It would have made sense if you were playing Great Britain, but he must have been there to watch a friend or something. I swear the cameras showed him nearly as much as they showed the game."

"Maybe he just likes soccer," I offered.

She hummed. "Maybe, but he could have just watched it on the CBS."

I smiled. "Listen, I need to shower. I'm about to lose consciousness from my own stench."

I promised I'd call her again the next day and she promised to watch the news for any mention of Frederick's attendance. After I hung up, I stripped off my jersey and threw it into my dirty clothes hamper. I went into the bathroom and turned the shower on as hot as it would go, feeling my muscles starting to ache from the game. There'd been a few hard blocks and diving saves. I could already feel the bruises forming as I rubbed my hands down my arms, massaging the muscles as I went. I stepped into the shower, wincing at the temperature, but left it there nonetheless. The water beat down my back as I rolled my neck and shoulders out. My wrist was a little swollen and tender to the touch, so I left it by my side and shampooed my hair with my other hand, lathering up twice before sliding it down to the rest of my body.

I stayed in the shower longer than necessary, replacing my sweat with the more subtle scent of lavender. I thought over the game, dissecting the few mistakes we'd made.

Once the water had all but cooled, I stepped out and reached for my towel. My phone was sitting on the bathroom sink and as I walked by, it buzzed with an incoming call. I glanced over and my heart dropped when Freddie's number lit up across the screen.

I'd been in denial about wanting to reach out to him. He'd gone out of his way to come to my first game, and even though I'd told him to stay away, it meant a lot knowing I'd had someone there rooting for me. That's why I swiped my finger across the screen to answer his call, or so I told myself.

"Andie," he said, as if surprised I'd answered.

"Hi."

"Have I caught you at a bad time?"

My eyes flitted around the room. "I just stepped out of the shower."

"Andie."

My cheeks flamed. *Stupid.* "Um…that wasn't supposed to sound as porny as it did, it's just the truth."

"Have you still got your towel on?"

"Freddie…"

"I'm just curious." I could tell he was smiling.

"I'm getting my clothes on right now."

"I'd rather you didn't."

I inhaled a shaky breath. "Freddie. Why did you call?"

He sighed. "I want to know how the last few minutes

of the game went. I had to leave to make it to my evening workout."

"We won."

"Good."

"Did your workout go well?"

He chuckled. "Brilliantly. Could've used a spotter."

"Right, well…" I said, eyeing myself in the mirror. My long hair fell down my back, in desperate need of a good brushing. My full lips were parted and my eyes were wide and curious. "I need to go now."

"You're lying. I can tell."

I rolled my eyes. "I'm not lying. I need to ice my wrist and put clothes on and generally ignore you."

"Stop saying you need to put clothes on."

"Well I do."

He sighed.

"Why'd you really call, Freddie?"

"I already told you."

I tightened my towel around my chest. "You could have watched the highlights on the news."

"Maybe I wanted to hear your voice then."

I avoided my reflection in my mirror.

He sounded so sincere. I hated that he sounded sincere; it only made the fight harder.

"I told you to stay away from me."

"I remember."

Silence.

"My brain can't keep up with you, Freddie," I said, turning away from the mirror. "You push me away one minute and then you show up at my game as if everything is okay and it's not."

"I know."

"This whole thing is too confusing for me to handle

right now. I'm in the middle of the Olympics for God's sake—"

"I'm not going to stay away from you, Andie."

The way he said my name sent a subtle shiver down my spine. His voice came across differently on the phone, a little more seductive and demanding.

"I need to hang up now."

"Lie down on your bed."

My stomach flipped.

Silence.

"Did you hear me? I want you to lie down on your bed."

"It hurt when you pushed me out of that bathroom, Freddie."

"I know, and I want to make it up to you," he continued, undeterred. "Lie down on your bed."

I stepped into my room and eyed my tangled sheets. I wasn't going to lay down, I knew that. *So then why am I stepping closer?*

"Are you still wet from the shower?"

I sat down on the edge of my bed, hardly on it at all, really.

"Answer me."

"My hair is."

"Is your body wet?"

I swallowed. "Ye…Yes."

"Run your fingers up your thigh, feel how soft your skin is there."

"Freddie—"

"Yes?"

"I think we should stop."

"Hang up if you want to, Andie."

Silence. I stared up at the ceiling and clutched the phone.

He knew I wasn't going to hang up.

"Are you touching yourself?" I asked with a soft voice, eyeing my closed bedroom door.

"Do you want me to be?" His voice was strained.

"I don't know. I've never done this before."

"You've never touched yourself?"

I smiled. "I've never had phone sex."

"Where's your hand right now?"

I glanced down. "Gripping the bottom of my towel."

"Let go and drag your fingers up the inside of your leg until I tell you to stop."

"Freddie…"

"Don't overthink it," he begged. "Let go."

I squeezed my eyes closed and moved my hand to my leg, just above my knee. It was a harmless spot. A nothing spot.

"Higher," he whispered into my ear. It sounded like he was right there, controlling my hand and dragging it higher for me. I could hear the pleasure in his voice as he told me to keep going, to let my fingers touch the groove of my hip. I squeezed my eyes tighter as a flush ran across my chest and neck. I was hot, burning up. I yanked the towel off and threw it aside, laying back on the bed, naked and alone.

"Open your legs."

"Freddie," I protested.

"Andie, slide your legs apart," he demanded, a little less patient this time.

My thighs slid across the soft sheets, just a few inches at first, not so far that I couldn't squeeze them closed if I wanted the call to end.

"I can hear you moving on those sheets and I wish I could be there to see how far you've spread your legs for me."

149

I opened my eyes to see what he would see. My entire body was flush, partly from the scalding shower and partly from Freddie's dark words. My hand rested on my flat stomach, rising and falling with my breath.

"Touch yourself, Andie. Drag your finger there and pretend it's me."

I pushed my hand lower, tentatively.

"Lower," he insisted.

I started turning slow circles, nothing much at first. I was too embarrassed to admit how turned on I was just from listening to him.

"I'd ask if you're wet, but I know that you are."

My heart fluttered.

"*Feel* yourself. Feel how tight you are."

My breaths were coming quicker. "Freddie."

"Andie…" He was begging.

My legs were trembling by that point, shaking with need.

"Spread your legs as wide as they'll go and slide your finger in and out. *Slowly*, Andie. Don't speed up until I tell you to."

I was seconds away from losing my mind.

"Do you like the way your fingers feel?"

I swallowed back a moan as my back arched off the bed.

"Answer me."

"Yes," I breathed. "But I need you here."

"I know. I can hear your breath picking up. You need a release, don't you? You're so fucking close."

My finger slid in and out, and I squeezed my eyes closed, listening to the sounds of my heady breaths.

"Tell me…what would you do to me if you were here?"

I could almost see his smirk as his dark voice filled the

silence. "I'd pull you down to the very edge of the bed and make you watch as I knelt between your thighs. Maybe you'd be shy, but I'd grip your legs and keep them apart so that I could see all of you."

His explicit promises consumed me.

"You'd watch me lick you. God, you'd taste so fucking good as you rode my mouth."

"*Freddie...I...*"

"I'd make you come like that, on your elbows with my mouth between your thighs. You'd beg me to end your agony, beg me to give you the release you so desperately need."

His words were dark embers, falling through the phone and setting fire to every single nerve inside my body.

"I want to hear you, Andie." His voice was strained, just as hot and breathy as mine was. "Give me that much..."

As if my body was under his command, I could feel my world starting to unravel. My toes curled, my eyes squeezed tighter, and I let the waves of pleasure roll through my body. The phone slipped from my hand as I moved to cover my mouth. I tried to stifle my moans, but it wasn't good enough. I'd come with Freddie on the phone and a moment later, a knock sounded on the door, just as I'd started to gather my senses.

"Andie, are you okay?" Kinsley shouted. "It sounds like you're strangling a cat in there."

I threw my phone across the room like it was on fire. It collided with my suitcase and clattered to the floor. I yanked my towel around my body and bolted off the bed.

"Yup!" I shouted back, praying she wouldn't open the door. "It's fine, I just...stubbed my toe."

"Do you need ice or something? Honestly, I thought you were sacrificing a goat or something."

"No, everything is fine!"

My phone buzzed on the floor across the room, but I didn't check it until I heard Kinsley walk back into the living room. It was a text from Freddie, short and foreboding.

Freddie: That was good, but not enough. Next time, I'll feel you come.

Chapter Twenty-One

ANDIE

I **HAD A** suspicion that my trainer Lisa was secretly an intern for the devil. She was tiny and adorable, but she made me cry like I was in the sixth circle of hell. I'd begun training with her my first day in Rio, and I'd figured we'd eventually work up to one of those great relationships where instead of rehabbing my wrist all day, we'd just sit around gossiping about celebrities and making fun of people.

"You have two more sets of mobility exercises, and we haven't even gotten to the strengthening segment," Lisa said, interrupting my short break in the training center.

Fuckkkk youuuuuuuuu.

"This is torture, Lisa."

She arched a perfectly sculpted brow. "Do you want to keep playing here or do you want to go home? The choice is yours."

I sneered. "Actually, I think I'm all set. I'll just go home."

She shook her head. "Too late."

I groaned and leaned forward onto the training table.

Lisa had it set up so that she stood on one side and I stood on the other, leaning toward her with my wrists hanging off the table.

"Ready?" she asked with a smirk.

I narrowed my eyes. "Whatever. Let's get this over with."

She stepped forward to adjust my form on my right hand. "Loosen up for a second."

I let her link her fingers through mine.

"Take a breath," she said, using her own wrist to rotate and loosen mine. I bit down on my lip to avoid cursing her to hell for all eternity.

Just then, I glanced up to see Freddie walking into the training room alongside his teammate, Thom. I could tell they'd just come from swim practice. Freddie's dark hair was still damp and he had his workout bag slung over his shoulder. He was wearing a white workout tank that cut down the side of his chest and loose gym shorts that sat low on his hips. He looked massive standing there beside Thom, tall, chiseled, and looking my way with curious eyes. Lisa still had her hands linked through mine, so I couldn't wave. I settled on a smile as he changed course and stepped closer.

"Hi," I said through clenched teeth. *Can't you ease up a bit, Lisa?*

"Hey," he said, glancing at my hand in Lisa's before meeting my eye. "How's the training?"

Lisa turned with narrowed eyes. "Bud, you mind coming back when we're done? We're kind of busy here."

I wasn't sure how "bud" translated over to UK English, but Lisa's body language made it clear that she wouldn't tolerate any distractions. There was a fleeting moment where I thought Freddie might escalate her unwarranted aggression, so I spoke up first, easing the tension with a feigned smile.

"Freddie, I'll come find you when I'm done," I promised.

"It'll be a while," Lisa cut in, still holding my hand. The situation couldn't have been more awkward, but fortunately Thom nudged Freddie's arm and pulled him away.

"Your trainer's looking for you," Thom said before nodding my way. "Hey Andie."

I smiled.

"Come on." Thom nudged him again. Freddie glanced back at me with a curious expression before heading off with Thom. I watched him go, taking in the slope of his powerful back. Swimmers had the most insane bodies.

I swore after they walked away, Lisa dialed up the punishment. She forced me to do double the normal amount of wrist turn-things, and four times the normal amount of my other least favorite exercise: something I called "holyfuckingshit" for short.

All the while, I tried to sneak peeks at Freddie. He was working with a trainer on the other side of the room, an older man who was helping him stretch out his arms and shoulders. Twice, I glanced over my shoulder and found him watching me. His trainer was jotting something on a sheet of paper, but Freddie was focused on me. I blushed and glanced away.

The third time I looked back, I thought I'd go into cardiac arrest on my training table. Freddie was in the middle of tugging his shirt off over his head. Time slowed as his arm and stomach muscles coiled and stretched. I'd seen a glimpse of his arms and back earlier, but when his shirt came off and I was met with his perfectly sculpted chest and abs, I nearly lost control of my vision.

"Andie, are you focusing?" Lisa asked.

No. Absolutely not. I was watching Freddie's trainer as he pressed an ice pack on the back of Freddie's right shoulder. He wove an elastic bandage over his chest and around his arm to keep it in place. I'd never wanted to change places with a human being as much as I did in that moment. He was getting the privilege of touching him. His hand was on his chest!

"Foster," Lisa snapped.

"Yep!" I said, jerking back to my table and trying to regain control of my tongue so I could answer her.

"Lisa! Phone call!" one of the training assistants called from across the room.

Lisa nodded and let go of my hand. "I need to take that. Rest for a minute and then we'll finish up."

"Oh thank god," I mumbled under my breath as she walked away. I'd been training with Lisa for eight days and each day I woke up with a little less pain than the day before. Still, her sessions were unbearable. Any break she offered, I'd take.

I stood up from the training table and shook out my arms. I reached for my water bottle and took a sip before giving in to the urge to steal a glance back toward Freddie. He was sitting on the edge of his training table, typing on his phone with one hand—THE PHONE HE'D USED THE NIGHT BEFORE…*oh god*. His trainer had left to help another athlete while he iced his shoulder, which meant I had a short window of time to talk to him alone. I scanned over to Lisa's office to find her gesticulating animatedly on the phone with the door shut. Without a second thought, I grabbed my water bottle and headed for Freddie.

He didn't notice me approaching until I was only a few feet away. He dropped his phone beside him and straightened up. I swallowed down a groan. Seriously, it wasn't real. The chest. The abs. His body was so sculpted it seemed to fit on the pages of an art history book better than it did in real life. I stepped closer and held my hand up to block everything from my view except for his face.

"What are you doing?" he asked with a smile.

"I can't talk to you if you aren't wearing a shirt. It's very distracting."

He laughed and reached for my hand to pull it away from my eyes. "You're mad."

"Fine, but if I start to drool or something, you can't hold it against me."

He shook his head and glanced away, almost as if he were embarrassed. Dear god, he couldn't look like that *and* be humble; my brain would short-circuit.

"Are you done with your training?" he asked, glancing back to me and dragging his gaze down my body. I was wearing yoga pants and a tank top, nothing too glamorous, but he seemed to like it well enough.

I shook my head. "Lisa wants me to do another set."

He arched a brow. "And do you always do what Lisa tells you?"

"It's easier if I don't test her."

Freddie nodded, taking in my answer for a moment before reaching for my good hand.

"Let me buy you dinner tonight."

His fingers were laced through mine the same way Lisa's had been, but Freddie's grip was tight enough to make my heart skip a beat. His thumb dragged up the inside of my palm, sending a shiver down my spine.

"Dinner?" he repeated.

No. I couldn't do dinner. Dinner was a bad idea. Dinner would be a slip in the wrong direction. Dinner would be me handing over another piece of myself, a piece he didn't deserve. Not after he'd kicked me out of that bathroom. Not with Caroline still in the picture.

"I'm busy," I said, meeting his eyes once again.

"With who?"

"The team," I lied.

"You're lying. Your hand, maybe."

I'd thought I was going to survive the conversation without him bringing up our phone call, but I was wrong. I bit back a smile and tried to keep my cheeks from burning red.

"Cancel. Tell them you've got something important to do," he continued.

It was so tempting. I mean, I was staring at shirtless Freddie, a sight more beautiful than any of the world's wonders. What was Giza compared to his chiseled, tan six-pack? Who needed the hanging gardens of Babylon when you could have the low-hanging fruit of his loom? I lingered on his abs, indulging in the sight for another moment before finally coming to my senses.

I shook my head. "I can't." Freddie and I couldn't just *date*.

He narrowed his eyes.

"What about after—"

"Foster."

I turned over my shoulder to find Lisa standing there with crossed arms and a deep frown marring her facial features. "I've been looking for you for the last five minutes. Are you ready to finish up? I have other athletes to train."

I blushed. "Oh, right. Okay."

I'd expected her to stay on the phone for a little longer.

I flashed Freddie a quick, grim smile and then moved to follow after Lisa with my head down, but before I could get far, Freddie reached out for my hand. He pulled me back with a gentle tug and kissed me square on the mouth.

It was shocking and the feeling of his mouth on mine was enough to erase the rest of the room. There was Freddie's lips on mine, his hand on my neck, and his claim on my heart. Lisa's annoyed huff? The whistle from across the room? They were the last thing on my mind as Freddie kissed me senseless.

I pulled back, fluttered my eyes open, and took a breath. "Umm…"

He smiled and let go of my hand. I hated that he had to let go of my hand.

"Better get back to that training session."

"Yup." I nodded, but I didn't move.

"Go Andie," he said with an amused smile.

"Yes. Right-o."

I turned back around on shaky legs. I didn't care that Lisa was about to put me through hell; I'd just experienced heaven.

Chapter Twenty-Two

FREDDIE

I WIPED MY towel down my face and tossed it aside. My water bottle was empty, so I reached for my t-shirt instead, pulling it over my head and shaking out the excess water from my hair. I'd just finished my last lap at practice; I was bone tired and ready for lunch.

"Your times are insane," Thom said, dropping his towel beside mine on the bench.

I nodded, but kept quiet. Good times are good times, nothing more. It was easy to psych myself out if I focused too much on the numbers.

"We've only got four more days before our races start," Thom added, reaching for his water bottle.

I threw him a glare over my shoulder. "Thanks for that."

"Oh c'mon, you can't be nervous. You've done this a million times."

He was right. This was my third Olympics games and I'd lost count of how many races I'd competed in over the years. "Expectations have never been higher."

He nodded. "True."

Everyone was looking to me to break my records from the last games. I'd had a team of trainers working with me for the last four years, helping me build strength through the offseason. I was stronger than I'd ever been, and my times were showing it. As long as I didn't muck it up during the races, I'd be going back home to London with six medals around my neck.

"How's the shoulder?" he asked as we carried our workout bags over to the water fountain.

I shrugged. "Better than yesterday. That ice really helped."

He laughed. "The ice on your shoulder, or that kiss with Andie?"

Andie.

Andie. Andie. Andie.

I shouldn't have kissed her in the training center the day before; it'd been bloody foolish. I knew we needed to lie low; we needed to keep this thing between us under the media's radar, but she had been wearing those tight workout pants. I could see the slight gap in her thighs and the curve of her ass when she turned back to follow her trainer. When she had first come over to talk to me, I'd nearly pulled her up to straddle me on the table. As far as I was concerned, I had shown saint-like restraint with that kiss, but Andie probably wouldn't agree.

"What are you going to do about that, mate?"

"I don't know. She declined dinner with me."

He laughed, the prick. "What's that? Your first refusal in history?"

"Glad you can have a laugh at my broken heart."

"All right, ease up. Just because she doesn't want to come to dinner doesn't mean you can't figure out some other way to spend time with her."

I arched a brow. "What do you mean?"

Over lunch in the food court, he laid out his diabolical plan. It was simple, but brilliant, and for a moment I was concerned that Thom had missed his calling as a Disney villain.

"You don't think she'll tell me to piss off when she shows up?"

He reached out and cupped my chin. "Wivva face like that?"

I jerked out of his grasp and punched his shoulder.

He laughed. "Text her, mate. Let's see what she says."

I grabbed my phone out of my pocket, stood up, and threw my workout bag over my shoulder.

"What?!" he protested. "You aren't even going to tell me how she responds?"

I flipped him off, stuffed my trash into the bin on the way out of the food court, and tried to decide what exactly I should text Andie. It wasn't until I'd stepped into the gym that I'd settled on something simple and easy.

Freddie: Thom and I are having a party at our flat later.

An hour went by and she hadn't responded, so I texted her again.

Freddie: I want you to come.
Andie: Sorry, we have our second game tomorrow morning. I can't go out.
Freddie: I'll have you in bed—your bed—by 9:00 PM. Swear.
Andie: Can't.
Freddie: I already phoned the Queen and let her know you'll be in attendance.

Georgie called then, jarring me out of the conversation

with Andie. I ignored the call and let it go to voicemail. A second later, she phoned again. Persistent little bugger.

Georgie: ANSWER YOUR BLOODY PHONE.

I deleted her text and instead, replied to Andie.

Freddie: I'm in flat 1120. Come over round 7:00 PM.
Andie: Jeez, now I get why we had to formally declare independence from you guys.

I laughed.

Freddie: See you then.
Andie: No you won't.
Freddie: 7:00 PM.

I turned my mobile off and tossed it into my workout bag before she or my sister could reply. After I'd gone through my afternoon workout, I ripped my sweaty clothes off and checked the clock on my bedside table. It was already after 5:30 PM, which meant I didn't have long to shower and get ready before Andie arrived. Her message said she wouldn't show, but something told me she was having as hard a time staying away from me as I was from her.

I showered quickly, lathering body wash over my tired muscles before rinsing them clean. I hadn't paid attention to the status of the flat when I'd first walked in, but I knew Thom wasn't always a shining beacon of tidiness. I frequently found his boxers in the dishwasher, and his drinking glasses in the laundry pile. After I hopped out and pulled on a white shirt and jeans, I stood in the living room, horrified at its current condition.

R.S. GREY

"When did you get in?" Thom asked from his perch on the couch. He hadn't been there when I'd arrived back home, but he'd managed to create a mess since then. He sat there, munching on crisps with his feet up on the coffee table. A pile of wrappers surrounded him on the floor and when I glanced over into the kitchen, the sink was full and nearly overflowing with our dishes.

"She's nearly going to be here."

He flipped the channel on the telly, less than concerned. "Who's that?"

"Andie, you twit. Remember the plan?"

"Right, that. It's only 6:00 PM."

I ripped the remote out of his hand. "And what comes after six, you wanker?"

He tossed the bag of crisps aside. "Fine, what do you want me to do?"

I put him to work tidying up the flat, starting with the area near the couch. I washed the dishes as quickly as I could, layering them into the dishwasher in tight stacks. I wiped down the counters and took the rubbish out to the chute in the hallway. When I went back into the flat, there was a distinctive smell I couldn't get rid of. I went round to the neighbors, begging for a candle or air freshener. A few English girls down the hall had a candle they lent me in exchange for an autograph. I lit it as soon as I returned and marveled at the ability of two grown men to spoil a brand new flat in only a few days.

"Thom, Jesus. My room doesn't smell like this. What do you do out here when I'm gone?"

He held his hands up in innocence. "You know I have a weakness for tuna. And sardines are some of the best sources of—"

"Sod it, I'm starting to think this was a mistake."

The place smelled like a fish market and there was no

changing it. I gave up and went back to work tidying up. By the time she was due to arrive, I'd completely forgotten about dinner. My stomach growled, letting me know how much it didn't appreciate not being fed on time.

"Mate, do me a favor: will you order something from the food court? I doubt Andie will have eaten and I'm starved."

"Anything in particular?"

I shook my head. "No, but she's got a match early tomorrow, so something with lots of protein."

He went off to his room and I reached for the supplies I'd picked up in the shop on the first floor. They had a small selection of birthday decorations—for the few sad sods who had to celebrate while they were competing in the games—but hopefully it would be just enough to convince Andie not to turn around once she opened the door and discovered I'd lied.

"Oh, and mate—don't you dare bring back fish!"

Chapter Twenty-Three

ANDIE

"**A**NDIE, YOU'RE IN the way. I can't see the movie."

"Well maybe that comes with the territory when *you* decide to watch a movie in *my* closet. Isn't there a better place?"

Becca rolled her eyes up at me from her spot on the ground like I was the crazy one. "We can't very well watch it in our closet—it's full of cute clothes that can't get wrinkled."

"Why do you have to watch it in a closet at all?" I demanded.

"It would be sacrilege to watch *The Notebook* under the glare of the harsh Rio sun," Kinsley said while drying her tears with one of my shirts.

Becca nodded. "Plus, this makes it feel like we're at the movies."

"Well I really need to find something to wear," I said, trying to hold my towel up while also maneuvering around them. The closet was already small, and with the two of them trying to use it as their own personal movie theater, there was no hope for me.

Kinsley groaned dramatically. "Pause it, Becca. We've missed the last five minutes."

"Yeah, I'm confused. Did they time travel, or were they old people the whole time?"

I flipped on the light overhead and the two of them hissed and covered their eyes like zombies seeing the first light of day. "Jesus! Rookies these days," Kinsley said, reaching past me to try to turn the light back off.

I held my hand up with a firm, "NO!"

They sat there, wearing their matching onesies as I tried to rifle through my clothes above their heads. I pulled out a light blue dress and held it up to the light.

"Not cute," Becca said.

"Nuh-uh," Kinsley agreed.

I shoved it back on the rack and reached for another one.

"Worse."

Becca nodded. "So much worse."

"Wow, film *and* fashion critics. You guys are very talented."

They sat quietly until I pulled out the next dress. It was black and short with spaghetti straps that crisscrossed in the back. I'd worn it so many times that the cotton-blend material had grown just soft enough to feel like pajamas. It was the perfect casual black dress for a party I still wasn't sure I'd be attending.

"Winner winner, chicken dinner," Kinsley said as I held it up to my body. It was even shorter than I remembered.

"Where are you going?" Becca asked, fidgeting with the unicorn horn on her hood.

"Out," I answered, turning to walk out of the closet in pursuit of my black strapless bra.

"*Out* out?" Kinsley asked. "We have a game in the morning!"

"No. Not *out* out. I'm staying in the building."

Actually, odds were I'd be staying in my room. All day I had gone back and forth on whether or not I wanted to attend Freddie's party. I wanted to see him and I wanted to make the most of my time in Rio, but I knew it wasn't a good idea to go. Even if there was a room full of people to buffer the tension between us, that also meant a room full of people to blab to Sophie Boyle.

"Did you shave? Because that dress is really short…"

I turned to find Becca and Kinsley lying on their stomachs at the door of the closet. They were watching me get ready with their heads propped up on their hands and their legs up in the air. They looked like the two kids at the slumber party that you only invited because your mom made you.

"Yes," I said, reaching down to confirm. "My legs are smooth."

"But your hair…are you going to leave it like that?"

I'd blown it dry after showering and put it in a loose braid down my back.

"Kins, you're literally dressed like a frumpy unicorn. I don't need any more input on my appearance."

"What about your makeup?" Becca asked, kicking her feet back and forth.

I was five seconds away from murdering the both of them.

I turned to Becca and smirked. "Guess what? At the end of that movie every—"

"No!" Becca yelled. "Don't ruin it." She shot up off the floor, cradling her laptop.

Kinsley trailed after her, but she paused at the door

and glanced back at me. "Should I even ask where you're going?"

I shook my head. "I wouldn't tell you if you did."

"Will you be having a... *jolly good time?*"

I smiled and turned away. "Maybe."

"I hope you know what you're doing, Andie."

I glanced down to the dress in my hand.

Yeah, me too.

———

I EXPECTED THERE to be music blaring on the eleventh floor, but when I stepped off the elevator, the hallway was quiet. I gripped my phone—the only thing I'd brought with me—and counted each room number I passed. 1101. 1102. Freddie was staying in 1120, and by the time I'd made it to his door, my hands were sweaty and my nerves were shot. I leaned forward and pressed my ear to the door, heard nothing, and cringed when I glanced down at the time. 7:01 PM. *Who shows up at a party right when it's just getting started??* For all I knew, I'd be the first one to arrive.

I walked past the door a few paces, trying to think of a plan. I could go linger around the gift shop for a few minutes and then head back up, or I could—

The door to his condo opened.

"Don't worry, mate. She'll show up," Thom called over his shoulder right before his body collided with mine. He'd been stepping back, not watching where he was going and I'd just turned around, also not paying attention.

"Blimey! I'm sorry," he said, reaching out to steady me before I tumbled to the floor. "Told ya, mate!"

I glanced down the hallway. Could I still make a run

for it? Thom's hand was on my arm, but I could yank it free with a few well-placed judo chops.

"What's going—" Freddie's sentence cut off when he stepped into the doorway and saw me standing there with wide eyes and cold feet. I really wanted to bolt, especially when his brown eyes assessed me from the doorway. He was wearing a cheeky smile across his freshly shaven face, and there were a few strands of brown hair that had fallen down across his forehead. More than anything else in the world, I wanted to step forward and brush them back.

Instead, I clenched my hands by my side and nodded. "Well, this has been fun. I'm going now."

He laughed then, a beautiful sound that made my toes curl inside my Converse.

"C'mon," he said, reaching out for my hand. "Thom's just ordered food for us. He's headed to go grab it right now."

Well it'd just be rude to leave without eating, so I let him usher me in and told myself I wouldn't stay for longer than four or five hours, or eternity. It was whatever.

"So this is our place," he said, extending his arm to encompass the small living room that looked identical to ours. Really everything was the same except for...

"What's that smell?" I asked, pinching my nose. "Is that tuna fish?"

His smile fell. "Thom ate a tuna sandwich for lunch and the bloody thing's soul is now haunting the whole place." He let go of my hand so he could walk to the coffee table and pick up the candle burning there. "Here, this should help with the exorcism."

I laughed and shook my head. "Really, it's not bad. It just smells like my meemaw's house."

He smiled quizzically. "What is a meemaw?"

"Nevermind."

"Right, well. I've kept my room closed off, so it's not nearly as bad in there."

I quirked a brow. "Subtle."

His smile widened.

"Oh, just come in here and slip under my covers to escape the smell of tuna! Oh, take off those clothes, the odor clings to the fabric!" I mocked. "Is that how you usually do it?"

"I quite like when you take the piss out of me," he said, stepping closer.

I held my hand up to stop him.

"Wait. Where's Thom gone?" He had apparently slipped by me during all the madness. "And wait, where are the other guests? Am I seriously the first person to get here?"

He rubbed his chin. "Right, well, about that. Like I've said, Thom's gone to get the food. And, well, it's set to be a small party."

I frowned. "How small?"

"Well…quite."

He dropped the candle on the kitchen table and whipped around the corner to grab something sitting on the counter. He held it behind his back as he walked back toward me, and then when he was just a few feet away, he lifted it up and slipped it around his head. A bright red paper party hat, sized for a five-year-old, sat sideways on his thick brown hair.

I burst out laughing.

"And look, here, this is for you," he said, handing me one of those cheap paper party horns you blow at midnight on New Year's Eve.

"You've got to be kidding me."

"I promised a party," he said, stepping forward and holding the party horn out for me to take. "Here's the party."

171

I shook my head, grabbed it, and blew. A sad "wooooo" sounded from the end before it rolled back toward my mouth.

That sad, weak sound made the dam burst; we couldn't catch our breaths for what felt like an hour. We laughed until tears filled the corner of my eyes and even then, I couldn't stop.

"Why'd you make up a fake party?" I asked, wiping beneath my eyes.

"To get you here."

That one sentence sobered me up fast. His brown eyes met mine and I watched his wide smile slowly fade into a flat, nervous line. "I knew you weren't keen on dinner, but this is different. This is an intimate soirée."

I dropped the party horn on the couch and took a shaky breath. "It's cute, but it's still not a good idea, Freddie. You kissed me yesterday in the middle of the training center. What if someone had taken a photo of that?"

"So what if they had? I want to be with you. I want to be kissing you."

He'd come to stand directly in front of me, leaning down so his gaze was level with mine. His hands gripped my arms, so strong and powerful I couldn't have pulled away even if I'd tried.

"I'm putting a stop to my betrothal, Andie. I've already talked to my mum and Georgie. It was all a sham and I should have seen that from the beginning. I just need to talk to Caroline and explain that I'm not going to roll over and marry some girl I don't love."

"Good." I nodded, unable to pull my gaze from his mouth. "I want you to be with someone you can love."

His eyes fell to my lips.

"What if I want to be with you?"

My gut clenched. "I'm currently…unavailable."

The edge of his mouth perked up like I'd just declared a challenge he couldn't pass up.

He bent forward and cradled my neck in his hand, bending low to whisper in my ear. "You didn't appear to be unavailable the other day." I dug my fingertips into his forearms and tried to form some kind of coherent response, but choppy stutters weren't enough to deter him.

"Freddie...I-I..."

He took my earlobe between his teeth, just gently enough to tilt my world. I squeezed my eyes closed.

"Tell me you don't want this."

Obviously, I couldn't. I wasn't that selfless. I wasn't even a little selfless. I needed Freddie so much my body hummed, and desire surged through me in time with the beat of my heart.

Stop.

Thump.

Walk away.

Thump.

This won't end well.

Thump.

Who.

Fucking.

Cares.

I turned and crashed my lips against his.

"Fuck," he hissed.

He gripped my loose braid and pulled me closer, tugging me flush against him. I could feel how hard he was. This was it. This desire tainting the air between us would finally see the light of day. I dug my fingers into his powerful back and he picked me up, forcing my legs around his waist. I wrapped my arms around his neck and kissed him, hard.

The front door opened then; I could hear Thom's

voice out in the hallway. I broke my mouth from Freddie's, expecting him to drop me, but he took three steps into the bedroom off to the side of the living room and kicked the door shut behind him.

His bedroom.

Chapter Twenty-Four

FREDDIE

ANDIE WAS COILED around me so tight I nearly had to rip her dress to get it over her head. I tossed it aside and pushed her up against my bedroom door. I gripped her hips and felt the dimples in her lower back as she rolled herself against me, teasing me. She was so accepting of my attack, no fight at all. I'd have welcomed a fight; it might have slowed me down.

I could feel her through my clothes. Her body was soft and her hands were tugging me closer, dipping into my shirt and dragging against my skin.

"Guys!" Thom called. "Food's here!"

"Piss off," I yelled through the door.

"It's going to get cold. And—I'm quite lonely at this shite party."

Andie laughed against my neck and I couldn't help but smile.

"Should we eat?" she asked with a wicked smile.

I yanked my shirt off over my head and tossed it aside. "We're not leaving this room."

Her eyes skimmed down my chest and the wicked smile

disappeared, replaced with dark, hot desire. Her tongue darted out to wet her lips and her hands reached out to touch me. My stomach flexed when her finger dragged along the top of my jeans, and then she popped the button and met my gaze with a wicked gleam.

"I hope you have a condom in these jeans, Freddie."

I laughed, and it was the sound of a wild man, one so far beyond the edges of control, he was hardly recognizable.

She slid her palm flush against my abs, pushed past my boxers, and continued down until she had me gripped in her palm. I squeezed her hips, needing something to hold on to as her soft hand stroked me up and down.

"Oh," she whispered with a teasing tone. "Olympic-sized."

I laughed right before her lips found mine again. I had a condom in my wallet I needed to grab, but I couldn't pull my hands off her. I reached for her bra and unclasped it, letting the soft material drag off her shoulders.

That first moment her naked chest hit mine was the moment my groan turned to a growl. She was tiny in my arms, receptive and eager. So much had separated us until now, and as she pressed her naked breasts flush against me, I knew she was appreciating the skin on skin just as much as I was.

I took her earlobe in my mouth and whispered everything I wanted to do to her…against that door…on the floor…in my bed. Her eyes fluttered closed as she listened to me, but I couldn't stop. I needed her to know how far she'd unwound me.

"What?" she asked, confused as I set her legs on the ground.

I pressed my hand against her stomach, feeling it

quiver beneath my touch. I kept my gaze on her as I slid down to my knees, registering her surprise with a smirk.

"Are you——"

Her question was cut off when my hand trailed up her calf, gently massaging her muscles. I bent forward and pressed a kiss against her hip. I could nearly taste her through the silky material, but I wanted it gone. I yanked down her knickers until they were on the ground and she was kicking them aside.

She held her hand in front of her waist, trying to conceal herself from my view. I looked up and met her eye.

"Nervous?"

She let her head fall back against the door and laughed. "Overwhelmed. You're like right…"

I let my hand drag up her thigh.

"Here?"

"Yup. Right there." She reached up to cover her eyes just as a rosy blush spread across her chest and neck.

"Have you ever been kissed here?" I said, reaching forward to lick the inside of her thigh.

"Oh sweet Jesus."

I kissed her again, this time a little higher, and her hips bucked forward. I pressed harder against her stomach, keeping her still as I dragged my tongue along the inside of her thigh.

"I…*oh*…*god*."

She sounded drunk with it, with us.

"Should we slow down?" I asked.

She yanked her hand away from her eyes and stared down at me. "Please don't," she begged, her voice nearly going hoarse.

She'd barely managed the last syllable before my mouth was on her again. She bit her lip to keep quiet, but I didn't care if she made noise. I slid one finger inside of her before leaning forward and gliding my tongue across her silk.

Her hands strung through my hair, tugging hard as I slid another finger inside, pumping them both slowly in and out. I owned her then. She was mine. She rolled her hips, sliding herself up and down my fingers, begging for more.

I dragged my tongue across her and I didn't slow down until she was withering against the door, pulsing around my fingers. She nearly ripped my hair out as she came and I let her rock herself against my mouth, taking her pleasure in her own hands. It was the sexiest bloody thing I'd ever seen.

I lost track of us after that. Her mouth was fire burning across my skin. My hands were everywhere, teasing and touching every patch of skin until I knew I could have fucked her with my eyes closed.

We put music on after Thom yelled, "They can hear you in São Paulo!"

I rolled on a condom, watching her walk back across the room, naked and flushed. I wished I could have stopped time to memorize every inch of her—that flat stomach, that slight gap in her thighs, her toned legs.

When she reached me, she drew close for a kiss. Before our lips could meet, I gripped her arm and spun her against the wall. She braced herself as I stepped behind her. One of my hands wrapped around her neck, so she couldn't turn away from me, and the other gripped her tiny waist.

"Freddie?" she asked as I caged her in with my hips, rolling my hardness against her. She was confused for only a moment before she tilted her ass back to meet me like a greedy little minx. I kicked her foot out to spread her legs and bent low to angle myself so I could slip inside of her.

"*Ahh.*"

Her head fell back against my chest and her eyes rolled closed. I could feel her rising onto her tiptoes, making it easier for me to sink all the way inside of her. With one quick thrust, she was mine.

I reached up to cup her breasts, rolling her nipples between my fingers as I pumped in and out of her.

"Fuck," she groaned. "*I can't...*"

She leaned back and wove her fingers through my hair, whispering how I was going to destroy her. I smirked and slid a finger down to stroke her.

"I already have."

She leaned forward and I forced her palms flat against the wall and told her to stay there. "Don't move."

With her in that position, I dragged a hand down her spine, feeling her shake from the sensation. Her back bowed and her head fell forward. She was weak and hungry for another orgasm. I wrapped a hand around her waist to support her, and then I tilted back to watch as I sank back into her.

"Like *heaven*," I whispered, closing my eyes and letting myself adjust to the feel of her wrapped around me. I'd never grow tired of it.

"Should we go to the bed?" she asked, bringing me back to life.

I wanted to keep her up against that wall and have my wicked way with her, but I'd let her decide.

"If you wish."

In lieu of an answer, she rolled her hips in a slow circle, teasing me until there was no other option. I slowly pulled out, gripped her hair in my hand, and then sank back into her with one hard thrust. She cried out and collapsed forward, but I caught her before she hit the wall.

Her hands clenched into tight fists and her toes started

to curl. I watched as beads of sweat dripped from her shoulder blades down to the small of her back.

I wanted to be gentle with her, but when she turned to look at me over her shoulder, I could see the wicked gleam in her eyes. She held my gaze as she moved a hand from the wall and dropped it to her neck, then *lower*. She slid it down her chest and cupped one of her breasts. I wanted to rip her hand away and replace it with my mouth, but she continued her descent before I could.

I knew what she was doing as she slid her palm past her navel. The idea of her touching herself while I was inside of her made it nearly impossible to take it slow.

"More," she whispered as I slid in and out. She was still getting used to me; I didn't want to hurt her. "*Please*. I'm so close."

She circled her fingers faster, moaning with need. Andie was the sexiest thing I'd ever felt. She was confident and sure of herself. After that shy moment against the door, there was no hiding her body. Everything she had was mine to touch and in return, I gave her everything I could. I pumped in and out of her so fucking hard. Her body shifted closer to the wall with every thrust and I reveled in it, loving how tight she felt around my dick. By the end, she was completely flush with the wall as I pounded into her from behind.

Our breaths echoed each other's, sweat dripped down my chest, and when she finally came undone around me, I pulled my mouth back to listen to every single sound that slipped past her lips. It was all it took to push me over the edge.

"Andie," I whispered, spent.

"Just give me a second," she said, letting her head fall against my shoulder.

I slid down to the floor and sat with her in my arms as we caught our breaths.

"My wrist hurts," she said.

"My shoulder hurts," I said.

"My lips hurt."

"I think we ought to do it again."

She laughed. "Obviously."

Chapter Twenty-Five

ANDIE

I **WAS INFATUATED** with Freddie. I was hopelessly obsessed with him. No matter how much I tried to get myself ready for my game, I kept replaying our night. Every time one of my Americanisms had confused him, he glanced up at me with an arched brow and I had to remind myself not to gape. For a man who regularly induced gawks and whispers from random passersby, he acted so normal.

"You have PRINCE HARRY'S phone number?" I asked as we lay on his bed.

He shrugged. "Prat hardly ever rings back."

I held up my hands, my mouth hanging open. I blinked and blinked again. My brain was short-circuiting and Freddie sat there, amused.

"So it's true then? You're a count, or prince or something?"

He reclaimed his spot beside me in bed, tossing the blankets over us and getting comfortable, leaving me hanging for what felt like a thousand hours.

"Freddie!"

He laughed. "No, I'm not a prince. My father was a duke, which made me a lord. My brother, as the eldest, was an earl, before he inherited the dukedom, but now—"

"You say it like it's so normal!"

"Andie, non-royal dukes aren't even in line for the throne. It hardly means anything anymore."

It was just like Freddie to downplay the glamour of his life. He wanted to be Freddie, just another normal swimmer, but he was Frederick, handsome duke with a phone full of numbers I could only dream of having.

"May we text him?" I asked politely, royally.

He glanced over. "Harry?"

"No! Baby George."

"Tired?" Kinsley asked from across the aisle of the bus, tearing me from my thoughts.

I shifted in my seat and shrugged. "No, not really."

"What time did you get in?"

I thought back to the night before when Freddie had yanked the clock off his nightstand and showed me the blinking red lights. *"12:01 AM and I promised I'd have you back by 9:00 PM."* I'd begged him to keep going, promising that great sex was a close enough approximation of a good night's sleep, but he'd kissed my head and pushed me out as politely as possible. He knew I needed rest. He knew that if I had an off game, he'd be the first person I blamed. So even though I would have happily stayed in his room all night, I'd reluctantly dragged myself back to my condo and slept alone. Luckily, I was so physically spent that I fell asleep the instant my head hit the pillow.

"Andie?" Kinsley asked.

"Oh." I shook away my thoughts. "Not late," I promised.

"Did you have fun?"

I tried desperately to keep the slow-crawling blush from

staining my cheeks. "Yup," I said nonchalantly, turning back toward the window.

"Ten more minutes!" our coach yelled from the front of the bus. "Time to get your heads in the game, ladies!"

Shit.

Coach Decker was right. I needed to focus. I plugged my headphones into my iPod and turned the volume as high as it would go. "Drive" by Halsey blasted everything else to the wayside.

The game against Colombia wouldn't be easy. They were rumored to be one of the best national teams in South America, and they'd proven it by knocking out Mexico in the qualifying tournament. The day before, we'd spent hours watching game footage, and I still wasn't sure our defense would be enough to stop their fast-paced onslaught on the goal.

I rolled my wrist left and right, getting a feel for the pain. The swelling had gone down since the last game, but I knew it'd puff right back up by the end of the day. I didn't have a choice though. I'd tape it and deal with the pain.

I propped it up on my left knee and gently massaged it, feeling my nerves start to eat away at me. Colombia was sure to break through at least a dozen times, and Liam said they averaged about six shots on goal per game. There was no option. My wrist couldn't take the day off.

———

THERE WAS NO getting around it. The team from Colombia was made up of superhuman cyborgs. They seemed to be built on size, each of them a giant, pumped-up killer I didn't want to see close up. I SWORE one of them had a mustache (and I'm not talking about a couple stray whiskers—homegirl was rivaling Ron Swanson).

My defenders had played stout defense through the first half, only allowing the Colombians to test my reflexes twice before the whistle. Their defense proved to be just as good up until the 42nd minute, when Kinsley finally scored with a crafty header. By the intermission, my wrist was on fire. The constant throb hadn't been as easily overcome by adrenaline as I'd hoped. Each time I connected for a block, I winced, and any attempt at covering up the injury was long gone. Coach Decker had pestered me about it during halftime.

"How bad is it on a scale of one to ten?"

Seven.

"Not bad. A three," I lied.

"Are you prepared to play the second half? Should I put Hollis in that goal?"

"No. I can handle it. I'm fine."

Fifteen minutes into the second half, my wrist had gone from a seven to an eight. The sound from the stands was deafening, made worse by the large Colombian contingent echoing Spanish chants all around me. There was a group of men, twenty or thirty of them, who'd made it their mission to taunt me. Their voices boomed behind me with thick Spanish accents. I wanted to win the game, but I also wanted them to shut the hell up. Fortunately, nothing would cut off their chants quicker than the taste of defeat.

I used their annoying-ass taunting as fuel to keep going.

My wrist is fine. Deep breath. Block. *Deep breath.*

At last, the 89th minute came and the score was still sitting at 1-0. I couldn't let Colombia score. *A few more minutes and we win.* The guys behind me were getting louder and Colombia had the ball. I stayed in the net, watching our defense try to keep up. Their legs were tired. Kinsley and Becca had played the entire game and clean tackles they'd made with ease in the first half were proving more difficult.

The ball was passing from one player to another so fast my eyes could hardly keep up. I watched as the ball kept falling in Colombia's favor, and I braced myself for the coming storm. I'd made every save so far. No matter the time on the clock, I could make one more.

28 seconds.

I'd studied their offensive schemes in the previous days. I knew Mustache Girl would be the primary scoring option in this last ditch effort, and I also knew that more often than not, she chose the bottom left corner of the net as her target.

I watched a midfielder set up the play and I loaded my weight onto my toes, shifting rapidly from side to side as she pivoted, striking inward behind her defender toward the penalty mark. Mustache Girl's eyes glanced up to mine. Her eye contact lasted less than a millisecond, but I saw them flick to my left. She was desperate for a goal and I debated whether she was mapping her shot or bluffing.

Fuck.

She reared back to kick and I dove to cover the left side of the goal. The entire stadium held its breath as the soccer ball sailed through the air. I'd guessed the direction correctly, but she'd kicked it higher than usual. Time slowed even further, and I could almost visualize the ball slipping past me for the goal. As the ball zoomed toward the top of the goal, I reached up with all my might. The ball grazed the tips of my fingers, deflecting up over the white crossbar and landing out of bounds.

I had a fleeting moment of internal celebration right before my body hit the ground and pain sliced through me.

White.

Hot.

Searing pain.

It was the sharpest, most acute sensation I'd ever felt. It brought vomit to my throat and blurred the world around me. I squeezed my eyes closed and collapsed back onto the turf, rocking back and forth with my wrist clutched against my chest. Curse words slipped from my lips, but I couldn't hear them. I cradled my wrist and tried to keep the vomit down, but it was no use. The pain gripped hold of me so tight I couldn't see past it.

"ANDIE!" Kinsley shouted. "Andie!"

I opened my eyes to see her crouched over me, concerned, but too happy to wipe the smile from her face. "WE WON! YOU DID IT!"

Becca was right behind her, and together, they tried to wedge themselves beneath me so I could stand. I was crying heavy tears I hadn't noticed until they started to slip off my chin and drop onto my sweaty jersey.

"Guys, I think…" I tried to get the words out, but I was out of breath and scared.

I can't…

If I said what I was thinking aloud, it would become reality.

My wrist is broken.

Done.

My Olympic career is over.

———

I ONLY REMEMBERED bits and pieces of them helping me off the field. A doctor inspected my wrist in the locker room, carefully removing the tape so the bruises hidden beneath were finally revealed to my coach. It looked bad, black and blue and so much worse than it had before the game.

Coach Decker was horrified.

"Was it like this before today?" She strung her fingers through her hair and tugged at the strands. "This stuff can be career ending, Andie! Do you understand that!?"

"I—"

My explanation was wasted on her anger. She'd just lost her star goalie. My team would suffer. Sure, we'd elimi-nated Colombia, but we still had two knockout games left: the semifinals and finals. Of course we had reserve goal-keepers on the roster, but as the competition got stiffer, our defense couldn't be running on backup power.

The doctor—I hadn't caught his name or maybe he hadn't even bothered with introductions—pulled his cell phone from his pocket. "Let's go down for x-rays. We'll know more after that."

The x-ray room was dark and small. The technician was a small girl who spoke choppy English and smelled like roses. She had me position my wrist beneath the x-ray machine and when she adjusted it, her dark eyes glanced up at me with pity.

"Any pain?"

I knew they needed to get the right angle to see the full extent of the damage.

"A little, but I'm fine," I said, lying through my clenched teeth.

Kinsley and Becca waited with me in the doctor's office while the radiologist inspected the x-ray. For the first few minutes we sat in silence, too worried to bother with small talk.

"Your mom has been calling nonstop. Do you want to call her back?" Kinsley asked, holding up my phone.

I shook my head and kept my eyes pinned on the wall

behind the doctor's desk. It was the spot where a diploma would have hung, but the office was temporary and the doctor would go back to the United States when the Olympics were over. No need for a diploma.

"It's going to be okay," Becca offered.

I ignored the sentiment. If my wrist was broken, it was over. The Olympics, Rio, soccer, all of it. I was good, but unless I was whole, I was replaceable. It was that simple.

A few minutes later, the doctor knocked on the door and entered the office.

"Andie, we've got good news and bad news," he said, curving around the desk and tossing my x-ray in front of me. He cut to the chase—no pleasantries or handshakes—and I appreciated that. "Your wrist isn't broken."

Kinsley, Becca, and I all let out a collective sigh as if it had been choreographed ahead of time.

"That said, you still can't play on it. You've sprained several ligaments, and you've further strained existing inflammation of your muscles and tendons. The only thing you can do, and what you should have been doing already, is ice, rest, and eventually—"

I shook my head, already determined. "What would happen if I played on it?"

"Andie," my coach hissed. I hadn't even noticed her sneak in behind the doctor.

"Certainly you'd see degradation of the soft tissue and advancement of your tendonitis, possibly into a chronic state. We're talking 'at best' here. The problem is, without proper flexibility and natural range of motion, any amount of pressure gets absorbed by the bony structures. You risk a catastrophic break, surgery, and a rocky recovery. So, I recommend taking at least six weeks off, rest, and PT, at which point we reevaluate."

I stood and shook my head. "No."

He reared back as if I'd slapped him. "Andie, we have to do what's best for your long—"

"I'm not going home. I'm staying and I'm playing the last two games."

"No, you aren't," my coach corrected with a tone that left no room for negotiation. "I'm sorry Andie, but you need to take some time to digest this information."

I whipped around to face her. She had her arms locked across her chest. Her white hair was pulled into a ponytail that looked tight enough to cut off circulation. She'd inspired fear in me since the first day of training camp, but I'd learned to read her tells. Those crossed arms, the severe look—it was all an act.

"You're young, and this is your first Olympics. If we play it safe now, you'll have plenty more to come. You can stay in Rio with your team and start physical therapy on your wrist. If all goes well, you'll be ready for the World Cup, and eventually the next Olympics."

No, no, no.

"No, Coach, I can play," I argued, turning around and holding up my wrist as evidence. There was no shudder or gasp of pain. "I'm fine."

She shook her head, annoyed. "Don't push this Andie, or I'll send you home."

"Keep me in the goal."

"It wouldn't hurt to keep her benched," Kinsley said. She was Coach's favorite player. If anyone could convince her to compromise, it was Kinsley. "Let her sit on the sidelines during the games. That's better than nothing."

"I agree," Becca said.

Coach glanced to the doctor then back down to me. Her head dipped and my heart plummeted in my chest before she replied.

"I'll consider it."

Chapter Twenty-Six

ANDIE

"**W**HOA. WHOA. WHOA.**"** Kinsley reached for the bottle of vodka before I could tip it back for another sip. "Slow down there, Andie."

I let her take the bottle; it didn't matter. There were four more lined up on the coffee table. I'd forced Becca and Kinsley to get them for me on the way home from the doctor's office. The liquor tasted like shit, but it helped dull both the pain in my wrist and the agony in my heart.

"You know what? I haven't had a real drink in months. Parties? Social life? NONE."

Kinsley leaned forward off the couch and adjusted the ice pack on my wrist.

"I sacrificed everything to be here and Coach Decker thinks she can send me home?! Fuck that."

Becca paced back in forth in front of us, trying to think of a plan to get me back in the game. "She won't send you home, she was just trying to get you to calm down."

"Andie, it'll be okay," Kinsley said. "I know it feels like the end of the world right now, but you'll see that it's not so bad."

"Not so bad?!" I argued.

"It could have been career ending, but it's not."

Perfect. I can use my wrist in FOUR YEARS! Would I even be alive in four years?

"I'll be twenty-five then, practically a washed-up has-been."

"HEY!" Kinsley and Becca shouted.

"No offense."

Becca laughed. "None taken."

"The point is, I don't care about the future. I'm mad and nothing you guys say will change that. So just let me have that liquor bottle and get me some firewood to burn this stupid wrist brace they're making me wear."

I leaned forward, trying to reach for the whiskey while simultaneously balancing the ice pack on my wrist.

"No. We aren't going to get you firewood."

"Scratch that then. Do either of you guys know how to give a tattoo? I'll get one that matches yours, Kinsley. Except instead of *She believed she could so she did,* it'll just say *Fuck this.*"

She laughed.

"Or what about a bellybutton piercing?" I asked, looking around. "We'll need a needle."

Becca gagged. "God no!"

Every single one of my ideas was met with sharp criticism: tattoos, piercings, prank calls to our coach.

"Okay, well then I want a haircut. Out with the old and in with the new! Right?" I said, looking at Becca. "Something that says 'fuck international athletics'."

Kinsley groaned, but Becca didn't seem wholeheartedly against the idea. "There *are* scissors out in the kitchen."

"Yes!" I said, holding the liquor bottle in the air.

"Becca, have you ever cut someone's hair before?" Kinsley asked.

She waved her off. "My own, when I was five. It didn't turn out well, but I've got to be at least…" She did the math in her head. "Five times better at it now."

Ten minutes later, I was sitting on a chair in my bathroom with a bed sheet wrapped around me as a makeshift smock. Becca circled my head, trying to figure out where to start.

"Aren't you going to ask what I want?" I asked, confused as to why there were two of her in the mirror.

Becca's eyes widened. "Let's just start small?"

My blonde hair was long. It'd grown for years, normally gathered in a ponytail for competition. Christy wouldn't hear of me cutting it when I was growing up.

"Chop it like it's hot," I said, motioning above my shoulder. "All of it. See if I give a FUCK."

Kinsley was on the other side of the bathroom door, banging away. "GUYS, let me in! I'm totally on board with the haircut, I just want to offer some pointers. I won't sabotage it."

Becca looked at me. I looked at her, and then I looked at the second Becca. They both seemed nice. "Do you guys trust her?"

"Guyssssssss. I swear!"

Becca number two shook her head, and I took another shot. I narrowed my eyes until the real Becca came into focus. "Leave her out there then."

———

TWO HOURS LATER, Kinsley walked past my room, dipped her head in to get a good look at me, and then laughed as she walked away. She'd been doing it all afternoon and her ridicule helped neither my hangover nor my hack job.

I didn't blame Becca when I looked in the mirror after my haircut. I mean, it definitely looked like a blind monkey had taken garden shears to my head. One side touched my shoulders while the other side sat an inch higher, but it wasn't all her fault. It was still greasy since I hadn't bothered to shower after my game, and there were pieces of trash in it from when I'd devoured a bag of Hershey's kisses instead of getting up to get a normal snack.

It had all seemed like a perfectly reasonable way to "stick it to the man" at the time. Now, of course, I had a splitting headache, a bum wrist, and the hair of a loony person.

"Coming down with us for dinner, Andie?" Becca asked, leaning into my room.

"What do you think?" I asked, picking a piece of foil from my hair.

She did her best not to laugh. "You know, I think it'll help if you shower. Maybe the hair will settle into place."

"That makes no sense," I argued.

"Okay, she was trying to be polite. You should actually shower because I can smell you from out here!" Kinsley yelled from the living room.

It was easy for them to go on with their lives. They were still playing in the Olympics, their lives progressing like movies. I was now a glorified equipment manager. Coach Decker had already emailed me a new, personal itinerary: 9:00 AM breakfast, 10:00 AM appointment with the trainer, 11:00 AM physical therapy, 12:00 PM lunch, 1:00 PM join team for afternoon meeting, 3:00 PM physical therapy, etc.

I planned on ignoring most of her orders. Instead, my itinerary would include the following: 9:00 AM sit on bed/general wallowing, 10:00 AM roll myself up in sheets and pretend I'm a mummy, 11:00 AM eat peanut butter from jar with fingers, 12:00 PM pick peanut butter out of greasy hair, 1:00 PM roll myself up in sheets and pretend I'm a Chipotle burrito, 3:00 PM throw myself in front of a moving bus.

"Okay, this is enough," Kinsley said, hitting the frame of my door with her hand so that I jumped. "You are going to get up and you are going to shower and you are going to come down to the food court with us. You need a decent meal."

I crossed my arms like a petulant child. "Go away."

She shook her head. "No. Let's go. I'll bet Freddie is down there and he'll be so happy to see you. He's been trying to get in touch with you all day."

I glanced around for my cell phone. "Wait, where's my phone?"

"In the living room. You threw it out there when your mom tried to call."

Oh.

"You really think he'll be down there?" I asked, suddenly desperate to see him. Did he know about the injury?

She nodded. "Maybe. Go shower and we'll wait for you."

I pushed off my bed and slid into the shower—yes, slid. I couldn't stand and I didn't feel like taking a bath. So instead, I turned the faucet to the hottest setting, sat at the end of the stream of scalding water, and let it beat down on me from above. I wasn't sure how long I sat there before Kinsley yanked the shower curtain aside and pulled me out.

"I get that you're drunk and injured, and I love you—but this is too much," she said, throwing a towel at me. "I just saw your entire vagina."

I smiled, drunk with self-pity. "Pretty good, right?"

———

I TRIED TO pull myself together after that. I mean, I couldn't brush my hair or put makeup on, but I threw my chopped hair into a passable ponytail and pulled on a pair of mismatched sweats. The alcohol had numbed the pain from my wrist, but I still cradled it in my other hand as Kinsley and Becca led the way to the elevators.

"Do you want to tell us about last night? To get your mind off today?"

I glanced over to take in Kinsley's gentle smile.

"We know you and Freddie have been sneaking around. You can tell us about it. We promise not to judge."

A slow, easy smile spread across my face before I could help it. That was the silver lining in all of this. Sure, I'd traveled all the way to Rio to win gold, and in the matter of one morning, that dream was gone. Finished.

But then I thought of Freddie, of how I would never have met him had I not traveled to Rio. Even if I wasn't going back to the U.S. with an earned medal, there was a good chance I'd return with a boyfriend—a super hot, super British boyfriend. Definitely better than nothing.

The elevator arrived on the first floor and we walked out into the lobby. I turned to Kinsley and Becca, trying to decide where to start. From the beginning? There was so much ground to cover and I couldn't wait to fill them in on all the juicy details, but something caught my attention in front of the complex before I could start. Right past the glass lobby doors, Freddie stood watching a limo roll to a stop near the curb. His back was to me, but I knew it was him. After the night before, I knew that body well enough to recognize it from any angle or position.

"Speak of the devil," I smiled, finally allowing myself to feel actual happiness after a day of misery. I broke off from Kinsley and Becca to step closer, excited to get to him. I hadn't seen him since he'd walked me back to my condo the night before, stealing one last kiss before I slipped inside.

I pressed my fingers to my lips, trying to remember what his kiss had felt like, but I came up short. There was no word for it.

So much had happened since then. I wanted to tell him about my injury and ask for his advice. I wanted him to yell and shout with me, do something crazy with me. He'd understand more than anyone, I just needed to get to him.

I was nearly to the door when Freddie reached forward to open the limo door. The driver was walking around to get to it, but Freddie couldn't wait. I stood in shock, watching through the clear glass as a tall, regal blonde stepped out. She was stylish and effervescent (whatever the hell that means) and I knew I didn't like her right away. Mature adults don't hate people on impulse, but I couldn't help myself. Her hair was long and silky, not chopped and damp. Her outfit was fitted and wrinkle free, not stained with melted Hershey's. I took a hesitant step back and succumbed to the feelings of inadequacy just as her identity sank in.

Caroline Montague in the flesh.

She was wearing a light blue wrap dress and nude heels. It was an outfit straight out of Kate Middleton's closet. For all I knew, it *was* Kate's dress; they were probably friends, after all.

"Frederick! Darling!" She squealed with excitement as she stepped forward and flung her arms around him. I lingered there in the lobby, watching from a distance, trying to connect the pieces of the puzzle. If the blonde "darling" *was* Caroline, betrothed goddess, then that meant the brunette climbing out of the limo was—

"Fred, you knobhead. I've been trying to phone you all day!"

Freddie's sister.

She stepped toward him, shoving past Caroline to get to him. Freddie bent to wrap her in a hug and she squeezed him tight before stepping back and peering up at him adoringly. It was in that moment that I realized she was beautiful—not the made up, altered beauty of Caroline. She was stunning all on her own, like the girl next door if the girl next door happened to be a supermodel.

"Andie," Kinsley said, reaching for my hand. She was trying to pull me away, but I wouldn't let her. I stood watching the small reunion. Until that moment, I'd foolishly felt like Freddie was mine. He'd become my fast friend and had told me some things I wanted to hear, but standing there, it became painfully clear that he had never been mine. Not in the least.

"Congratulations are in order, sir," the limo driver said, winking at Freddie. "Your fiancée told me during the drive over." His voice was slightly distorted through the glass, but I could hear him loud and clear. He scanned from Caroline to Freddie. "Have you two decided on a wedding date yet?"

Caroline clapped excitedly. "Early winter hopefully! As soon as Frederick has time to devote to the wedding, we'll get to planning."

She turned to him with stars in her eyes and I slowly processed how careful and specific her answer had been, as if they'd gone over it a thousand times before. I felt like the wind had been knocked out of me.

Early winter.

Wedding.

And worse yet, Freddie didn't deny it. He tucked his hands into his pockets and rocked back on his heels. I couldn't see his face, but I could imagine that perfect smile stretched across his perfect mouth. His mouth. The mouth he'd used on me the night before. It'd been on my neck and my chest and my stomach and my…

I couldn't breathe.

My breaths were coming short and shaky and I pressed my hand to my chest as images flooded my mind. He'd carried me into his room knowing full well that his betrothed—no, his *fiancée*—was due to arrive the very next morning. He'd dropped me onto his bed and tangled me up in his sheets—the same sheets he planned on using with her. Had he even bothered to wash them?

I missed the last half of their conversation, but I watched the driver tip his hat and turn, adding a few parting words over his shoulder. "Welcome to the games!"

"I'm going to be sick."

I turned and ran for the nearest bathroom—there was one tucked away in a corner of the lobby—and I shoved past an open stall door. I was barely hunched over the toilet when my stomach turned over. I kneeled there, dry heaving and wiping away the tears that insisted on streaming down my cheeks. I couldn't handle it. I couldn't understand how quickly my life had gone to shit.

My wrist burned from the pressure of holding myself up over the toilet, but I didn't ease off it. I let the pain sear through me.

"Andie, are you okay?"

Kinsley was there, rubbing my back and trying to console me.

I couldn't form words. The dry heaves wouldn't stop.

My Olympic dreams were over…

And Freddie was a fucking liar.

Welcome to the games, indeed.

Chapter Twenty-Seven

FREDDIE

I RAKED MY hands through my hair and tried to get ahold of the situation as best as I could. Georgie and Caroline were in Rio. They were in Rio, *together*. In my flat. I paced back and forth in Thom's room, trying to figure out what to do.

"This is a bloody mess," I said, keeping my voice down so it wouldn't travel across the flat. Caroline was in my room, returning the phone calls she'd missed during the flight. Fortunately, it gave me a few minutes alone with Georgie.

My sister leveled me with a narrowed stare. "Obviously, you twat! Why do you think I've been trying so hard to get ahold of you over the past two days!"

"I told Mum the betrothal was over!"

"Yes, and like always, Mum has ignored you and sent Caroline anyway. This is precisely how she used to get what she wanted with Dad—sheer stubbornness. She thinks you'll see Caroline and be overcome with unbridled love for her."

I wiped my hand down my face. "I did nearly pass out when I saw her get out of that limo before you."

Georgie laughed. "Maybe that's what unbridled love feels like?"

I groaned. "I assure you, it's not."

"Well what do you want me to do?"

"Keep her occupied. I need to talk to Andie and warn her that Caroline is here."

Her smile fell. "I saw a story about her injury while we were in the limo. Do you think it's serious?"

I wouldn't know. I'd watched the game on the TV during my workout. I'd stood immobile as they replayed her bad landing over and over again in slow motion. Her pain was written across her face as they walked her off the field with her friends in tow, looking more dejected than the losing team. I'd cut my workout off early and tried to reach her.

"Freddie? Have you heard from her? What's going to happen?"

"I don't know, Georgie. I haven't managed to reach her all day. She's been ignoring my texts."

Georgie laughed. "Probably because you're a miserable sod. Maybe you ought to keep Caroline around. She could be all you've got."

"You aren't helping."

She threw her hands up. "Fine. I'll go distract Caroline, but you owe me big time. I've already been on a flight with the turtle for a million hours. I had to occupy myself with one of her corny inspirational books the entire way. It was my own personal purgatory."

Caroline was still in my room with the door closed, so hopefully she couldn't hear Georgie.

"Wait, did you say 'turtle'?"

She smiled, proud of herself. "She's got the personality of a sea turtle so I've taken to addressing her as such."

"Georgie," I scolded.

"What? The book she lent me was called *Becoming Boring: Volume III.* She's clearly already memorized the first two."

"I doubt that was the name of the book."

She waved me off. "I've forgotten. Anyway, have you got a granola bar or something? Caroline wanted to grab dinner at the airport but I couldn't stand another minute alone with her."

I led her out into the kitchen and tossed her one of Thom's protein bars. The mumbles from my room cut off and then a moment later Caroline whipped open the door. I cringed thinking of everything she might have overheard, but she was all smiles as she came out to join us.

"How about we all go get dinner? I saw this great little place on the way in."

Georgie waved her protein bar. "I'm all set, but you go ahead."

Caroline's smile fell as her gaze swept to me and I actually felt sympathy for her. Caroline was a nice person, and she didn't deserve to be led on. I needed to carve out time to pull her aside and chat with her, but at the moment, my priority was Andie. I needed to find out if she was okay. I needed to tell her Caroline had arrived and promise her that everything would be sorted shortly.

I took a deep breath and met Caroline's gaze. "I have a few things I need to do with the team, and you must be tired from the flight. Rest up, then I think we should sit down and talk tomorrow."

Her features perked up at the idea. "Okay. How about we talk over dinner?"

I swallowed down my desire to turn her down. The

chat needed to be short and respectful. We didn't need to sit down for a four-course meal, but she looked so hopeful and it was easier to say yes. With the plans made, I moved on to the next item on my list: Andie.

I took the elevator down to her floor, thankful to know the way after I'd walked her home the night before. My mobile rang midway down the hallway—Thom. I nearly ignored it, too anxious to reach Andie, but I swiped my hand across the screen and said hello as I scanned the flat numbers on the wall.

"How's Andie?"

"I wouldn't know. She's still not replying to my messages."

"That's because they're probably still running a billion tests on her. She'll ring you when she's done."

I ignored him and knocked on her door.

"We have practice soon," he continued. "Are you planning on bunking off?"

"Shit."

I had my first race in a week; I couldn't skip practice.

"Just give me a minute to—"

My sentence was clipped by the sound of someone unlocking the door. Kinsley pulled the door open then blocked my entry with an unwelcoming gaze. I hung up on Thom and swallowed down her annoyance.

"Is Andie here?" I asked.

Becca walked up behind her, further blocking me from entry.

"Yes."

The two of them both looked like they'd been through hell and back.

"Could I talk to her?"

Kinsley crossed her arms. "She's had a tough day, Freddie. Give her a second to catch her breath."

I took a step closer. She could catch her breath *with* me.

"I just need to talk to her for a second. I need to know how she is."

Kinsley shook her head. "Not good. She's out for the rest of the games."

My heart sank. "Is it broken? Her wrist?"

She shook her head. "No, but the doctor thinks it will be if she keeps playing on it."

I couldn't imagine how upset she was. She'd worked her entire life to earn a spot on that team and with one tough save, it was over. I tugged my hand through my hair, trying to think up some way to make it better for her.

"How is she handling it?"

Why the bloody hell were they keeping me out in the hallway? I needed to talk to Andie. I needed to see her and promise her everything would be all right. Doctors are paid to be overly cautious. Maybe if she—

"Listen, Freddie," Kinsley continued. "Andie doesn't want to speak with you. Your actions have spoken louder than any words you might have to say."

My brows furrowed. "What do you mean she doesn't want to see me?"

Kinsley sighed, glanced behind her, and then leaned in close, dropping her voice to a whisper. "We all saw you with Caroline this afternoon. Andie was there, looking for you for comfort. You are a new level of asshole."

My heart dropped. They didn't understand.

"No." I shook my head. "No. I need to talk to her. I'll explain it."

I pushed my hand against the door to slide past Kinsley, and I shoved it harder than I'd meant to. It whipped out of Kinsley's hand and slammed against the wall, hard.

Kinsley's eyes went round as saucers and Becca stepped closer, protecting her. *From me.*

Fuck, this was going wrong.

"Andie!" I shouted, trying to get her to come out and talk to me.

"Stop it, you lunatic!" Kinsley stepped forward and held her hand up to my chest. "Jesus, she's had the worst day of her life. Don't make this harder for her."

I stepped back and slid my hands through my hair, feeling powerless on the threshold of their flat.

"Look, I wasn't lying about ending my betrothal." I raised my voice. "ANDIE! I WASN'T LYING."

Kinsley winced. "Stop! Jesus, Freddie. You're making a scene."

She had the door in her hand again and she was trying to close it, to push me out of the flat and out of Andie's life. I wouldn't let her do it.

"Kinsley, you have to tell her I didn't invite Caroline here. I didn't know she'd be in that limo with Georgie. This is all a jumbled mess, but I'll figure it out. I'll…"

Kinsley was shaking her head and staring up at me with a mixture of pity and—worse—hatred. I sounded crazy, and she didn't believe me. *Bloody hell.*

I wasn't going to let them speak for me. I wasn't going to let them muddle the facts and confuse Andie. I already looked crazy, so I shoved past them. I didn't know which bedroom was Andie's, but two of the doors off the living room were open and empty, so the one closest to me, the one with the closed door had to be hers. I knew she was in there, but I wasn't going to barge in. I'd give her that much. I stood outside the door as Kinsley and Becca shouted at me that they were going to call whatever the Brazilian 911 was. God, I was causing a scene. I knew I was being a prick, but I couldn't let this get any further out of hand. I was falling for Andie. I was falling for her so bloody hard and so bloody fast that the idea of losing her over a misunderstanding seemed unfathomable.

"Andie, please come talk to me," I begged.

Kinsley gripped my arm with surprising strength, trying to tug me back. I hardly recognized this version of myself, this lovesick dog.

"Andie, please," I begged again, pressing my hand up to the door as if she could see it through the cheap particle board. "Last night was the best night of my life. I need you to know that…"

There were no sounds coming from her room, nothing to indicate my pleas were even reaching her. I was pouring my heart out to a white door.

"Freddie, you need to go…" Kinsley said, holding up her phone. "My husband Liam is on his way."

I squeezed my eyes closed and fisted my hand against her door. I had to leave. I had practice and I wasn't about to get escorted out like a psychopath. I turned away from her door and brushed past Kinsley and Becca without another word. I walked up to my flat and gathered my swimming gear. I was late for practice and Coach was going to chew me out…but I couldn't seem to care.

A heavy fog lingered around me, even in the pool. The water was usually my escape, but that day, my heart wasn't in it. I swam slow, ignored my coach, and left right after practice, not even bothering to wait for Thom.

I tried to reach out to her one last time before bed.

Freddie: Please give me a few days to get this sorted. I never lied to you. I'm ending my betrothal.

She responded right away.

Andie: Of course you are. Is that before or after your "winter wedding"?

Freddie: Where are you? Can we meet somewhere? We need to talk.

Andie: Save it for your fiancée.

Chapter Twenty-Eight

ANDIE

THE **ANGER I** felt toward Freddie paled in comparison to the self-loathing that had settled in the pit of my stomach since the day before. I had known Freddie was betrothed. He'd been perfectly honest about that from the start. I'd been the one to fall into a fairytale. I'd let my fantasies get the better of me, until reality sank in like a hot sharp knife.

The harshest reality?

That I was stupid enough to fall for a man who'd been unavailable from the start. I was surrounded by a fucking all-you-can-eat buffet of sexy single athletes, yet I'd chosen one of the few that were off limits.

That's stupidity at its finest.

I hadn't left my room the night before. After leaving the bathroom in the lobby, I'd locked my door and barricaded myself inside. When Freddie had pounded his fist on the other side and begged me to come talk to him, I'd stared at my wall and prayed he'd go away. I needed him to go back to Caroline and leave me alone. It would make it so much easier for me to squash my delusions. I needed him to cut me off cold turkey.

But he was messaging me constantly. Every time I looked down at my phone, I had a new text from him that I had to delete. Since he wasn't going to leave me alone, I did the next best thing: I googled Caroline Montague incessantly. For hours, I sat on my bed—alternating between icing and heating my wrist—and scrolled through articles about the English socialite. There was no shortage of information about her. I read up on everything from her fifth birthday party (her family had thrown a lavish affair at her family's country castle) to her sweet sixteen (in lieu of a party, she'd asked friends to donate gifts to the children's hospital in London). Honestly, it would have felt very good to find some salacious gossip or a mug shot after a drunken night out on the town, but instead of skeletons in her closet, TMZ only reported that she was pleasant to everyone she encountered.

At first, I didn't believe it. Every celebrity poses for feel-good photo-ops every now and then, but with Caroline, they didn't seem staged. She didn't even have her own social media accounts. The stories were spread from the people she met—the surprised children, elated to have gifts from Caroline on Christmas Eve, or an elderly woman who intimated that Caroline had helped her shop for groceries each Saturday morning for the past five years.

I forced myself to read every article there was about her, including one about her betrothal to Freddie. It'd been posted recently, only three weeks before Freddie's arrival in Rio. The reporter highlighted the fact that the setup was a bit old-fashioned (even by British standards), but that "it was an earthly formality only meant to celebrate the match that had so clearly been made in heaven".

I wanted to paint Caroline as the villain. It would have

been so nice to hate her, but by the end of the night, I felt
nothing nothing but confusion and sadness: confusion over
why Freddie *didn't* love Caroline—for god's sake, after
internet stalking her for a few hours, *I* was willing to toss
my life aside and marry her myself—and sadness, because,
at the end of this all, one of us was going to end up
brokenhearted.

"Ready, Andie?"

I turned to find Lisa standing a few feet from the
training table, looking fresh-faced and ready to get to work.
Her black polo nearly matched the color of her eyes as she
assessed my wrist. I'd been icing it for the last fifteen
minutes, but it was time to start my training session for the
day.

"No rest for the weary."

She nodded. "Let's have a look at it. Sit and scoot
back."

I followed her directions and propped myself up on the
leather table. She came around the side so she could
unwind the wrapping as gently as possible. The bruising
was already more faded than the day before.

"Tell me when it starts to hurt," she said, turning the
wrist slowly counterclockwise. "I'm trying to get a feel for
the mobility."

She kept going, working my hand in different directions and applying varying amounts of pressure before I
finally couldn't take it.

"There." I winced.

"Okay." She nodded. "Your doctor sent over your x-
rays. In his email he recommended that you sit out for the
rest of the Olympic games…?"

Her black eyes darted up to me for confirmation, but I
shook my head.

"Well that was his recommendation, but I have a different plan."

She reached beneath the trainer's table for a blue elastic band. "Is that so?"

She seemed amused, which was a first. From what I'd gathered during our training sessions, Lisa wasn't someone who laughed easily.

"Yes. I know my body and I know how far I can push it."

"So you think you can play in two days? Isn't that when your next game is?"

I bit my lip, thinking over her question. I hadn't been able to put any pressure on my wrist the day before, and it'd only improved slightly overnight.

"Okay, not that game," I relented. "But definitely the final."

"When's the final?"

"Next week."

She scoffed. "You're asking for trouble."

I leaned back. "So you're not going to help?"

Her dark eyes met mine. "Oh no, I didn't say that. If you're willing to put in the time, then so am I. I'm not saying you'll be ready for the final game, but together, we can try."

I smiled. "All right. What first?"

She tossed the blue elastic band at me. "This thing. And rest assured, you aren't going to like it."

———

MY TRAINING SESSION with Lisa was about as enjoyable as a bikini wax paired with a nipple piercing (the latter being something I could only make assumptions about), but it felt good to have a goal again, and the pain distracted me from thinking of Freddie. After she was done torturing me, I dragged myself back to our condo, showered, and threw on the first thing I touched: the unicorn onesie Becca had insisted on hanging in my closet. I had to hand it to her though—after I slipped it on and zipped that sucker up, I decided I'd wear it for the rest of my life. It was soft, and it did make me feel a little bit better. Glitter will do that to you.

Kinsley and Becca were still at their evening practice, and if I had my timing right, they were probably in the middle of watching footage for their game against Canada. I'd been excused from the practice so I could attend my physical therapy session, but also because Coach Decker didn't want to see me. I'd already sent her three emails and left two voicemails. She knew how I felt about the situation. She could get her way with the semifinal—I wasn't prepared; I couldn't play—but I'd be damned if I was missing that final. I'd be at every practice and I'd go to therapy twice a day. I'd play through a compound fracture with my bones sticking out if I had to.

I pulled out a prepared meal from the fridge and popped it in the microwave. Though I wasn't really looking forward to a heaping plate of chicken and vegetables, I didn't have a choice. If I wanted to play in that final game, everything had to stay the same. I had to keep up my work-outs and diet. Sure, I'd nearly chugged a bottle of vodka the day before, but sometimes vodka counts as medicine.

The microwave dinged and I pulled out my meal just as a soft knock sounded at the front door.

"One sec!" I yelled as I set the plate on the counter. *Ouch.* The plate had been scalding and I'd nearly burned off my hand pulling it out without an oven mitt. I ran my fingers under cold water and shouted over my shoulder. "Just a minute!"

Whoever it was, it wasn't Kinsley or Becca. They'd have been shouting at me to hurry up already. I peered through the peephole and spied a heap of honey-brown hair just before a soft British voice spoke up.

"Hello? I know you're in there, I have a keen sense of smell for asparagus."

I yanked the door open and stood back to find Freddie's sister standing on the other side, wearing a friendly smile.

"Georgia?"

She shook her head. "Jor-jee, not Jor-juh." She stepped past me and plopped her purse on the kitchen counter like she'd done it a thousand times before. "Well, I mean, Georgia is my real name, but I despise it, so please, call me Georgie. And may I call you Andie?"

I nodded, still standing with the door in my hand.

"Cute onesie," she said with no hint of sarcasm. She was already moving around the condo, taking in the space and flipping through a stack of papers on the table. Her cool brown eyes met mine and I was momentarily silenced. She looked so much like her brother, but smaller and—obviously—feminine.

"Well, Andie, I've been dying to meet you, of course."

She grinned and stepped close so she could wrap me in a tight hug. I stood frozen, confused by her obvious approval. Wasn't she friends with Princess Caroline? "You're just as gorgeous as I imagined," she said before stepping back and holding me at arm's length. "The photo I saw online had you with long hair. Have you gone and chopped it?" She reached up to feel one of the uneven strands. It was still damp from the shower, so hopefully she couldn't tell how terrible it looked.

When I didn't answer right away, her smile fell. "Oh no, I'm scaring you already, aren't I?" She spun around and went back to rifling through the condo. "Or not…if my mangy brother hasn't frightened you away, I couldn't possibly deter you. Although why are you even hanging with him? In just a few hours, I've spied dozens of better-looking blokes roaming about. Have you seen that Argentinian basketball player, the one with a bum like—"

"Why are you here?" I asked, interrupting her.

She didn't seem to mind. She turned back and glanced at me over her shoulder. She truly was gorgeous, all big brown eyes and pink cheeks. "Because Caroline is a naff cow, of course."

I smiled, appreciating the sentiment even though I had no clue what it actually meant.

"I take it you two aren't friends?"

Georgie leveled me with a serious gaze. "Caroline Montague has the brain of a dim weasel and the personality of a dead mouse."

I burst out laughing and Georgie smiled. "Was that a bit harsh?" She shrugged. "Ah, well, sometimes the truth hurts. Now, go put some shoes on because I need a tour guide to take me around the village so I can find a handsome athlete of my own."

I frowned. "What? I can't…"

My gaze drifted to the chicken growing cold over on the counter.

She eyed it like it was last year's fruitcake. "Right. That. How about we get a real dinner too while we're out?"

I could have said no. I could have sat down at my kitchen table and ate chewy chicken by myself, moping around until Kinsley and Becca finally got home, but I was too intrigued. "Okay, just let me change out of this onesie really quick."

She frowned. "But then you're just as boring as everyone else."

I spent the next hour leading Georgie around our complex. I showed her the gym, the computer room, and the food court, all the while wondering how a person like Georgie Archibald actually existed. She was outspoken, beautiful, and slightly insane. When we poked our heads into the gym, she clapped her hands loudly and shouted, "Keep up the good work, ol' chaps!" Every head turned in her direction, but she'd already turned and walked away, leaving me with the awkward task of waving before ducking out after her.

"You're a brilliant guide, I promise, but so far, you've shown me every boring destination on Mt. Olympus. Where are the sex rooms?" She turned to me with wide eyes before rapping her foot on the solid ground. "Is there a dungeon?"

I shot her a skeptical glare. "If there is such a place, I haven't found it."

She pouted. "Well poo. Maybe we'll have to make one then."

"Were you and Freddie raised in the same house?" I asked with a half smile.

She nodded. "Yes, up until he went off to swim camps and all that. Why do you ask?"

I shrugged. "You're just much spunkier than him."

Spunky was the only word I could think of that wouldn't offend her.

She nodded. "I haven't a clue what 'spunky' means, but I accept your crude American compliment."

She poked her nose into a room we were passing. A sign on the door read *No Trespassing*, but she didn't seem to care.

I smiled.

She hummed and scanned over me again. "You know, you're not Freddie's usual type." She waved her hand in front of my face. "He usually fancies girls a bit more…"

I waited for her to fill in the end of her sentence.

"Posh."

"Posh?"

She glanced over. "Girls like Caroline."

My heart sank. "Right, well, I'm definitely *not* Caroline."

"Thank god," she rasped, stringing her arm around mine. "I know it must have been a shock to have us arrive yesterday. We weren't due for another week, but Caroline insisted on coming early. I wasn't going to let her come alone and muck everything up, so here I am."

I nodded. "Well, thanks for coming."

"Has Freddie filled you in on the dreadful situation?"

I glanced away, ashamed to admit that I hadn't spoken to Freddie since Georgie's arrival. "Um, a little bit, I guess. I know the betrothal wasn't his doing and that he wanted to break it off, I'm just not sure what he's telling Caroline. For all I know, he could be feeding her the same bullshit in reverse."

"Bull-shit," she repeated, testing the word on her tongue for what seemed like the first time. "That's a fabulous word." She nodded before glancing back at me. "Oh, yes, I understand where you're coming from, but I assure you that Freddie isn't some kind of womanizing playboy. He's been truly moaning on about you since he arrived in Rio. It's been quite nice to hear him fancy someone, but the whole Caroline situation does ruin it a bit. He's taking her to dinner right now actually to—"

I stopped walking. "He's taking her to dinner?"

Georgie frowned once she glanced back and saw my face. "No, no. Not as a date! He's taking her out so that they can have the conversation. Y'know, the whole 'betrothal over, piss off, I don't like you, yada yada yada.' It's all very mature of him, really."

I took a deep breath. "Right. Okay. So you think she'll just go away?" I snapped my fingers. "Like that?"

Georgie smiled. "See, that's the brilliant part. Caroline Montague is as dim as a box of bricks. I'll bet by tomorrow morning she'll be back on a plane to London sipping a mimosa and reading *He's Just Not That into You: Duchess Edition.*"

Chapter Twenty-Nine

FREDDIE

I **ADJUSTED MY** shirt. The thing was starched and stuffy—something I wore during interviews and ripped off the minute I got home. Caroline had come to my flat prior to dinner wearing a fancy dress and heels. When she'd seen my jeans and t-shirt, she'd laughed and told me she'd wait for me to change. Now, I regretted the slacks and button-down. It was too formal; the whole night was, really. The restaurant Caroline had picked was too fancy and quiet. The waiters fluttered around with champagne and wine glasses. Heavy chandeliers hung from the ceiling and there was a harpist in the corner, plucking away at a song that sounded like it belonged in a funeral dirge.

"Isn't this place divine, Frederick?" Caroline asked, reaching her hand up onto the table for mine.

I nearly yanked it away, but I didn't want to embarrass her. I left it there for a second or two and then pretended to cough so I could pull it away and cover my mouth.

"I didn't think places like this even existed in Rio." At least not the part I'd seen. We'd driven by flip-flop stands and beach shops on the way in, nothing nearly this fancy. It almost seemed like a place like this didn't belong in the easy party atmosphere in Rio.

Caroline batted her manicured hand like I was crazy. "These places exist everywhere, you just have to know where to look."

I nodded and fought the urge to tug at the collar of my shirt.

"Actually, Caroline, I'm glad we have a quiet moment. I've been discussing things with my mother—"

"Are you ready to order?"

I glanced up to see a waiter hovering over us, dressed in black with a protruding belly and an oily mustache. He didn't even notice that he'd cut me off.

"I think—"

Caroline nodded, anxiously. "Yes, I'm starved." I studied her as she rattled off a few appetizers and entrees for us. She looked to me for approval, and I just shrugged and let her order; it was easier that way. She'd really done herself up for the dinner. Her long wheat-blonde hair was curled in loose waves and she'd coated her lips in enough red stain to last ten years. Her eyes were dark and heavy. I couldn't imagine keeping mine open with all the stuff she had smudged on them.

Andie wore makeup to events, but most of the time when I saw her, she'd just come from practice. She was light, fresh, freckly, and tan. She was a breath of fresh air and I would have traded all the money in the world to have her sitting across from me at that fancy restaurant. She'd make fun of the place, swearing she didn't need a different fork for each bite. We'd pretend to like our overpriced salmon, and then we'd sneak out for a burger afterward.

I wanted that so badly, which is why I needed to be honest with Caroline.

"Listen, Caroline…"

She took a long sip from her water and leveled her gaze on me. The conversation wouldn't be easy, and the longer I stalled, the worse it would become.

"I've spoken with my mother about breaking off our betrothal."

"You've spoken with your mother?"

Why had I said it like that?

"I'd like to break off our betrothal," I repeated, a bit more determined.

She swallowed and set down her glass, eyeing its placement on the table.

"You're serious?" she asked, finally meeting my eye.

I nodded. "Yes."

"Is there someone else you're interested in?"

Her voice was calm, but there was a hint of something behind her eyes. Jealousy? Annoyance? Caroline and I had known each other our whole lives, but I wouldn't have called her a friend. Her family knew mine, and we were occasionally invited to the same events. I'd seen her around every now and then after it'd been announced that she and Henry would marry, but after his death, she'd nearly fallen off the face of the earth as far as I was concerned. Then, my mother had brought her up casually one day. *"Have you heard from Caroline lately?"* I'd ignored her interest then, but she hadn't let that deter her. My mother continued to bring Caroline up for months before she finally came out and said it during breakfast one day.

"I think you should marry Caroline Montague."

I nearly choked on my piece of bacon. "What do you mean, marry her?"

"She was intended for Henry for a reason…she's a wonderful match. Anyone would be lucky to have her."

I shook my head. "So then, let anyone have her. I'm not going to agree to an arranged marriage."

She halted then, but didn't retreat. "Right."

But that wasn't the last I heard about it. For months, she brought up the idea. I'd push her away and change the subject, but she kept on prodding. She'd drop hints about familial responsibility.

"Whether you like it or not, you are a duke, and one day, running this family's affairs will be your fulltime job."

I'd never wanted that part of my legacy. I was happy to sit back and let Henry take the reins, but after his untimely death, the decision wasn't mine to make anymore.

Georgie had been the one shouting at Mum after she went behind my back and discussed the betrothal with Caroline and her family. She couldn't believe how unfair it all was. Me? I'd sat quietly in the corner, trying to find the path of least resistance. I'd had a few weeks until I was supposed to leave for Rio and I couldn't concentrate on betrothals or weddings when I had my records to beat. I'd shoved the announcement to the side and walked out of the room, intent on focusing on swimming until after the Olympics were over.

It'd been a good plan up until I ran into Caroline at a friend's flat two days later. I was piss drunk, annoyed at my mum, and stressed about the future. The tequila wasn't sitting well with me and then I'd glanced up and spotted Caroline having a laugh with one of her friends across the room. Caroline. My betrothed. How odd that she was there and she hadn't even come to say hi to me, her future husband.

The details after that were fuzzy, but I remembered standing and walking toward her with the idea of chatting. She was pretty in a done-up way, and she was always extremely nice. I had a fleeting moment where I thought, why not? Why not Caroline? A man could do much worse for himself. She'd laughed at my drunken state, not the least bit perturbed. She'd helped me get a glass of water and directed me to a couch in the corner.

That night was the last time I'd had communication with her up until she'd stepped out of the limo in Rio. My mother had been the driving force behind our relationship from the start, and it was time I assessed the situation with my own eyes. Caroline was pretty and kind and wonderful, but I didn't want her, and I wouldn't marry her out of some misplaced ideal of familial duty.

"You know, I'm not surprised," Caroline said from across the table.

I shook my head clear and glanced up to see her soft smile.

"Honestly, Frederick. We hardly know each other."

I let out a sigh of relief.

"I would be lying if I said I hadn't expected that this would come soon enough. We're still young and we've got all the time in the world to fall in love. I'd gone along with the betrothal because my parents had pressured me into it—"

I laughed. "Seems our parents are very similar."

She smiled. "But if you'd like to break it off, I completely respect your decision."

I inhaled a deep breath, shocked at how well she was handling it all.

Her smile fell suddenly. "Oh dear. I *am* expected at that media dinner tomorrow night though…"

Right.

"I could still attend it, I suppose…if it will make it easier on you. That way you can delay the news of the broken betrothal until after you've finished competing."

She had a point. Was it so wrong to want my successes highlighted in the news more than my failures? Once the media got wind that I was breaking off our betrothal, there'd be no stopping them. I knew that better than anyone.

"So you'll go to the media dinner."

She nodded. "Right. There's no sense in hopping on a flight right back home after I've just arrived. I'd like to stay and enjoy the games with Georgie. There are so many people in the city. Who knows, maybe I'll meet the *true* love of my life while I'm here!"

She laughed at her joke, but I stared down at the table and thought of Andie.

Chapter Thirty

ANDIE

I REALLY WANTED to text Freddie. I wanted to tell him I'd met Georgie and she'd filled me in on his plan for ending things with Caroline. I wanted to tell him I'd be at the media dinner and I hoped he'd be there too. It'd been one day since he'd banged on my door, trying hard to get me to listen to him. I'd gone through two PT sessions, glancing up every time an athlete walked through the doors, only to bury the disappointment when it wasn't him. I desperately wanted to reach out, but it wasn't right. As long as he was with Caroline, I needed to keep my distance. Georgie insisted Freddie was trying to make it right and his text had said as much. I had to wait. He needed to come to me when he'd sorted everything out.

So, I deleted an unsent text message and shoved my phone back into my clutch. Kinsley was across the room, applying makeup. She'd asked me a few days ago if I'd be willing to go to the media dinner. We'd all been invited, but Becca had zero interest in putting on a cocktail dress and Liam said he'd had enough of reporters to last him a lifetime.

"Tell me again why we have to go to this thing?" I asked.

"Because while reporters aren't allowed in the village, they still need something to write about. The committee thought this would make everyone happy. We get good food and they get interviews."

I smiled. "You already know what they're going to ask you."

She offered up her best broken record impression. *"When are you and Liam going to start a family? When will you get pregnant? Are you pregnant NOW?"*

I laughed. "It's all anyone cares about."

"Including Liam," she added, turning back to the mirror so she could finish her makeup.

"*What?* Really?"

She nodded. "He's turning thirty soon and he thinks after the Olympics we should *start trying*. You know, uh, take away the goalie."

"Oh my god. I'm going to be an aunt."

She laughed. "Hold your horses, I'm not pregnant yet." I guessed she could see that my face fell because she continued, "but I promise you'll be an aunt when the time comes. Becca already claimed both godmother and fairy godmother privileges, but we might have an opening for you in the diaper changing department."

I laughed. "Well at least I won't have to worry about anyone focusing on me during this stupid dinner tonight."

"Don't be so sure, Andie. The Olympic season is the only time the whole of America really falls in love with soccer, and you're the fresh face of the brand. You have millions of little girls looking up to you now, and even though you're injured, the media will want to tell your story of perseverance." She paused, applying her makeup.

"Plus, you forgot one other person who will be focusing on you tonight—Freddie."

"Oh, he's going?" I asked while I rifled through my makeup bag. I thought I was doing a good job of looking like I hardly cared. Freddie Schmeddie, right?

"Mhmm," she said, passing her blush off to me when it was clear I couldn't find mine. "And I'm almost tempted to disinvite you because of it."

"*What?* I've spent the last hour getting ready with you. I DID MY HAIR."

Well, truthfully, *I* hadn't done my hair. Becca and I had gone to the salon in the village after practice so a stylist could fix my hack job. In the end, I liked it. It was short, just at my shoulders, and it'd be much easier to style.

"Do you know how rare that is?"

"Andie—"

"And I'm wearing a stupid cocktail dress!" I stepped back from the mirror and took deep, dramatic inhales to show her how tight the bodice of the dress fit. Each inhale only filled my lungs to like 2%. I'd probably pass out from lack of oxygen by the end of the evening.

She laughed. "You look gorgeous and it's too late to disinvite you, so just stick by me and ignore him. This isn't the place you want to have a scene. There will be cameras and microphones everywhere."

I narrowed my eyes. "You sound like you have no faith in me."

"It's not that, really." She spun around and flashed me a small, sympathetic smile. "I've just seen Freddie Archibald up close and it's clear that he has a way of separating a woman from her senses. It doesn't take a rocket scientist to recognize a bomb looking for its fuse."

"Well tonight, I'll only have eyes for food."

She eyed me skeptically, but I ignored her and turned

to check my appearance in the mirror one last time. My blonde hair was short and sleek, like that of a secret agent. I'd applied a smidgen more makeup than usual and it was making my gray eyes pop. My tight dress was doing wonders for my cleavage, something I usually tried to avoid, but tonight, it felt right. I felt beautiful, albeit uncomfortable. *But who needs to breathe when your boobs look this good, right?*

I turned to find my sky-high heels, the ones that made my legs go on for days, and then glanced back at Kinsley.

"Ready when you are, *baby mama*."

"That is NOT funny!"

———

KINSLEY HAD PREPPED me as best as she could on the way over, but as I stepped out of the cab and into the madness, I was still taken aback. There were so many reporters stuffed inside the press box that as Kinsley and I walked down the carpet, shouts and grunts could be heard over the snapping shutters. I smiled through the audible oooomphs and laughed when one of the photographers tripped on his way to the front of the line.

"Kinsley!"

"Right here!" the photographers yelled, vying for her attention. I stepped back and gave her the limelight, smiling just enough that I wouldn't suffer from Resting Bitch Face in any of the photos; I'd learned that the hard way. I used to think I was invisible when the paparazzi were snapping Liam and Kinsley, but then one day my mom called and asked me why it looked like I was picking my nose on the cover of US Weekly. From that day on, I kept my hands tucked by my side and a casual smile plastered on my face.

"Andie! Andie Foster!"

I nearly swallowed my tongue when a few of the photographers turned from Kinsley and aimed their flashing cameras at me.

I laughed like I thought it was a joke and waved them off.

"No thanks, I'm okay."

"They're not *asking*, Andie," Kinsley laughed before reaching back to my hand. She tugged me forward and tucked me into her side. "Just smile," she whispered out of the corner of her mouth.

"This is a mistake," I whispered back.

But it wasn't a mistake. The photographers wouldn't leave us alone, and I couldn't settle back into Resting Bitch Face until I was well within the confines of the banquet hall.

I stretched out my jaw. "Jeez, pretending to be happy is hard work."

Kinsley laughed. "Now you know why I wear shades all the time. It makes it much easier to pretend they aren't there when they snap photos."

I pocketed that bit of knowledge for later and then followed Kinsley through the party. Soft music played in the background and servers were walking around in black suits, serving hors d'oeuvres on silver trays. I reached for something that looked like a shrimp and then froze as half a dozen camera flashes went off in my direction.

"Don't put anything in your mouth that you can't eat in one bite," Kinsley warned, tilting her head toward the cameras. Jesus, I couldn't even enjoy the food?

The banquet hall was jam-packed with members of the press, all wearing official Olympic-sanctioned badges. Even if they hadn't been wearing lanyards, they still stuck out like sore, pudgy thumbs compared to the athletes in attendance. We wove through the crowd and I kept an eye out for Freddie. She'd said he'd be there, but by the time we made it to our table, I hadn't found him yet.

"Looks like we'll have to endure the press through dinner," Kinsley groaned, reaching forward for her name card on the table. I was assigned to the seat next to her, but I couldn't see the other name cards from where I stood. For all I knew I'd be sitting next to a Bulgarian shot putter. *Joy*.

"I'll go get us some drinks. Will you be okay here?" Kinsley asked.

I made a show of rolling my eyes. "Honestly, I'm fine. What do you think? I'm going to run over and hump Freddie the first chance I get?"

She smiled. "Either that or slap him."

As she left for the bar, I turned back to the crowd and recommenced my search for Freddie. It shouldn't have been hard filtering through the balding reporters, but it wasn't until there was a commotion near the door that I realized why I hadn't found him yet.

He'd only just arrived.

He and Thom breezed into the banquet hall and every camera within a ten-mile radius turned and flashed in their direction. He stood for a moment in the doorway. His suit was tailored to his long swimmer's physique and his smile was just wide enough to make my toes curl. He wore his suit with ease and confidence and even from across the room, I wanted to hump him. *Sorry, Kinsley. I lied.*

He smiled good-naturedly for the cameras for another few seconds and then waved them off so he could step into the party. I stood frozen to my spot, watching him walk and recklessly hoping he'd eventually find his way to me.

"Andie Foster! We meet again!"

My name, spoken in a shrill English accent, forced my attention away from Freddie. Sophie Boyle, the sour-faced reporter who'd tried to interview me in the food court, was back, and she was standing behind a chair across the table from me. As if on cue, she reached for her name card and turned it around. Sophie Boyle was written in scrolling gold cursive.

"Looks like we'll be tablemates," she said with a twisted smirk.

I shook my head. We were the only two people at the table and I'd be damned if I stuck around to deal with her harassment. I turned, prepared to find the nearest bar, and stopped short right before I ran into Freddie's wide, powerful chest.

He reached out to steady me, but I stepped out of his grasp quickly, too aware of Sophie Boyle right behind us. She already suspected something was going on; we didn't need to add fuel to the fire.

"Andie," he said, breathing life back into my name.

"Excuse me—"

Sophie Boyle cleared her throat behind me. "No need to be shy you two. Freddie, your name card is on this table as well. It looks like we'll all be well-acquainted by the time they've served dessert."

I shook my head. "I need a drink."

Freddie followed after me and I didn't stop him. The bar in the far corner of the banquet hall was dark, quiet, and most importantly, free of reporters. They were all hovering around the entrance of the room, ready to pounce on the next athlete that walked through the doors.

"I came to see you the other day," he said.

I winced at the sadness in his voice. "It was a really bad day, Freddie—"

"I know. How is your wrist?"

"Not better yet."

He nodded. "I'm so sorry, Andie."

I brushed away his apology. We both knew I didn't want to discuss my wrist.

"You have to know that I'm ending this betrothal," he said. "I wasn't lying."

"I know," I said just as we reached the bar. "I spoke with Georgie."

I put in an order for a ginger ale—though I would have loved a shot of tequila—and Freddie requested a water.

"So you forgive me?" he whispered.

I tried to conceal my slow-spreading smile.

When the bartender turned his back, Freddie slid his hand around my waist and pulled me flush against him. He was impossible to resist—his chest, his thighs, his stomach. He was hard edges and toned lines, but his touch was soft and warm.

"You look beautiful, Andie. This *dress*…"

His hand slid up my stomach, pressing the soft material to my skin just above my navel.

I swallowed and shook my head. The corner was dark, but not that dark. "Not here, Freddie, and definitely not now."

His brow furrowed. "Then when? I've been trying to reach you for the last two days."

I turned to glance over his shoulder, but no one was paying us any attention. "Have you spoken to Caroline?"

He stuffed his hands into his pockets and nodded. "Yes. I told you I'd take care of it, didn't I?"

His brown eyes burned into me.

"I want you, Andie."

My stomach flipped.

"Do you hear me? I want you." He leaned forward so that the next few words were whispered right up against my ear. "I choose *you*."

His hand was on my lower back, gathering me against

him. There was no hesitation in his voice, no second-guessing. Just because Caroline was in Rio didn't necessarily mean he'd lied to me.

I pressed my hands to his chest and glanced up. "After the dinner, meet me back at your condo. We can talk there."

A slow smirk unraveled across his lips—we both knew we'd be doing more than talking.

"Here are your drinks," the bartender said with a bored tone. If he'd noticed our flirtation, he didn't act like it. We reached for our cups and walked back to the table with a healthy distance between us.

"There's just one hitch: Caroline will be here."

My heart sunk. "*Here* here?"

He nodded. "She was invited by the organizers after our families released the news of the betrothal. It would be bigger news if she didn't show up, so we agreed that we would show up separately and ignore questions about the betrothal."

I frowned. "Am I missing something? If it's over, can't you just say it's over?"

He shook his head. "It's not that simple. The press in England are ruthless. When the story breaks, it won't be simple and it won't be pleasant. I'd rather not deal with it until after I'm done swimming next week. She's agreed to play along for now and keep the separation discreet."

My heart sank. Of course. Freddie hadn't even started competing. He had his first race the very next day, and where most of the athletes were focused solely on swimming, Freddie might as well have been trying to put a stop to World War III. He didn't deserve to have all this petty drama on his plate, and I was partly to blame for putting it there. I couldn't help but feel disappointed and insecure, but I swallowed my doubts once again. If he told me he'd talked to Caroline, then he had. I could deal with our relationship being a secret for a few more days, especially when I took a moment to admire him as we walked back.

I smiled. "I like your suit."

It was black and fitted, and with his British accent, it almost felt like I was flirting with James Bond himself.

He pressed his hand to my lower back, guiding me to my seat. "I think you'll like it more once I've taken it off."

My cheeks flushed. We were back at the table where Kinsley and Sophie were talking. Another few athletes had found their seats. If any of them had been paying close attention, they would have heard him.

"Freddie," I warned, trying to contain my blush.

"Oh my goodness, finally," a soft British accent spoke behind me. "This place is like a circus."

I spun toward the voice and inhaled a shaky breath as my eyes locked with Caroline Montague. Coifed blonde hair, discreetly sexy black cocktail dress, impossibly expensive shoes—she was hard to absorb in person, like seeing a Monet for the first time. Her plump lips spread into a smile as her eyes slid over Freddie, then she looked down, down, down, and paused when her gaze hit Freddie's hand resting on the small of my back. I stepped forward to introduce myself, but she beat me to it with a harmonic string of practiced words and a smile that only made her more radiant.

"You must be Andie Foster."

Chapter Thirty-One

ANDIE

THE ORGANIZERS OF the media dinner either had a very sadistic sense of humor, or they were setting me up for a hidden camera prank show; there was no other way to explain the seating arrangement. Out of all the tables in the banquet hall, I was assigned to the one with Sophie Boyle, Freddie, and Caroline. Worse yet, Caroline was assigned to the seat directly beside mine. When she'd walked up to find her name card, she'd smiled good-naturedly, but my body had filled with dread. I felt like the dirty mistress. *Am I the dirty mistress?* They weren't even dating. They hardly knew each other. She had agreed to end the betrothal. So why couldn't I meet Caroline's eyes?

"More water?"

I gripped my napkin in my lap and stared down at my place setting, trying to think of how I could get out of having to sit through the rest of dinner. They hadn't even served the first course yet, and they were still seating people across the room. I couldn't do it. My stomach hurt and I was fairly sure that if I tried to eat anything, it'd just come right back up.

"Andie," Kinsley said, jostling my arm. "She's asking if you want more water."

"Oh." I glanced behind me to find a small woman with a pitcher of water in her hand. I'd guzzled down my glass when I'd first sat down, more out of nerves than real thirst. I grabbed my glass and handed it back to her. "Yes, please. Thank you."

"Andie, you have to tell me more about your...*soccer* career," Caroline winked, adorably adopting the American name for the sport. When she spoke, she pressed her hand to my uninjured forearm to get my attention. It should have left a mark when she pulled away, but there was nothing, no burn or scar to show how painfully awkward her touch was.

"Umm..." I fidgeted in my seat and tried to pull the hem of my cocktail dress down. It wouldn't budge. "What do you want to know?"

"I've just always wished I could play a sport like that. You must be so talented."

Freddie smiled on the other side of her, watching her praise me. He had assured me Caroline knew nothing about our relationship, but I still would have given anything to disappear. The waiter handed back my water and I set it down beside my plate.

I glanced up to find Sophie Boyle watching me with a small self-serving smile from across the table. She had a tape recorder set out right beside her plate and the small blinking red light served as a reminder that anything I said, she could quote in an article. That was the whole point of the media dinner.

"Soccer isn't so hard," I said, swallowing past the frog in my throat. "I just started playing at a young age and it seemed natural, even back then."

"She's being modest," Freddie insisted.

"Well it obviously keeps you in great shape," Caroline said. I kept my gaze forward but I could feel her eyes on me.

"Thank you."

"You must run ten miles a day to have a body like that."

I forced a laugh and reached for my water glass. Why was the attention on me? There were eight people at the table, six other athletes worth talking about, and yet everyone was happy to listen to Caroline.

"I'm sorry, I don't mean to put you on the spot," she continued with an apologetic smile. "I've just been watching your games and I was so excited to meet you. Now I'm making a fool of myself."

I glanced over to see a slight blush dotting her cheeks. Was she really as nervous as I was? I reached out to touch her arm and smiled genuinely for the first time since she'd arrived. "It's fine. That's really cool that you've been watching the games."

Her features perked up again. "Do you think you'll be able to play tomorrow?"

I shook my head. "Not tomorrow, no. I won't be ready."

She nodded, but kept quiet.

Kinsley leaned forward. "Freddie, you race tomorrow, don't you?"

After that, the conversation turned to Freddie and his first day of racing. For a week straight he'd have to compete in multiple races per day. He'd take the pool fifteen times before he was finished and though he seemed confident sitting at that table with his fitted suit and his wide smile, I knew the pressure had to be getting to him, even just a tiny bit. I'd played in thousands of games over the years, but these big events never got easier. The world was anxious to watch him compete, and the other swimmers naturally put a target on his back. It wasn't every day that an Olympian came back for his third games poised to break the records he'd set four years earlier, and yet when I glanced over, there was no hint of anxiety behind his eyes. He winked and I melted, dropping my face so that Sophie Boyle wouldn't notice my secret smile.

Caroline leaned closer. "Would you mind coming with me to get a drink? Between the two of us, we ought to be able to fight our way to the bar."

I smiled. "Of course. I actually need to use the restroom too."

I dropped my napkin on the table and nodded to Kinsley. "I'll be right back. Bathroom."

Caroline linked her arm through mine and led me away from the table. We wove through the crowd, trying to stay out of the way of the waitstaff flitting around the room. There was a bathroom tucked away in the corner next to the bar, and I tilted my head toward it.

"Bathroom first?"

She smiled. "Sounds good."

I pushed through the door and Caroline stepped in after me. I slipped into the first stall and listened to her heels clap against the tile as she moved around the small space. She pushed open the other three stall doors, as if to decide which one was most suitable for her use. I smiled at the idea just before I heard her walk back toward the bathroom door. I listened to the distinct metallic clink of a lock sliding into place, and the smile dissolved from my face. Silence filled the small fluorescent space as my blood turned to ice.

I stood and flushed, trying to stay as calm as possible. Surely it was just another quirk of aristocracy, to reserve a public restroom for the duration of her private use. My heart pounded against my chest, as if sensing before my brain that something was seriously wrong. I slid the lock on my stall door and stepped out to wash my hands. Caroline was posed up against the bathroom door with her arms crossed.

"Didn't need...to go?" I asked with a shaky voice.

Even to me, it didn't sound natural.

"You know, I have to hand it to you Andie," she said, uncrossing her arms and stepping away from the door. For those few seconds, all I could focus on was the sound of her heels on the tile. "For a girl who prides herself on keeping nets empty, you've shown yourself to be quite good at filling them. Why, it took you no time at all to ensnare poor Frederick. The dim bastard never really stood a chance once you stumbled into his life, did he?"

She came up to stand directly beside me and I met her cool blue eyes in the mirror. She reached forward and gripped a few strands of my hair, sliding her fingers slowly down. I stood still, breathing shakily and praying that the situation would turn, that she'd laugh and step away, joke about the whole thing and lead me out of the bathroom in front of her. But she didn't. She let the strands fall back against my cheek and smiled, a slow sardonic smile that proved how far from freedom I truly was.

"I don't know what—"

She held up her hand. "Save it."

The water was still running, so I leaned forward to turn it off. Caroline shoved me forward and stepped up to force my hip bones into the hard ceramic sink. I hissed as the hard surface bit into me, and steadied myself by placing my palms down on the counter. Caroline stayed there, caging me against the sink. I couldn't get past her without shoving her aside, and I didn't want to take it to that level. She was taller and heavier, but more importantly, her eyes were desperate, feral. I was alone in that bathroom with a wild animal.

"You knew he was mine and yet you pushed and you pushed." She dragged her fingernail down my bare arm as she spoke, causing an angry red line to form in its wake. "What a little whore you are."

I shook my head, more indignant than afraid. She had guessed right that Freddie was interested in me, but I'd had nothing to do with his decision to break it off with her. However, I wasn't about to argue semantics with someone that seemed more and more like a psychopath.

"Did you think I would roll over and let you take him from me? Do you know how hard I've worked for this marriage?"

I couldn't wrap my head around this woman. She'd been so polite and gentle at the table, just as the world believed her to be. Now, here, alone and riled up, I had no clue of what she was capable.

"So listen well: Frederick Archibald is mine. He and I are going to get married and I won't let you get in the way of that." She lightly trailed her fingertips down my arm until she'd clenched her fist around my injured wrist. I cried out and grabbed her forearm, but when I yanked to loosen it, the pain in my wrist doubled. With her free arm she pulled my hair back until my neck was exposed to her. My breaths were coming loud and heavy, echoing across the space. "If you think you're hurting now, just wait until everyone thinks you're breaking up my engagement. They might know of you, but they *love* me, Andie." She whispered the words seductively in my ear as if she was a siren. "If you break up this betrothal, I'll make sure they crucify you. Your name will be synonymous with *Olympic whore*. Your budding brand, your sponsorships, your beloved fans…they'll leave you so fast you won't know what hit you."

She let go of my hair and wrist at all once, and I'd been resisting her so hard that when the tension was gone, my head yanked forward, nearly colliding with the mirror. I winced and tried to keep the tears at bay. This was all too much.

"So choose wisely Andie," she said, stepping back and tilting her head. Her feral smile was crumbling and in its place, I could just barely make out the innocent, doe-eyed philanthropist. Jesus, she was two-faced.

"Is Freddie worth everything to you?" she asked.

I swallowed.

"Decide now, because he is to me."

She turned, checked herself in the mirror, and walked out of the bathroom, leaving me to stare at my reflection in the mirror as tears slid down my cheeks. I tried to wipe them away and get ahold of my emotions. My entire body shook with anger, with the shock of seeing Caroline's true colors. She was a fucking psychopath and I was the only one who knew it.

I inhaled two shaky breaths and then swallowed down my nerves. I considered calling the police and reporting an assault, but since she'd carefully inflicted pain on my wrist where I already had bruising, it would be her word against mine.

Still, I wouldn't let her win. She was bluffing; I knew it. She couldn't possibly have proof that Freddie and I were together. I leaned forward and wiped away the mascara that had clouded beneath my eyes.

Caroline was about to learn that Andie Foster didn't intimidate that easily.

I shoved my way through the bathroom door and strutted confidently back to our table. Caroline might have wanted Freddie, she might have thought he belonged to her, but the fact remained: he wanted me. *He chose me.*

By the time I arrived back at the table, everyone was listening to Caroline tell a story. She was smiling and laughing along with Freddie and Kinsley. What a crazy bitch. I leaned forward, cut her off midsentence, and flashed a seductive smile at Freddie.

"Freddie, could I speak to you for a second?"

Caroline's sharp eyes flashed up to me in shock. I smiled. What do bullying bitches do when you stand up to them? They run and keep quiet. They slink into the background and convince themselves it's not worth it anyway. I wasn't going to stay quiet. Caroline wanted me to cower in fear, but I was stronger than her. I'd tell Freddie about Caroline and we'd deal with her together.

I was going to win.

Caroline reached out and gripped my arm, digging her nails in just gently enough so that no one would notice. I bit down on the inside of my mouth to keep my expression normal.

"Actually, Andie, I was hoping you could settle something for me." She pulled her phone out of her purse with her free hand and held it up, angled so that only I could see the small screen. "Is this you in the photo? It's such a great action shot. They must have taken it during one of your games."

I slid down into my seat and felt the color drain from my face.

She wasn't showing me a photo from a game; she was showing me a photo of Freddie and me from Mascarada. My red mask had slipped off just enough to make me recognizable in the hazy light. My red dress was bunched up on my thighs, and though you couldn't see anything past the hem, Freddie's hand up my dress was damning evidence all on its own. I had no clue how she'd found it, but she'd made it perfectly clear what she planned on doing with it. As if to prove her point, it was already preloaded into an email on her phone with a subject line that made my stomach drop.

Soccer Slut Seduces Frederick Archibald

"Is that you?" Caroline asked again, sending a chill down my spine. To the outside world, she was a happy, smiling angel. Only I could feel her fingers digging into my thigh beneath the table. Only I could see the email she was prepared to send if I didn't leave Freddie alone.

"Yes. It's me."

"Andie?" Freddie asked. His voice sounded a million miles away. "Do you want to go talk?"

I shook my head quickly. "No...no. Never mind."

Caroline smiled and leaned closer. "How wonderful. I do *love* that photo."

Chapter Thirty-Two

ANDIE

I **'D SUDDENLY FOUND** myself in the middle of a minefield. I could have grabbed the phone from Caroline and showed the table what she was doing, but Sophie Boyle was there, smiling and observing the entire scene from her perch across the table. Every move I made had to be perfectly calculated. If Caroline had that photo from the club, there was no telling what else she had packed away in her arsenal. I needed to tread lightly and respect Caroline's psychosis.

"You hardly touched your dinner," Kinsley said later as we walked out of the media dinner and slipped back into the car waiting for us out front. I had half a mind to check the brakes, but I shook away the thought. She didn't want to kill me; she wanted me to leave Freddie alone, and that was exactly what I'd done.

I'd avoided him for the rest of dinner, all but ignoring his questions, even when they were specifically directed at me. He'd joined me when I stood to leave, offering to walk me out, but I'd avoided his hand and shook my head. He was so beautiful there, tall and commanding. He wanted to walk me out and I couldn't let him. I had to walk away without so much as a promise.

As soon as my seatbelt was buckled into place, I reached for my phone in my clutch and started typing a text for him.

Andie: I'm sorry I pulled away from you as I was leaving. This isn't going to make sense, but Caroline is a fucking crazy person. She cornered me in the bathroom and threatened to expose us if I didn't stay away from you.

"So did you think the dinner—"
I cut Kinsley off. "Hold on."
I could only concentrate on one thing at a time.

Andie: I thought she was bluffing, but she has a photo of you and me from Mascarada on her phone. That's the picture she showed me when I got back to the table.

My fingers were flying over the keyboard; I had to let him know about everything as quickly as possible.

"Jesus, who are you texting?" Kinsley asked.

I tilted my phone screen so she could read what I'd already sent, and then I continued typing.

Andie: Do not trust her. She doesn't want you to break off the betrothal and I think she's prepared to go to extreme lengths to keep you. Please believe me. I know she seems meek and innocent, but she's not, Freddie. She's insane.

"ARE YOU KIDDING ME? She did that?!" Kinsley shouted, grabbing the phone out of my hand and scrolling up to reread the messages. "How could you keep quiet through all this?"

I inhaled a breath, feeling better now that two people knew about Caroline. "Because Caroline and Sophie were both sitting at that table."

"So for the last hour you just had to sit on this?"

"Why do you think I was so quiet?"

She shook her head. "No, no. This isn't right, Andie."

"I'm going to figure it out."

My phone buzzed in her hand and she handed it back to me.

Freddie: I believe you. Of course I believe you. I'm so sorry, Andie. I can't call now. I'm in a car with her. I'll ring after I drop her off at her hotel.

My blood boiled at the idea of them sitting in the back of a car together. Why did he have to drive her home? Couldn't she just slither back to whatever hellhole had spawned her on her own?

Kinsley and I made it back to our condo and I stormed into my room. It was 9:00 PM, and we had a game at 8:00 AM the next morning. Freddie's first race was just as early and instead of focusing and getting in the zone, we were dealing with Crazy Caroline. It wasn't fair.

I threw my clutch across my room and yanked off my cocktail dress. It still had remnants of Caroline's perfume on it and I knew washing it wouldn't help. I kicked it aside and glanced up to Kinsley. She'd followed me into the room and called Becca in to join us.

I stepped into the shower and quickly worked at washing away Caroline's vile touch. By the time I'd dried off and tugged on sweats, Kinsley had filled Becca in on everything that had gone down during dinner. They sat side by side on my bed, watching me pace in small circles.

"I can't believe I missed it. I was Skyping with Penn,

but I would have definitely gone had I known this Jerry Springer shit was going to go down."

I leveled her with a narrowed gaze. "This isn't funny, Becca."

Her eyes widened. "No, I know. I'm sorry Andie. I just wish I had been there to help."

"Do you think she'll expose that photo?" Kinsley asked, turning to me with sad eyes.

I raked my hands through my damp hair and reached for my phone. Freddie still hadn't called me and I was starting to get worried. The dinner had ended a while ago and he should have already dropped her off by then.

I shook my head. "I don't know. It's a standoff. I've fired first by telling Freddie what happened, so if he confronts her…there's no telling what she'll do."

Chapter Thirty-Three

FREDDIE

I READ ANDIE'S text messages just as our car pulled away from the media dinner.

"Everything okay?" Caroline asked, tipping an easy smile in my direction.

I nodded and kept my eyes glued on my mobile, reading Andie's messages as they popped up one after another.

...she cornered me in the bathroom...

...she has a photo of you and me...

...do not trust her...

"Who's trying to reach you this late?" Caroline asked, scooting closer to try to get a look at my screen.

I pocketed my phone and tried to plaster on a genuine smile. I knew it wasn't right. My muscles were strained and taut. "Just my manager. To her, workdays never end."

She laughed. "Ah, the life of a famous athlete, I suppose."

I kept my gaze on her as she looked out the window. I tried to see her as the villain Andie had just described in her messages. She was so delicate and kind. I'd never seen

247

her raise her voice to anyone. If someone had asked me ten minutes earlier, I would have assumed Caroline Montague was incapable of killing a fly. Had I really misjudged her so much?

She turned to assess me with her crystal blue eyes. "What?" she said with a light giggle.

I shook my head. "Nothing, just taking in the view."

"It's magical, isn't it?"

I wouldn't know. I was too preoccupied to care about the coastline flying by us.

"Listen, Frederick…" She turned to me as the car rolled to a stop beneath a small portico in front of her hotel. "I know you've got a race really early tomorrow, but I do think it'd be good to chat for a minute about the betrothal and everything. Y'know, we should figure out how we'll navigate the rest of the games so the media doesn't catch wind of anything. I still think it'd be best if we keep it to ourselves for now."

Of course she thought that. I should have realized she had ulterior motives as soon as she'd arrived in Rio.

"I've really got to get back to my flat," I said, anxiety laced through every word. I didn't care about sleep; I just wanted to get back to Andie as soon as possible.

"C'mon, just for a minute," she said with a hopeful smile. "There's a cute little bar right inside."

I opened my mouth to turn her down but then Andie's messages flashed through my mind. What would she do if I said no? Would she take it as a personal insult? It was better to go along as if everything was normal until Andie and I got a grip on the situation.

"All right, just for a moment," I relented, sliding out of the back seat of the car and then holding open the hotel door for her.

She made a real show of it once we were inside. She

insisted on ordering drinks, though I didn't touch mine. I didn't drink anything other than water this close to a race, but she didn't seem to care. She sipped on her cocktail and then leaned close with an easy smile.

"This isn't so bad, right?"

A chill ran down my spine. I should've realized earlier that her easy smile was something more manipulative.

I shrugged. "What is it you wanted to talk about? I've really got to get back."

I wanted to text Andie and tell her it would be a little longer than I'd expected, but I wasn't going to text her when I was sitting this close to Caroline. I'd already been able to tell she suspected something when I mentioned my manager in the car.

"I just know you're under a lot of stress right now, and I want to make sure you've thought everything through—breaking off the betrothal, I mean."

She played with the rim of her glass, slowly swirling her fingertip along the edge. It gave off a piercing ring, just barely noticeable. I reached forward and gripped her hand to force her to stop.

She laughed. "Sorry, old habit."

I let go of her hand and sat back. "I'm going to be very honest with you, Caroline. I'm not ready to get married. Half of my stress is thanks to my mother insisting that we push forward with the betrothal without my consent. You don't want to marry a man who's not in love with you, do you?"

Her smile fell like I'd just wounded her. "We could fall in love."

My gut clenched with the amount of sincerity in her voice. She really thought we could work out. How had I missed that before? That subtle desperation in her voice?

"I'm not—I won't ever—be in love with you," I said. Clear and concise.

She inhaled sharply, as if my blade had finally pierced her skin. All at once, she leaned back in her chair and dropped the innocent mask. It was like watching a snake shed its skin, the way her smile twisted into something sour and her kind eyes narrowed into thin slits.

"Right, well just remember that I offered the easy way. Tell me, Frederick: do you love Andie, or do you love the fact that she's been spreading her legs for you every five seconds?"

I scraped my chair away from the table and stood. "Leave her out of this. She has nothing to do with my decision."

"No Frederick, I don't think I will." She was so calm then, running her finger along the rim of the glass once again. The high-pitched sound was back, forcing my hands into fists by my side. "The moment you picked her over me, you made that impossible."

"What do you want?" I growled.

She picked her hand up off the glass and reached for the end of my tie, feeling the material between her fingers. "What I've always wanted."

Her gaze flashed up to lock with mine.

"*You.*"

Chapter Thirty-Four

ANDIE

I STAYED UP late waiting for Freddie. I tried his phone a few times and even left a message with Georgie (she'd loaded her number in after our tour of the village), but she hadn't heard from him either. I was close to calling the police or alerting the officials, but he finally texted me back just before midnight.

Freddie: I promised you I would handle this situation, and I will. Get some sleep, we'll talk tomorrow. XX

I clutched my phone to my chest and read as deeply into his message as those two little Xs would allow. He still wanted me; Caroline hadn't convinced him otherwise.

I went to bed and dreamt of Caroline's contorted smile staring back at me in the mirror. I woke up three times throughout the night, jarring myself out of nightmares that never seemed to end. By the time I was awake for good, it was thirty minutes before my alarm was due to sound. I turned it off and wiped the sleep from my eyes. I didn't bother brushing my teeth or looking in the mirror. I went straight out into the living room to brew some coffee so it'd be ready by the time Kinsley and Becca finally forced themselves out bed. I was halfway to the kitchen counter when I saw a few newspaper pages lying just inside the doorway. They were scattered as though someone had stuffed them beneath the door one at a time. I walked toward it hesitantly and paused when I saw the headline that ran in bold font across the top of the page closest to me. It was just as she had threatened.

Olympic-Sized Affair Leaves Archibald in Hot Water

Fiancée-to-be Devastated to Learn he is "Fostering" International Relations

My knees buckled and I collapsed there, pulling the newspaper onto my lap. Caroline had slipped a note on top, just below the headline.

"Rise and Shine. Kisses, C."

I ripped the note off and crumpled it up. It'd been blocking part of the photo they'd printed along with the headline. It was the one Caroline had showed me the night before, of us inside Mascarada, blown up to a full page. I blinked and blinked again, confused about why the image was distorted. It wasn't until my tears started to smear a few words of the story that I realized I was crying.

I wiped my tears away and forced myself to read every detail they'd printed, though my stomach threatened to give halfway through. The newspaper hadn't held back. Every gory, salacious detail was printed there for people to read, from our rumored meet-ups to my soccer history. They started by contrasting my history with Caroline's, painting me as the Whore of Babylon and Caroline as Mother Theresa. They juxtaposed an image of me in my sports bra, sweaty and tired after practice with a photo of Caroline in a perfectly tailored pantsuit handing out bread at a freaking orphanage in Croatia. Honestly, by the end of the article, even I hated myself.

I sat on the floor in the entryway and read the article twice before reaching for my phone and googling my name. The day before there'd been a few random interviews from small-scale magazines. My college soccer profile had still been on the front page along with a story my town's newspaper had printed about me going to the Olympics. All of that was gone. Gossip site after gossip site, magazine after magazine, Facebook post after Facebook post…I was officially the most hated person on the internet.

She'll never be Caroline.

Shouldn't she be focused on the games?! How does she have time to become a mistress?

She's pure trash. She couldn't keep her legs closed for a few weeks? What part of ENGAGED didn't she understand?

I refuse to watch the game today! I won't be supporting her OR her career. #Loser

She's pretty, but she's nothing compared to Caroline. #TeamCaroline

Is anyone else boycotting the soccer game today?

My daughter looks up to these girls.

How does #AndieFoster still have any sponsorships?

What a whore.

I was still reading through #AndieFoster on Twitter when Kinsley and Becca pulled my phone out of my hand.

"Stop! I was reading those."

Kinsley shook her head. "No. It's not healthy, Andie.

Those people don't know you. They're bored and stupid. Ignore them. They'll be on to the next story in a few days."

I stared back down at the paper, wrinkly and smeared with tears. "She sent the story."

"I saw it."

Of course she'd seen it. Everyone had fucking seen it. Every person I'd gone to high school with, every girl on my college soccer team, my parents, grandparents, enemies, friends. Every single person was waking up across the world and reading the #1 headline on every major news outlet: *me*.

Kinsley dropped to the floor and wrapped me up in her arms. "I'm so sorry, Andie."

My tears mixed into her hair as she held me there, keeping her arms wrapped tightly around me.

"What happens now, Kinsley?"

"I honestly don't know, but there was a media shitshow after everyone found out I was seeing Liam while he was my coach, and here's what I wish someone had told me then: you're an adult, and you haven't done anything wrong—even though they want you to think you have. There's a little bit of blood in the water, and they think they're sharks, but they're actually vultures, Andie, and if you don't give them anything, they're powerless. Hold your head up high."

Easier said than done.

As I got ready for the game—well, got ready to sit on the bench and *watch* the game—I fielded phone calls from my mom, my dad, my manager, Coach Decker, and a dozen or so unknown numbers that kept hounding me. I ignored everyone I could and spoke briefly with everyone I couldn't. My nerves were shot and my emotions were raw. I finally stopped crying long enough to dab concealer under my eyes and brush on a bit of mascara, but I knew it'd be gone well before the end of the day. Kinsley and Becca had everything waiting for me by the door when I was ready to leave. We walked in silence to the elevators and then stepped inside when the heavy doors slid open. There were already people inside and when I took a spot near the doors, all conversation came to a screeching halt.

"Are you Andie Foster?" one guy asked.

I kept my eyes on the doors and stayed silent.

"Hey baby, where's that mask?"

"That's enough," Kinsley snapped, turning around and leveling him with a sharp stare. I could feel the tears starting again, but I took a shaky breath and willed them away. Stupid Elevator Guy was only the start of it. As we made our way through the lobby, I heard the whispers and chatter.

"She doesn't look like a slut," one girl said to her friend before they both broke out into laughter.

I ignored them and pushed through the glass doors, anxious to step into our team's bus. Kinsley and Becca led the way and I took the first full breath of the morning once the door closed behind me. Coach Decker was sitting up front with Liam. She offered me a short nod.

"Chin up, Foster. Let today be about soccer and nothing else."

I nodded, trying to absorb her words, but it didn't help. As I walked down the aisle of our bus, I felt the stares from my teammates. Most of the people who should have been there for me the most were just as curious, wide-eyed, and annoyed with me as anyone else. They might've stood behind me before the injury, but now I was no more than a distraction to them. I moved to take a spot beside Michelle near the back, but she reached for her gym bag and tossed it on the seat just before I moved to sit.

R.S. GREY

"Sorry, need the space," she said, slipping her earbuds in and turning to face the window.

I walked on and took the last seat at the back of the bus, and that's where the tears continued to fall. In a matter of hours, life had spun me on my head, and though I tried to hang on for dear life, I knew there was no point. This was only the beginning.

Chapter Thirty-Five

FREDDIE

THEY KEPT THE swimmers tucked away in the locker room until it was time to announce our teams one by one for the semifinal relay race. I was ready, warmed up, and focused, but my heart pounded a heavy rhythm as the announcer called our names and beckoned us into the stadium. I followed Thom out of the locker room, and even though my music blared in my ears, the fans screamed loud enough that I could feel the vibrations hum in my chest.

An Olympic official led us toward the swim platforms and we slipped off our jackets and warm-up pants. Reluctantly, I pulled the headphones off my ears and was met with deafening cheers. One of the team managers came around to gather our clothes and as I handed him my jacket, he pointed up. I followed his finger and found myself blown up on the jumbotron in the center of the stadium—wide eyes hidden beneath goggles and a tense frown. In less than thirty seconds, I'd take my position on the podium for my first race and they wanted me to wave or smile, but I gave them nothing. Other swimmers could flash them chummy smiles; I needed to focus.

Thom nudged my shoulder and gave me a nod. I adjusted my swim cap and goggles until they were secure. I stepped up to the podium and inhaled the sharp smell of chlorine. Swimming had been a part of my life for as long as I could remember, and the smell of the chemical brought the race into razor-sharp focus.

The warning whistle blew and I stepped onto the podium to take my starting stance. I cracked my knuckles and inhaled another deep breath. I bent forward and swung my arms back and forth, loosening the muscles.

"Take your mark," the announcer shouted.

I bent lower and gripped the edge of the podium. The water was all I could see through my goggles; the small waves beckoned me closer. I could hear the shouts from the stadium in the distance. I could hear the deep breaths from the swimmers positioned on either side of me, but there was nothing louder than the buzzer as it DINGED to the start the race. I pushed off the podium, propelled myself into the water, and let my body do what it did best.

Swim.

Chapter Thirty-Six

ANDIE

BY THE TIME our bus arrived at the stadium, I wasn't sure how much more I could handle. I trailed after my team, fidgeting in the awkward pantsuit I had to wear. I'd specifically asked Coach Decker if I could dress out with the team, but she'd insisted on the suit, probably because she assumed it would keep me from running onto the field midgame.

There was a cluster of reporters hovering outside the back entrance of the stadium. Kinsley and Becca huddled around me and helped me block my face from their camera flashes. I had my earbuds in and my music blaring so that even if they had shouted inappropriate questions, I couldn't hear them. I followed my team into the locker room and set down my bag. There were pregame interviews I had to get through, but Kinsley assured me they would keep the focus on soccer.

She was wrong.

I stepped up behind the small podium and glanced out at the reporters standing and waiting to ask their questions. Before the first two games, there'd been three or four reporters there. I counted a dozen that day before Coach Decker stepped forward and announced that I would be answering questions for five minutes, "so please keep it brief."

"Andie!"

"ANDIE!"

"Foster!"

I pointed to a short balding man in the back row.

"Do you have any response to the allegations made against you this morning concerning the affair with Frederick Archibald?"

I opened my mouth, stunned.

"Andie! When did you and Frederick start the affair? Were you two together prior to arriving for the games?"

My resolve was cracking with each question they slung my way. They didn't care about soccer or my injury. They wanted to know every sordid detail of my "affair" with Freddie.

Liam stepped forward and yanked the mic across the podium. "Unless anyone has a question pertaining to the game today or Andie's injury, I'll be ending this interview right now."

One long, thin hand reached up into the air. I followed the lanky arm down to a head of curly red hair and inhaled sharply as Sophie Boyle stood up with a commanding smile.

"I've got a question, Andie. Now that your injury will preclude you from participating in the remainder of the games, why exactly are you still in Rio?" Her eyes narrowed. "Hmm...surely you'd find better doctors and treatment back home in Los Angeles?"

Her question wasn't about Freddie, but it might as well have been. The other reporters jumped on board.

"Are you staying in Rio because of Freddie!?"

They couldn't help themselves. Even after Liam's threat, the reporters clamored over one another to shout their questions about Freddie. Liam signaled for me to leave. I hadn't uttered a single word and somehow, I felt like I'd just dug myself a foot deeper. Was staying quiet about an alleged affair just as bad as owning up to it? Was that what Freddie and I had been the last two weeks? An affair?

The second I was out of view from the press, I lost it. I dug my hand into my hair to keep the shouts lodged deep down in my throat. I wanted to curse and punch and yell my way out of the situation. I wanted to call Caroline out for being a conniving bitch and I wanted to prove to the world that even if I did have an illicit relationship with Freddie, it didn't define me. I was still a good soccer player, regardless of what I did off the field.

My life had gone to shit and I couldn't see a way to fix it. Freddie was supposed to be a fling. He brought out something in me that was exhilarating and sexy. But this? Dealing with a media frenzy and trying to defend my character to the entire world was never part of the plan.

I felt like I couldn't breathe. I ripped at the collar of my blazer, trying to fill my lungs with air. The corners of my vision grew fuzzy and I pinched my eyes closed, willing the panic attack to pass.

"Andie, are you okay?"

Liam was standing there, holding my shoulders against the wall and trying to get my attention.

"Andie."

I shook my head. "I can't…fuck, this thing is too tight."

I ripped off my blazer.

"Focus on the game, Andie. Not the press. Not anything else."

I still couldn't catch my breath. My chest burned with the struggle.

"I just wanted to be a soccer player," I said, hearing the words through a distorted tunnel. "I've chased this dream my entire life and now everything is ruined."

He shushed me. "Trust me, Andie. It's not over. These situations always seem like they'll last forever, but the media will move on when they realize the story isn't half as interesting as they thought it was. Just get better, kick ass on the field, and make your success a bigger story. This will all be over before you know it."

He was lying because he wanted to make me feel better. He was scared that I couldn't breathe and he was saying anything to calm me down; I knew better though. Even after I'd dried my tears—for the tenth time that day—and pushed myself off that wall, I knew my life as I'd known it before Freddie was over. I would never again be Andie Foster, Cinderella of the Olympics.

I was now Andie with a scarlet A.

————

WATCHING MY TEAM take the field without me was absolute torture. I reclined on the bench and crossed my arms as my teammates prepared to compete. Erin, a seasoned vet, was taking my spot in the goal, but this would be her first cap in years. I'd earned the starting position from her because of my speed and agility, and though she'd served as my mentor, there was still an air of saltiness.

My removal from the game was our team's greatest weakness and Canada was going to try and exploit it. Coach Decker had run conservative defensive drills at the last few practices, but I still worried it wouldn't be enough.

If we lost this game, my rehabbing wouldn't be necessary; there'd be no championship game.

"This will be good for you," Coach Decker said, nodding to me before the officials started the game.

Good for me?

Nothing about that day was good for me.

An hour later, I leaned forward and gripped the edge of the bench. I was about to break off a chunk of the cold aluminum—either that or break my hand, whichever came first.

"Girls, pick it up!" our coach yelled from the sidelines.

Her shouts were tame compared to what I was screaming in my head. My team was playing like complete shit. After Michelle had missed three easy shots, Kinsley started trying to do too much by herself. Erin kept getting screened by her own defenders, and she'd let two goals sail past her in the first half. I knew she was trying her hardest, but it was clear that the chemistry and communication was completely off.

Early in the second half, we got our act together defensively and started increasing pressure on the other end. I scooted farther off the bench, watching Becca kick ass with her practiced footwork to turn opponents and penetrate Canada's side. Near the goal, she kicked it hard to Michelle, but missed the mark. The other team cleared the ball and effortlessly guided it back toward Erin. With no defenders left between her and the attacker, she charged forward and slid face first at the ball. I squeezed my eyes closed, but she'd miraculously made the save.

We were down 2-1 and if we didn't start picking up the pace, we'd be the first US Women's National Team to miss out on gold since 2000, and the first to ever miss out on a medal completely.

For the remainder of the game, I was in a constant

state of panic. I stood, sat, paced, pinched my eyes closed, even covered them with my hand in the final minutes of the game. My worrying had been in vain though. We won thanks to Kinsley's 11th hour heroics, which ended up being the only silver lining to an otherwise terrible day.

I trailed after my team as they headed off the field toward the idling bus. They were elated, high-fiving and clapping each other's shoulders. Kinsley and Becca had their arms wrapped around one another, and though I was happy for them, I couldn't shake the dark cloud hanging over my head.

The game had been entirely too close for comfort, but we'd pulled through and won by the skin of our teeth—well, *they* had won by the skin of *their* teeth. I had sat on the bench by the skin of my ass.

I couldn't conquer my bad mood. I wanted them to win, and yet when Erin had pulled through and blocked the last two goals, I'd felt useless. I was supposed to be an integral part of this team, and yet they'd shown they could win without me. I was working my ass off to rehab my injury for the championship game, but now there was a good chance they wouldn't even want me.

"Andie!" Kinsley shouted, waving for me to catch up to them.

I tucked my head and joined them, letting them fold me in their arms even though I would rather have hung back by myself.

"We're going to grab dinner. Want to come?"

I shook my head.

"You guys go on ahead. I've got a training session with Lisa."

I wanted to go home, fall into bed, and never wake up again, but I couldn't skip my training session. I dragged myself to the training center and changed into workout clothes. Lisa still hadn't arrived by the time I was ready to start, but I wasn't going to go out and look for her. I couldn't stand walking around the village any more than I had to; the stares and whispers were getting worse, and I could only ignore them for so long. Fortunately, the training center was all but empty. It was the thick of the Olympic games and most athletes were out competing or watching the events.

I pushed up onto the training table Lisa usually assigned me and dug around in my bag until I felt my phone. I'd purposely avoided looking at it all day, and as I powered it on, that decision was confirmed as a good one. I had thirty missed calls, fifteen voicemails, and forty-six text messages waiting for me.

"Fuck," I groaned under my breath, trying to triage the messages. I skipped over the texts from random high school friends wanting an inside scoop about the drama and opened an email from my agent.

I've hired a publicist to handle the media backlash. We won't lose sponsorships—this might even help you. We'll get this figured out. Good luck at the game. -Holly

I took a breath and scrolled down to open a message from my mom.

Mom: When Meemaw asked for a photo, she didn't mean *that* kind of photo. (Is it too soon to joke?) I'm sorry, sweetie. This will all pass. We love you. Call me.

There were dozens more from her, but I dropped my phone on the table behind me just as I caught sight of someone walking into the training center out of the corner of my eye.

I glanced up and my breath caught in my throat. Freddie stood in the middle of the doorway, frozen and staring at me. His chocolate-brown hair was damp and a few strands had fallen down across his forehead. His eyes were a dark mixture of shame and desire. I got the two mixed up as he stepped closer, tugging the headphones from around his neck and dropping them on top of his workout bag. He was in his swimming clothes, the warm-up outfit that made him look even more the part of the powerful Olympian.

He stopped when he was right in front of me, but I pulled my gaze away from his eyes and focused on the center of his broad chest. I felt safe there, staring at that red, white, and blue jacket covering up his powerful body.

"Andie, look at me."

I hadn't expected the tears. Jesus, I'd cried all day. Couldn't the world cut me a break at some point?

"Andie…"

He bent down to level his gaze with mine, and this time I didn't look away. I let him see it all; the horrors of the day were written across my face, plain to see.

"I can't do this, Freddie."

He shook his head and reached out for me, but thought better of it and tucked his hands back by his sides. His full bottom lip was between his teeth. He was trying to think of a solution, but there was no way to fix this.

"Jesus, she's probably watching us right now for all we know."

Just the thought sent a shiver down my spine.

He raked his hand through his damp hair and stood back to his full height. "She's not here. Only athletes are allowed to enter these facilities."

"I've already made the mistake of underestimating her. I'm not doing it again."

"I'm taking care of it, Andie. Just don't give up on me."

Too late.

"I was falling for you, Freddie, but I can't do this. It's not worth it. The stories paint you as a sexy playboy, juggling two girls and your Olympic dreams, but do you have any idea what I've been called today?"

He shook his head, wanting me to stop, but I didn't.

"Whore…slut…bitch." He inhaled a sharp breath listening to the words as they slipped off my tongue. "That's just page one. I've heard it all, and not just from the media. I can't walk out of my room without someone whispering behind my back."

"Stop, Andie."

Was it hard for him to stomach? Poor Freddie.

He reached forward to pull me off the table. I let him drag me out of the main training room and into a dim hallway before I stopped short and pulled out of his grasp.

"You know what, Freddie? I came to Rio to win gold, not hearts. You know best of all what the Olympic village is supposed to be like. I wanted to have fun and focus on soccer, but you pushed and you pushed and you pushed and I *let* you…" My gaze swept across his features, across the high cheekbones that had seduced me, across the jaw that had made my knees weak, across the eyes I'd assumed always told the truth. I could read him like an open book if only I stared into those dark eyes. I was breaking his heart.

He pushed open a door off the hallway and pulled me in after him. He flipped on the lights and I blinked as my eyes adjusted. He'd pulled me into a messy supply closet.

"I can't let you leave, Andie. Not now…"

I let out an exhausted laugh.

"I'm not giving you a choice."

Chapter Thirty-Seven

FREDDIE

I RAKED MY hands through my hair and spun around to look at Andie. The effects of the day were etched across her features. Her red, puffy eyes. Her splotchy cheeks and messy hair. She'd been through hell and back and now she was pulling away from me. Of course she was pulling away. She wanted her old life back, she wanted the stories and articles to disappear, but that wouldn't happen. Leaving me wouldn't make that happen.

I stepped forward and tilted her chin up. She resisted, the fire inside her not quite extinguished by the storm of the day. She'd been through so much. I could only imagine what her day had been like, but I wanted to make her feel better.

"Let me erase it all," I said, bending low and kissing the sensitive skin just below her ear.

She shivered against my hand.

"This won't change anything, Freddie."

"Let me try…"

Her eyes pinched close as I dipped down and trailed kisses along her neck. Her tank top was tight and I could see her nipples pebble beneath the surface. She didn't want anything from the day, but she wanted me.

"I won't let her take you from me."

She shook her head. She didn't believe me. All day the world had chipped away at her. My confident Andie was gone and in her place was a broken shell of a girl. I wanted to remind her what I saw when I looked at her. I needed her to remember that the gossip and the names didn't define her.

I gripped her arms in my hands and massaged them, loosening the clenched muscles. She was poised and taut after an entire day spent in fight-or-flight mode. I eased the tension out of her limbs. "These arms are so strong. They're so powerful. They're the arms of a woman who beat out hundreds—thousands to be where she is today."

She squeezed her eyes closed, but a tear slipped out then, trailing down her cheek. I brushed it away and kissed the spot where it had landed. I trailed my hands down her arms and bent down. She opened her eyes to watch me trail my finger up behind her Achilles tendon and around her calves.

"These legs belong to the most confident, beautiful woman I've ever met. Do you feel how strong they are? Do you remember how hard you've worked for these?"

She watched me worshipping her with her bottom lip tugged between her teeth.

"Do you, Andie?"

She nodded, hesitantly.

"These legs are so beautiful; I could worship them every day."

The edge of her mouth tipped up; I was getting to her. I stood and dragged my hand up over her chest and pressed down against her rapidly beating heart.

"This heart, Andie…"

She let go of her bottom lip and inhaled a shaky breath.

"I want this heart all for myself."

"Freddie…"

I didn't give her time to push me away. "This smile. This is what unwound me. I'm powerless when it comes to this smile."

I dragged my finger across her bottom lip. I could feel her breath against the pad of my finger and I wanted to kiss her. I wanted to steal that mouth and show her what she meant to me.

"You're confident and you're funny and they don't know that, Andie. You're more than what they see."

She leaned forward then, pushing her body against mine and wrapping her arms around my neck. I cradled her against me and whispered in her ear. "I promise you that, Andie. You're more than what they see."

She laughed. "Is that why we're kissing in a supply closet?"

I smiled and shook my head, slipping my hand into the waistband of her pants. "Just close your eyes."

She smiled sadly against my neck, easing her fingers into my hair. "I don't know what's going to happen with us Freddie."

I wanted to tell her everything would be easy from here on out, that we could be together and tell the world to piss off, but truthfully, I wasn't any surer than she was.

"Just give me this," I said, kissing her neck. "This is all we need."

It was a lie. Secret sex in a broom closet wouldn't sustain us for long. Andie deserved so much more, but it was the only thing I could give her that wouldn't make things worse. I could make her happy for that one moment. I could drag her out of the terrible day and make her remember why the fight was worth it.

My hands were everywhere, feeling her smooth stomach beneath her tank top and sliding up higher to palm her breast. I needed her more than I needed my next race. The water was soothing, but Andie lit me on fire. Her touch on my arms was enough to send me over the edge.

"Kiss me," she begged.

I crashed my mouth against hers and hauled her up against my body. I picked her up and she wound her legs around my waist. I wanted to take my time and make love to her on soft sheets, but there was no bed and no time.

I nibbled on her bottom lip until she opened for me. My tongue slipped past her lips and she moaned against me, sending vibrations down my throat. Her hand found its way down the front of my pants, so soft and warm I had to stifle a heady growl.

"I need you."

"*I need you*," she repeated as her hand stroked me up and down.

I cradled her neck in my hands and dragged my finger across the center of her thighs. "I want you to come first. I want you to feel how good it can be with us."

Her fingers dug into the back of my neck, mimicking my movements. I spun my finger in a slow circle, working her up, and she circled her finger around the back of my neck, showing me what she wanted. She didn't tell me she was about to fall; I could *feel* her falling. Her body shook against mine and I watched her unravel, fixated on her delicate features and the sensual way she came apart around me.

"Again," she begged.

Eventually we slid down onto the floor. I laid back on the

cold concrete and Andie straddled my hips. A single light bulb swayed back and forth overheard, casting Andie in bright light one second and then dipping her into the shadow the next. I gripped her hips and pulled her down onto me. Her mouth opened, but no sound came out. I thought I was hurting her, but she gripped my chest and moved up and down, taking our pleasure into her own hands.

I watched her roll her hips as she glided herself onto me. Up and down she went as I gripped her tiny waist.

"Fuck, Andie…"

Her breasts bounced while she rode me. I wanted to taste them, but she fell forward and dropped her mouth to my neck with whispered moans. Her nipples rubbed against my chest; her soft cries told me how much it was turning her on. Her hands clawed at me as I wrapped my arms around her. I held Andie there, and her hips pressed down on me as I pumped into her harder and faster.

There were no promises made in that dark closet, but everything we felt for each other was spelled out as clear as day. She lifted her head so she could stare down into my eyes. Her gaze flitted back and forth, trying to find something hidden beneath them.

That was when I realized the only promise I could make was to myself.

I would protect Andie no matter what.

Chapter Thirty-Eight

FREDDIE

"**FRED, SHOULDN'T YOU** be at your race?" my lawyer asked as soon as the call connected.

"I'm headed to the stadium now."

"Jesus."

"Listen, Dave, I need you to start looking into this situation with Caroline. I need to try and get a handle—"

"Fred, you're in the middle of the Olympics."

"And Caroline is doing everything she can to ruin my life."

"You've cut off communication with her, right?"

"I haven't spoken to her since two nights ago, at the bar."

"What about Andie? I've advised you to—"

"I'm not going to cut off communication with Andie."

The night before, hours after the broom closet, I'd called her. I'd assumed she'd ignore it, but when the call clicked on and her voice filled my ears, I was filled with hope once again. We couldn't talk long. She had an early morning practice and I had a race first thing.

"I know I've already promised you a hundred times, but I will figure this out."

She didn't reply.

"Do you trust me, Andie?"

"Of course, but I don't know what you want me to say."

"Tell me you aren't going to give up on us. Tell me this afternoon meant as much to you as it meant to me."

"Everyone is telling me to stay away from you."

"And is that what you want to do?"

She sighed. "I should! Any sane person would have given up days ago. I've only known you for a little while, Freddie. This is crazy, what we're trying to pull off."

I didn't have a counter for that, because it was the truth. A sane person would walk away.

"Tell me something good, Andie. Tell me something about your day that doesn't include this shit."

She laughed. "Lisa gave me a hard time for being late to my training session."

I smiled. "Did she realize you were in the closet?"

"No."

Even the silence was soothing.

"I'm going to try and play in the final in four days," she continued. "Lisa's helping me get my wrist ready."

My brows shot up. "I thought you said the doctor—"

"I'm not going to listen to him."

I smiled. "You're different than any woman I've ever met."

I could practically hear her smile as she spoke. "Don't you forget it."

Dave sighed on the phone, bringing me back to the topic at hand. "You only have a few days left before the games are wrapped up. I'll get my team on Caroline, and in the meantime, I need you to keep your head focused on swimming—if not for your sake, for Andie's."

Chapter Thirty-Nine

ANDIE

"**A** NDIE, SIT OUT for these next couple of drills."

"But I can—"

My coach shot me a glare. "Not a request."

I balled my hands and ignored the pain in my wrist as I headed for the bench. It was three days until the final game and Coach Decker was still treating me like I was made of glass. She'd forced me to sit out of warm-ups, so instead I'd jogged around the field, sending defiant glares her way with every lap I completed. Since then, she'd excused me from nearly every other drill. My legs would fall off if I ran another lap, so I had nothing left to do but sit on the bench like a loser.

"Line up ladies!" she shouted, directing everyone's attention back to practice.

I turned away and popped the top off my water bottle with more force than necessary.

I'd already done double my usual cardio and there was another hour left of practice.

"Andie, just rest."

I resisted the urge to flip her off and tossed my water

bottle on the ground. Times of rest had become my most agonizing, because the burn I felt while being active helped take my mind off the crush of the world. Coach Decker was either coldhearted or genuinely oblivious to how painful it was to attend practices for a team I was no longer a part of.

———

TWO HOURS LATER, I dragged myself back to my condo, more frustrated than ever. I wished I could have called Freddie to tell him about my day, but he was at his races, probably winning races and breaking records. I'd seen on the news that he already had two gold medals to his name. *What a life*. Instead, I settled on a phone call with my mom.

The phone rang twice before she answered and went straight into her sentence. With her, the phone calls never really started. In her mind, we were talking all day, every day.

"Andie, Meemaw is just beside herself. The ladies at the bridge club are talking about kicking her out of the group."

"Well, we're all suffering."

"You and Freddie are the talk of the world. I thought it would settle down after that ping pong player got caught doping, but you guys are still the bigger story."

"Well I have that Sports Illustrated party tonight. I'll try and calm things down a bit."

She sighed heavily. "Are you sure it's a good idea to go to that thing? It seems like you'll only add fuel to the fire."

"The PR team said in the mind's eye, you're only as guilty as you act in public. So if I hide out for too long, people will assume I have reason to."

"Well you need to be careful."

If even one more person told me to be careful, focus on soccer, or stay away from Freddie, I'd rip my hair out. Fortunately, a musical knocking sounded on my bedroom door before I could tell her that.

"All right, I've got to go now, Mom." I opened my bedroom door, surprised to find Georgie in the living room. She was wearing short denim cutoffs and a loose tank top. She'd pushed her sunglasses onto her head to keep her long brown hair out of her face, and resting in her arms were two cartons of takeout, the smell of which immediately made my mouth water.

"Sweetie, I'm not done. I was going to—"

"I'll talk to you later."

"Promise me you'll focus on soccer, and if you are with Freddie, be sure to practice safe—"

Oh, Jesus.

I hung up on her and eyed Georgie tentatively.

"I come with gifts," she said, holding up the takeout. "First, some Chinese food, as interpreted by Brazil. There was a language barrier, so I'm not sure what I've ordered. Fortunately, I've also nabbed a bottle of wine to help us wash it down."

I laughed. "Oh boy…"

Before I even invited her in, she stepped inside my room and kicked the door closed with her foot. I had half a mind to turn her away—I didn't really feel up to company —but she'd already taken up residence on my floor and pulled open one of the cartons. Salty, spicy goodness wafted around my room and I knew there was no way I'd be asking her to leave. I was starving. I hadn't had lunch yet and I was avoiding the food court at all costs. I'd planned on begging food from Kinsley or Becca, but this was much more convenient.

"How'd you get in my condo?" I asked as I took a seat across from her on the floor.

She was already sitting cross-legged and tearing into one of the cartons with chopsticks. She had noodles sticking out of her mouth when she titled her head toward the living room.

"Through the door," she said in a tone devoid of sarcasm.

I made a mental note to berate my roommates for leaving the doors unlocked.

"Here, eat up," she said, passing me one of the takeout cartons. "It looks like chicken fried rice, but I can't be sure. Anyway, are you…all right?"

I shrugged.

"Freddie told me Caroline gave that photo to the press. That's part of why I'm here; he wants to make sure you're doing okay."

I kept my gaze on my rice. Georgie had called Caroline all sorts of names when I'd first met her, but I had no clue if she was genuinely friends with her or not. I called Kinsley and Becca names all the time, but they were the closest thing I had to sisters; maybe that was how she felt about Caroline.

"Just so you know," she continued after I didn't offer up a response. "Excluding the fact that it's my brother, I thought that photo was very sexy. Everyone on the internet is obsessed with you now."

I narrowed my eyes. "Obsessed with their hatred of me."

She laughed. "Some of them, but when you start to dig into the blogs and hashtags, you'll find that there's a quiet contingent that's quite besotted with you."

I shook my head. "Well, no more photo talk, seriously."

It'd only been one day since the story broke and I still

didn't have a real grip on my emotions. I'd crashed early the night before and slept in as late as I could. Having a solid eight hours seemed to help, but my eyes were still puffy and the story still wasn't anywhere close to being my favorite topic of conversation.

"Freddie mentioned that Sports Illustrated party is tonight. Do you have to go?"

I frowned. "Sadly."

She nodded. "Caroline is going too. She told me about it at breakfast."

I paused with my chopsticks midway to my mouth. "You had breakfast with her?"

"Yes." She laughed. "Have you forgotten that she was commissioned by my mother to be my chaperone while I'm here? We're staying in one big suite at the hotel and everything."

My eyes widened. "Lock your door at night."

The jab slipped out before I could stop it, but when I glanced up to Georgie, she didn't look offended. She was smiling.

"Don't worry, I have been. I always knew Caroline was a bore, and the fact that she's bonkers isn't that surprising. It actually came as somewhat of a relief to know that there is something going on in that alarmingly sized skull of hers, even if it is just plotting and scheming."

"You two weren't friends in London?"

Georgie's eyes nearly fell out of her skull. "I'd rather cut my right arm off than loll around with Caroline. Her idea of a fun Friday night is reorganizing her closet and then sipping on a bit of bubbly while she watches her laundry spin."

I laughed. God, it felt good to laugh again, especially when my new archenemy was the butt of the joke.

"I'm actually sort of glad we're sharing the suite though because now I can keep better watch over her."

I nodded. "Good point."

"For instance, I know she'll be wearing a killer dress to the event tonight."

My glaze flitted over to the two dresses hanging up on my closet door. Sometime during practice, a designer had dropped off dresses for Kinsley, Becca, and me to wear to the party later. It was a glamorous affair, and something I had been looking forward to before C-Day 2K16. (i.e. the day Caroline released the story to the press. Also, to be clear, the C stands for Caroline, not for the other "c" word, though it would be fitting in this instance…)

"Are those your options?" Georgie asked, pointing to the garment bags. I nodded. One was a white dress with simple beading and an A-line fit. The other was black and short, with a strapless bodice and a loose skirt that hugged my hips when I moved.

"What color is she wearing?" I asked.

"Pale pink." She feigned a gag. "The woman has the whole 'innocent virgin' act down pat. I swear."

I narrowed my eyes. "Looks like I'm wearing black then." My PR team wanted me to dress conservatively and the white dress was a better option, but there was power in the color black. Caroline wanted me to cower and hide, but I wasn't ready to run just yet.

Georgie clapped her hands together and then reached forward to yank the Chinese food carton out of my hand.

"Hey! I was eating that."

She shook her head. "Nope. No more Chinese. If you're going to that event with Caroline, you're going to look bloody hot."

I wanted to remind her that I worked out multiple times a day, that I could eat anything I wanted while I was training, but she was already pushing to stand up off the floor.

She eyed my appearance. "A little makeup and a bit of hairspray will be good for you...maybe a good scrub as well."

She scrunched her nose.

"What? I was training," I said, brushing stray hairs away from my face.

"Guess it doesn't matter anyway." She shrugged. "My brother fancies you, sweat and all."

My chest tightened at the mention of Freddie. "Right," I said, glancing away.

I didn't want to talk about Freddie. I didn't want to consider how handsome and sweet he was. Until he got things settled with Caroline, there was no point in daydreaming about him. Unfortunately, it seemed like there was no forgetting Freddie—especially not when I had his sister sitting across from me, shooting me a smug smile.

"He's been a mess the last two days, trying to focus on swimming as much as possible. Caroline has tried to get in touch with him nonstop, but he's been ignoring her calls. She moaned on and on about it during breakfast."

"Does she realize you know she's crazy?"

Georgie shook her head. "I'm keeping up appearances. Y'know, the whole 'friends close, but enemies closer' thing."

"Good." I dropped my bag on the table. "I'm getting in the shower."

"Fine, I'll go down and get us something less bloating to eat."

I waved over my shoulder.

"Don't forget to moisturize! I'll help with that rat's nest on your head when I get back! We don't have any time to waste."

"Georgie, it's only 2:00 PM. The event isn't until 6:00."

She sighed, exasperated with me already. "Exactly! We're already running behind."

I was still in the shower when she got back, but she didn't let that stop her. She sat on the other side of the curtain and talked to me about the event.

"Good news," she said while typing on her phone's keypad. "Fred just asked if I'd attend the party with him tonight. He said it'd be fun for me, but I think he's just hoping to put a buffer between him and Caroline."

I worked the conditioner through my hair. "Good, I'm glad I'll have an ally."

"I didn't bring a dress, though."

"You can wear the white one hanging on the door."

She laughed. "Good, someone should look more angelic than Caroline. She'll hate that."

Chapter Forty

FREDDIE

A **BLACK TOWNCAR** pulled up in front of the complex and I held the door open so Georgie could slide into the back seat. We were running behind for the Sports Illustrated party—the medal ceremony and interview after my last race had run over on time—and Georgie was anxious to get there.

"Come on, Fred," she said as I bent down and slid into the car after her. "We've got to hurry or we won't arrive before Andie."

She was checking her phone, probably texting Andie that very minute. I wanted to lean over and add my own message, but I held off and glanced up at Georgie instead. She looked so much older than when I'd left her in London a few weeks earlier. In her white dress and heels, it was almost easy to forget that she'd once been my snot-nosed little sister. I could still recall her running after my mates, trying to land a solid punch or kiss. (More often than not, it was the former.) She was always such a confident bugger growing up, and it hadn't dimmed with age. Even now, no one could stand in her way if she set her mind on something.

"You look pretty, Georgie."

She waved me away and kept texting.

I laughed and glanced out the window. "How did Andie seem when you left her?"

Georgie had texted me to let me know she was getting ready with Andie. The fact that the two of them had become friends definitely made my life easier. I was in the middle of my races and away from my phone most of the day.

"What?" Georgie asked, sliding her pale green eyes to me. "Do you mean to ask if she was moaning on about how much she missed you and all that?"

I smiled. "A little bit of moaning never hurt anybody."

"Well that's too bad. She went on about a dozen or so footballers she'd like to romp around with."

"Georgie…"

She groaned. "Fine. Actually, she's smitten, though God knows why. She's much prettier than you and could have any bloke she fancied, with half the trouble."

"Have you ever thought maybe she finds me good-looking and worth the trouble?"

She narrowed her eyes on me as if trying to assess me in a new light, then shook her head. "No, that's not it. She must really like the accent. Or maybe it's the gold medals."

"Thanks for the vote of confidence, G."

She reached out and touched my hand. "In all honesty, I really like Andie. She's funny and beautiful, and you and her really appear to be meant for one another."

Flashing cameras drew my attention away from Georgie before I could agree. The driver had pulled up in front of the event space and suddenly I found myself faced with another red carpet. The Olympics were trying enough—what with fifteen races (heats, semifinals, and finals) taking place over six days—without all the extracurricular events they piled onto us night after night. At the end of it all, more than wanting to party and celebrate, I knew I'd crave a decent weekend back in my flat in London: no press, no cameras, no intrusive questions. Just time alone with Andie.

The driver opened the back door and I stepped out then reached back to lend Georgie my arm. They'd started shouting my name the moment our car had pulled up, but with Georgie in tow, the frenzy kicked up another notch.

"Georgie who are you wearing?!"

"Who designed those shoes?"

I pushed her ahead of me on the carpet, letting her taste the limelight for a little while. At home, the press couldn't get enough of Georgie. She was the youngest member of the Archibald family, and after the deaths of our father and Henry, the press were keen to see Georgie unravel into the emotional wild child. She did generally assume rules didn't apply to her, but she had a better head on her shoulders than most adults.

"I'm proud of you, Georgie," I said, leaning in and giving her a tight hug.

For once I was glad the cameras were firing. I'd have appreciated a copy of that photo, if only because Georgie wasn't a fan of public displays of affection and there was a fifty percent chance she'd pulled a sour face as soon as I hugged her.

"What an adorable family reunion."

I released Georgie and turned to find Caroline standing a few feet away, dressed as if she'd just stepped off the top of a frilly cupcake. Her light pink dress looked like something a year one student would wear to a dance recital. To solidify the look, she'd added on a delicate pearl necklace.

"Caroline!" the cameraman called.

She turned to pose for photos and I used the opportunity to push Georgie toward the end of the red carpet. There was a group of reporters hovering near the entrance, and though I wished I could ignored them, one of them shouted out a question about the betrothal that I couldn't ignore.

"Did she forgive you, Freddie? Are you still set to marry Caroline?"

I motioned for Georgie to continue on inside and then I turned toward the cameras. If I wanted to shut Caroline down, this was the simplest way. Live television couldn't lie.

"Freddie! Could you tell us any details about the wedding?"

"There will not be a wed—"

I felt a hand hit my lower back as Caroline swooped in to interrupt me.

She coughed, a light airy ahem that made my stomach churn. "We're still working through this challenging time, and we would appreciate it if you would respect our privacy."

"Are you two engaged?" they asked anyway.

"No," I answered.

Cameras fired.

"Is the wedding off because of the cheating scandal!?"

She laughed again and shook her head. "If you'll excuse me, I really must speak with my fiancé."

"There is no wedding," I continued, staring straight into one of the cameras so my words couldn't be misconstrued. "There is no betro—"

"Freddie!" Caroline shrieked, suddenly on the brink of tears. "Please don't do this."

Her hand was pressed to her stomach as if she were about to be sick, and then there were actual tears slipping down her cheeks.

I reached back and gripped her arm to drag her off the carpet. There would be no honest interviews as long as she was present. I pulled her into the party and bypassed the coat check and the cocktails. I found the first quiet corner and turned to lay into her.

"I'm not playing this game, Caroline."

She laughed, all signs of tears and sickness completely gone. I knew it'd been an act, but it was still jarring to see how quickly she could change characters. Truly, I'd have nominated her for an Oscar had she not been attempting to ruin my life.

"Do you hear me, Caroline? This isn't a game."

"I know, Frederick. Games have multiple outcomes, but the sport we're playing only has one."

She was pulling something out of her purse then, a small, square piece of paper. It took me a fraction of a second to realize what it was. A fraction of a second was all it took for my life to come screeching to a halt before my eyes. A fraction of a second was all it took…

"I was hoping to surprise you under more positive circumstances, but after your little outburst, I suppose tonight will do." She held the square photo up against her stomach for me to see. "Meet your future child, Freddie."

———

I HELD THE sonogram in my hand, stunned. "But how…"

She laughed. "When two people have unprotected intercourse, Frederick, sometimes——"

"Shut up. Just shut up."

I couldn't stand her mocking me.

"What a way to speak to the mother of your child."

"I'm going to be sick."

"Do try not to get anything on your suit. I'd like to get a few photos of the two of us dressed up. They'll need a proper photo to run with the pregnancy news."

My body was shaking with an angry, uncontrollable current. "I won't let you do this to me."

She smiled. "Oh yes you will Frederick. You know why? Because you love that little American whore, and you wouldn't want to make things worse for her."

I nearly slapped her then. My hand stopped within an inch of her cheek before I remembered we were in the middle of a party.

She tutted. "Striking a pregnant woman?" She brushed my hand away. "Really, Frederick? Don't make this harder for yourself than it has to be."

"I won't ever love you."

She laughed. "I don't want your *love*. I just want to be Her Grace, the Duchess of Farlington."

Her words hardly surprised me any more. "I'm getting a paternity test."

"Wise." She smiled before leaning forward and grabbing hold of my tie. "I assure you though, my dear fiancé, you are the father of this baby."

The color drained from my face. If this was true and Caroline was pregnant with my child, I had no one to blame but myself. I always used protection, but that last night I'd seen Caroline before Rio was fuzzy. We'd been at my friend's flat together. I'd spotted her across the room and once I'd stumbled over, she'd gotten me a glass of water and sat me down. Sometime after that, I'd invited her back to my flat so we could have a chat. I wanted to get to know the woman I was supposed to marry. I wanted to know if she was funny or dull, shy or confident.

I had thought she'd turn me down, but she'd come willingly. She'd taken a seat on my couch and unbuttoned her shirt all on her own. I remembered grappling with my equilibrium as I watched her undress. The details were so muddled; I wasn't sure who made the first move, but I did remember fucking her there, too drunk to register the gravity of the situation.

She was gone in the morning, but she'd left a note beneath a pastry on my kitchen counter.

Perhaps this doesn't have to be so bad… - C

I saw red. Caroline stared up at me with her big, round eyes. I wanted to kill her then. I could have killed her. The supposed mother of my child. She was evil incarnate and I wanted her out of my life once and for all. I reached down and squeezed the hand she had clamped around my tie. Her brows furrowed and her delicate features contorted in pain.

"That hurts, Frederick."

Her voice was smaller then, lighter and panicked. It felt good to remind her how quickly the tables could turn. She could plot her moves and weasel her way into my life, but there was no denying how easy it would be take back control. One hand around her neck and Caroline would be gone.

"Frederick, you're scaring me."

I squeezed tighter. I wanted to break her like she was breaking me. "Even if you have this child, I'm going to stay with Andie. I will never marry you, Caroline."

Her eyes narrowed.

"We'll share custody and communicate through solicitors, nothing more," I continued.

"No, Frederick, once again you're too slow," she said,

scraping her nails against my hand until I finally released her. She took two steps back and slid the sonogram into her purse. "You'll realize soon enough that you have no choice but to marry me and make me your wife."

Her sly smile was enough to do me in.

I raked my hands through my hair. "How could you be so bloody delusional?"

"Because if you think the world hates your precious Andie for being the object of your disloyal desires for one night, just think how much they'll despise her once they hear she's conspiring to break up a *family*."

"No." I shook my head.

She sent a smile to a wandering party guest then glanced back at me. "If you don't stop, I won't stop. Not until you've lost everything, Frederick." She leaned forward and tipped her heels to kiss my cheek. "The sooner you realize that, the better."

She slipped back into the party and I stood rooted to my spot in the corner. The entire world continued on around me, but I stood there with numb senses. Waiters passed with trays of drinks and food. Party guests stepped around me. Laughter and chatter and music and life continued on, but I stared at a singular spot on the wall. The sound of my rapidly beating heart was enough to fill my ears. I didn't hear Georgie when she stepped up beside me and jostled my arm. I watched her lips move, but I was a world away.

Was I truly about to become a father?

Had Caroline manipulated my life so easily that there was no way out?

I blinked and Georgie was there, trying to gain my attention. I blinked again and she was gone.

Eventually, I moved. I turned for the doors of the party and walked toward them in a daze. Someone reached out to grab my arm and ask me a question, but I jerked away from them and continued on without so much as a second glance. People were flooding through the doors, smiling and laughing. How could everyone else be so happy? Couldn't they see what was happening? Couldn't they see?

"Freddie."

Andie's voice was the first thing to break through the static. Her fingers wove through mine as she pulled me aside. I'd nearly stepped out of the party, but she was there, pulling me toward her, pulling me out of the fog.

"I have to go," I said, staring at her lips. They were always an irresistible shade of pink, plump and beautiful. I'd miss her lips.

"No," she said, shaking her head and trying to catch my eye. I wouldn't let her leave me. "The party just started. Stay. I need to see you. *Stay.*"

She was magnificent in that black dress, small, and subtle, and real. I reached out to run my finger along her collarbone, feeling her inhale a sharp breath. I'd miss that skin, just above her breasts. She was extra sensitive there and I knew if I leaned down and pressed my mouth against her, she'd crumble in my arms.

"I'm leaving," I said, my voice nearly unrecognizable.

Her hand squeezed around mine, trying to force me to stay. It wasn't the same as Caroline's touch. When Caroline grabbed my tie, it was with a vengeance. Andie touched with love and need and passion. I'd miss her touch.

"Caroline is pregnant."

Her hand slipped away from mine.

One second she was there, begging me to stay, and the next she was stepping back and shaking her head, already losing sight of us. I'd taken her into that broom closet and I'd tried to show her how good we could be together. This was too much though, even for my Andie.

"What do you mean?" Her voice was shaking.

She was crying and I was stepping back, giving her the space Caroline demanded.

"She's pregnant."

I leaned forward to wipe the tears from her cheeks, but she turned her head away before I could.

"Don't."

I'd never had my heart broken by a single word before.

She spun around and walked away from me then. I wanted to shout out after her.

Don't go.

Don't leave me.

Don't end this.

She was already gone though, weaving through the party as fast as she could. She was putting as much distance between us as possible, building on *don't* until it wasn't just a word, it was a wall.

Chapter Forty-One

FREDDIE

I LEANED FORWARD in the elevator and punched the number for Andie's floor before I could change my mind. The Sports Illustrated party had ended a few hours before, but I'd left early and taken a cab around Rio. I'd been in the city for weeks and had yet to see anything beyond the village and the pool. The city was alive in a way I hadn't realized before. The streets were warm and colorful and loud. Music streamed out of the bars and restaurants we passed, setting a backdrop for the drive. I watched as friends and couples fell out of bars, laughing and hanging on one another. Everyone was out on the town, partying and inhaling life in a way I never had before. I found myself wishing I could be one of the people on the streets, a normal bloke with a pint in his hand, without a worry in the world.

I told the cabbie to keep driving until we'd wound through what felt like most of the city's streets. By the time we made it back to the village, I could finally breathe again. It'd been nearly three hours since Andie had walked away from me and I already missed her.

I leaned forward and punched the number for her floor again, willing the elevator to speed up.

I'd had time to think, and now I needed to see her.

The hallway leading to her door was quiet enough that as I knocked, I could hear voices murmuring inside.

I couldn't help but smile a little as Becca whipped the door open and tilted her head, confused.

"Freddie? What are you doing here?"

"Is Andie here?" I asked tentatively. I wasn't sure if Andie had already told her the pregnancy news or not; I had half a mind to cover my face in case a punch was coming my way.

"Is that Andie?" Kinsley shouted from the living room. "Tell her that I'm mad at her for disappearing at the party!"

Becca rolled her eyes. "No! It's Freddie!"

"Oh! HI FREDDIE!"

I tugged my hands through my hair. "Becca, is Andie in there?"

She frowned and glanced back to Andie's open bedroom door. "No. Didn't she tell you? She's hanging out with Georgie. I'm not sure when they'll be back."

Ah. That explained the aggressive text messages I'd been receiving from Georgie for the last two hours.

Georgie: You've royally screwed up this time. I mean honestly, Fred, what were you thinking?!

Georgie: I'll strangle you myself if you got that mad cow pregnant. She's bonkers and her spawn will be bonkers too.

Georgie: Oh my god. She's probably going to call it Paprika, or Apple, or god forbid—Caroline Jr.

Georgie: I will not have a niece called CAROLINE JR!

"Right." I fisted my hands to keep from dragging them through my hair for the hundredth time. "Could you tell her I stopped by when she gets home?"

I could see the pity in her eyes as she nodded. She felt sorry for me, the bloke chasing after Andie. It was an unfamiliar sensation to lose the chase, and as I walked back to the elevator bank, defeated, I wondered if maybe I'd never had Andie at all.

"Freddie!"

I turned back to see Becca running down the hall after me. She gripped my arm once she'd reached me and her gaze flitted back and forth between my eyes.

"You aren't just toying with her, are you? Andie?"

I frowned.

"The last few days have been hell for her. She's been so stressed about her wrist. She's got that doctor's appointment tomorrow; did she tell you?" I shook my head and she continued. "Yeah. They're going to do a full MRI, and then she's got to hope they clear her for the final game. And that's not even half of it, Freddie. She can hardly leave our condo without people trying to take her picture or call her names. Even the girls on our team have turned on her the past few days." I winced and she gripped my arm tighter. "I'm not blaming you, and I'm not even telling you to back off or anything. I just want to know. I want you to look me in the eye and tell me you aren't subjecting her to slings and arrows for sport."

She was staring up at me with such earnest desperation that three little words slipped out before I'd even fully thought them over.

"I love her."

Her mouth dropped open. She shook her head and stuttered, "Y-you what?"

I sighed. "Becca, I love her. Tell her I stopped by, will you. Please?"

"Of course."

I nodded and turned away.

"If it matters, Freddie," she called out behind me. "I'm rooting for you two."

Chapter Forty-Two

ANDIE

"**A**NDIE, THERE'S NO shame in coming home to take care of yourself. Your dad and I have been making calls, and we've found the best orthopedic wrist specialist in the country—Dr. Weinberg. He worked with both of the Williams sisters!"

"I'll think about it, Mom."

I knew it'd been a mistake to answer her call while I waited for the doctor to see me. I'd done it on purpose, assuming she'd be a good distraction from thoughts of Freddie, but now I wasn't sure which I preferred: listening to my mom tell me to give up or losing myself in thoughts about a pregnant Caroline.

"You can fly home and Dad and I can pick you up from the airport. You can watch the final game here, with us."

She was basically describing my worst nightmare, and she didn't even realize it.

"Mom. I'm staying in Rio. I'm going to play in the final."

"I don't think that's a smart idea, sweetie."

I was angry at her dismissiveness, but I figured it was out of ignorance, not condescension. She'd never played soccer at an Olympic level. She thought she knew how hard I'd worked to get to where I was, but she wasn't inside my body. Every late night practice, every extra mile, every extra rep, every single drop of sweat and blood my body had given would all be for nothing if I left Rio without playing in the final. Soccer took so much out of me. Sprains, bruises, strains— there wasn't a part of my body soccer had left untouched.

"Mom, the doctor is coming in. I have to go."

It was a lie, but it got her off the phone. She made me promise to call her after the appointment wrapped up, but I knew I wouldn't.

"Ms. Foster."

A soft knock sounded on the door behind me and I turned to look over my shoulder as the doctor strolled in. He had my chart tucked under his arm; inside it, he had my MRI scans and injury reports—everything he needed to stamp out my dreams for good.

"How are you?" he asked, glancing at me over the top of his black-framed glasses after he'd taken a seat in his leather chair.

I cradled my wrist in my lap and nodded. "It feels fine."

"I meant how are *you*, overall. Your team played quite well in their last game," he noted.

During our last appointment, he hadn't bothered with small talk. Why was he doing it this time?

I shrugged. "I'm fine. And it wasn't pretty, but a win is a win."

He nodded. "Right. Well, Lisa has updated me on your physical therapy and I've taken a look at today's imaging."

He motioned to my wrist. "Let's do a quick exam and then we can continue talking."

I'd prepared myself for this moment. I knew he'd do the same exercises he'd done during the first exam and I'd trained myself to mask every single emotion. When he pressed on my wrist and asked if it hurt, I shook my head. "No."

"What about now?" he asked, gently rotating my wrist in a circle.

It wasn't necessarily a lie when I told him it didn't hurt. A week earlier, the same motion would have inspired every curse word known to man. Now, it was nothing more than a dull ache—completely manageable in my opinion.

"You understand that this appointment was set up so that I could clear you for the final in two days?"

I nodded.

"I don't think the sprain has fully healed. You've told me it feels better, but the body doesn't lie." He pointed to my two wrists lying flat on his desk. "You can still see the swelling surrounding your wrist. It's gone down, but it's clear you're still healing from the injury."

I pulled my hands off the table tucked them beneath the desk. "So what are you saying?"

"I can't clear you for the game." He tugged off his glasses and massaged his nose like he was the one in pain.

"Are you kidding?"

"Lisa has said you've improved—"

"More than improved. My wrist is fine. The swelling is from the exercises, not the injury."

His mouth pulled into a tight, grim line. "I'm sorry, Ms. Foster, but your coach will want to know my opinion and I'll have to tell her my conclusion, based on the evidence."

I jerked up from my chair and the metal feet scraped

against the floor. "Is anything broken?"

He sat back in shock. "Well, no—"

"Then that's all you need to report. Whether or not I play isn't your call."

He furrowed his brows, and I swallowed, hoping I was getting through to him.

"I know my body better than anyone. I know how far I can push myself, so please don't make this decision for me. Just tell her that the MRI confirmed no broken bones, and that you've noticed improvement. That's all I'm asking."

I stood and walked out of his office before he could make a decision. I needed him to think on it, to consider what he was doing to my career if he didn't clear me for the game. I hadn't asked him to lie; I wanted him to relay the facts. I could fill in the rest myself.

"How'd it go?"

I turned to see Lisa posted against the wall outside the doctor's office.

"Not great," I said, shaking my head.

"Did he say whether or not he was going to clear you?"

"I left before he could."

She smirked. "Right. Well, let's get to work."

I followed her over to our training table and hopped up to sit on the edge.

"We won't train for too long this morning," she said, reaching out to grab hold of my wrist. "I'm going to wrap your wrist in ice at the end and see if we can't get some of that inflammation to go down."

I stared down at my wrist as she worked it in her hands. I took a deep breath, surprised to find tears clouding the corner of my eyes. My chest tightened and I could hardly swallow. Everything was getting to be too much. Deep down, I had convinced myself that the media scandal, the situation with Freddie, the faith of my teammates—they would all resolve themselves if only I could get back on the field. But with one phone call to my coach, the doctor could end that hope.

"Andie?" Lisa ducked to stare up at my downcast eyes. "Andie. What's wrong?"

I shook my head and tried to escape her questioning. "It's nothing."

But it was too late; the floodgates had opened and there was no stopping the tears from slipping down my cheeks. I was tired, so fucking tired of fighting a losing battle. My body ached, my heart ached, my wrist ached, and no one seemed to believe I had any fight left in me. Maybe they were right.

"Andie." Lisa ran a hand up and down my back, trying to soothe me. "It's okay. It's been a tough time."

Her words only made me cry harder. She reached out to wrap me in her arms. I leaned forward and dropped my head on her shoulders, giving in to the feeling of defeat. It was all too much for one person to handle. Freddie's announcement the night before had broken whatever resolve I had left. Caroline was pregnant with his baby and there was nothing I could do. I had no problem stepping between Freddie and a woman he didn't love, but I wouldn't step between him and his unborn child. Caroline was the vilest woman I'd ever met, but Freddie couldn't abandon his child. Even if he wanted to be with me, I wasn't sure I wanted to oppose Caroline for the rest of my life.

I had nothing left but soccer and I was not giving up. The final was in two days. I was going to take the field with my team whether the doctor cleared me or not. I inhaled a deep breath, sat up, and forcefully wiped away my tears.

"Let's get on with it already," I said, holding out my wrist for Lisa to take. "I'm playing in that final."

Chapter Forty-Three

FREDDIE

I TOOK THE last seat on my team's bus and put my headphones in before anyone could ask about my foul mood. It's been two days since I'd seen or spoken to Andie at the SI party and she'd been ignoring my calls and texts. I would have gladly cut my right arm off just to receive something from her—a text, a smoke signal, a carrier pigeon. Georgie insisted that I needed to give her space and focus on my races, and she was right; I knew the farther away I stayed from Andie, the safer she'd be.

It wasn't easy though; I could still remember the feel of her pressed against me, the sound she made when I kissed the inside of her thighs. She'd walked away from me at the party and life had gone on. I'd competed in two races the day before and I was on my way to more. I knew I needed to focus on swimming, but I wasn't interested in life continuing on without Andie. The gold medals weren't going to be enough.

A hand hit my shoulder, drawing me out of my thoughts. I paused my music and glanced up to see Thom looming over me.

"Ready mate?" he asked with an amused smile.

We were at the stadium and the bus had completely emptied out without me noticing. I was the only one still on it, sitting up front like a fool. Thom nudged my shoulder and I stood up to follow after him. I hadn't prepared myself for the barrage of cameras waiting for me outside. I held my hand up to block the flashes, but it was no use. By the time I stepped into the locker room, bright circles danced in my vision.

"Archibald, your race is first. Clear your thick head, or else you're liable to sink," Coach Cox said playfully, pounding his fist against my shoulder as he passed. I bit back a slew of curse words.

"No one asked for your advice," I spat, rolling out my shoulder.

He spun around to face me. "Excuse me?"

Thom stepped between us, trying to cut the tension. "He'll be ready to race."

"That's your first warning, Archibald. Another outburst like that and you'll be on a plane back to London."

"Right, better send off your fastest anchor before the relay. Fuck off," I hissed beneath my breath as he walked away.

Thom spun around and leveled his gaze on me. "What the hell is your problem?"

"He's a prick."

"Right well, he's also your coach, but not for long if you keep on at him like that."

I shoved past Thom and walked to the back of the locker room. Anyone with half a brain could sense the anger rolling off of me. I was a live wire and I needed to channel my rage, not subdue it for the event. I found a spare locker and shoved my bag inside. I turned the volume up on my music until the world around me was completely drowned out.

I slammed my locker door closed and turned to find a quiet place to warm up. I let my music's rhythm harmonize with my anger as I stretched. In that quiet corner, facing the cement wall, I finally found my focus. I thought of the laps, of the calm that washed over me in the pool. In that lane, there were no mind games or ultimatums. Just water.

This was the easy part.

———

CAMERA FLASHES WENT off around me as I held up my gold medal. It was the fourth one I'd earned since the start of the games and it hung just as heavy around my neck as the first. I'd broken my world record in the 100m butterfly by finishing a full two-tenths of a second faster than I had four years prior. Every other swimmer had lagged after me; I was untouchable in the water and it felt good to stand on the podium with the stadium erupting in cheers around me.

The media always asked if the winning got old, if my twentieth medal felt as good as the first one had. I glanced down and stared at the ribbon hanging around my neck and smiled.

No, winning never got old.

"Freddie!"

"Archibald!"

"Please Freddie!"

I stepped down from the podium as the reporters shouted at me, trying to get my attention. There was a guy right up front, a little younger and less polished than the rest. He was trying hard to capture my attention and when I met his eyes, I could see the desperation there.

"Freddie, please. Do you have time for a quick interview?"

The media knew I detested interviews. What answers I gave were short and clipped, but something about this young reporter made me want to cut him some slack.

I waved off our team manager—who was trying to lead me back to the locker room through the chaos—and stepped closer to the reporter.

"You have three questions," I said with a nod. "What's your name?"

His blue eyes widened in shock and for a second, he stood immobile. The reporters around him shoved forward, trying to steal my interview away from the kid, but I ignored their pestering.

"Mauricio."

"Good to meet you. Let's get on with it."

He shook his head clear of shock and held the small tape recorder out to me. His hand shook violently as he asked his first question.

"Were you n-nervous about the race today?"

The reporters erupted behind him, annoyed with his question.

"C'mon Freddie," a reporter spoke behind him. I recognized him from races in the past. He was a tall, older man with white hair and thick-framed glasses. He was always ready with a standard question and never took no for an answer. This time, I ignored him completely and answered Mauricio.

"No, I wasn't nervous. Once I hit the water, my body knew what to do."

He nodded and glanced down at a small notebook clutched in his hand.

"Did the Olympic level of competition contribute to your record-breaking effort today?" he asked, glancing back up at me. "Or was it something else?"

I inhaled a deep breath. *Good question.*

"The competitors are great, but today I was able to clear my mind of distractions that tend to slow one down."

"Can you elaborate on what's been distracting you?" he asked, hopeful.

"Is it Andie Foster?" the older reporter asked, shoving his tape recorder over Mauricio's shoulder.

I shook my head and took a step back. "I'm here to win gold, not hearts."

Those were her words. She'd tossed them at me and now I was using them, trying to get to her through the TV. I wanted to shout from the rooftops about how much I missed her, but until Caroline stopped dropping bomb after atomic bomb, I needed it to look as if Andie meant nothing to me.

Mauricio frowned. "So does that mean the rumors about you and Andie Foster aren't true?"

I tried to keep my face calm, resolute. "Your three questions are up, but my focus is on swimming, not American football players."

The reporters jumped forward, clamoring over one another to get their questions in.

"Freddie!" a reporter yelled. "C'mon, just five more minutes!"

I felt a tug on my arm and glanced back to see my team manager trying to lead me out of the madness, and this time, I let her.

Chapter Forty-Four

ANDIE

I SPREAD PEANUT butter on a slice of bread, taking my time to smooth it evenly across the surface. I liked peanut butter. Peanut butter never got another woman pregnant. Peanut butter never made me cry. Nobody cared if you were photographed in a club with a jar of Jif. (I mean, it'd be weird, but no one would call you a whore because of it.) I dipped the knife back into the jar and glanced up to find three pairs of eyes watching me with concern.

"What?" I asked, biting out the word in a hard tone.

Becca glanced down at her magazine and Liam turned back to the TV, but Kinsley held her gaze without so much as a blink.

"How's that sandwich coming?" she asked, tilting her head.

I glanced down to survey the kitchen counter. There were over a dozen pieces of bread sitting in front of me, each one piled with more peanut butter than the last. I'd been lost in thought, but I'd be damned if I told Kinsley that. I turned and yanked the jelly out of the refrigerator.

"Excuse me for making an afternoon snack for everyone," I said, coating jelly on fresh pieces of bread and then plopping each finished sandwich onto a plate. When I was done, I dropped the plate of sandwiches on the coffee table and reached for the one on top.

No one else seemed quite as eager to eat them.

"What?" I asked. "They're good."

Becca and Kinsley exchanged a wary glance, but I ignored them and took a bite of my sandwich. It was good, but there was so much peanut butter inside, I could hardly swallow the bite.

"Let me get you some water," Liam said, pushing off the couch and heading into the kitchen.

"Are you okay?" Kinsley asked, leaning forward so Liam couldn't hear her.

I shrugged. "I'm fine."

"You're not having a nervous breakdown?"

"Why would you think that?" I asked.

She leveled her gaze on my chest and I glanced down. Sure, I was wearing my game jersey, complete with knee high socks and shin guards, but didn't everyone do that now and again?

"I just like the way it feels," I said, taking another bite of my mostly-peanut butter sandwich.

Liam walked back into the living room and held out a glass of water for me to take. "Here you go, champ."

I offered him a smile. "Thank you."

"Oh look! The race is about to start," Becca said, grabbing the remote and unmuting the TV. I focused on my sandwich as the announcers droned on about Freddie. I already knew he was planning on breaking his previous records. I didn't need to listen to them going on about how he could possibly end up as the most decorated Olympian in history.

"I was scared we'd missed it during our workout," Kinsley added giddily. "Andie, can you see okay?"

I glanced up to see them all staring at me again. Why did they keep doing that?

I smiled and shot them a thumbs up. Sure, the chair I'd picked was facing away from the TV, but I'd already seen enough already. The cameras had zoomed in on Freddie during his warm-up. He already had his jacket off, so every inch of his tan chest was being broadcast in HD. His swim cap covered his hair and his goggles concealed his eyes, but his sharp cheekbones and strong jaw were enough to make my stomach hurt. I twisted back around and stared at my sandwich. Somehow I doubted I'd be able to manage another bite.

"It's starting, Andie!" Kinsley exclaimed.

I nodded and tried on a plastic smile. It felt tight and uncomfortable, but at least no one seemed to notice. I hadn't filled them in on my break from Freddie or the pregnancy. Part of me was happy to keep it closer to my heart, and part of me was sick of thinking about it at all. For the last two days, I'd analyzed his announcement. Had he seemed happy? Lost? Excited? Anxious?

"Aren't you going to watch?!" Becca asked.

"Take your marks," the announcer said through the TV.

I glanced over my shoulder and watched Freddie bend down and grip his podium. His shoulders and back flexed with the effort. His strong muscles rippled and I bit down on the inside of my cheek. The camera zoomed out, the buzzer went off, and Freddie dove into the water.

My heart raced as he swam, though it looked so effortless to him. He was nothing but beautiful lines and hard muscles slicing through the water with unbelievable speed. The other swimmers stayed close, but Freddie seemed to be on another level. He cleared the first lap, hit the wall, and spun around, all before I'd taken a single breath.

Every part of Freddie was meant to be in the water. His speed and grace were mesmerizing, and before I'd fully wrapped my head around his skill, he'd touched the start wall and finished the race. Gold. Freddie surfaced from the water, pulled the goggles from his eyes, and glanced up the scoreboard. My heart pounded against my chest and I pressed my hand to feel the rhythm of it.

He was beautiful, glistening with water and beaming from ear to ear. A drop of water slid down his cheekbone and I found myself smiling along with him, grinning despite my broken heart.

"Andie?"

I spun around at the sound of my name. Kinsley, Becca, and Liam were staring up at me again, but this time it was because I was blocking the TV. Sometime during his race, I'd moved from my chair to stand within an inch of the screen.

"Oh, sorry," I said, stepping back and taking the seat beside Kinsley on the couch.

She wrapped her arm around my shoulder and shook me back and forth. "I can't believe he's won four gold medals already! He's amazing."

"And he lo...*likes* you!" Becca said with a look of amazement. "Don't you feel special?"

My smile fell, but everyone had turned back to the TV to watch the celebration. "Something like that," I nodded. "Anyway, that's probably enough for now," I said, reaching for the remote.

"Wait!" Becca said, blocking my path and grabbing it before I could. "He's about to do interviews."

Oh lord. "I doubt it. He's pretty private."

But I was wrong. I'd barely stepped into my room when

I heard him speak through the TV. The last time I'd heard his accent, he'd torn my heart in two, but as he greeted the reporter, he sounded like his normal self, confident and sexy. I stood just inside my door, listening to him out of sight of the others.

"Do you care to elaborate on what's been distracting you?" the young reporter asked in response to Freddie's answer as to why he'd been able to swim faster than usual.

Another reporter spoke over him. "Is it Andie Foster?"

My gut clenched at the mention of my name. I stared up at my ceiling and waited with bated breath for his answer.

"I'm here to win gold, not hearts," Freddie answered with a clipped tone.

My breath caught short in my chest. It was the right thing to say, but that didn't make it any easier to hear.

"So does that mean the rumors about you and Andie Foster aren't true?"

"…my focus is on swimming, not American football players."

I stepped away from the door before I could hear another word. My heart was already ripped apart; there was no need to rub salt in the wound. I reached for my phone and locked myself in my bathroom before Kinsley and Becca could pester me with questions about the interview. They were smart girls; they could connect the dots without having to see the hurt in my eyes.

I turned on the faucet of the bathtub and turned to my phone to silence it. Just before I could set it down by the tub, a text from Georgia caught my eye.

Georgie: He's only saying that so Caroline leaves you alone. REMEMBER THAT.

I typed out *Does it even matter?* but deleted it without hitting send. I already knew the answer.

Chapter Forty-Five

ANDIE

I WAS ON my way to the last practice before our final game when the news of Caroline's pregnancy broke. I knew something was different the minute I stepped out of our complex. There were paparazzi hovering outside the perimeter of the village, snapping photo after photo as we loaded onto the bus. They were far more desperate than usual. An Olympic official was shouting at them to get back, but they kept right on snapping photos until the bus doors closed behind me. I could only imagine what the headline read that morning: *Mother Theresa Step Aside, There's a New Mum in Town.* Gag me.

She'd probably given them an array of photos to choose from, all of which solidified her image as a wolf in sheep's clothing. Virginal white, pale pink, pearls, diamonds, nude flats—she knew exactly what she was doing, I'd give her that.

As I walked down the aisle of the bus, I heard whispers about her pregnancy, but no one had the guts to stand up and ask me. Even Kinsley and Becca danced around the issue, focusing on my wrist instead.

R.S. GREY

"What did the doctor say at your appointment yesterday?"

I shrugged. Truthfully, I wasn't sure what his final decision had been, but I was still proceeding as planned. If Coach Decker asked, I'd lie. There was no other option. Soccer was the only thing I had left.

When we arrived at the practice stadium, I trailed the rest of my team members off the bus, annoyed to find more paparazzi waiting there for me. I shoved my earbuds in and turned up the volume on my music, but I could still hear them shouting.

"Andie!"

"Andie! Are you and Freddie still seeing each other?"

"What do you think about the pregnancy news, Andie?!"

Kinsley reached back and tugged me through the door before they could ask anything else.

The mood inside the stadium was different than it'd been in the weeks since we'd arrived in Rio. Everyone was tired and anxious. The final game was the next day and the tension emanating from the group was nearly tangible. We'd made it to the final round, which meant we were at least guaranteed silver. Even if we lost the game, we'd be the second best women's soccer team in the world, but that didn't matter. We only had eyes for gold.

"Huddle up first," Coach Decker shouted as we dropped our bags on the benches. "We need to go over a few things before we start warm-ups."

I grabbed for my water bottle and my shin guards then took a seat beside Kinsley on the scratchy turf. The other girls joined us, giving me a wide berth, which didn't surprise me. Other than Kinsley and Becca, most of my teammates had treated me like a leper the last few days.

"I'm going to cut right to the chase here," Coach

Decker said, clutching her clipboard to her chest. "The doctor didn't clear Foster for the game tomorrow, which means Erin will have to sub in—"

She said it so calmly I nearly missed it the first time around.

"Wait, I'm sorry," Kinsley spoke up. "Her doctor didn't clear her?"

Coach Decker finally glanced my way. "I spoke to him on the phone this morning and he thinks—

"That's bullshit!" I said, standing up. "I'm ready to play."

I hadn't realized I'd yelled until Coach Decker narrowed her eyes. "Andie, calm down, or I'll ask you to leave."

Kinsley reached for my hand and squeezed it before she continued in a diplomatic tone. "What did he say exactly? Is it broken?

Coach Decker shook her head. "It's sprained."

Becca groaned. "Are you kidding me? I've played with sprained ankles more times than I can count."

"Exactly!" I added. "Kerri Strug won gold in '96 by vaulting on a sprained ankle. Tiger Woods played 91 holes and won the US Open on a broken leg and torn ACL." (Clearly, I'd done my research over the last few days.) "My wrist is nothing."

Coach Decker shot me a warning glare. "That's neither here nor—"

"Please let me finish. Some goalie in Manchester named Trautmann finished a match with a freaking broken neck. I'm just trying to say that this isn't the time to play it safe. I will do anything for this team…if it will have me." Kinsley tugged my hand until I finally relented and sat back down beside her, then she spoke up.

"Andie's right. This should be a team vote."

My gut clenched. My team had pulled away from me the moment news about Freddie and I had spread. It wasn't that they thought I was some home-wrecking whore, they just hated the negative attention my relationship with Freddie was bringing to the team. As if to nail home my doubt, I glanced down to Michelle to gauge her reaction, and she glanced away, too embarrassed to even make eye contact. Yeah, great idea, Kinsley. *Let's put it to a vote.*

Liam stepped forward. "I think a vote is a good idea. I think they have a right to decide who's defending their goal."

Coach Decker shook her head, but Kinsley stood and cut her off. "It's nothing against you, Erin. You carried this team through the 2000s, but Andie was named starter for a reason, and injury or not, we're a better team with her in the net. She's worked her ass off to rehab her wrist. She's been at every practice and every team meeting. She knows Japan backward and forward. She's as prepared as any of us to take the field tomorrow. Now, set aside the bullshit you guys have heard the past few days and remember that Andie is one of our own. She's our last line of defense and she's the person I want walking onto that field beside me tomorrow. Raise your hand if you agree."

Kinsley raised her hand and Becca followed right after her. I braced myself for the worst and prepared to handle yet another defeat. They had every right to keep their hands tucked by their sides. After all, the doctor hadn't even cleared me.

For those first few seconds after Kinsley and Becca raised their hands, no one moved. There were heavy breaths and cleared throats, but not a single one of my teammates raised their hands for me. For all my passion, I knew that if my teammates didn't want me on the field, then I wouldn't play. That was it.

Erin stood up and walked over to me, and for a second I feared she was going to laugh and tell me to leave. To my surprise, she took my left hand and wordlessly raised it with her right. We only had 4 out of the 18 women on the roster, but Erin's vote was obviously a game changer.

"I think Andie should play." My heart dropped as my gaze flew to Michelle. She had her hand stretched in the air, straight and confident. When our eyes locked, she nodded. "Sprained wrist or not, you're one of the best players we have."

I swallowed down tears as Nina raised her hand beside her. "Yeah, I agree. Andie should play."

Like slowly falling dominoes, every single teammate huddled in that circle raised their hands. One by one by one they all agreed that I should take the field with them the following day.

Becca nodded to Coach Decker. "I think that settles it, right?"

Chapter Forty-Six

FREDDIE

CAROLINE WAS MORE cunning and ruthless than I could have imagined. I had assumed she'd tried to rush the betrothal because she was anxious to get married before I changed my mind, but now it was clear she'd had everything planned from the start. Every single part of Caroline's life was meticulously designed.

The drunken sex was part of her plan. The more I thought of it, the more my stomach twisted with the hazy memories. Had I been the one to invite her to my flat or had she suggested the idea? How could I have been so careless?

I wasn't pushing all the blame onto her; I was merely learning to respect her devilry. She and my mother had timed the betrothal news so perfectly. By pushing it forward and announcing it to the world right before I left for Rio, they knew I'd be too distracted to give it my full attention.

I'd never agreed to marry Caroline Montague, but I'd never put a stop to it either. Now, if the paternity test came back with me as the father, there would be no getting rid of Caroline. She'd be completely untouchable.

I swam two races the same day the story of Caroline's pregnancy broke. I woke up early, rode a bus to the Olympic stadium, and warmed up alone. I dove into the water and let it take me in like a security blanket.

"Freddie Archibald!" the announcer yelled hours later. "GOLD!"

I couldn't hear the crowd over the sound of my heart beating in my ears, reminding me of its true desire.

———

I READ THROUGH the article about Caroline's pregnancy for the fourth time that day, confirming she hadn't said anything to harm Andie. She rambled on about how excited she was to be pregnant, how much she was looking forward to our wedding, and how happy she'd be to raise a child on my family's estate. None of that bothered me. I was immune to her insanity and my lawyer was already working on retracting the article.

Apparently Caroline had appreciated my interview the day before though, because she'd quashed any rumors about Andie in the article. Sure, she was lying, but when the reporters asked her if she knew anything about my alleged affair with Andie, she'd smiled and reveled in the martyrdom. *"The past is the past, and Freddie and I are looking forward to a bright future for our family."*

I hated playing her game. I hated having to tell that reporter Andie meant nothing to me, but I did it because I had to. If Caroline announced to the world that I had any kind of relationship with Andie now that I knew that Caroline was pregnant, they'd crucify Andie. I couldn't let that happen.

I stretched and adjusted the ice pack on my shoulder. "Georgie, listen—I have a plan, but I need your help."

She put her phone down and perked up.

"I hope your plan involves a time machine so you can go back and kill baby Caroline—and baby Hitler too, I suppose, if there's time," Georgie said.

It was late, I was knackered, and if I hadn't needed Georgie's help, I would have told her to bugger off.

"I have a million things on my plate," I said, motioning toward the growing pile of medals on the counter. "And no matter what I've done to fix this, Caroline always seems to be one step ahead of me. But you're not busy, and you have an advantage I don't: you're living with her."

Georgie nodded in agreement as I continued, "I think you can help me find some dirt to undermine her efforts."

Her eyes grew wide. "So I'd be like a…proper investigator?"

I shook my head. "No cloak-and-dagger stuff, Georgie. The last thing we need to do is give Caroline more leverage. I just need you to keep your eyes and ears open, in case she lets something slip."

"Fine I'll do it."

That was easier than expected.

"I've had plenty of time to think about about how looney Caroline is," she continued. "And I've come to one conclusion."

"What it is?"

"She's obviously lying about the baby."

My brows arched. "Lying?"

Georgie rounded the coffee table and took a seat beside me on the couch. Her light brown hair was pulled up into a bun with a pencil shoved through the center. Her t-shirt was stained with what looked to be jam and I couldn't be sure, but I thought she hadn't changed her socks in two days.

"G, have you showered yet today?"

She held up her hand. "No. Given the impending doom of a lifetime with Caroline, my hygiene is the least of my concerns."

"I figured the baby might not be mine, but what would she have to gain by lying about the pregnancy entirely? She'd lose everything when it becomes apparent."

Georgie threw her hands into the air like she was done with me. "It's not what she stood to gain, it's what she stood to lose as soon as Andie came into the picture. She had to do something that would at once sever you from Andie and bind you to her. And guess what—it's working."

I let my head fall back on the couch, considering her theory.

"Well if you are right, we'll know eventually, right?"

Georgie jumped up. "Well I for one won't be waiting for *eventually*. I want to crack this case wide open."

"You know Andie has her final game tomorrow," I said, tilting my head to look back at Georgie. "I can't go and watch because I've got my races."

"Think she'll stay after that? For the closing ceremonies?"

My heart dropped; I hadn't even thought of that. Would she really leave as soon as she was done competing?

"I don't know. I haven't spoken to her since the party," I admitted.

Georgie finally glanced up with a frown. "She's been busy. You know that."

I nodded.

"But now that you've promoted me from sister to

Minister of Espionage, I could probably help arrange a meeting if you want me to…"

I shot up off the couch. "Georgie, you're brilliant."

She smiled. "I know."

"After her game tomorrow, could you try and figure out where she is? I have a race in the afternoon, but I'm free after that."

"What are you going to do?" she laughed. "Kidnap her? If she wins the game she'll be celebrating with her team."

I nodded. "Right, well, I'll have to work that part out later. For now, I just need you to promise me you'll help me. I can't let her leave Rio without knowing how I feel."

"Okay, but you owe me. I'm already up to my ears in detective work and now you want me to help you win Andie back too?"

"What do you want in exchange?"

"A proper detecting hat, like Sherlock Holmes has got. Oh, and there's this new Chloé purse…"

I extended my hand for her to shake. "Fine, it's yours."

She smirked as we shook on it.

"Georgie Archibald, Detective/Love Guru, at your service."

Chapter Forty-Seven

ANDIE

EVERY SEAT IN the stadium was filled by 80,000 loud, rowdy fans. From the top of the rafters to the exclusive field-side seats, there wasn't a free spot anywhere. The announcers were pumping party music through the speakers, making it that much harder to keep my nerves at bay. My heart was already beating in time with the techno. Everyone in the crowd waved American and Japanese flags overhead and their screams echoed around the field well before the game had even started.

I turned my head in a circle, trying to absorb the frenzy while Lisa wrapped my wrist. The crowd was like nothing I'd ever seen before. Their energy was electric and even though I tried to take deep breaths and stay calm, it was useless. I was just as hyped as they were.

A group of girls in the front row caught me glancing over and they started screaming and jumping up and down. They had ponytails, braces, and fresh-faced smiles. All five of them were wearing white t-shirts with giant black letters covering the front.

A-N-D-I-E.

"We love you ANDIE!" they screamed in unison.

Lisa laughed. "Looks like you have a little fan club there."

I smiled and waved, making a mental note to take a photo with them after the game—hopefully during a victory lap.

"How's your wrist feel?"

"Fine."

"Andie, are you lying?"

I rolled my eyes. "Honestly, I can't feel my feet. I can't feel my face. I can't feel my freaking wrist. I'm about to play in the final game of the Olympics."

Lisa laughed and tossed her roll of tape on the back of the training table. "Well good luck. I wrapped it as best as I could."

"Thanks," I said, sliding off the table and testing out the tape. There was a dull ache, but the tape definitely helped.

"Oh, and Lisa—" I turned to glance back at her over my shoulder. "You've been a really good trainer."

She tilted her head and studied me with a smile. "I thought you hated me."

"Oh, I do," I winked.

"Foster!" Coach Decker called. "C'mon. Huddle up."

My team was already circled around Coach Decker and Liam. They stood just off the side of the field, adjusting shin guards and tightening cleats. My stomach dipped when I joined them. Each second that passed meant we were a second closer to game time. This was it. The final.

"This stadium is yours, ladies. This game is yours, just like all the games that brought you here. So act like you own the field, and trust one another." Her cool, confident gaze swept across the circle. "Do you hear me?"

We all nodded and she continued. The energy spreading through us was enough to make me feel as if Kinsley had accidentally given me a tablet of ecstasy instead of an Excedrin that morning. I was hopping back and forth on my legs, keeping my body warm.

"Hands in!" Coach Decker shouted.

We stacked hands on hands until all of us were woven together in a tight circle. Our hearts were beating in time, our bodies were humming together, excited and nervous. Our eyes locked and our heads nodded. *We got this.*

————

KINSLEY AND I took off for the field, jogging in tandem. "You good, Foster?"

"Other than the fact that I'm about to throw up?" I laughed. "I'm great."

She shook her head. "Do you hear that?"

I held my ear up to the stadium and listened.

"That's the sound of eighty thousand people who seriously don't want to see your breakfast."

I shoved her shoulder and took off for the goal.

"Keep that net clean!" Kinsley shouted after me.

"Get theirs dirty!"

I stepped past the goal line and inhaled a deep breath. This was it. This was my space. For twenty years I'd worked to earn a spot standing inside that net and as I turned toward the crowd and listened to them shouting my name, I knew that win or lose, I'd done it.

I was an Olympian.

————

"USA! USA! USA!"

The entire crowd inside the bar was shouting the three-letter chant, holding their beers overhead and sloshing them around. There was a mix of athletes and fans congratulating us. Japan had knocked Brazil out earlier in the tournament, so Rio residents were more than happy to join in our celebration. Kinsley stood on top of the bar, leading the crowd through the chant another few times before she cut her hand through the air to silence everyone.

"Gather round! Gather round!" she said, swirling her hand so that everyone pushed closer to the bar. She was on her way to being plastered, but it didn't matter. We were world champions.

"You all saw it! The game was neck and neck," Kinsley said, jumping into her tenth dramatic retelling of the game. No one stopped her though. It was like gathering around a campfire the way she dropped her voice and built up the suspense. "The score was zero-zero. Japan turned up the heat, pounding and pounding away—"

"Stop making it sexual!" Becca yelled beside me. "Get to the good part!"

The crowd laughed as Kinsley continued, "Okay so after my goal—off of Becca's *team-leading* fifth assist of the Olympic games—we were up one-nil! But that only made them angrier after the half."

Becca wrapped her arm around my shoulder and pulled me into the crook of her neck. She stank—god, we all did. We hadn't stopped celebrating since the end of the game, but no one seemed to care.

"They came storming back, first with the header, which Andie tipped off the crossbar, and then with the penalty kick, which Andie blocked as well. But Japan wasn't going down without a fight. After Kawasumi tackled the shit out of me," Kinsley said, holding up her bloody and bruised knee to prove it. "And breezed right past Michelle—"

"Hey!"

"—nothing stood between her and our own little Andie in the net."

"I KNEW ANDIE HAD HER!" Michelle shouted, tossing her beer into the air so that most of it spilled out onto the crowd around her.

I laughed and shook my head, trying my best to hide against Becca's shoulder.

"But did Andie panic? Did she charge out at her like we were all shouting at her to do? No! She stood poised, daring her to take the shot!"

Becca jostled me around. "And it worked! She got a little too confident, drove a little too deep, then what happened Kins?"

"Andie pounced and blocked that ball like it was the easiest thing she'd ever done!"

I could feel my cheeks burning red with all the attention. I wasn't nearly drunk enough to have an entire bar full of people focused on me.

"Kawasumi was no match for our Andie!"

"TO ANDIE!" Nina shouted, and the bar echoed back. "ANDIE!"

Kinsley was embellishing the story a little bit. I hadn't blocked the shot that easily. I'd blindly dove, praying it'd be enough to stop it. And it had. But we hadn't won the game because of me. Our offense was the reason we had two scores on the board by the time the whistles blew.

"Andie! Andie! Andie!"

Oh Jesus. No matter how much I tried to quell the chanting, the crowd just grew louder. I assumed it couldn't possibly get any worse, until I heard a loud Scottish brogue bellow my name behind me. I turned in time to find the same pack of Viking rugby players I'd met my very first night in Rio. They looked just as tall and thick and bearded as when I'd last seen them. Gareth—the redheaded giant who'd accidentally dropped me—was leading the way and he didn't waste any time.

Becca shouted at them to haul me up to the bar beside Kinsley and they followed her directions.

"Holy—" I shouted as Gareth tossed me up onto his shoulder like a rag doll. I felt like his pet parrot.

"It's okay!" I shouted in his ear. "I can walk!"

"Nonsense, las! I shan't drop you this time!"

I'd assumed he would take me straight to the bar so I could hop up there beside Kinsley, but instead he paraded me around the room as people continued to chant. It was all very embarrassing, and I needed a drink. We passed by Becca again and I reached down for her beer. I chugged down a quarter of it, desperately needing liquid courage to make it through the night.

"Here you are, Andie!" Gareth said as we approached the bar—except he actually bellowed my name like "AHH-HHHNNNNDDDDDEEEEEEEHHH." I swore he'd missed his calling as a seafaring pirate.

Kinsley helped pull me up beside her and I leaned in to whisper in her ear. "I'm actually going to kill you for this, so enjoy your fun while you can."

She laughed and grabbed hold of my arm. "Oh come on! You're the best goalie in the world! You're a national treasure! You're Andie freaking—"

"Foster."

My heart stopped.

My breath caught.

My smile fell as I slowly turned to find Freddie standing in front of the bar, positioned right beneath me with his hand over his heart and a smile that tipped my world upside down. He had a little American flag tucked in the front pocket of his white shirt and when I didn't make any move to welcome him, he pulled it out and waved it back and forth like a little peace offering.

Seeing him there, with his earnest gaze, his bashful smile, his one isolated dimple, was enough to make the last few days all but disappear. I'd tried my best to forget about him, including ignoring his calls and his text messages. But there he stood, waving his little American flag and breaking his way back into my heart.

I pressed my lips together to keep from smiling.

He shook his head and glanced around him, recognizing that everyone within a ten-foot radius had stopped to stare at us. He glanced back to me and dropped the American flag on the bar.

Maybe I should have asked what he was doing there —*what about Caroline, what about the baby*—but I didn't. I stared down at him, nervous for his next move.

"I know I owe you an explanation," he said just before he reached up to grip my waist. He pulled me off the bar and I reached out to grab his shoulders so I wouldn't fall. Our bodies were flush by the time I had my toes back on the ground.

"Not here," I said, conscious of all the people around us.

"Then let me steal you."

He wound his hand around mine before I could reply.

"Where are you taking her?!" Kinsley shouted as he pulled me through the crowd.

He waved over his shoulder. "I'll have her back in a few minutes!"

My heart dropped. I didn't want him to "have me back" in a few minutes. I'd had enough celebrating with my team and I'd see Kinsley and Becca bright and early the next day anyway. I wanted to spend the rest of my night with Freddie. I wanted his hand clutched tight around my mine for as long as possible, but I didn't know what he planned to do about people that might see us together.

He pushed through the front door of the bar and led me toward the curb. There was a cherry-red Vespa sitting there.

"Is that for us?" I asked with a laugh.

He nodded and reached for one of the helmets locked onto the side. I stood, waiting patiently as he slipped it onto my head. He leaned forward and tightened the strap beneath my chin. He was so close to me, his lips were inches away, and it'd been three days since he'd last kissed me. I could hardly remember what his lips felt like; he needed to remind me.

"I lied," he said, taking a step back and sliding the dark visor down to cover my face.

I frowned. "About what?"

"I won't have you back in a minute." His dark eyes gleamed. "Now that nobody knows it's us, I'm going to keep you for the rest of the night."

Chapter Forty-Eight

ANDIE

I GOT MY first taste of the real Rio on the back of that cherry-red Vespa. We wove down ocean boulevards and I closed my eyes, letting the wind whip against me. I could taste the salt in the air as Freddie pulled over and parked on Avenida Atlântica. The sun was heading south and dusk was in full effect. The sunset painted the ocean waves in orange hues and for a minute, I stood mesmerized.

There were thousands of people out on the beach and walking along the avenue. It was a bustling street with six lanes of traffic and honking cars and confident pedestrians weaving in and out. Vendors lined the shore, selling everything from fried corn to flip-flops. On the other side of the street, there were hotels and condos—all tan and stucco with large windows.

In the Olympic village, it'd been easy to miss how far from home I'd been for the last few weeks, but on Avenida Atlântica, there was no mistaking it. The thick humidity, the salty air, and the mountains standing tall in the background—it was all unfamiliar and new and exhilarating.

Freddie took my hand and led me along the walkway. We skipped over the shops with the woven friendship bracelets and colorful ceramic trinkets until we stumbled upon a shop a little bigger than the rest. It was set up along the beach, surrounded on four sides by a thin white tarp that whipped in the wind as we stepped inside. There were sarongs lining an entire side of the tent. Small, cheap ones for children sat up front, but I reached out for one at the very top. It was soft and purple, with tiny tassels lining the edges.

"That's a good one," Freddie said, coming up behind me.

I smiled. "For you."

"What?" I ignored the adorable shock on his face and pointed back to the sarong.

"You can't be serious," he continued.

I nodded.

"I'll look like an arse."

I angled around him to find the shopkeeper. He was a short man propped behind the counter, scrolling through his iPhone until I held the purple sarong right up in front of him.

"How much for this?" I asked, hoping he spoke enough English to understand my question.

"Thirty-eight," he said with a thick accent.

My eyes almost bulged out of my head. "DOLLARS?!"

"Reais."

"That's not much," Freddie said, coming up behind me with something blue clutched in his right hand. He tossed it up on the counter, on top of the sarong, and then threw two pair of cheap black aviators onto the pile. "We'll take the lot."

"What's this thing?" I asked, picking up the corner of

what looked to be a blue bungee cord. Or was it a small bracelet…"DEAR GOD."

"*Fio dental.*" The shopkeeper laughed, pointing at what I could only assume was a bikini that was supposed to go under another, more modest bikini.

After Freddie paid, he picked up our bag of embarrassing items from the counter and led me out of the store.

"I think the literal translation is dental floss." Freddie laughed.

I shot him a side-eyed glare. "You're insane if you think I'm putting that thing on."

He didn't reply. Instead, he reached into the bag, pulled the tag off the aviators, and slipped them on, handing the other pair to me in case anyone recognized us. It wasn't fair how easily he made cheap sunglasses look good.

"Seems we both have things we'd rather not wear," he said, taking my hand. "I think that's called a stalemate."

"Fine, let's switch. You'll wear the bikini and I'll wear the sarong."

He tossed his head back and laughed. It was an infectious sound that had me smiling as he pulled us out of the store. With our sunglasses in place, we walked until we found a small beachside restaurant that had an intoxicating smell wafting out the front door. We ate leisurely, appreciating the fact that nobody thus far had recognized either of us.

"Probably time to slip on that sarong," I winked, picking up my coconut water.

He ignored my teasing. "Should we swim for a bit after this?"

I shrugged. "It'd be a shame not to go into the ocean at least once while we're here."

He hummed in agreement.

"I'm not sure you could handle it though…"

I laughed. "Handle what?"

"Seeing me in that bikini."

―――――

ANYWHERE ELSE IN the world, wearing the bikini Freddie had picked out would have been 100% off the table, but in Rio, most of the women clearly subscribed to the "less is more" mentality. Like way, *way less*. Just walking along the avenida that evening, I'd seen enough butt cheeks to last me a lifetime. Freddie, to his credit, didn't make a fuss about it, but he didn't need to. "LOOK AT THAT BUTT!" I'd whisper excitedly every time one came into view, and these weren't your mom's butt cheeks. If I didn't know better, I'd have assumed Brazil was manufacturing Kim Kardashian clones.

"You okay in there, Andie?" Freddie asked from the other side of the door.

He was waiting outside the restaurant's bathroom while I changed into the bikini.

"Fine!" I shouted, trying to angle myself in the mirror so I could see all the parts of my skin the bikini *wasn't* covering. The top was hopeless. The blue triangles covered me as much as they could, but my boobs were just…everywhere. Side boob, middle boob, top boob. All of the boobs. And if that didn't seem bad enough, the real issue remained with the bottoms.

"How's it coming?"

I shifted to get a better look in the mirror. "I have no clue. I put it on, but then it disappeared."

He laughed. "I'm sure it's not so bad."

He was very, very wrong. I practiced most days in my soccer shorts and sports bra, so about six inches above my knee, my skin turned from tan to PALE. SO PALE. My butt cheeks practically glowed in the dark. Beneath the blue triangles of my bikini top, you could make out a perfect silhouette of where my sports bra usually rested.

Whatever sex appeal the bikini offered was counterbalanced by the fact that I looked like I'd been dip-dyed in tan paint.

I opened the door of the bathroom and peeked my head around to find Freddie leaning against the adjacent wall with his arms crossed. He'd taken off his shirt so I could see the full extent of his Olympic workouts. He was tall and built, with broad, tan shoulders. His chest was toned in a way that made me shiver and I made my eyes stay three inches above his six-pack. Once I looked, there really was no going back.

He heard the door open and glanced over with a curious gaze. With my head the only thing visible, I gave him a warning.

"What you're about to see *is* objectively funny, but if you laugh, I will never speak to you again."

He smiled wryly. "You have to give me a bit of an explanation. I'm not that good at keeping a straight face."

I sighed and let the bathroom door swing open. His eyes widened as he swept down my body, and to my surprise, he didn't laugh. Not once.

"Were you nervous about the tan lines?" he asked as he led me down to the beach with my hand in his.

"It's pretty funny, you have to admit."

"It's really not bad. You should see my bum."

I smiled and shook my head. "I have."

By the time we made it out onto the sand, the sun had nearly set, but the beach was still crowded. We passed hundreds of colorful umbrellas on our way to the water, but no one paid us much attention. With less clothes on, we blended in with the tan, scantily clad masses.

Freddie decided to swim in his boxer briefs and I pretended to be intrigued by a seagull pecking away at some chips while he dropped his shorts. I told myself my heart was racing because the seagull was really going to town on the chips, but when Freddie reached out to lead me into the ocean, I had a dangerous thought. *What happens to us after tonight?* I knew what I wanted, but I didn't know how to secure it before I left.

So while we slipped into the water and waves lapped up against us, I thought of questions that would give me the answers I was seeking.

"Have you had many girlfriends, Freddie?"

"A few over the years. No one too memorable."

A giant wave was headed for us and he dove in head first, slipping beneath the wave as I floated over it. When he came back up, he whipped his wet hair out of his face and flashed me a wide smile.

"What about Americans? Have you ever dated one of them?"

He laughed. "Andie, is this a quiz?"

By then, he was practically supporting my full weight while he continued to tread water. Our legs were getting tangled beneath the surface and every now and then my hip would brush his. I couldn't pay attention to the sensuality of the moment though; I needed him to answer my question.

"I'm just wondering," I said, glancing to the horizon over his shoulder. "We haven't talked about it really."

He nodded. "You're the first American girl I've ever fancied."

FANCIED.

"And what exactly does it mean to fancy someone?"

He tightened his hold around my waist so that our stomachs were flush. He was nothing but warm, hard lines against my body. "So Becca didn't tell you then? I figured she would have."

I frowned. "Tell me what?"

He smiled and glanced away. "I'll tell you later."

"There is no later."

It wasn't a teasing ploy to lure the words out of him, it was a real threat. I was leaving. Gone.

He brushed a few wet strands of my hair away from my eyes. "What do you mean?"

"Kinsley and Becca and I are headed back to the States in like six hours."

It hurt to say the words out loud.

His hold tightened around my waist. "You what?"

I shook my head. "My mom got me an appointment with this exclusive doctor in L.A. He's supposed to be a world-renowned orthopedic surgeon who specializes in wrists. He's already taken a look at my MRI—"

"So you're leaving in the middle of the night to see him? This doctor?" His brows were furrowed in confusion. "That makes no sense."

"He's booked solid for the next six months, but he has *one* opening tomorrow afternoon and I'm taking it."

"You're leaving Rio in six hours?" He glanced out at the darkening horizon and then back at me. Whatever happiness he'd had a moment earlier was gone now.

"Yeah." I nodded. "I have to go. I've put off treatment because I wanted to play in the final, but now that I'm finished, I have to make my wrist my priority. I don't want to be known as the promising goalkeeper that had her career cut short by chronic injury."

I'd worked too hard to walk away from the sport now.

"Stay," he pleaded, walking us back a few feet so he

could touch the ocean floor. I stayed wrapped around him, letting him carry my weight beneath the waves.

"I can't."

His brown eyes implored me to stay, but I couldn't. I should have seen the doctor a week ago. I could have already damaged my wrist past the point of full repair.

"I have to make that appointment."

For a few minutes we stayed quiet. The briny sea lapped against us, pushing us up to shore and then dragging us back out toward the horizon. The waves were loud, filling the silence between us until I spoke up and suggested something I hoped he'd agree to.

"You could come to L.A."

I cringed at the desperation in my tone. Freddie turned his head to look at me and I shrugged.

"After the ceremonies wrap up, I mean." I continued filling the silence, though my brain was yelling at me to shut up. "You could see where I live and spend some time in America."

His dark eyes told me no even before he did. "I would love that, but...I've got to get home and figure out this Caroline thing. If she's really pregnant with my child..."

Caroline.

Caroline.

Caroline...

We'd gone so long without mentioning the glaring obstacle sitting between us, the dragon that had yet to be slayed.

"Right," I said, turning my head so he couldn't see the hurt in my eyes.

"Andie. I only slept with her once and I was drunk. It meant nothing."

"But now it might mean everything."

Silence.

I stared out at the waves and worked up the courage to ask my next question. "Will you marry her? I mean will you marry her if she *is* pregnant?"

"No. Never." He seemed shocked by the notion, which made me feel a little better. "But I've got to get the paternity test sorted, see my lawyer, and have a chat with my mum. She hasn't spoken to me since I decided to cut off the betrothal."

I nodded. "Right. So you're going back to London."

"And you're headed back to L.A."

The words sounded final, even if we didn't want them to be.

"Why does this feel like the end?" I asked, leaning forward to drop my head on his shoulder.

"It's not," he promised.

A wave crashed against us and Freddie tightened his grip on me. I felt so small there, fighting against the waves and the end of us and the tears that were falling for no reason.

"Do you think this thing between us is real? Or is it just part of the magic of Rio?"

"I *know* it's real."

I tipped my head up and nuzzled my nose against his neck, inhaling the scent of salt water on his skin. He smelled so divine. I stayed there, with my lips against his throat.

"Don't forget about me once you go back to London."

He bent and dropped a kiss to my shoulder. "How could I?"

"Even if you escape from Caroline, there'll be lots of *fanciable* girls pining after you once you go back home with six more gold medals around your neck."

His hand cupped my neck, dragging it up and down

and warming my skin. I hadn't realized I'd started to shake against him.

"I only have four so far," he said, mocking himself.

"Girls or medals?" I joked.

He smiled. "Will you call me after your appointment and let me know how it goes?"

"You'll probably be racing."

"How about later…"

I shook my head and skimmed my lips up to his mouth. "I don't want to talk about later. Let's just stay here in this ocean forever."

He laughed. "We'd turn into prunes."

I slipped my hand along the hard ridges of his stomach. "You don't feel pruney to me."

His sharp inhale told me how much he loved my touch. His head turned and he captured my mouth in a kiss so powerful, I lost track of my breaking heart. With his lips on mine, it felt like there was only us, the two of us standing in an ocean with our bodies wrapped up and our hearts on our sleeves. I loved him in a hopeless sort of way, the type of love you feel for what could have been. I wasn't giving up on him, or us. I was giving up on the promise of more. In six hours, we'd be worlds apart.

"I don't even know your middle name."

"William."

"Or your favorite food."

"Spaghetti."

"Or your favorite song."

"Anything by Jake Bugg."

I was crying, but he was kissing away the tears and answering my questions as if it would actually help. His hand pressed against my heart, trying to calm me down, but it didn't work. I told him I didn't want to think about the future. I wanted to stay in that ocean forever, but I knew life wouldn't pause for us—the setting sun was a constant reminder of that.

When the night had turned black and the only light we could see was from the moon and the cafes along the avenue, Freddie carried me out of the ocean and into a hotel across the street. We took the last room they had, a shabby beachside suite for tourists on a budget. The carpet was old and stained. The drapes were stiff and smelly. The bed was small and hard, but Freddie stripped off the old comforter. We tossed the pillows to the ground and he pushed me down onto the sheets. The mattress dipped with his weight as he crawled over me. We hadn't bothered with a lamp; he was hardly visible in the darkness, but half his face was illuminated from the light slipping through the closed curtains. I reached up to touch him, feeling for the features obscured in the shadows.

"I know it's not much," he whispered as his mouth traveled down my bare stomach.

I shook my head and clenched the sheet as his hands untied my bikini bottom. He pulled it off and cast it onto the floor with the rest of our mess.

"Freddie…"

I needed him to look up at me. I needed to tell him how I felt before it was too late.

"Freddie, I—"

"I know." He glanced up to me, but I couldn't make out his eyes in the darkness. His hands pressed against my thighs, pushing them apart.

———

MY PHONE BUZZED on the bedside table, jolting me awake. I blinked in the darkness and reached over to silence it before it woke Freddie up as well. Kinsley's name flashed across the screen and though I was tempted to ignore her call, I knew she'd probably been trying to get ahold of me all night.

I pushed up off the bed and walked into the bathroom. Once the door was shut, I answered with a hushed tone.

"Kinsley, hey—"

"Where are you, Andie?" She sounded frantic. "We need to leave."

I pulled the phone from my face to look at the time: 2:00 AM. How was it already 2:00 AM?

"I can't leave yet, Kinsley."

She sighed. "Andie, where are you? Becca and I already packed up all your stuff. We'll come pick you up and then head straight for the airport."

She wasn't listening to me.

"I can't go. I have to stay here."

"Andie, you can't stay in Rio. This thing with Freddie, if it's real, you two will find each other again. Right now, you need to focus on yourself. You have that doctor's appointment tomorrow and then we have to meet up with the rest of our team in a few days for interviews. On Friday we're flying to the White House for a special dinner with the president."

My heart was splitting in two, but she kept on talking. "Life goes on. You have to be at these interviews. The world needs to be reminded that you're a soccer star with your own hopes and dreams, not just another one of Freddie's groupies."

I closed my eyes and leaned my head against the bathroom wall. I didn't want her to be right. I wanted to stay in Rio.

"Now, where are you?"

I rattled off the name of the hotel and she promised

they'd pick me up in five minutes. I had just enough time to slip out of the bathroom and pull on my dirty clothes. I hadn't showered since the game, but the ocean had washed away the sweat. My skin was sticky and warm and when I sniffed my arm, it smelled like Freddie. I'd sit on a ten-hour flight back to the United States with his scent wrapped around me.

Kinsley called when they were outside the hotel and I scrambled to gather up my things inside the dark hotel room. Freddie was still asleep, laying on his stomach with his body splayed out over the bed. I made sure his phone had two alarms set so he wouldn't oversleep, and then I leaned down to kiss his cheek.

A part of me wanted him to wake up and pull him down onto me. I wanted him to hold me down so I couldn't leave. The plane could take off without me and I'd stay in Rio forever with Freddie.

He didn't wake though, even after I whispered his name in the dark.

Kinsley called me again and my phone buzzed in my hand. Freddie stirred and rolled over. I froze, but he didn't wake up. I walked to the door and resisted the urge to look back at him. I had a thousand images to remember him by; one more would only only make it harder to walk away.

To their credit, Kinsley and Becca didn't berate me when I finally made it into the van. They directed the driver to the airport and I stared out the window, mesmerized by the rolling waves. If I closed my eyes, I could still feel them lapping against me. Kinsley pressed her hand to my shoulder and squeezed. I shook my head and brushed her off. It was too early for condolences. I wasn't ready to accept that I was actually in a van, on the way to the airport, leaving Rio without Freddie.

We arrived outside the empty airport and the driver popped the trunk to grab our bags.

"Thanks for packing my stuff K—"

"Andie!"

The sound of my name shouted from a few yards away nearly sent me into cardiac arrest. It didn't matter that the British accent was light and feminine, or that I knew Freddie was still in dreamland. I heard my name called outside of an airport and I assumed it was Freddie running after me until I turned and saw Georgie nearly falling out of a cab to get to me in time. Her brown hair whipped in the wind and her flip-flops clapped against the concrete.

"Wait!" she yelled, though I wasn't going anywhere.

"We don't have a ton of time, Andie," Kinsley reminded me. I nodded and turned back to Georgie just as she'd made it to me.

"Give me a second." She leaned over and clutched her knees, calming her breath. "I know you wouldn't know it, given my enviable physique," she said. "But I'm quite out of shape."

I laughed and shook my head. "What are you doing here?"

"I heard you were leaving early, and I needed to tell you this in person. I know Caroline's faking the pregnancy. I KNOW IT. I just have to prove it."

Her determination made my heart break even more.

"It's okay, Georgie," I said, pulling her up to stand so I could wrap her in a hug. "Caroline has won the battle. I'm going home."

"The battle, yes, but not the war. You can't give up."

I smiled, a wistful, flat smile. "Maybe you're my true love, Georgie." I laughed. "You chased me down at the airport in the middle of the night. If that's not love, I don't know what is."

"Stop, that's not funny." Her light green eyes implored me to take her seriously. "You're the one he's meant to be with, not her."

I inhaled a shaky breath and took a step back. "I'll call you when I land. Look after him for me, will ya?"

"Don't give up yet, Andie."

I shook my head as Kinsley nudged my shoulder. The plane wouldn't wait for me.

"I've got to go, Georgie," I said, taking a step back.

"He's a complete knobhead if he lets you slip away, Andie."

I laughed and shook my head, letting Kinsley pull me toward the airport doors.

"Do you hear me, Andie?!" Georgie shouted after me. "A COMPLETE KNOBHEAD."

Chapter Forty-Nine

FREDDIE

BEEP. BEEP. BEEP.
 I threw my hand over to silence my alarm, feeling for my mobile on the bedside table where I usually left it to charge. Nothing was there. I sighed and sat up, realizing as I blinked my eyes open that I wasn't in the Olympic village. Andie and I had fallen asleep in the hotel, on old scratchy blankets that had seemed like clouds at the time. I tried to recall the last moments of the night, when I had Andie tucked into the crook of my arm, pressed so tightly against me that she'd complained about not being able to breathe. I'd eased up and let her fall to her side of the bed, and she'd smiled over at me in the dark.

"Think we can manage one more time before I have to leave?"

I'd nodded and draped my arm around her stomach. She spooned against me and we must have fallen asleep soon after that.

Now, I sat up and rubbed my eyes, calling out her name into the dark room. The blackout curtains were doing a fairly good job of keeping the sun out, but once I whipped them open, there was no denying that Andie was

346

gone. The hotel room was quiet and stale—and as the dust settled, I realized she hadn't woken me up before she'd left. She'd told me her flight was in the middle of the night and instead of waking me up, she'd snuck out while I was asleep.

We'd pushed off the goodbye so long that I never got one. I didn't get the chance to beg her to wait for me. I never told her I loved her, not in a way that would fade once I left Rio, but the real kind, the sort of love you fight to keep. I wanted to promise her that as soon as I had my life in order, I'd fly across to America and drag her out to see me if I had to.

I didn't get to say those things because Andie had left and I was alone in that room.

A quick glance at my mobile confirmed that she hadn't tried to ring, and though I was tempted, I didn't phone her. I collected my stuff from around the room and slipped into the clothes I'd been wearing the day before. My boxer briefs were still damp from the ocean, but I forced them on anyway. I checked around the room twice, confirming I'd snatched up everything, and then I was about to head for the door when I turned for the bed instead. I bent and picked up the pillow she'd slept on—it still had the indent from her head—and I held it up to my face and inhaled. It was like a punch to the gut. It still smelled like the coconut shampoo I'd grown accustomed to over the last few weeks and the scent alone was enough to make my knees crumble. I sat on the edge of the bed and hugged the pillow like a mad fool. Why had we made no plans about the future? Why had I not promised her it would work out? That somehow, someway, she and I would be together?

When I finally left that hotel room, I was running late for my first race of the day. I already had a few missed calls from Caroline, my manager, my agent, my mum, Thom, and Georgie. I sat in the back of the cab and dialed my manager.

"Freddie, where have you been? Your coach has been looking for you."

I let my head fall against the window of the cab. "I was out. I'm headed to the race now."

"Jesus, Fred. They give you a long leash because you're Mr. Dependable. Now you've got everyone worried."

I squeezed my eyes shut. "Is that all you wanted to talk about?"

She sighed heavily, annoyed with my clipped tone. "I've been trying to contact you about appearances for after the games wrap up. You've got interview offers left and right. There are parties and brunches and tea with the royals. Everyone is hounding me to get to you and you've been MIA."

"I'm not doing any of it. Let everyone know that after the Olympics, Freddie Archibald has set a media moratorium. I've got some personal stuff to work through once I get home."

Two slow, steady inhales later, she asked for clarification. "I'm sorry, are you saying you won't be doing a single interview after Rio?"

My eyes were still closed as I leaned against the window and if I listened hard enough, I swore I could hear the waves breaking against the shore. I held my breath and tried harder to listen. I needed to hear the waves.

"Freddie!?"

She was nearly hysterical, but I couldn't work up the same feeling. "That's right. No interviews. I'll keep up my sponsorship duties, but that's it."

"You do realize this will only make them want you more. What is the point of going and winning all those medals if you don't share your experiences with the world? You owe your fans at least one—"

"I'm done living my life like I owe anyone anything."

I hung up on her then and dropped my mobile on my lap.

"Just a few more minutes," the cabbie said, sensing my anxiety.

"Thanks."

I opened my eyes and stared out at the landscape whipping by. I wanted to tell the cabbie to drive to the airport. I wanted to get on a plane to America and find Andie and convince her that she and I were worth more than three weeks in Rio. I couldn't though, and I'd never felt as trapped as I did as I gathered my swim gear and headed to the stadium.

I was trapped with Caroline and I was trapped in Rio. I had two more days of racing. Two long days of focusing on the pool and not much else. Swimming had gotten in the way of my life many times before, but I'd never minded. After my father had passed, the pool was my therapy. After Henry's accident, the pool became my best friend. It was so easy to lose myself in my workouts and my competitions. Now, for once, I didn't want to lose myself. I wanted to stay dry and settle the loose ends of my life.

"You good, mate?" Thom asked as I stepped into the locker room.

I nodded and shrugged him off.

The entire team was there, changing and getting ready for the races. They looked up at me when I walked in, their eyes scanning me up and down like I was a loose cannon getting ready to fire.

"Fred, you're thirty minutes late."

I nodded and tossed my gym bag on the floor so I could lean forward and splash cold water on my face.

"You good to compete?"

I laughed. Out of everything in my life—Andie, Caroline, love, pregnancies, marriage—swimming was the one thing I still had any control over. I patted my face dry with a paper towel before meeting my coach's eyes in the mirror.

"Have I ever not shown up ready to compete?"

He frowned. "No."

I pushed off the sink and reached for my bag. "Then let's go."

Chapter Fifty

ANDIE

I **FELT A** change the second the plane took off. I stared out the window and tried to convince myself that Freddie and I could make it work, but my hands still shook with nerves.

Kinsley and Becca didn't have doctor's appointments to get back to, but they flew home with me anyway. Becca was anxious to see her husband Penn, and Kinsley swore she didn't care about missing the closing ceremonies. She said the closing ceremonies were basically just the start of the final rounds of the debauchery the village was known for. As a married woman, she said she'd rather be there with me for my appointment.

"Can I get you anything?" the flight attendant asked with a gentle tone. Half the plane was already asleep; I was one of the last stragglers clinging to the night. I shook my head and adjusted in my seat to get comfortable.

I slept for a few fitful hours, but it was the kind of sleep where when you woke up, you weren't sure if you were ever out at all. I'd been thinking of Freddie when I'd closed my eyes, and when I opened them a few hours later, he was still on my mind. The plane was dark and Kinsley was snoring gently beside me. I wanted to jostle her awake and have her convince me that things would be okay. Instead, I felt for one of the magazines she'd stuffed in her seatback pocket. I turned on my dim overhead light and tilted it away from Kinsley so it would only illuminate the magazine on my lap.

It was a trashy tabloid, something Kinsley only ever had when she was trying to kill ten hours on a flight. Two pages in, I saw my first glimpse of Caroline. They had done a whole four-page spread about her stay in Rio. They highlighted her *"Olympic Fashion!"* and blew up a photo of her walking into her hotel. They speculated about who she was using as a wedding coordinator and which top designer she'd commission to create her custom gown.

I crumbled the magazine up and shoved it back in the pocket, disgusted.

"Ma'am, are you still doing okay?"

The flight attendant was back and I needed her to leave me the fuck alone. I nodded again, and then I turned away and flipped off my overhead light. I felt sick and I wanted to reach for the vomit bag no one ever uses, but it was dark and I couldn't see it. Instead, I squeezed my neck pillow to my chest and stared out the window, willing the nausea to pass.

By the time we touched down in L.A., there was no denying reality. Freddie and I were separated by 6,299 miles. *I'd looked it up.* Not to mention my injury, his family, Caroline, a blackmail wedding, and now a baby. *A baby.* Fuck.

A car took Kinsley, Becca, and I straight from the airport to Central L.A. Orthopedic Group. I slipped on a baseball cap in an effort to hide the dark circles under my eyes, but the receptionist didn't mention them. She was practically vibrating in her chair, staring up at us with wide eyes.

"Barbara! Did you see!?" she bellowed to the woman working behind her. "We have three gold medalists in the office today!"

By the time I was turning to find a seat, there was a short line of fans formed to the side of us with their iPhones and pens at the ready. I put on my best attempt at a genuine smile and let Kinsley take the lead with them. Luckily, the nurse called me back for imaging right away, before my facade could crack.

"You must be so excited to get back home," the nurse said as she walked me to the x-ray room.

I glanced over at her.

"What with all that craziness in Rio," she continued. "I tried to keep up with it, but every day they were reporting something new. Your name was, uh…everywhere during the games."

My stomach rolled as she ushered me into the dark room. "Yeah, I guess I am glad to be back."

After my x-rays, they led me into the doctor's office and promised I wouldn't have to wait too much longer. I nodded as I settled into the leather chair across from his desk. There was a TV perched in the top right corner of his room, set to mute and showing news about the Olympics Games.

"Freddie Archibald, three-time Olympian and a member of Great Britain's swim team, just broke his world record in the 200-meter freestyle earlier this afternoon," the closed captions read. "This race brings him to five gold medals for the 2016 games, and ups his all-time medal count to 21."

The footage showed Freddie as he walked to the

podium, took his start, and dove into the water. I'd been with him less than twelve hours earlier, and the way my body ached as I watched him race made no sense. Maybe it was because I was tired and he hadn't called or texted me since I'd left. A part of me had hoped there'd be a message waiting for me once I walked off the plane, but there was nothing. Maybe it was because I knew the magic we felt was bound to Rio, and that the odds of me ever seeing Freddie again were slim to none. Or maybe it was the fact that they were highlighting footage of Caroline in the audience, jumping up and down and cheering Freddie on during his race. They flashed a little banner beneath her that read "Caroline Montague, Frederick Archibald's Fiancée." I wanted to throw up as they shoved the camera and microphone in her face. It was Sophie Boyle doing the interview and she gushed about how excited she was for Caroline and Freddie. I tried to watch Caroline answering, but my phone vibrated in my purse, magnified by the silence in the room.

I reached down for it in my purse and nearly dropped it when I saw a text from Freddie waiting for me.

Freddie: How did the appointment go?

That's all. How did the appointment go? Five words that were innocuous and gentle and thoughtful, and yet I hated every syllable. How was I supposed to flip through magazines and turn on the TV and see Caroline splashed across every page and every channel and pretend that it was okay? How was I supposed to handle small talk when what I really wanted to do was pick up my phone, call him, and shout that things like appointments and races and "how was your afternoon" and "what did you eat for dinner" didn't fucking matter.

Fuck.

I was crying and I was so sick of crying. With my luck, the doctor was going to do that two knuckled knock on the door soon. I didn't want to be a blubbering mess while he tried to talk to me about my wrist.

I couldn't do it. I opened his text and read it over again, feeling more angry than dejected.

There were things Freddie and I needed to talk about, none of which included him asking me about my appointment. I didn't want to see his name pop up on my phone unless it was him announcing that he had found some resolution for the Caroline dilemma. The little banter, the small talk hurt too much. They were empty words and I told him so. I typed out everything I'd been thinking since I'd left Rio. *There's no way this will work. You're a million miles away. What if Caroline IS pregnant and what if it IS your baby? Caroline will never let us be happy. The world will never let us be happy. Every magazine and newspaper and TV show is reporting your engagement to her. How could this possibly end well for us?* And then I capped it off with a final text.

Andie: For now, I need to focus on my wrist and my career.

It was as solid as a breakup. I'd completely come to terms with the fact that Caroline had won. Unless she got hit by a meteorite, she wasn't going to let Freddie and I be together. So what was the point of ignoring the inevitable?

The doctor knocked just as I'd slipped my phone back into my purse.

"Ms. Foster?" he asked as he strolled inside.

I took a deep breath. It was time to focus on something other than Freddie.

———

KINSLEY, BECCA, AND I spent three days in L.A. before we flew to New York to meet the rest of our team for a Good Morning America interview. We were scheduled for a week-long tour around the United States that I'd been looking forward to like a death sentence. Kinsley pushed me onto the plane in L.A. and once we landed, there were cars waiting outside the airport to whisk us directly to the studio. I needed sleep, a shower, and a decent meal, but there was no time.

Right before we went on air, Becca handed me two espresso shots.

"Because you literally look like death," she said with a laugh.

I downed them like water and within a minute, I knew it'd been a mistake. I was already nervous enough to go on live TV. I didn't want to talk about Freddie. I hadn't responded to his text messages, though I'd read every single one.

...please don't do this...

...give me time...

...just give me something here...

He still hadn't gotten a handle on Caroline, which meant there was no reason to respond.

As the hosts announced us and we walked out onto the stage to patriotic music, I thought I'd have a heart attack. I took a seat beside Kinsley and tried to contain my nerves.

In the end, I thought I'd answered the questions normally, but Kinsley and Becca wouldn't stop making fun of how jittery I'd been. I pulled off the fake eyelashes the makeup team had made me wear and scrubbed the makeup off my face.

"It's Becca's fault!" I said. "She gave me enough caffeine to kill me."

Becca laughed. "Well you can thank me later. This week is going to be insane, so I suggest resting up and staying caffeinated."

She wasn't kidding.

After our interview with Good Morning America, we did a fan meet-and-greet. Immediately after that, we flew to Washington D.C. where, over the next few days, we were honored with a special dinner and a parade around the capital. I shook the President's hand and tried not to say anything inappropriate or gushy to Michelle Obama.

During the parade, Kinsley leaned over and nudged me.

"Make sure to soak this all up while you can. These moments are once in a lifetime."

I stared out over the crowd surroundings the streets. They were all waving small American flags, screaming and shouting as we drove by on top of a fire truck. There were little girls wearing jerseys with my number on them, crying as I tossed candy and necklaces with tiny soccer balls hanging off like charms. I soaked in the moment, trying to smile and wave at every fan who was there to support us, and yet all the while, a part of me was 6,299 miles away in Rio.

Every chance I got, I'd check my phone for messages from Freddie. I craved his messages as much as I hated them.

...I miss you...

...I'm off to London tomorrow and I'll be meeting with my lawyers right away...

IT WAS FOUR days after I'd cut off communication that he called me. I was alone, in my shared hotel room, and I glanced down to find his name flashing across my phone's screen. I knew it would only make matters worse if I answered it, and yet I couldn't resist.

"Andie?" he answered in shock.

My name, spoken from his lips, was enough to make me tear up.

"Andie?" he asked again when I didn't speak up.

"I'm here," I said, hearing the sadness in my voice.

"I can't believe I'm finally talking to you."

I inhaled a shaky breath and tried to pull it together. I knew I only had a few minutes before Kinsley and Becca returned to our hotel with food from a diner down the street.

"How are you?" he asked, so desperately hopeful that I had to answer, even though I hated the small talk.

"I'm good. I watched your final race today," I said, staring up at the popcorn ceiling. "Well, not live obviously. We were visiting one of the children's hospitals in D.C. and they were playing the footage from a few days ago."

"It was a good race," he said; I could hear the exhaustion in his voice.

There were so many questions I wanted to ask him. How's London? How's Georgie? How's that sixth gold medal feel around your neck? Did you go to the closing ceremonies? Have you talked to Caroline? Have you thought about me as much as I've thought about you?

"Freddie, I—"

"Andie, hold on." I could hear him talking to someone in the background, but I couldn't tell who it was. "Give me a second," he told the other person.

The hotel door opened with laughter as Kinsley and Becca entered the room, arms overflowing with takeout.

"I hope you're hungry!" Kinsley said, dropping two togo containers at the bottom of my queen bed before glancing up and realizing I was on the phone. "Oops!" she said, covering her mouth.

I shook my head and mouthed, "It's fine," before slipping into the bathroom and locking the door.

"Freddie, are you still ther—"

My question was cut off by his own statement. "Andie, I've got to run. I've got a meeting with my PR team in the morning and my lawyer wants to go over a few things."

"Oh, okay right," I said, meeting my own sad reflection in the mirror.

"Yeah, I'll try and reach you la—"

His sentence cut off.

"Freddie?" I asked, to no reply.

I stared down at the black screen. It'd taken four days to get a thirty second phone call. Four days of watching Caroline's face splashed across every magazine, TV, and news story I stumbled upon. Four days of watching her dip into wedding boutiques and baby boutiques around London. Four days and all I had to show for it was a thirty second phone call.

It wasn't enough.

I missed him so much and the more days that passed, the farther apart we felt. Thirty seconds couldn't sustain me. Thirty seconds wouldn't reassure me that he and I would work out. Thirty seconds was nothing.

"Andie, are you okay?"

I'd sunk down to the bathroom floor. Could they hear me out there?

I inhaled and swiped at my cheeks, trying desperately to get rid of the evidence. I couldn't keep crying over Freddie. I was really fucking sick of crying over Freddie. This was supposed to be the best week of my life and I was sitting on the bathroom of a five-star hotel where the towels were warmed and the soap was designer, and I was crying about stupid Frederick Archibald and his stupidly beautiful face.

I felt something hit my butt and I turned to find a piece of paper they'd slid under the bathroom door.

Chapter Fifty-One

FREDDIE

MY FIRST NIGHT back in London, I started unpacking my things, amazed that I'd been able to bring so much shite with me across the ocean. I worked my way through a pile of stuff sitting on a chair in the corner, but paused when I caught a glimpse of red lace peeking out from the very bottom. It was the red mask Andie had worn to Mascarada. I'd pocketed it on our way out of the club. She couldn't wait to take it off and had nearly tossed it in a bin, but I'd caught it first.

It was beautiful and she'd looked beautiful wearing it. Caroline had done her best to taint that moment in the club, but she couldn't erase the memories we'd made on that leather couch. I'd had Andie under my thumb in the dim lights and if I closed my eyes and ran my hand over the red lace, I could still feel the lust take hold.

I picked it up off the chair and cradled it in my hand. The red lace was torn in one corner and the black silk ribbon was crinkled, but other than that, it was no worse for wear.

"I know Caroline is faking the pregnancy and I'm THIS close to proving it!"

That's how Georgie entered my room, with an accusation and a tone that warned me not to argue. I turned from the chair to see her standing with her hands on her hips in my bedroom doorway, no smile, no nod.

I shook my head. "I just went over it with Dave, Georgie. She's shown me the ultrasound photos, and records from a legit doctor in London. And we can't do a paternity test until she's a little further along in the pregnancy. I'm meeting with him again tomorrow but—"

She wiped her hand down her face. "You aren't listening! You told me to keep tabs on her, and I've been doing just that. I think she's faking the whole thing."

"Do you have proof?" I asked, hopeful.

"No, but—"

I turned back to continue unpacking, but she whipped around me and jumped between me and my suitcase. "I lived with Caroline in that suite for the last few weeks. We avoided each other at all costs, but I was always there when she sat down to go through her emails in the morning."

"So?"

"So…" She smirked. "I hovered in the kitchen, pretending to drink coffee, and secretly watched her type in her computer's password for nearly a week before I finally had it figured out. When I was on the plane today, I logged in and took a look around."

I dropped the red mask on top of my suitcase and let my lungs fill with hope. "Georgie, what'd you find in her email?"

She held up her hands to slow me down. "It's not proof of her faking the pregnancy, but it's definitely fishy. I rooted around her deleted emails—thank goodness Caroline is too dim to know how to properly use Gmail—and I found an email exchange between her and that 'legit doctor' in London. She sent him £100,000 and they're supposed to meet tomorrow for coffee. How weird is that?"

I dropped the red mask on top of my suitcase and took a deep breath. For the first time since the pregnancy announcement, I sensed a chink in Caroline's armor.

"£100,000?"

She nodded excitedly.

"How'd she send it?"

"PayPal! To his *personal* email address!"

I nodded, thinking. "G, I admit that sounds suspicious, but I need some kind of concrete proof of wrongdoing. If we go public with stolen emails, she'll probably just reveal that the money was more of her philanthropy, some donation sent to Doctors Without Borders or UNICEF. Besides, hacking someone's email is probably illegal."

"Who cares if it's bloody illegal? So is extortion!" she shouted.

"I know." I leveled my gaze on her. "Which is why I want you to go and stake out that coffee shop tomorrow. We need to figure out what's going on between them. I know I said no cloak-and-dagger, but—"

"No need to justify, Fred. I think it's a brilliant plan. I'll be there."

She seemed too eager.

"Georgie. I'm serious. No actual daggers at the coffee shop," I warned.

She smirked. "I wouldn't dream of it. We all know justice is best served hot and foamy."

Chapter Fifty-Two

FREDDIE

FIRST THING THE following morning, I walked into my lawyer's office in Hanover Square. He was already set up in a large conference room on the first floor. He took up nearly half of the large oak table and my PR team was spread out across the other half. Together they made up my brain trust, responsible for both legally extricating myself from Caroline's grasp regardless of the baby situation and minimizing the collateral damage Andie would feel. It was early, but it looked like everyone had been there since the crack of dawn.

I slid a coffee in front of Dave and he barely looked up from the pile of work in front of him. I had no bloody clue what he was up to, but he had files and papers and two empty cups of coffees spread out before him. At the very least, he looked busy.

"Could I get you a coffee or a cup of tea?" his assistant asked me from the doorway.

I held up my half-full cup. "I'm good, Kathleen. Thank you."

I felt rather useless standing there, watching them all

work. I pulled out one of the chairs closest to Dave and waited for someone to take a break and fill me in on what they'd been doing all morning. Truly, it wasn't necessary for me to be there, but I wanted to be as close to the solution as possible. For too long, my focus had been elsewhere, but with the games finished, it was time to show Caroline that playtime was over.

A few minutes later, Dave finally glanced up from his work.

"Fred, first of all, you're a hell of a swimmer."

I nodded in thanks and pulled my chair closer to him.

"That being said, you've worked yourself into a shite situation here."

"I know that. Have the PR people worked out how to get me out of it yet?"

He shook his head and rifled through a few papers to get to a yellow legal pad buried underneath. "It just doesn't look good. You see, if we ignore the fact that Caroline has behaved criminally and present the separation as a result of irreconcilable differences, you come out looking like an ass, and Andie is sure to receive more vitriol than ever."

"And what about the stuff Georgie found?"

"Up against the story of the cheating father of her unborn baby? Nobody will care. Like you mentioned on the phone, she's likely to pass it off as a charitable donation, or as paying the premium for top obstetrical care."

I shook my head and fell back into my chair.

"We're working on it, Fred, but without evidence of Caroline's extortion, we can't weaken her position in the public eye. And if we can't reverse this perception, any pain we inflict on Caroline will inexorably pale in comparison to the hurt Ms. Foster will endure in the aftermath."

———

IT WAS NEARLY lunchtime before I got a chance to step out of the conference room and check my mobile. I'd gone over every detail of Rio with my PR team. They'd listened and shaken their heads, more than convinced Caroline was a lunatic, but they agreed with Dave that there wasn't enough objective evidence to bring her down.

I was knackered and hungry, but Georgie had already called four times that morning, the last of which had only been a few minutes earlier.

"Georgie, you there?" I asked as soon as the call picked up.

"FRED."

She sounded out of breath and excited. I shoved against the hallway wall, giving space to the lawyers flooding out of the building for lunch.

"What is it, G? Have you gone to the coffee shop yet?"

"Yes! I've been sitting at the table right behind Caroline and her dopey doctor for the last fifteen minutes and she hasn't even noticed!"

"How is that possible?"

"I've got a red wig on and everything. I think I look quite cute. Might have to give it a go one of these nights when I've the time."

I pinched the bridge of my nose. "Georgie, have you heard anything?"

She practically squealed. "SO MUCH! I can't tell you everything right now. I'm in one of the bathrooms and someone's already knocking on the door. But Fred, get this —the doctor went to university with Caroline, and he's obviously in love with her. I just know he's been helping her falsify the pregnancy! It makes so much sense."

"Has he said that?"

"They only just started talking about it when you called."

"Get back in there Georgie, and call back on my lawyer's conference line so I can have him record their conversation. I'll text you the number."

The chance that Caroline would say anything incriminating in a public setting was slim to none, but regardless, I ran back into the conference room and explained the situation to Dave as quickly as possible. Just as I finished, the phone rang in the center of the conference table, and for the next thirty minutes we were all privy to Caroline's conversation. We sat, stunned as Caroline spoke with her friend, Dr. Dunn.

I didn't care that my stomach was growling with hunger; I hovered over that conference table and listened to Caroline's voice through the speaker. She was laying on the charm like I'd never heard before, sweet and innocent and disgustingly pleasant as she droned on with her friend.

At first, I thought Georgie had overestimated the content of their conversation.

"This reminds me of the good old days in Cambridge," he said with a wistful tone.

Caroline giggled and Georgie cleared her throat.

"You know those are some of the fondest memories I have."

Dr. Dunn leaned closer to the phone. "I did receive your payment the other day, but it would be quite unnecessary if you were amenable to my alternative. Honestly, Caroline. You know I'm mad about you—are you sure it's worth faking a paternity test just to be with a man who doesn't love you? You and I could have—"

"Hush, Nick. You know how much this marriage means to me. I love you, you know I do, but I'm too stressed to think about all of this right now. Please don't make this more difficult than it has to be. You and I will always have something special between us, truly."

Their tone wouldn't have drawn the attention of the patrons around them, but to me, her words were good as gold. From "darling, I adore you", they slipped so easily into the conversation we'd all been waiting for. Dave practically chomped at the bit, hovering over the conference table, tirelessly taking notes on the things we were overhearing.

"We must keep this between us, darling…"

"You've been such a good friend to me through this all, you must know how much your help means to me…"

"Freddie insisted on the paternity test as we assumed he would, but he would never suspect your involvement…"

"Sophie will run the story as soon as I give her the go-ahead…"

Caroline had finally slipped up and dug her own grave, and Georgie, the brilliant little detective, had been there to listen to her do it. I'd known for weeks that Caroline Montague was a manipulative, conspiratorial, dishonest woman, and now the world would know too. It was time to finish this whole thing once and for all.

———

CAROLINE AGREED TO dinner right away. She answered my call with a 'darling, I'm so happy to hear from you' and she'd crooned into my mobile about how she'd been hoping for a reconciliation once we'd arrived back in London. She admitted that the circumstances of the pregnancy must have come as quite a shock, but that she knew, in time, I would come to understand her reasoning behind putting a wedge between Andie and I.

"I just couldn't lose you like this Freddie," she said, reaching across the table at the restaurant Georgie and I had agreed upon. We'd only been sitting at the table for ten minutes and I'd already had enough. Her hand fell on top of mine and I took in the sharp shade of red covering her nails. It was the same shade she'd smeared across her lips—lips that were currently tipped up in an innocent little smile. She was dressed in a silky cream dress, back to looking the part of the innocent angel. I wasn't sure how much longer I could let her get away with it.

"I think you'll make a wonderful father, Freddie."

Had I eaten the bread they'd brought to our table, it would have come back up with that comment.

"How is the pregnancy going so far?" I asked, careful to watch her face for any sort of tell.

She pressed her hand to her stomach as if there was really something there other than the French baguette she'd stuffed down her throat a second earlier. "I've been having bouts of morning sickness off and on, but everything I read says that's normal."

I nodded.

"I'm just glad I was able to make it to all of your races." Of course she was. They couldn't resist showing her on the stadium screen. She played the role of the nervous fiancée just the way they wanted her to. "You were brilliant, Frederick," she continued.

I nodded and took a sip of water.

"How has your mom taken the baby news?" she asked.

I thought back to the call I'd had with her the day before. It'd been strained and short. *What will you do now that you've returned from Rio, Frederick? You've turned down every event. The press are beside themselves to get an exclusive with you. I think you ought to come out and clear the air. You need to let the world know that Caroline is your fiancée and the mother of your child, and that you're not leaving her for some girl you met four weeks ago.*

Four weeks.

How had so much changed in four weeks?

"Freddie?"

I shook my head, glanced back up at Caroline, and lied. "I haven't spoken to her in a few days."

Her brow perked. "Ah, well, I'm sure she's so excited."

I couldn't sit there any longer. I'd gotten her to the restaurant and she had her guard down; sitting there any longer wouldn't serve any purpose.

"Georgie can't wait to become an aunt."

She swallowed down a piece of bread slowly and then reached for her glass of water. After a long, drawn out sip, she finally glanced up to me. "Oh, that's such good news."

I leaned forward so that the nice couple at the table beside us—people who were actually enjoying their dinner —wouldn't hear me. "It's a shame she won't become one for quite some time."

Her eyes narrowed, but her tone stayed light. "What do you mean?"

I rolled my eyes. "Oh, give it a rest already, Caroline. You aren't pregnant." She set her glass on the table as I continued. "Georgie found the emails you sent to your friend, Dr. Dunn. Nice guy with a practice in central London? He must have had no trouble adding your name to the ultrasound photos." I never gave her a chance to cut me off. "Tell me, was he going to lie to my face when we returned to London? Pass along forged medical records with your name on them? What about a paternity test? Would we have seen him about that as well?"

Caroline picked up her napkin and dabbed at the corners of her mouth. She seemed wholly unaffected by the news. She didn't blush or fidget. When she'd finished wiping away the imaginary crumbs, she dropped her napkin to her lap and leaned over the table confidently.

"This is ridiculous. You can't prove any of this nonsense."

I laughed. "I haven't needed proof since you first showed your true colors. I'm announcing our separation as soon as I leave tonight."

Her demeanor shifted then. The polite, anxious expression was wiped clean like she'd taken a towel to her features. She looked like a snake ready to strike. Her eyes narrowed and her lips pressed tightly together.

"The fact that you still think you're in control right now is truly the sad part of all of this." I focused on the slow-spreading smirk as it overtook her features. "Don't you think I planned for this?" She laughed and flattened her hand across her stomach. "Whoops! I've lost the baby. Look at that." She shook her head and shot me a pitiful glare. "I suppose the stress of having a cheating fiancé would cause any woman to miscarry, don't you think?" She didn't give me time to reply. "Tell me dear: how do you think the world will treat your little slut when they find out that she's not just taken my husband and ruined my fairy-tale life, but also killed my sweet baby?"

She had a valid point, but she'd underestimated me. She assumed I still thought she had an ounce of humanity left inside her, but I knew better. There was no negotiating with Caroline. I knew that if I sat her down at dinner and revealed my hand, she'd reveal hers with a gloating laugh. I could try and be gentle and persuade her to back off, but it would get me nowhere.

"Her fate is linked to mine, Frederick. If you try to pull away from me, it will only tighten the noose around Andie's neck. But you have an alternative: I know the media will love to hear about how you've stood by my side through a devastating miscarriage. Sure, you'll do some groveling and they'll make you pay for the affair, but in the end it'll all work out." She smiled. "Don't you see, Freddie? You'll never get rid of me."

I shook my head and reached into the pocket of my trousers for my mobile. At first, I'd wanted to keep the press out of it, but Georgie, Dave, and my PR team had convinced me that transparency was our ally. I already had the article pulled up on my mobile. It'd been published twenty minutes earlier, as soon as Caroline's ass had hit the chair inside the restaurant.

She took the mobile from my hand, but I was too anxious to watch her read the whole thing. The article was long—part interview, part exposé—and it touched on everything from my Olympic records to Andie and Caroline.

"It's an exposé," I said, reaching over and swiping my hand across the screen so an image of the fake ultrasound photo popped up, full-screen. "You see, for the last few months, I've largely ignored the press. They've been hounding my family and my manager to get to me." I saw the mobile shaking in her hand, but I didn't feel bad for her. "This time I answered every question they wanted to know: the forced arrangement between you and I, my involvement with Andie, and, most importantly, how you lied to the world about a baby that never existed."

The color drained from her face and she dropped the mobile to the table. It shook the stemware, drawing the attention of the guests around us, but I trudged on, mostly because at that point, it felt bloody good to unravel the snake that'd been coiled around me for the last few months.

"Oh and we contacted Dr. Dunn—well, I should say, my lawyer contacted him. He signed an affidavit that details his involvement in your lies. Since he was so cooperative, we won't pursue criminal charges, though he surely won't get off so easily with the Medical Council."

She reached for her mobile in her purse, but I shook my head.

"If you're about to contact Sophie Boyle, I wouldn't bother. She's actually the person who interviewed me." I could see the shock sink in. "Wasn't she a friend of yours? Nice girl—bit of a mercenary, don't you think? I would say you should pick your friends a bit more wisely in the future."

She let go of her mobile and closed her clutch.

"Fuck you, Freddie," she spat before sliding her chair away from the table. "This isn't over."

A part of me felt bad for her then—a small, tiny iota that diminished the longer she stared daggers at me.

"You've done this to yourself, Caroline. What happened to you?"

Her eyes were filled with such hatred. She reared back as if she were about to backhand me, but Georgie was already there, holding up her phone with one hand and catching Caroline's arm in the other.

"Hey roomie! I'll never forget the wonderful memories we've shared—this one in particular."

Caroline shoved Georgie back so hard that Georgie nearly lost her footing and fell onto the table behind her.

"Get that camera out of my face!" Caroline yelled.

I stood up and rounded the table to put myself between the two of them. The restaurant's manager was already approaching us, concerned about the commotion. We'd overstayed our welcome, and I had no intention of ruining the night for everyone around us. I threw more than enough money on the table and turned to escort Georgie from the restaurant.

"Let's go, G."

She held up her phone. "I got every single word! And that near-slap at the end. That was pure magic."

"This isn't over Freddie!" Caroline yelled out after me.

I shook my head and kept walking.

She was wrong. It *was* over, and once the shock of the news wore off, she'd realize it as well. With the article, the doctor's signed confession, and Georgie's video, Caroline had undone herself. She could trash me in the news all she wanted, but no one with half a brain would take her seriously after the reality of her insanity spread. She'd assumed that lies about infidelity and pregnancies would trump all, but it turned out truth burned far hotter than Caroline's fiction. London socialite turned absolute whacko? I couldn't have made it up better if I'd tried. Sophie Boyle had practically salivated over the phone when I'd started to lay out the story for her.

As I escorted Georgie out of the restaurant and toward a waiting cab, she glanced back at me. "How do you feel?"

I inhaled a breath of night air.

Free.

I felt free. For the first time since Henry's death, I finally felt like I was ready to handle the responsibility of my title without caving to my mum's demands. I could be Freddie Archibald, swimmer, duke, and normal bloke. She hadn't thrown Caroline at me out of malice. She'd suffered in the last few years, more than she let on to Georgie and me. She'd lost her husband and her son and she wanted something to look forward to, she wanted an engagement and a wedding and future grandchildren. She wanted a new daughter-in-law she could welcome into the family and dote on, and when I'd broken the news about Caroline to her on the way to dinner, I'd promised her that soon enough, she'd have one.

Chapter Fifty-Three

ANDIE

A **FEW DAYS** after we'd returned to the States, life had returned to normal (as much as it ever would). We'd wrapped up our final interview as a team and parted ways in D.C. Everyone headed back to the lives they'd dropped upon getting called up to play for the Women's National Team. For most of my teammates, it'd been a tough few months away from their families. For me, it had been ideal timing. Before the games, I'd wrapped up my final year of playing college soccer and had started planning for my life after graduation.

I had a few offers from club teams around the United States including Orlando, Seattle, and Houston, but I was more interested in the offers from soccer clubs abroad. Arsenal and Chelsea were the two I'd actually started to consider before the games had ramped up. They were both great teams, and Chelsea was in need of a goalkeeper immediately—which meant if I signed with them, I'd get to start right away. I'd get a ton of field time and I'd get the opportunity to hone my skills against international competition before the next World Cup in a few years.

Kinsley padded into the kitchen and sent me a sleepy nod that I half-heartedly returned. I'd been hard at work creating a list of pros and cons for the five club teams I was still considering. Currently, the list only included food. In Houston, I would get great BBQ, but in Chelsea, I'd get fish and chips.

"How's the cereal?" she asked.

"Stale and gross," I said, dipping my spoon in and taking another bite. It tasted like cardboard, but I was too hungry to care.

She laughed and looked in the fridge, though I knew she wouldn't find anything inside. We'd cleared it out before we'd left for Rio, and unless she wanted to eat a pickle or a jar of mustard for breakfast, she was shit out of luck. I'd rifled through the pantry until I found a lone box of Cheerios that had expired two months earlier.

"Where's Liam?" I asked.

"Sleeping."

I nodded.

She shut the refrigerator door after reaching the same disappointing conclusion I had thirty minutes earlier: nothing inside was edible. I shook the box of Cheerios in the air and she rounded the kitchen island, pulling back the chair beside mine at the table. I didn't hide my pros and cons list; Kinsley already knew I had a difficult decision ahead of me.

"Have you put any thought to what you'll do now that the games are over?"

I tapped my pen on the notepad. "A little bit."

"With Chelsea you'd be close to Freddie in London."

Freddie.

She was watching me with a hopeful glint in her eye, like I would rip up the empty list and toss it in the garbage for Freddie. Freddie. Freddie. Freddie. What did she not

376

understand about Psycho Caroline and her desire to murder me in my sleep? Did she really think I wanted to move to London and play for Chelsea, all so I could continue to deal with Caroline's crap? It sounded like a nightmare, even with Freddie by my side.

I shrugged. "I'm not sure where I want to play yet, and I doubt anyone would want me on their team until after I've finished rehabbing my wrist."

"That's a copout and you know it."

I stared up at her over my cereal bowl.

"Chelsea will sign you right now," she continued. "Hurt wrist or not. You're just scared of actually putting yourself out there."

"Maybe I want to play for Houston."

She rolled her eyes. "Oh yeah? Name one thing about that city."

"They have a lot of cowboys."

"Exactly," she said, tipping the cereal box over so she could get a handful of Cheerios. "If you're not going to make a move with Freddie now that Caroline is finally out of the picture, then you need to choose a team based on your needs. Chelsea is a good place to start."

I narrowed my eyes. "Wait, back up."

"Were you not listening that whole time?" She sighed. "You need to figure out what you want for your career—"

I shushed her. "No! Not that stupid part. What did you just say about Caroline?"

She furrowed her brow. "You didn't see the news this morning?"

"What news?"

"I thought you had a Google alert on Freddie?"

My heart dropped.

In an effort to get a grip on my life, I'd placed a Freddie filter on my computer as soon as I'd returned to the US.

No Googling, no Yahooing, no Binging. It wasn't healthy to spend all day scrolling through every photo of him I could find.

It'd been a few days since I'd gone Freddie-free and my life was already starting to look up. I'd brushed my hair and my teeth that morning, left my room, and I even had plans to go for a run after I finished eating my stale cereal. See? *Progress*.

Kinsley pushed my cereal bowl out of the way and handed me her phone with three tabs already pulled up.

"Pick one and read it."

CAROLINE'S CONCEPTION CONSPIRACY
Freddie freed following shocking report of fiancée's fraud, extortion

CAROLINE'S INACCURATE CONCEPTION
Aspiring duchess faked pregnancy

A WOLF IN CHIC CLOTHING
Socialite Caroline Montague unmasked as liar, extortionist

Olympian and Duke Freddie Archibald has been embroiled in a love triangle controversy of late involving his betrothed bride-to-be Caroline Montague and American acquaintance Andie Foster. Earlier reports detailing Archibald's alleged infidelity at the Olympic games brought sharp backlash and scathing public outcry against Foster, the young American goalkeeper, particularly after Montague revealed that she was expecting a child. However, new evidence suggests the pregnancy was a fabrication used to coerce Archibald into an arranged marriage he never agreed to.

"I'm glad the truth of Caroline's poisonous actions have come to light," said Archibald, speaking to Sky News reporter Sophie Boyle. "For weeks, she has extorted me for my silence and cooperation by

using threats and false medical records created in concert with a sympathetic doctor."

The madness began when three weeks prior to leaving for the Olympic Games in Rio, the Archibald family put out a statement announcing Frederick's official betrothal to Montague, a longtime family friend and London socialite. The betrothal came as no surprise to most of London, as Caroline had previously been linked with Henry Archibald prior to his death, but not everything was as it seemed, says Archibald.

"I never agreed to marry her. My mother suggested it after my brother passed away, but I didn't want any part of it—the estate, the family legacy. I just wanted to train and swim for my country. The betrothal was announced without my consent."

It had been widely speculated that the betrothal would become an engagement after Montague flew to Rio de Janeiro to cheer on her duke, but Archibald reportedly broke the news of his wishes the same day of her arrival.

"It was after I told her I wanted to end the betrothal that she let down the façade of the soft-spoken, charitable girl the world knew and embraced the role of scheming extortionist. She didn't care that I would never love her. She would stop at nothing to see the wedding through and to have her title set in stone."

With the Olympics finished, the entire conspiracy might have gone unreported, but for the efforts of the amateur detective and youngest Archibald, Georgia.

"I honestly didn't care about exposing [Caroline] as a criminal," she said. *"I just couldn't swallow the thought of 60 or 70 more years of her boring me to tears at Christmas."*

"Are you done yet? Skip to the end!" Kinsley said, pacing back and forth in front of the kitchen table.

. . .

Boyle pushed Frederick on the subject of Andie and their future together.

He smiled. "I'm not quite sure what the future holds for us. She and I never really had a chance while Caroline was in the picture, but she's an amazing person and hopefully once the dust settles on this story, she and I can have a fresh start."

I glanced up. "Is this real life? Did he just tell the world he wants a fresh start with me?"

She yanked the phone out of my hand. "EXACTLY! He's in love with you and you've been sitting at this table eating moldy Cheerios instead of packing your bags."

I leapt out of my chair. "Look up flights to London! I want to be on the next one that leaves LAX."

She nodded and waved her hand for me to hurry up. "Go pack and I'll book the ticket."

I ran down the hallway toward my room, already trying to think of what I should take. I needed cute clothes if I was going to fly across the ocean and show up on someone's doorstep.

Wait…

"What did the other articles say?" I shouted down the hall.

"There was a part about the doctor being in love with Caroline since college. Oh, and apparently Georgie dressed up and recorded them admitting to faking the pregnancy!"

Holy shit. Georgie did it.

I LOVE YOU GEORGIE.

"You can read the rest on the plane!" Kinsley continued. "Get to packing!"

Chapter Fifty-Four

ANDIE

THINGS I CARRIED with me off the plane in London:

- The 2mg Xanax my seatmate offered upon hearing the condensed version of my story
- An abysmal understanding of the London transit system
- A healthy dose of panic and anxiety (see: why I held on to the Xanax)
- My iPhone loaded with the theme song from *Rocky*, *Wonderwall* by Oasis, and *Your Song* covered by Ellie Goulding
- A text message from my mom that read: "This is crazy. You cannot fly halfway across the world and show up on the doorstep of a man you hardly know. What do you think will happen once you get to London?! You need to call him first! Meemaw is having heart palpitations."

My mom was wrong. She had to be. Freddie's article was his way of putting the ball in my court. He'd gotten rid of Caroline and he'd all but shouted to the world that he

381

wanted to be with me. It was my turn to show him I was capable of a grand gesture. After my plane landed in London later that same day, I pulled my luggage into the first bathroom I found and glanced in the mirror. *Oh, sweet Jesus.* The long flight had done a number on me, and without a deep clean in a shower, there wasn't much I could do. I washed my face and swiped on some mascara and blush. I could feel the woman beside me watching me freshen up, and when I finally glanced over and met her eyes, she smiled.

"Going somewhere fun?" she asked as she washed the soap from her hands.

"Umm...well." For some reason I couldn't come up with a lie on the spot, so I shrugged and told her the truth. "I'm going to try to find the man that might be the love of my life, now that his ex has been outed as a psychopath."

Her mouth dropped open in shock and I laughed, trying to ease the awkwardness.

"Oh my lord...you're—"

I cleared my throat and nodded before she could even say it.

"Right," she said with a conspiratorial smile. She rifled through her purse and handed me a can of dry shampoo. "Here, take this dear."

I glanced up at my reflection and took note of my rat's nest. "Ah, good thinking."

She nodded and patted my shoulder. "You'll knock his socks off, I'm sure."

I sprayed in some dry shampoo and pulled my hair up into a messy bun. After a dab of perfume behind my ear, I pulled my luggage out of the bathroom behind me and headed for the taxi line out front.

I felt good, like maybe I wasn't a crazy person for flying to London without Freddie knowing. If Random Bathroom Lady believed in me, then this would surely work out in my favor.

"Where to?" the cabbie asked as I slid into his back seat and pulled my suitcase in after me.

"Miss? Where to?"

He stared back at me in the rearview mirror and I froze, unable to give him an answer.

"Oh. Right."

I had no clue where Freddie lived. How had I not thought this far ahead? Maybe because I'd shoved clothes into a suitcase, hightailed it to the airport, and jumped on the plane just as they announced the final boarding call. Now I was in London with nowhere to go.

"Ma'am, where do you want to go?"

"I actually have no idea," I said with a tight, strained laugh as I opened the backdoor and pushed my luggage back out onto the sidewalk. I probably looked like a whack job, and truthfully, I was starting to feel like one.

I stepped back up onto the curb and dropped my suitcase beside me. It was 9:00 PM London time, and I wasn't sure if Georgie would have her phone on her, but I tried her anyway. The traffic around the airport made it hard to hear the phone ring, and for two seconds I feared I'd be stuck on that sidewalk with nowhere to go. I'd have to find a random hotel and stay the night like a lonely loser.

"ANDIE!" Georgie squealed into the phone. "Took you long enough!"

I sighed with relief at the sound of her voice. "Hi Georgie."

"I take it you're phoning to shower me with praise on my excellent detectivating?"

"Uh, well…yes, something like that." I glanced around. "I'm actually in London."

She screamed so loudly into the phone I had to hold it

away from my ear to keep from going deaf. The few people hovering on the curb beside me, waiting for their taxis, sent me awkward glares.

"Georgie, stop screeching."

"Where are you!? I'll come round and pick you up."

"I'm still at the airport. My plane landed like thirty minutes ago."

"You've come for him haven't you?" She sounded so excited by the prospect.

"Unless he's already found someone else?" I joked with a flat, anxious laugh.

"Are you kidding me? The prat has been lolling around his flat like the world is ending. He's clearly been waiting for you to call, and any time I try to go over he nearly bites my head off about giving him space and what not. It's all been very dramatic, I assure you."

I smiled. "Well if you wouldn't mind giving me his address, I think I'll just head straight there."

Chapter Fifty-Five

FREDDIE

"**O**PEN UP, FRED!**"**
I groaned at the sound of Georgie banging on my door. "Go away, G. I'm not up for company."

She ignored me, used her key, and shoved her way into my flat like a Tasmanian devil. I kept my head tucked in the fridge—looking for something to eat—but she strolled past me and picked up an empty bag of crisps from the kitchen counter.

"Listen, you insufferable hermit," she said, crumbling up the empty bag. "You need to tidy this place up and then maybe consider having a shower yourself."

I picked up my shirt, sniffed it, and only recoiled a bit. "It's not so bad," I said, returning to my search for food. I'd already eaten dinner a few hours earlier, but food was distracting and since Andie was on my mind, a distraction was more than welcome. I shoved the vegetables aside and reached for a cheese stick.

I let the refrigerator door fall closed and then glanced over to see Georgie drop a heavy paper sack at the base of the kitchen island. It sounded like there was a bowling ball stuffed inside.

"What've you brought, G?"

She ignored my question and walked toward me with determination. I'd barely pulled back the cellophane wrapper on my cheese stick when she slapped it out of my hand. It fell to the ground with a sad *thump*.

"Hey," I moaned. "I was going to eat that."

"Are you listening to me?! Leave the cheese stick!" she said with fire in her eyes. "You need to shower! Now!"

I'd seen a few different versions of Georgie over the years. She was excitable and loud and opinionated and crass, but this was Georgie on a whole new level. Her bright eyes were wide and anxious, urging me to take her seriously.

When I didn't move quick enough, she groaned and shoved past me to get a bin bag out of the broom closet. She whipped it open with a loud POP and tore through the kitchen, throwing away anything in her sight: trash, papers, an empty pizza box. She nearly tossed one of my gold medals (I hadn't gotten around to putting them up with the others yet) but I reached out and caught it before it fell into the bag.

"Georgie, you've gone completely mental. Should I ring a doctor?"

She ignored my teasing and turned back for the broom closet where she'd found the bag.

"Do you have a candle or something?" she asked, pinching her nose closed with her fingers.

"What's going on?"

She shook her head. "Nothing. Just…" She glanced around, trying to think up a lie. "I think you needed to freshen up a bit."

"I have a housekeeper who comes twice a week. Now fess up. What's gotten into you?"

She was a terrible liar, made worse by the anxious energy she put off when she was up to something.

I pulled the bag out of her hand and let it drop to the floor. "You're being really weird. Either tell me what's going on or—"

A loud knock on my front door interrupted my ultimatum. Georgie's eyes widened even more as she swept her gaze to the door.

"Oh no." Her hands covered her mouth. "I'm too late. You'll mess it all up with your manky apartment."

"Mess what up, Georgie?"

She didn't respond.

"Who's at the door?"

She shrugged and turned back for the broom closet, rooting through my cleaning products. "Go see for yourself," she said. "I've got work to do."

I wiped my hand down my face, annoyed at the idea of company. I didn't know what Georgie was up to, but the person at the door was knocking again, so I stepped over the bin bag to go answer it. I'd barely turned the knob when I heard Georgie spraying something in the kitchen. She'd truly gone off the deep end. I shook my head and whipped the door open.

Time stopped as Andie came into focus on my doorstep. I was gripping the door, mouth ajar, breath frozen, heart pounding.

I blinked, and blinked again.

It couldn't be her. She was supposed to be half a world away, and yet she was here, standing a foot away from me and waving a small British flag back and forth in front of her chest.

I couldn't quite wrap my head around her being here.

In London. At my flat. Her luggage was tucked behind her and she was wearing a small, tentative smile. Her gray eyes were gleaming with hope and her hand was shaking around the flag. Her pale blonde hair was falling out of a messy bun and she had on jeans and a wrinkled white blouse. She should have looked weary from her flight, but she was radiant. I wanted to reach out to touch her, but I was scared she'd disappear like a mirage.

"Andie?" I asked, hearing the hope in my voice.

Question after question sprang to mind (How did you get here? When did you plan this? Where are you staying? How long will you be here?), but I settled on a simple statement. "You're here."

A loud crash sounded in the kitchen and her smile dropped. Her eyes scanned past me, trying to find the source of the commotion. "Is this a bad time?"

I shook my head and pulled the door open wider. "No, it's just Georgie. Come in."

We hadn't touched. She'd been on my doorstep for one whole minute and I hadn't kissed her and I wanted to kiss her.

I held the door open and she stepped inside with a hesitant laugh. I reached for her suitcase before she could and rolled it in the foyer for the time being.

"Pretend like I'm not even here!" Georgie shouted from somewhere in the flat just before a door slammed. I had no clue what she was up to, but I didn't care. I closed the front door and focused on Andie as she inspected the photos hanging in the foyer.

"So this your place," she said, leaning forward on her toes to inspect a photo of Georgie and me from when we were little. Georgie had urged me to hire a decorator after I'd purchased the flat a few years back; as Andie turned to take in the living room, I made a mental note to thank her. "It's really nice, Freddie."

How had I still not touched her? She was walking around the place, smiling at the furniture when she should have been smiling at me. I stepped forward to break the separation and give her the greeting I should have at the door, but suddenly her face contorted as we both caught a whiff of air freshener coming from the kitchen. No, not a whiff. A plume of the noxious gas nearly knocked us off our feet. Georgie had sprayed enough of it that it smelled like a Febreeze factory had exploded in my flat.

Andie coughed and waved her hand in front of her face. "What in the world is that?"

"That will have been Georgie. She came around to tidy up just before you got here. It's supposed to smell like…" I checked the spray bottle. "*Summer citrus.*"

She laughed. "It smells like shitrus."

I shook my head and walked over to push open the balcony door. It was a bit chilly out, but we'd have to make do until the flat aired out.

I waved for Andie to follow me out onto the balcony and I watched in wonder as she took in the view of London. I'd grown accustomed to it over the years, but seeing it through her eyes reminded me how overwhelming it could be at first. She leaned against the railing and stared out at the London Eye.

"Georgie knew I was coming," she admitted, peering over at me from the corner of her eyes. "That's why she came to clean up, I think."

I stepped closer. "You called her, but not me?"

Her cheeks flushed. "I wanted it to be a surprise," she said, wrapping her arms around herself to keep warm. I stepped forward and rubbed my hand up and down her back, warming her skin beneath her blouse.

"It's a wonderful surprise," I assured her. I was still in shock.

She tilted her head to look at me over her shoulder. For a moment we hovered there with my hand on her back and her eyes pinned on my mouth.

"Typically when one makes a grand romantic gesture like this, they get kissed," she said wistfully.

"I still can't believe you're here. My lips haven't caught up with my eyes," I said, skimming my hand up her back so I could cup the base of her neck and tilt her mouth to mine.

"Well tell them to hurry."

It hadn't even been a month since she'd left me in that hotel in Rio, but as I bent down and pressed my lips to hers, it felt like years had separated us. Her hand pressed to my chest, gripping my shirt. She tugged me closer and I cradled her head, bringing her body closer to mine so I could bring her bottom lip into my mouth and show her how much I'd missed her.

She moaned against me and I pushed her back against the balcony railing. I knew the metal would bite into her back, but she didn't care. She was lost in the kiss as much as I was.

When I finally pulled back to catch my breath, she fit herself against me so her head was tucked beneath my chin and her cheek was pressed against my chest. "I read the article today. I read it and I got on a plane an hour later."

I smiled.

"Is that crazy?" she asked.

Crazy?

I tilted back to get a good look at her. Her lips were full, bright red, and so bloody kissable I couldn't help leaning forward and stealing a quick peck. I knew that wasn't what she wanted though. Her wide eyes were vulnerable and her heart was right there, splayed across her features. She was waiting for an answer, but I didn't want to scare her away. I didn't want to tell her the last few days without her had been miserable. I didn't want to tell her she was the reason I suddenly felt like life was more than races and medals and records. She was the reason I wanted more and if I told her that, I was scared she'd fight it, saying a month wasn't enough time to fall in love, but I was in love.

"You're not crazy," I promised. "If I hadn't heard from you by tomorrow, I was going to fly to L.A. I already had my ticket."

She smiled. "This is better."

I nodded. "Much better."

I brushed away a few strands of hair the wind had blown across her cheek. She fell into my touch, closing her eyes and inhaling the moment as much as I was. When she glanced back up at me a few seconds later, there was a playful edge to her smile.

"You know, there was one thing you left out in the article."

"Oh?"

She nodded. "You said you wanted another chance with me, but you weren't very explicit about your feelings."

I smiled and traced my knuckle back and forth across her cheek.

"I told you how I felt the night before you left Rio."

She sighed. "Yes, but that was in the moment, in the magic of Rio and the games…" She sighed. "I wondered whether you would feel the same in the light of day."

I bent down so I was at her eye level and spoke the next few words as clearly as I could. "Andie, I love you."

She grinned. "Okay, just checking."

I laughed. "That's it?"

I needed to hear her say it just as badly.

"Well, I'm here," she said, sweeping her hand across the London skyline. "Obviously that counts for something...and I do like your flat...and this view is pretty killer."

"Andie..."

Her eyes gleamed with mischief as she glanced back up to me. "And okay, fine. Frederick Archibald, though your name is slightly pretentious, I love you."

Georgie whipped my bedroom door open then, and we both turned to watch her walking out of my bedroom with one hand covering her eyes and the other stuck out straight, trying to keep from tripping over my living room furniture.

"La la la, I'm not here!" she sang. "I wasn't listening very much, and I only heard the last bit about how you two love each other. It was all very nauseating and I nearly puked up my dinner in Fred's room."

"Georgie—"

She cut me off. "I'm leaving! Can't you see I'm leaving?!"

I watched her move through the living room with her hand over her eyes and just before she made it to the door, she tripped over the bag of rubbish she'd left by the kitchen island with an audible "oomph!"

I pushed down a laugh and moved to help her out, but she waved me away.

"Don't let me ruin your night. I just set up a few items in your room and now I'm going to see myself out."

Andie laughed. "What do you mean? A few items?"

She turned back and parted the fingers she was using to cover her eyes. She peeked through them to look at us and shrugged. "Oh, you know, just some stuff to get the romance going. Seeing as how my brother is dreadfully naff, I had to take things into my own hands—though I was fairly limited. The corner shop I went to hardly had anything to…how shall I say…" She waved her hand in the air. "Set the mood."

I groaned. "I don't really want to know what you've done in there, G."

"You should be thanking me!" she shouted as she grabbed her purse from the kitchen island and headed for the door. "I drew a bath because you stink—even if Andie is too polite to say so!"

Andie laughed as Georgie slipped out of the door. "BYE! We'll get breakfast in the morning and then pop into Chloé for that bag you promised!"

Once she was gone and I'd locked the door after her, Andie met me outside my bedroom door.

"Your sister is insane," she said with a laugh.

I nodded. "But you can't argue with her results."

She nodded toward my room. "C'mon, let's go see what she's done."

Andie pushed my door open and I prepared myself for the worst; turned out I hadn't been far off. As my gaze swept across the space, I hadn't a clue where to begin. There were cheap chocolates strewn around the room—not with any sort of rhyme or reason, just there, scattered so that you could hardly walk without stepping on one.

On the base of the bed, she'd taken a few dozen lemons and arranged them so they spelled out S-N-O-G.

"Lemons?" Andie asked as she stepped closer, sidestepping the candy minefield on the ground.

That wasn't even the worst of it. She'd tried to set the mood with a few candles lit on the bedside tables, but apparently the shop she'd gone to was out of standard tea candles. Instead, she'd purchased a dozen of those tall religious candles with Jesus, Mary, and a few other saintly blokes I probably should have known splayed out on the sides. Apparently, according to Georgie, the illuminated figure of a crucified Jesus was supposed to set the mood.

"In all fairness, she did say the shop was lacking a romantic selection," Andie said, picking up one of the lemons and glancing over to me.

I laughed and stepped closer to wrap my arms around her.

"Is this what life will be like?" she asked.

I smiled. "I'm afraid so. She used to live on the estate with my mum, but now that she's almost eighteen, she'll be getting a flat in the city."

Andie smiled. "That will be really fun."

She said it as though she'd be a part of the fun, like she'd be staying in London when Georgie moved down the street.

"How long can you stay?"

She glanced down as she dropped the lemon back onto my bed. "Actually I have a meeting tomorrow with Chelsea."

"The ladies football club?"

She nodded. "They offered me a spot before the games and—"

I crashed my lips against hers and stole the end of her sentence.

When I pulled back, she laughed and shook her head. "Nothing's been signed, and there's a real chance they won't want me after my physical, because of the wrist."

I shook my head. "They'll want you."

She'd just helped the best team in the world secure a gold medal in the Olympics. There wasn't a better keeper out there.

"If I do make the team," she continued, "then London

might be seeing a lot more of me."

I inhaled her words, trying not to look as if they were the best thing I'd heard in a decade. I'd already thought over all our options. I'd worked myself up to the idea of flying to L.A. once or twice a month to see her, but this? Her moving to London was something I hadn't dared imagine.

I cupped her cheeks in my palms and leaned down to steal another kiss.

"Something is buzzing," she said, jumping back.

"Oh god, what else did Georgie buy?"

She laughed and shook her head. "No, it's your phone."

It was buzzing on the nightstand and when Andie handed it over to me, a text from Georgie lit up the screen. I read it aloud.

"Georgie says, 'Oops might want to check the bath. Forgot to turn off the faucet before I left.'"

Andie spun for the bathroom. "Oh shit!"

Oh shit was right. There was water and bubbles everywhere. Water sloshed over the sides of the bathtub, making the marble around it a slippery hazard zone. The faucet was still running, and there were enough foamy bubbles to make it impossible to see Andie as she bent down to turn it off. I reached for a few towels beneath the sink and dropped them on the floor right as my mobile buzzed again.

Georgie: Oh! And I poured an entire bottle of bubble bath in the tub. I've always wanted to do that... :)

"I'll kill her," I said, tossing my mobile onto the sink and getting to work soaking up the water.

Andie laughed. "It's kind of fun." She pushed around

one of the towels with her feet. "It reminds me of foam parties back in college.

I scrunched my brows. "Foam parties?"

"You've never been?!"

I shook my head and bent down to push around one of the towels, blowing bubbles out of my path so I could actually see what I was doing. Andie bent down beside me and we worked together, mopping up the floor as best as possible. Our shoulders bumped together and she sent a smile my way. I shook my head, thinking of all the ways I'd murder Georgie in the morning.

I picked up one of the towels and carried it over to the sink to wring it out. Just as I started to twist it in my hands, Andie's white blouse landed with a splat on the counter beside me. I stared at it for a second and then glanced up to meet her reflection in the mirror. She was half hidden in the mass of bubbles, but her wicked smile was easy to see.

"Is this what happens at those parties?" I teased.

She fingered the straps of her bra and I watched, enraptured.

"Not quite…at least not while I was there."

She was being shy, taking her time with her bra. She met my eyes in the mirror as she pushed the straps off her shoulders. Her chest rose and fell with her nervous breath, straining against the top of her bra.

"Take it off," I said with a subtle nod.

She twisted her hand behind her back and unhooked the clasp. The creamy lace slid away and a second later, her bra landed beside her blouse.

The bathroom was full of steam and bubbles and water and the scent of that damn bubble bath. I turned from the sink and she bent to push off her jeans.

"Andie…"

She looked up through the veil of the bubbles. "Will

the water ruin your floors?"

I shook my head. "I don't care."

"Then I see no reason to let this bubble bath go to waste."

She let her jeans fall to the floor, and then she was gloriously naked. The bubbles shrouded her tan skin as she stepped back and put one leg in the tub.

"Mmm," she hummed, drawing a finger out and trying to lure me closer. "It's warm."

I reached behind my neck and pulled my shirt off over my head with one smooth pull.

"Coming in?" she asked as she bent and disappeared behind the bubbles. More water splashed out over the sides and I knew I'd displace even more when I joined her. We'd have quite a cleanup job, but I had a singular focus. My jeans hit the floor and my boxer briefs went next. I walked to the tub and Andie popped her head out of the bubbles. I had to hold back a laugh as I stepped in and sank into the warm water.

I could barely make her out on the other side of the mountain of bubbles.

"Where are you?" she asked, reaching out for me under the water. Her hand hit my upper thigh and I hissed and reached for it. I brought her palm to my mouth and pressed my lips to the very center.

"This bath won't last very long if you touch me there."

She laughed and scooted closer. I pushed some of the bubbles out of the way just as her chest fell against mine.

"You're right. Hop out and grab a few of those Jesus candles to keep us chaste."

I laughed and pulled her down onto me. My hands slid up her back and her chest hit mine. She was so warm and soft and wet. Her legs wound around my waist and her lips found mine. She was complete fucking heaven and I knew

I'd let the whole bathroom flood if only I could keep her there with me forever.

"Andie?" I whispered as I broke our kiss.

She nuzzled her head against my neck. "Hmm?"

I tangled my hands in her hair and pulled her head back so I could look her in the eye. "I want you to stay in London regardless of the meeting tomorrow. I know it's fast, but I want you to stay here. The flat is big and there's more than enough room for your things."

I thought I saw her nod but it was hard to see through the bubbles.

"Andie?"

She cursed under breath.

"What's wrong?"

No one should be upset in bubbles.

"This is supposed to be a happy moment," I said, bringing her against my chest and soothing her back.

"It is," she insisted, hugging me back just as fiercely. "I'm so happy but also…I lost a bet I made with Kinsley."

I laughed. "What bet?"

She tilted her head back and let out a heavy sigh.

"When she dropped me off at the airport, I told her I'd see her in a week, but she bet me a million dollars I wouldn't be coming back."

"Yikes." I smiled and pulled her close. "Where do you think you'll get that kind of cash?"

She kissed my chest and shrugged. "Maybe I'll ask Caroline to help me forge some bank documents."

I smiled. "Too soon."

She laughed. "Then let's stop talking and get to the things we really want to be doing."

I slipped my hand down her stomach and watched as she inhaled a shaky breath. Her smile slipped and her nostrils flared. Just like that, she was mine…*for good*.

Epilogue

ANDIE

"**FREDDIE! HAVE YOU** seen my cleats?!"

I threw a pair of stilettos aside and then pushed a few dresses out of the way to look in the back corner of the closet. There were heels and flats and sneakers, but my team cleats were nowhere to be found. I didn't even bother looking over on Freddie's side of the closet; it was always immaculate. I had no clue how he kept up with everything. My clothes and shoes usually landed somewhere in the vicinity of the closet, but hanging things up at night wasn't a priority when I had Freddie Archibald waiting for me in bed.

"Have you already looked in the kitchen?" Freddie asked, tipping his head into the doorway and offering me one of his trademark smiles.

I rolled my eyes for extra emphasis. "Of course I looked there."

It was a lie, but his smile was so confident and I wasn't going to give in that easily. He loved being right and I loved pushing his buttons. I stood up and swept past him to get out into the hallway.

His hand reached out to grab my waist to block my path. "Where are you going?"

I stared past his shoulder. "To grab a granola bar."

I could see his smile widen out of the corner of my eye. "You just had breakfast."

"Did I?" I scrunched my nose. "Hmm, wasn't very filling."

His hand tightened around my waist. "We both know you're going to have a look for your cleats in the kitchen."

I turned and pressed a kiss to his cheek. "Don't be silly. I really, really want a granola bar."

With that, I wrestled myself out of his grip and took off to the kitchen as fast as I could. If I could get them in my bag before he saw them in the kitchen, *technically* he wouldn't be right.

He shouted after me as I rounded the corner and I saw them sitting on the floor near the kitchen island, grass-stained and untied. I lunged for them and threw them in my bag, glancing up just in time to see Freddie standing in the doorway.

"Find them?"

I patted my bag. "They were in here the whole time."

He arched a dark brow. "Were they?"

I smiled, proud. "Yes, Archibald; you're not right *all* the time."

He pushed off the doorway and strolled to stand in the kitchen. (I swore it looked like he was gloating, though he had no reason to.) I watched him fill my water bottle and then reach into the pantry for a granola bar we both knew I didn't want.

"Here you go," he said, handing them both over to me.

I averted eye contact and grabbed for them before offering a deadpan, "Yum."

I was running a little behind so Freddie offered to drive

me. He reached for his keys and I slipped on my sneakers. Just as we were walking out the door, he laced his fingers through mine.

"You're sure the cleats weren't in the kitchen?"

I could see the devilish glint in his eyes, the small smirk he was trying desperately to squash.

"Positive," I lied.

He nodded and his smirk widened. "That's a shame. If they *were*, I was thinking of having you pay for it later."

"P-pay…"

My stomach dropped with anticipation as the meaning behind his sentiment sank in.

"I guess you still could?" I offered. "I mean, even though the cleats *were* in my bag."

He laughed and then reached up to cradle my neck so he could press a quick kiss to the corner of my mouth.

"First we have to get you to your game."

I smiled. "You're able to take me?" I asked. "I thought you had a meeting with the construction team for the swim club?"

Since the Olympics, Freddie had been in no rush to jump back into the limelight. He took time off before deciding his next move would be to open a swim club for the underprivileged in central London. His foundation had partnered with Nike and they were due to break ground on the project in a week.

"I had the team move it to another day. I couldn't miss your final."

I smiled and popped up onto my toes to plant a kiss on his cheek. "We should go out with Georgie and your mum after the game to celebrate."

He peered at me out of the corner of his eye. "Brilliant idea. I have a feeling there will be a lot to celebrate."

———

"WE BELIEVE, WE believe, we believe in ANDIE!"

"We believe, we believe, we believe in ANDIE!"

The entire stadium was on their feet for the final seconds of our game. Fans were chanting behind me. Arsenal's offense was making their way down the field so I stepped out in front of the goal line and watched as the ball made its way closer to me. I'd been bored, waiting for this moment for 89 minutes; my teammates had owned the field and I hadn't touched the ball once. Now, in the final seconds of the game as the other team got desperate to even the score, maybe I'd actually get to play my part.

I rolled out my wrist, testing it out of habit. It still gave me trouble every now and then, but nothing compared to how it'd felt during the Olympic Games. I bent my knees and loaded my weight onto the balls of my toes. I had to be light on my feet, ready to leap at a moment's notice. The ball slipped down the field, closer and closer.

"WE BELIEVE, WE BELIEVE, WE BELIEVE IN ANDIE!"

Arsenal's left-side striker moved the ball across the field and wove through defenders. She broke away and instead of crossing it to a streaking teammate, she reared back and rocketed the ball for the net. It was low and headed to the right. In microseconds my body reacted, throwing itself into the calculated trajectory of the ball. It ripped through my hands but hit my chest with a heavy thud and I wrapped myself around it. Seconds later, the shouts from the crowd finally sank in. The game hadn't been called yet, but I knew we'd won. I could let go.

My teammates were there, pulling me to my feet and throwing themselves against me. I laughed, too full of adrenaline to register the excitement. It was the final game of the Women's Champions League, which meant I'd made it through my rookie season with my new club undefeated. They'd announce us as the league champions, and more than likely, there would be a giant trophy waiting for us after the game wrapped up.

"You did it, Foster!" my teammate Sasha shouted before throwing her arms around me. She was a tiny thing and the best striker we had. It was because of her that we had our only point on the board.

"You killed it out there."

She laughed. "Yeah, well hopefully we can give you some more wiggle room next time."

I slung my arm around her shoulders. "I'll remember you said that."

We walked in tandem toward the center of the field. Both teams were congregating there, shaking hands and offering pleasantries to one another before Arsenal's coach led them off the field. We always stayed in the center so our assistant coach could lead us through some quick post-game stretches.

I glanced back to the stands to look for Freddie and Georgie—a habit I'd acquired after my first game in London. The day after I signed the contract with the team, Freddie announced that he'd purchased season tickets in the front row on the sideline. I'd laughed as he held up the printed tickets in the kitchen, too excited to wait for the official ones in the mail. They had private boxes in the stadium that would have afforded Freddie more privacy, but he'd shaken his head and insisted the sideline was where he wanted to be. And he had been. For every single home game, Freddie and Georgie sat in those seats.

In the beginning, their mom had joined as well, but soccer really wasn't her thing. She pretended to like it for my sake, but after seeing her squirm on the sidelines in her

cashmere sweater, Freddie and I had freed her of the oblig-
ation. *"Too gritty for my taste, though you are very talented and quite
pretty in your uniform, dear!"* She was happy to stay home and
clip out details of the games from the newspapers. We'd
flip through the clippings together over tea on Sunday
mornings. Oddly enough, I realized growing up with
Christy and Conan Foster had perfectly prepared me for
life with a dowager duchess.

Usually after my games wrapped up, Freddie and
Georgie would wait for me to finish stretching and we'd
meet out back of the stadium to ride home together (with a
pizza in tow), but when I glanced up into the stands after
the game, their seats were empty.

I knew they'd both planned on attending the game;
Freddie had confirmed it in the kitchen just before we'd
left.

"I have a feeling there will be a lot to celebrate."

Apparently not, since he and Georgie hadn't even
waited for me. All the other fans were still lingering in the
stands, but Freddie and Georgie's seats were glaringly
empty.

"Why the long face, Foster?" Sasha asked from beside
me. We'd moved on to a new stretch and I hadn't noticed.

I rolled out my neck as our assistant coach continued
to lead us through a few final stretches. I couldn't shake the
feeling that something was off, though. Not only were
Georgie and Freddie gone, the rest of the stadium hadn't
budged. Normally fans cleared out quickly, anxious to beat
the crowds, but not that night. I glanced around to check
out the other side of the stadium and everyone was
standing up, angled toward the tunnel that led to the
locker rooms as if they were waiting for something to
happen.

"Do you know what's going on?" I asked Sasha.

She pressed her lips together and averted eye contact, a universal sign for 'I know something you don't know.'

"Not sure."

I laughed. "Seriously, what's happening? Are they going to do the trophy ceremony early?"

She turned away and kept stretching, determined that I not see her face.

"Sasha!" I said, trying to get her to turn toward me, but then I saw him.

Freddie. Walking out of the dark tunnel. Half cloaked in shadows and then gloriously lit under the stadium lights. He was wearing a fitted navy suit with brown leather oxfords. He was clean-shaven and his thick chestnut-brown hair was styled back with a smooth wave. I'd gotten used to how devilishly handsome he was day to day. At home, he usually walked around shirtless in a pair of sweatpants that had seen better days. I'd roll out of bed and find him in front of the stove, flipping pancakes, eggs, or bacon. He loved cooking breakfast and I never got tired of watching him from my perch across the kitchen island.

Home Freddie wasn't the version I saw walking toward me from the tunnel. This was a smooth, refined version of the man I loved. A version that made my hands shake as he continued walking toward me. The stadium erupted when they saw him, and I started to walk toward him with my hand pressed against my heart. I was trying to force it to calm down, but it was too late. Once I caught a glimpse of the line of people trailing out of the tunnel behind Freddie, the first tears were already falling. Kinsley, Liam, my parents (in their summer whites), Becca, Penn, Georgie, and Freddie's mom; each of them trailed out after Freddie, smiling and waving as I shook my head in disbelief. I hadn't seen my mom and dad in a few months, and I hadn't seen Kinsley and Becca in twice as long. Moving to

London and leaving them behind had been one of the hardest things I'd ever had to do, but it'd been worth it.

I locked eyes with Freddie when we were only a few feet apart. My heart kicked up a rapid beat and he smiled wider. I shook my head and asked him what was going on. As soon as he reached me, he pulled me into a tight hug and I inhaled his clean, sharp scent. It was the smell that brought me peace at the end of a long day. It was the smell of a man who was supportive, and loyal, and loving. He bent to kiss my cheek and then he pulled back to look at me. His warm brown eyes assured me that everything would be okay.

My family and friends were around us then, circled up and watching from a few feet away as I completely lost it in a fit of tears.

"I can't stop," I said with a laugh and a hiccup.

Freddie smiled and bent forward to wipe a tear from my face. "It's okay."

"You look cute!" Kinsley shouted.

"Dang, girl!" echoed Becca.

I laughed and then inhaled a shaky breath as Freddie took a knee before me on the turf.

Oh my god.

"Andie Foster…"

Oh, Jesus I could hardly hear him over the sound of my sobs. He took my hand and pressed his lips to the center.

"The first time I met you, you asked me for my knickers…" Everyone around us laughed, but my hands shook and my heart beat wildly. "But you took my heart instead."

I inhaled a breath and shook my head. I couldn't do it. He was kneeling there, staring up at me with earnest eyes and an open heart, and I couldn't wait for him to finish. I knew how much he loved me; he showed me every single day. I knew he wanted to spend his life with me; he told me whenever he got the chance. I knew he and I were a perfect pair. We loved going for runs in the morning right after breakfast. We loved teaching and coaching one another. Freddie had greatly improved my skills in the pool, but teaching him to kick around a soccer ball was all but hopeless. We loved trying new recipes, subsequently failing, and then hopping in a cab to the nearest restaurant. We loved hanging out with Georgie and going to pubs with friends. We'd sit across from each other, laughing and talking, he'd glance over to me and I'd reach out for his hand, and it was enough. It didn't matter where we were, Freddie and I were in it together. His struggles were mine. My triumphs were his.

"In those first few weeks," he continued, "you made me work for every smile and every word. I had to fight for you to give me the time of day, but even then, I think I knew I was fighting for my future wife."

I crumbled to the turf and threw myself against him. He was in the middle of his proposal and I was sure the words he was about to say were beautiful and compelling, but I didn't need them.

"Yes," I whispered against his neck. "Yes. Yes. *Yes*."

He laughed and wrapped his arms around me to keep me against him. "You didn't let me get to the good part."

I turned and pressed a kiss to his cheek. "This *is* the good part."

Epilogue to the Epilogue

ANDIE

FREDDIE AND I both agreed that we wanted a low-key destination wedding, preferably somewhere tropical.

Georgie was an early advocate of the plan. "Yo quiero mucho rum y shirtless hombres" were her exact words on the subject. I hope she takes her maid of honor duties more seriously than her Spanish lessons.

Coach Decker retired after the games, and Liam replaced her as head coach of the Women's National Team. Kinsley took a break from her club team in Los Angeles, as she and Liam are expecting their first little soccer prodigy (!!!) this summer.

Becca responded to Kinsley's news with just one text: "Umm, looks like we might have two soccer prodigies in the making. SURPRISE."

Two weeks after the Olympics, Caroline sued Freddie and Sophie for libel and defamation. After losing the case, she was forced to pay for court costs and legal fees. She then checked herself into a hospital retreat for exhaustion. (Who could blame her?)

One week into her stay, she was arrested for biting a nurse who refused to sneak her extra Tramadol. After posting bail, she fled the country and subsequently announced her engagement to some prince living in Dubai.

I pray for an invitation to their wedding every time I open the mailbox.

Want more of Georgie?! (Who wouldn't?)
Follow her journey to find love in
A PLACE IN THE SUN.

SYNOPSIS:

When her mother's incessant matchmaking hits an all-time high, Georgie Archibald does what any sensible woman would do: she flees the country.

Seeking refuge in the picturesque seaside village of Vernazza, Italy, Georgie's only plan is to lie low, gorge herself on gelato, and let the wine and waves wash her troubles away...that is until she wakes up in a bed that belongs to the most romantic-looking man she's ever seen.

Gianluca.

After going out of his way to rescue her, the former London financier turned mysterious recluse makes it clear that despite acting as her white knight, he has no plans to co-star in her fairytale.

But Georgie isn't asking for his heart—she's merely intrigued.

After all, Gianluca isn't just gorgeous—tall and tan from days spent in the sun—his touch sets her world on fire. With him, Georgie experiences the most intoxicating passion she's ever known, and it only takes a few steamy nights for her to realize that sometimes running away from trouble is the best way to find it.

Chapter One

GEORGIE

HOW WAS NO *one else seeing this?*

The two middle-aged tourists in queue to enter the Colosseum were going at it like randy teenagers. The woman had her leg coiled up around her lover's waist and his hand had disappeared beneath her skirt fifteen minutes ago—the thing hadn't come up for air since.

She moaned into his mouth and fingered his hair. He growled like an undersexed werewolf, and then went back in for another snog with enough tenacity to suck her lips off.

I sat ensconced from my vantage point a few yards away, picking at a croissant and pretending to pay attention to a travel podcast about the Colosseum. In the last few minutes, the spirited performance had completely stolen my focus. Surely their oxygen levels were getting pretty low.

In all my twenty-six years, I'd never once kissed someone the way they were kissing each other. It was as if they were newlyweds on a transatlantic flight and the pilot had just announced that they'd lost both engines. God, if they went at it like that in full public view at the foot of a crusty old ruin, what on Earth did they do in private?

I blushed just thinking about it.

Eventually, a security guard with a red, pudgy face and an awkward manner asked the couple to politely refrain from boning in line, or so I imagined—his words were in Italian, so I couldn't be sure. The unflinching lovebirds disappeared inside the Colosseum and I was left with my pastry once again. *It's just me and you, carbs.*

"Seat taken?"

I glanced up to find a devastatingly handsome Italian man with cool trainers and slicked-back hair. He was smiling down at me, pointing to the bit of stone to my left. I tossed my croissant aside and yanked my earbuds out so quickly they nearly took my ears with them.

In front of the Colosseum, there's not much in the way of seating. It's all brash vendors peddling plastic crap, pale-thighed sightseers running after their bored children, and pushy groups of veteran tourists spilling out of buses with expensive cameras around their necks. I'd sought refuge from the swirling sea of humanity on a distant rock in the only bit of shade I could find.

"Oh, yeah. All yours," I said with a big smile.

The man sat down beside me, pulled out a water bottle, and took a long swig.

"*Bellissima*," he said, tipping his water bottle in my direction, and for one tiny moment, my heart leapt. I didn't know much Italian—nearly none in fact—but every woman on Earth knows that word.

I blushed and opened my mouth to thank him before he pointed to the Colosseum. "It's beautiful," he repeated, this time in thickly accented English.

Oh.

Of course. *The crumbling heap.*

"It's all right," I grumbled, glancing back to the Colosseum so he wouldn't see my frown. Truthfully, it wasn't what I had expected. The street was crowded, the sun was blazing overhead, and the street performers waltzing around in skimpy gladiator outfits for photo-ops weren't half as sexy as I'd assumed they'd be. The latter was the issue that bothered me the most.

"You aren't going in?" he asked, tilting his head to the queue spiraling around the base of the building.

I scrunched my nose. "It seems fairly self-explanatory from the outside."

"You're missing out," he said before stuffing his water bottle back into his backpack and turning his full attention to me.

I shrugged. Maybe I was cheating myself, or maybe I was smarter than the sweaty masses filing in. Perching on my rock with my croissant and my podcast had been pretty nice up until the canoodlers had distracted me with their tonsil tennis.

"How long are you in Rome?" he asked, flashing a wide smirk in my direction.

This man was handsome, *really* handsome, and though I was due to leave the next day, I was hesitant to tell him that. If he wanted to sweep me off my feet and put his hand up my skirt while we stood in line at the Colosseum, I'd consider extending my stay.

"Well, actually I…"

My sentence faded out as a glamorous woman appeared behind him. The sun shaded her face so I couldn't really make her out until she'd bent low and wrapped a possessive arm around the Italian man's shoulders. There, with his head shading her face, I suddenly saw her dark eyes narrow into little slits right at me.

"Luciana, look, I've found us a new friend," he smiled.

Luciana didn't share his excitement.

I'll spare the superfluous details and cut to the chase: Italian man had a girlfriend. The good ones always do. After a few minutes of terribly awkward conversation in which I tried to pretend Luciana wasn't wishing me a swift, sudden death, my phone rang on my lap and I seized the excuse to flee. I scooted off the rock, gave my spot to Luciana, and promised to come back after I'd finished my call. It was a lie—there was a better chance of me sacrificing myself in the arena.

I curled around the side of the colosseum, using the massive structure to shade me as I answered the call.

"Georgie, finally!"

My brother sounded exasperated.

"Hello ol' chum. What do you want?"

"When will you be at Mum's? We're waiting for you before we sit down for dinner."

Oh, oops. Had I forgotten to phone and cancel?

"Don't bother waiting for me, Fred. Eat up."

"You aren't coming? Mom's expecting you." He sounded a bit sad about it, which made me feel good. He used to find me so annoying when we were younger, but he was finally coming around. *As he should.* I was (objectively) the only person in our family with any personality.

"No, I'm not coming. You go on ahead."

A group of young, rowdy American tourists ran past me then, shouting and pretending to be gladiators fighting one another. I tried to muffle the sound of their shouts through the phone, but it was no use. Freddie heard them.

"Georgie, where are you?"

"Oh, well actually…"

I glanced around me, trying to conjure up the name of a street back home in London. I'd lived there my whole life but my brain wasn't cooperating.

"Georgie."

"Well, as a matter of fact, I've gone to Italy."

A massive moment of silence hung between us before he flipped out.

"*Italy?!* Since when?"

"Just yesterday. I meant to tell you."

"Georgie, have you gone insane?"

I smiled. "No, brother. All is well."

"Then why on Earth are you in Italy?"

"To find love, of course."

―――――

I found myself in Italy the way I find myself in most places: by chance. The week before, I'd been sitting in a restaurant in London, partaking in another miserable blind date set up by my mother. The man sitting across from me was chewing with his mouth open. His massive chompers were spewing steak at a rate that concerned me—and the diners sitting within a five-yard radius.

In a moment of panic (I was particularly worried I'd become a new statistic taught to medical students: the first case of mad cow disease transmitted by sirloin to the eye), I realized I couldn't allow my mum to control my love life any longer. She was concerned for me, laboring under the outdated perception that if I were to remain single past twenty-six, I'd be branded a hopeless spinster, destined to spend my days scouring the streets for love.

Unbeknownst to him, Chompers served as a perfect example of why I needed to take my love life into my own hands. He was nearing forty in both years of life and strands of hair. His job was something like "insurance for insurance" and though he tried to explain it to me while chewing, after thirty minutes, I still didn't quite understand any of it.

It really wasn't fair to poor Chompers. He hadn't chosen to be the latest in the long string of terrible blind dates my mother had forced upon me, but in that role, he suddenly had to bear the cumulative weight of disappointment of all those who'd come before him. There was Mitch—the gouty muppet who had the personality of a dull housefly, Thom—my brother's naff friend who smelled perpetually of tuna fish, and Celso—a Spaniard who, despite looking fairly tidy, wouldn't let go of my hand through the entire dinner. I made it through the appetizers all right, but when I'd tried to cut my chicken one-handed, I only succeeded in flinging it off my plate and onto his lap.

The real problem lay in the fact that my brother—the golden child of our family—had found love and married years ago. He and his wife, Andie, had three chubby-cheeked children, and thus my mother was able to focus the full power of her matrimonial death beam onto me.

"You're in your prime, Georgie!"

As if this was the seventeenth century.

"You're getting older every day!"

She'd said this to me at my twentieth birthday party, just before gifting me an actual antique hourglass, making sure to emphasize the symbolism by flipping it upside down in my hands.

"You really ought to loosen your standards. That man who comes round your house every now and then is so handsome and in quite good shape."

She'd been referring to the postman.

A few years ago, fearing that my status as single was a permanent problem, my mum had started enlisting the help of her friends and their "eligible" sons. I'd been a good sport about it, going on dates with men from nearly every county in England, but in the years since then, the novelty had lost its luster. Though I was no closer to marrying, I *had* developed a very clear list of requirements in a future husband. For instance, he must chew with his mouth closed. He must wash a few times a week and be taller than he is round. I used to think a sense of a humor would have been nice. I wasn't asking for a Russell Brand or a Ricky Gervais, just a man who wasn't a complete bump on a log. But those days were coming to a close—if my mother had her way, I would settle down with a well-meaning bump on a very average log.

After my date with Chompers, I'd left him on the curbside after dodging—*you guessed it*—an open-mouthed kiss. I took the long way home, puzzling over my problem. I wanted to find love as much as my mother wanted it for me. At twenty-six, I *obviously* wasn't a spinster, but I was becoming a bit lonely. I hadn't ever experienced a gut-clenching, obsessive, swoony kind of romance.

Obviously, it was time for a change.

But the need for change wasn't new. After each of these bad dates, I'd head home, working out how I'd break the news to my mother: no more dates. No more matchmaking. A week or two would pass, she'd bat her eyelashes, and I'd cave. I always caved, but not this time.

I knew if I was really going to make a change, I had to get out of London. My mother, bless her, would never leave me alone as long as I stayed within her reach.

So I'd done what any rational girl would have.

I spun a globe in our estate's library and promised myself I'd travel to whichever country my finger landed on. The globe's colors had blended together in a mess of blue and green and then I'd dropped my finger, abruptly stopping its rotation.

Syria.

Er, right. Minor hiccup.

I spun again and *voila!*

Italy!

Specifically, *Vernazza.*

———

Even though I'd never heard of Vernazza and needed a magnifying glass to see it on the map, I didn't spin the globe for a third time—I didn't want to get on destiny's bad side. Instead, I wrote down the name and rolled it over my tongue to get a feel for the pronunciation.

After a bit of research, I learned that Vernazza is one of five seaside villages that make up Cinque Terre. All five of the centuries-old villages are tucked into the rugged Ligurian coastline, and are only easily accessible by train— lovely, considering motion sickness was my fiercest enemy.

In an effort to break up the trip and spare my poor stomach, I'd flown into Rome first and planned a day of exploring the ancient city. After escaping the Colosseum, I walked along the cobblestone streets, turning the paper map in my hand and trying to maneuver around the crowds. I saw all the important sights that day. I stood in the center of the Pantheon under the massive oculus, boiling. It was noon and the sun was right overhead, blinding everyone in the room.

"Not incredibly practical to cut a hole in the roof if you ask me," I deadpanned to the ten-year-old beside me.

She sighed heavily and rolled her eyes, walking away with *Architecture of the Italian Renaissance* shoved underneath her arm. Very cultured, these kids today.

After that, I toured the Vatican and got in trouble for talking in the Sistine Chapel. They shuffled a thousand of

419

us into the room at once, told us to zip it, and threatened to start chopping fingers if we tried to take photos. Still, an elderly Italian woman prodded my arm with her cane and pointed at her iPhone like she wanted me to help her take an illegal photo.

"Oh, I don't think you're allow—"

A baritone voice boomed overhead. *"SILENCIO! SIII-ILLLEEENNNCE."*

I'd jumped a mile in the air, assuming it was the voice of God himself.

My final stop of the day was the Trevi Fountain. I chucked a euro over the crowds, but my aim was crap, and it ended up striking a woman in the forehead as she stood for a photo-op in front of the fountain. I shrugged—my wish had been to make the crowds disappear, and as the woman hurried off angrily, I counted it as a win.

Confident that I'd consumed the best bits of Rome and also anxious to flee the area in case the woman with the coin-shaped bruise on her forehead came back looking for vengeance, I turned back for my hotel. The sun was setting and my feet were aching.

In the morning, I would head to Vernazza and see what fate had in store for me.

———

In true Georgie Archibald form, I slept right through my alarm the following morning. It BEEPED BEEPED BEEPED over and over again and my brain—still exhausted from traveling—had assumed it was some annoying Italian songbird outside my window. Eventually, my subconscious brain realized that birds don't even sound remotely like alarm clocks, and I shot out of bed.

I looked at the time. "Arse! Bugger! SHITE!"

If I missed my first train of the day, I'd have a hell of a time making my connections. I tossed anything and everything into my suitcase, nearly taking half the hotel room with me. The train station was only a few minutes away, so I didn't bother with a cab. I shot across streets without looking both ways, nearly collided with a few cars, and made it past security with ten minutes to spare before the train departed.

It was an 11:20 AM departure for Pisa, packed with families on holiday. I took a deep breath, telling myself, *I made it.* I stowed my luggage then wandered down the aisle, glancing at the numbers posted above each seat. I was assigned to 11A and when my eyes landed on my backward-facing seat, I groaned. It wouldn't do; I had to face the direction the train was moving or I'd get sick.

I glanced around for an opening, but my late arrival had ensured that every last seat on the train was full except for mine.

"Sir," I said, turning to the distinguished-looking man sitting in 11C. His seat was opposite mine, facing the right direction. It was a small move, but it would ensure I didn't spew up the granola bar I'd stuffed down my throat on the way over from my hotel.

He tilted his head up, a bit annoyed to be pulled out of his crossword.

I offered him a massive, pleading smile. "Is there any way I could convince you to swap seats with me? I get motion sickness on trains and I—"

He shook his head before I'd even finished.

"This is my assigned seat."

"Of course, and I'm assigned to 11A."

I pointed between the two seats as if trying to convince him of how small the distance was. He'd just have to pop up, rotate that impressively large bottom of his, and plop back down across the gap. Easy peasy.

"Then 11A is where I suggest you sit."

On that note, he held up his crossword to cover his face.

I moved on to my next target: the woman sitting in 11D, but unfortunately, she was snoozing against the window, a bit of drool already rolling down her chin. I could have forced her awake and asked her to swap seats, but it seemed like bad form.

I tried one last glance around the train, displaying the most desperately tragic face I could muster, but everyone turned away, avoided eye contact, or offered up a blatant shake of their head.

Fine.

I sat down in 11A, dropped my backpack between my feet, and yanked out the supplies I carried with me whenever I traveled: chewing gum, ginger candy, peppermints, and Dramamine. I began to fortify myself for my impending doom, but it was no use.

By the time we'd chugged away from the station in Rome, dizziness had taken hold of my head and wouldn't let go. I squeezed my eyes closed, willing the sensation to pass, but it only grew worse. I managed to make it to the toilet before throwing up the first time, but the second time, I made sure to look right in 11C's eyes as I hurled into the paper bag. *See? See what you've done to me?*

Fortunately for me—and everyone else assigned to my car—I had a forward-facing seat for the next leg of the journey, from Pisa to La Spezia, but it didn't matter. By that point, my head was swimming and my stomach was rejecting everything I put in it. I considered stopping in La Spezia for the night, but it was still early afternoon and I'd intended on making it all the way to Vernazza before calling it quits for the day. I wanted to crash, but a bigger part of me just wanted to get the journey over with. I wanted a hotel room. I wanted a proper shower and a bed to collapse into.

Unfortunately, I'd underestimated how difficult the final leg of my journey would be. It was a short train journey between La Spezia and Vernazza, but the regional train was small and all the seats were full by the time I lugged my suitcases onboard. I was forced to stand, packed like a sardine, in the small compartment between two cars. My body was crushed against the side door, facing out. I desperately willed my nausea to pass; I'd used my last sick bag on the train to La Spezia and I really didn't want to traumatize the family of five laughing behind me.

The small train sped along the coast of Italy, through long, dark tunnels cut through rock. I caught my own reflection in the door's window and cringed. My brown eyes, usually bright and lively, had heavy circles beneath them. Strands of my long chestnut brown hair were coated with sweat and stuck to my cheeks. All color had faded from my face and the bit of throw-up crusted below my bottom lip served as the *pièce de résistance* to my entire haggard appearance.

I nearly caved then. It would have been so easy to call Freddie and beg him to come collect me, but in the blink of an eye the tunnel broke open and my vision was filled with an expanse of turquoise water.

It was blue in every direction, different hues painted across the landscape as far as my eyes could see. A cloud-less sky met crystal clear waters. Angry waves crashed against the shore, spilling white sea foam over massive granite rocks that had tumbled down from the mountains over the centuries. I pressed my hands to the glass, leaned forward, and gasped, nearly lost in the beauty of it, right before another bout of motion sickness overtook me.

Oh bloody hell.

"Mom! The crazy lady just threw up on me!"

Want to read the rest of A PLACE IN THE SUN? You can buy it now or read it for FREE in Kindle Unlimited!

A PLACE IN THE SUN

Acknowledgments

Thank you to all my readers, especially the Little Reds. I know there are so many books to choose from these days, and I don't take it for granted that you all chose to spend a day or two reading mine.

XO, Rachel

Made in the USA
Monee, IL
25 July 2024

62602761R00256